STAR TREK®
AVENGER

Also by William Shatner

TekWar
TekLords
TekLab
Tek Vengeance
Tek Secret
Tek Power
Tek Money
Tek Kill
Man o' War
Believe (with Michael Tobias)
Star Trek Memories
Star Trek Movie Memories
The Ashes of Eden (with Judith and Garfield Reeves-Stevens)
The Return (with Judith and Garfield Reeves-Stevens)

WILLIAM SHATNER

STAR TREK®
AVENGER

with
Judith Reeves-Stevens &
Garfield Reeves-Stevens

POCKET BOOKS
New York   London   Toronto   Sydney   Tokyo   Singapore

POCKET BOOKS, a division of Simon & Schuster Inc.
1230 Avenue of the Americas, New York, NY 10020

STAR TREK is a Registered Trademark of
Paramount Pictures.

This book is published by Pocket Books, a division of
Simon & Schuster Inc., under exclusive license from
Paramount Pictures.

ISBN: 0-671-55132-9

First Pocket Books hardcover printing May 1997

10 9 8 7 6 5 4 3 2 1

POCKET and colophon are registered trademarks of
Simon & Schuster Inc.

Printed in the U.S.A.

Three is a lucky number. This is the third of a trilogy of novels. And I also have three editors to whom I wish to dedicate this novel: Kevin Ryan, John Ordover, and Margaret Clark, members of the illustrious clan of Simon & Schuster. All good things come in threes. Now just to louse things up, the publisher has asked for another two novels. I've got to find me a couple of editors!

ACKNOWLEDGMENTS

Gar and Judy Reeves-Stevens deserve accolades,
not acknowledgments.
What would I have done without them?

STAR TREK®
AVENGER

PROLOGUE

☆

Kirk knew it was over . . .

. . . in Yosemite. The rocky face of El Capitan blurring past him . . .

. . . on the Enterprise-B. *The bulkhead of the deflector room ripped away by the unfathomable power of the Nexus, pulling him into space . . .*

. . . on Veridian III. Plunging downward, twisting, in a tangle of torn metal as Picard defeated Tolian Soran . . .

. . . and on the Borg homeworld. The two captains of the Enterprise, *Kirk and Picard, each ready to throw the switch that would shut off all power to the collective's Central Node. The power feedback would be immediate. Whoever threw that switch would die.*

"It's my job to do it," Picard insisted. "You've done enough."

But Kirk's course was chosen. His body was being inexorably damaged from within by the Borg nanites that had reconstructed him and brought him back from that undiscovered country that lies beyond life.

"Jean-Luc," he said, "I'm dying." The nanites would see to that in less than a day.

1

But Picard would not be swayed. "Who isn't?"

Spock's voice crackled out of Kirk's comm badge. "Enterprise to away team. We are at thirty seconds to emergency beam-out. What is your status?"

Picard locked eyes with Kirk. Touched his own comm badge. "This is Picard, Enterprise. Break off your approach. Repeat—"

Kirk pushed Picard's hand away from his comm badge, hit his own.

"Ignore that last order, Spock. Bring that ship in."

"I am not leaving!" Picard said.

Kirk was about to shout back, when he suddenly stood down.

"Did you ever try to save the Kobayashi Maru at the Academy?"

Picard regarded Kirk with deep suspicion. "Yesss . . . But it can't be done. It's a no-win scenario designed for cadets."

Kirk smiled. "That's what they'd like you to believe. But there is a strategy that can win it. It's just that nobody in your time seems to do it anymore. Spock tells me it's a lost art now."

"Are you suggesting a compromise?"

Kirk thought it over. "You could call it that."

"Well," Picard said. "Go ahead. I'm always open to suggestions."

Kirk nodded. "Good."

Then he slugged Picard in the jaw as hard as he could.

Picard dropped like deadweight.

Kirk dragged Picard by his collar, until he was well away from the power conduit.

He pulled off his own comm badge, touched the front to activate it.

"Kirk to Enterprise," he said.

"Spock here."

Kirk smiled.

He felt better already.

"Keep the ship out of danger, Mr. Spock." He studied the

Starfleet delta in his hand. Remembered when it had belonged only to the Enterprise. *But some things had to change. It was the way of the world. Of the universe.*

He was glad to have been part of it.

"Lock on to my signal," Kirk said. "One to beam up." Then he tossed his comm badge onto Picard's chest and stepped back.

Picard reacted to the impact of the badge. His eyes opened. He looked up. Started to speak.

Then dissolved in the transporter as the Enterprise *once more claimed her own.*

Kirk turned back to the power conduit. Grabbed the lever in both hands. Tested it once to see how much force he might need. Felt it move easily.

"A second chance," he said aloud.

Then he closed his eyes.

Squeezed his hands tight.

Pulled.

Heard a sudden, deafening roar of thunder coming from the dome.

Then a scrape as quiet as a footstep behind him.

Kirk turned.

Opened his eyes.

Saw the shimmer of an energy beam sweep across the floor like a searchlight. Whatever that beam touched glowed as if lit from within, then disappeared.

As if the shimmer were a transporter beam.

Or a phaser set to disintegrate.

The dome above him cracked open with an explosive blossom of energy.

Kirk felt the floor rise up beneath him.

Less than a heartbeat remained before the energy feedback that he had set in motion would destroy the Central Node.

There was no time for Spock's logic. No time for McCoy's emotion. There was only time for action.

3

And Kirk responded, even in what might be his last moment of existence.

He threw himself forward, dissolving in the beam as all around him was vaporized.

Whatever the beam's origins, whatever it was, Kirk was still alive. Within it.

Once more he fell.

From El Capitan . . .

From the Enterprise-*B . . .*

From the Veridian precipice . . .

Alone to his death.

As he had always known he must.

But without knowing why *he knew.*

Or how *he knew.*

Until now *. . .*

ONE

---------------- ☆ ----------------

This was the first time.

When it had all begun.

When it hurt even to breathe the icy air of Tarsus IV.

Blinding snow swirled around him, glistening in the light of the planet's twin moons, covering his tracks as quickly as he made them. He was weak with hunger, shaking with fear and bitter cold as he fled into the darkness, knowing that he could not run forever.

This first time, he was thirteen years old. He was alone and the shadow was behind him. Running even faster.

There could be no doubt. Death pursued him. Relentless. Inescapable.

The boy lost his footing in the snow, slammed into the ice-prickled bark of a daggertree, thudded backward to the ground with a gasp of pain.

He lost his breath. Tasted blood from a sudden cut on his cheek.

Tears ran from his eyes.

His whole body ached with the cold, with frustration, with fear, more than any child, any man, anyone should bear.

Sprawled in the snow, the boy gave up, closed his eyes.

Saw the face of Kodos staring back at him. A face he would never forget.

. . . boy . . . keep running . . .

Jimmy Kirk's eyes flew open. He looked up, startled, expecting to stare into the glowing barrel of a laser rifle. Whoever had just whispered in his ear could only have been centimeters away.

But there was no one near him.

The boy struggled to his feet, convinced he was not alone. But all he saw was the stabbing shaft of light dancing through the dark silhouettes of the trees, coming from the handtorch of his pursuer.

. . . keep running . . .

The boy stumbled forward, sobbing. His toes burned with the cold in his frozen boots.

But he ran.

Eight thousand people had lived on this planet when he had arrived here.

It was a colony world. His parents had friends here. He was to spend a semester with them, then meet his father to travel back home. To Earth.

But the Romulans had done something in the Neutral Zone. His father's leave from Starfleet had been canceled. The shipping lanes closed.

And then the fungus struck.

It destroyed the grain. Poisoned the animals.

Four thousand people survived on Tarsus IV now.

Governor Kodos had killed the other four thousand to extend the food supply.

It was a "necessity," the governor had told those gathered by the open pits that would be their graves.

The boy still heard the lasers. The screams.

And still there was not enough food.

So thirteen-year-old Jimmy Kirk, with no parents to protect him, no ration book to feed him, no one to speak up for him, was selected for the second list.

Out of necessity, said the governor.

A beam of light flashed over him.

The boy almost fell, knowing he had been found.

But the near yet distant voice whispered once more . . . *keep running. . . .*

The boy wavered, confused. It was almost as if he were hearing someone else's thoughts.

A shaft of light locked on to him.

He tried to twist away, but it followed him.

He tensed, waiting for the searing pain of a laser, lost his footing, slipped in the ice and the snow, tumbling wildly, arms waving, screaming out for his father as he fell . . . alone—

—into two strong arms that caught him.

Saved him.

Then a caring voice spoke, calm, reassuring, soothing beyond any rational explanation. The same voice that had whispered to his mind now spoke to him in person.

"Let me help," that voice said, three words which would resonate in the boy's life forever.

The boy stopped struggling. He knew it wasn't Kodos who held him, nor one of the governor's men.

He looked around, suddenly realizing that his run through the woods had led him to the field where the landing pads were.

There was a new ship there, its outline barely visible through the blowing snow. But its viewports and loading bay were clearly defined by the blinding shafts of brilliant light that streamed from them, swirling snowflakes into streaks like stars seen from warp.

Silhouetted against that light, dark figures unloaded crates with antigravs.

WILLIAM SHATNER

Supplies. The colony was saved.

With relief greater than he could express, the boy looked up at the tall stranger who had caught him, half-expecting to see his own father.

"Are you from Starfleet?" the boy asked, his teeth chattering with the cold.

The stranger tugged back the hood of his parka.

The boy's gaze fixed on the points of the man's ears.

"You're a Vulcanian?" the boy stammered.

"I am Sarek," the Vulcan said. "And you are safe now."

For a moment, Jimmy Kirk almost believed him.

But then from behind, Kodos spoke: "The boy was a witness. He must die."

Jimmy Kirk twisted in Sarek's grip to see Kodos three meters away, laser rifle unslung, barrel glowing. There was a handtorch clipped to the rifle's sight. The boy squinted at its brightness.

But Sarek didn't turn away from the light. "No more will die," he said. "We were wrong."

Kodos raised his rifle. "What is it you are so fond of saying . . . ? About the needs of the many outweighing the needs of the few?"

Sarek kept his hand locked around the boy's wrist, to keep him close. At the same time, he stepped forward, placing his body as a shield between the boy and Kodos.

"The experiment must end," Sarek said. "The Romulan action was not anticipated."

"Not anticipated? That was the point of the lesson. Safeguards must be taken. They have to learn. The boy must die, like the others."

Kirk's eyes widened as Sarek drew a compact laser pistol and aimed it directly at Kodos. From the governor's reaction, the sight of a Vulcanian brandishing a weapon was as remarkable to Kodos as it was to the boy.

But Kodos did not lower his rifle.

"We will permit you to leave on our vessel," Sarek said.

"There are four thousand who know me back in the colony."

"We will provide you with a new identity, passage to a different sector."

"And what of the cause?" Kodos demanded.

The boy heard hesitation in Sarek's reply.

"It must be . . . reexamined."

"Vulcanians." Kodos frowned. "Your logic is a mask for your cowardice."

Sarek's arm was like duranium, his aim unmoved.

The boy leaned out from behind Sarek to stare at Kodos. The governor looked directly at him. "Even if I never see any of the colonists again, this boy's heard every word we've said about my leaving."

"He will not remember them."

The boy didn't like the sound of that. Neither did Kodos. "And if he does?"

"Then I shall be at equal risk with you. Just as I am now."

For long moments, the boy shivered. Then Kodos turned off his rifle, removed the attached handtorch, and slung the rifle over his back. He directed the handtorch downward, at the ground. The shadows cast upward were unsettling to the boy. He did his best to ignore them.

Sarek returned his laser pistol to the folds of his parka.

Kodos moved threateningly close to Sarek, held up his hand in the Vulcanian salute.

"Live long and prosper." The governor's voice was heavy with sarcasm. He stared down at Jimmy Kirk. "If you ever speak about what you've seen here, boy, I'll know. And the Vulcanians can't protect you forever. Someday you'll be alone, and I promise you, that will be the day you *will* die."

Sarek pulled the boy closer. Somehow, at the Vulcanian's touch, Jimmy Kirk felt his unreasoning urge to run back into the woods begin to fade.

"Leave, Governor. We shall not meet again."

"For the sake of the cause, you had better hope you're right."

Then Kodos pushed past them, striding off toward the Vulcanian ship on the landing pad.

Jimmy Kirk stared after him, his shivering almost gone. But not his fear or his anger. "Why are you letting him go?"

Sarek looked down with eyes that seemed far older than the rest of him. "I have a son, only a few years older than you."

The boy never understood the way adults talked about children. What did the Vulcanian's answer have to do with his question? He struggled in Sarek's grip. "He's getting away! You're letting him get away!"

But Sarek's hold was unbreakable. "No one escapes his fate, young human. Neither Kodos. Nor I." Even to a thirteen-year-old whose knowledge of Vulcanians came primarily from schoolboy jokes, the sadness in Sarek's words was unmistakable.

"What about me?" the boy asked with all the bitterness of youth unjustly ignored.

Sarek bit the edge of a glove and tugged it off, baring his hand to the icy wind of Tarsus IV. "No one can know the future," he said.

Then, to the boy, it suddenly seemed as if the two of them were somewhere else, on a blistering desert, or in a quiet forest, or . . . The middle-aged Vulcanian seemed centuries old, sallow and shrunken.

Jimmy Kirk shook his head, clearing his mind of the strange images that had filled it. "I know my future," he said indignantly.

"Then let us share it," Sarek replied. He reached out to touch his fingers to precise points on the boy's face.

"What are you doing?" The boy was nervous. He had heard stories about Vulcanians and their strange mental powers. They could change shape, fly, even—

"Shh," Sarek whispered. "Your mind to my mind . . ."

The touch of the Vulcanian's fingertips was electric. The boy felt his body relax instantly, as if the Vulcanian had drained him of emotions.

For a few moments, he seemed to be observing images through someone else's eyes. He saw . . . the Plains of Gol? A red desert? Words came to him from another language, as if his thoughts were mixing with another's.

"Our minds are one," Sarek intoned.

The boy heard a whispered voice ask his name.

"We are one, James Kirk," Sarek said aloud.

Just then, the boy experienced, felt, saw an image of a Vulcanian boy, a teenager, sharp-featured, with a human woman at his side.

The teenager's unpronounceable Vulcanian name flashed into Jimmy Kirk's consciousness as he suddenly understood that Sarek and he had somehow merged their minds. That desert was on Vulcan! The teenager was Sarek's son! He was seeing through *Sarek's* eyes.

The boy was astounded, amazed, excited. Overwhelmed with alien thoughts and concepts. He wanted more. To see more. To *know* more.

But something held him back.

No, James Kirk, Sarek's thoughts whispered. *This meld is not for knowledge. This meld is to help you forget that which you should never have known.*

No, the boy thought.

Forget, Sarek commanded.

"Never," the boy said aloud.

But the struggle was unequal and the boy's last conscious memory of that night was Sarek reflecting on an unexpected discovery: *How like my son. . . .*

In his mind, in his memory, Kirk continued to fall from the Borg homeworld.

He wondered whose arms would save him this time.

11

TWO

─────────────── ☆ ───────────────

It was not supposed to be this way.

Picard knew it.

He could sense the same frustration in each member of his bridge crew as the *Enterprise*-E screamed through space, all weapons systems locked on to a sister ship of the Federation. Of Starfleet.

The captain of the *Enterprise* gripped the arms of his command chair, willing himself to stay focused on his mission.

But he felt poised on the brink of a precipice, and at any moment he knew he would slip and fall and there would be no way back.

Not for anyone.

The *Enterprise* shuddered as Data banked the mighty *Sovereign*-class vessel to slip past an asteroid at better than five hundred kilometers per second—a fraction of the speed the ship was capable of achieving, but as fast as the asteroid belt of the Alta Vista system made practical.

The ship's deflectors nudged the asteroid aside, but the imperfect momentum exchange between starship and space rock made the internal dampeners lag, jarring the bridge crew to the side. Ever since the deflector array had been replaced, after Picard's last encounter with the Borg in Earth's twenty-first century, the navigational deflectors remained slightly, though maddeningly, out of phase.

The unsettling vibration that imbalance brought to the ship was a constant reminder to Picard of what all of Starfleet faced: the lack of resources to correct what should have been a simple problem.

The fleet was stretched too thin, and not even the genius of Chief Engineer La Forge could work miracles when he was denied the most basic supplies and replacement parts.

"Coming up on Alta Vista two five seven," Data announced.

Picard gave his order, knowing how useless it was. "Stand by on tractor beams." From the corner of his eye, he saw Will Riker turn in his first officer's chair.

"Using the tractor beams won't work," Riker said.

Picard felt his anger escape, unwanted, so close to being uncontrollable. "I am not prepared to fire on a Starfleet vessel."

Riker did not turn away from his commanding officer. "Captain Picard, we do not have a choice. The blockade *must* be held or . . ."

There was no need for Riker to finish.

Everyone knew what he meant. Picard's orders were clear.

"Or this will spread," Picard said.

On the viewscreen, the asteroid field dead ahead spun dizzyingly as Data rolled the *Enterprise* through a narrow gap between two irregular carbonaceous chunks of stone, each ten times the size of the ship.

Directly beyond them was the nickel-iron crescent of Alta Vista 257—the fifteen-kilometer-long asteroid behind which their quarry hid, her master no doubt hoping to be shielded from the *Enterprise*'s sensors.

Picard set the approach. "One-eighth impulse, Mr. Data.

Course change: bearing mark eight seven. I want to come in from the side."

Data's android fingers moved easily over the smooth control panels of the navigation console. "That is the longest way around, sir. There is a chance the *Bennett* will run again before we lock our tractor beam on her."

Picard felt an inexplicable wave of sadness come over him. At his left, Deanna Troi looked away from him, clearly sensing his emotions but not wishing to intrude upon them. As if there were anything she, or any of the others, could do.

"The *Bennett* will not run," Picard said. They were at the edge of the asteroid belt. There were no more hiding places left in the Alta Vista system. "She has nowhere else to go."

"Coming about on course change," Data said. His tone betrayed that he still had far to go in integrating his emotion chip with the rest of his personality programming, in order to keep some of his feelings to himself. It was obvious that the android did not believe his captain's assessment of the situation any more than Picard did.

For in truth, the commander of the *Bennett* did have one last option open, other than that of surrendering.

"Ready on tractor beam," Riker said.

Lieutenant Rolk acknowledged Riker's orders from her tactical station behind the command chairs. The blue-skinned Bolian security officer was a promising replacement for Worf: brusque, confident, inhumanly competent.

Data swung the ship about. "Coming up on target."

The pockmarked surface of the asteroid flew by the viewscreen.

"Asteroid horizon at eight hundred meters and . . . target acquired!"

The viewscreen flared as the blue glow of the *Enterprise*'s tractor beam shot out through space and locked on the *Bennett*—a *Fernandes*-class cruiser escort, named for one of the great admirals of the twenty-third century.

The viewscreen image instantly expanded to show the smaller vessel, an elongated disk half the size of the *Enterprise*-E's saucer section, with twin warp nacelles trailing from short, tapered pylons.

"We have her, sir," Rolk stated, but with so little conviction that Picard knew they would not have their quarry for long.

"Hailing frequencies," Picard ordered.

"She is releasing additional mines," Data said.

That was what the cruiser escort had done the last time the *Enterprise* had snared her, three hours earlier on the other side of the asteroid belt.

The spherical mines, each a meter across, had been jettisoned into the tractor beam, where they had been swiftly drawn toward the *Enterprise*. As Rolk had taken each out with a precision phaser hit, the resulting explosions had disrupted the beam enough for the *Bennett* to escape.

"Targeting mines," Rolk announced.

"Do not fire," Picard said. "Full power to forward shields."

"Sir," Data warned, "they are antimatter mines."

"And our shields are at one hundred percent," Picard said. Under these conditions, his new *Enterprise* could withstand multiple impacts with minimal damage. The *Bennett* would not escape him again.

Picard stood to address his unseen captive.

"This is Captain Jean-Luc Picard of the *Enterprise*—"

"First impact in two seconds," Data interrupted.

"—requesting contact with the commander of the *Bennett.*"

The viewscreen flashed white and the bridge shook as the first mine detonated against the forward shields.

"The *Bennett*'s impulse engines are going to full power," Data said.

"Add auxiliary tractor beams," Picard ordered. "But watch

the *Bennett's* structural integrity. We don't want to crack her hull."

"Two more detonations—"

The jarring thunder of a double explosion echoed through the bridge, replaced by the rising whine of the straining tractor generators.

"—imminent," Data completed.

"Commander of the *Bennett,*" Picard said. "You cannot escape. Please, power down your engines and drop your shields for boarding."

Data turned in his chair to face Picard. "Captain, the *Bennett's* warp engines are powering up."

Riker stood up beside Picard. "He's in a tractor beam."

"*Bennett* acknowledge!" Picard urged. Other ships might attempt such a maneuver against a *Sovereign*-class vessel and survive, but not a cruiser escort. "If you attempt to go to warp while in our tractor beam, you will destroy yourself."

"Receiving a transmission from the *Bennett,*" Rolk announced.

"Onscreen," Picard said even as the bridge shook with the final cluster of mine impacts and the tractor beam's whine soared in response to the *Bennett's* continued impulse thrust.

When the viewscreen flickered to display the image from the *Bennett's* bridge, Picard's concern and frustration became shock and bewilderment.

How was this possible?

The master of the *Bennett,* the commander who had led the *Enterprise* on a near-suicidal chase and who now held his ship a hairsbreadth from destruction, was a *Vulcan*—young, male, and in a *Starfleet* uniform.

"Captain Picard, I request that you disengage your tractor beam and release my vessel."

The Vulcan's words were calm, unhurried, though every action he had taken this day had been tinged with reckless desperation.

"May I know who I am addressing?" Picard asked. At the very least, a Vulcan could be counted upon to negotiate, if not explain. And, even more important, to listen to logic.

"I am Stron," the Vulcan replied.

Picard read the pips on the Vulcan's collar. "Lieutenant Commander Stron," he began.

But the Vulcan would not let him finish.

"I have resigned my commission. I am no longer part of Starfleet."

"Perhaps you would care to reconsider," Picard said, feeling his way through this inexplicable situation. "Otherwise, you will be charged with the theft of a Starfleet vessel, instead of simply misusing it."

"I will not be charged with anything."

With the briefest of glances, Picard looked past Data's shoulders to check the status of the *Bennett*. Her impulse engines still warred against the *Enterprise*'s tractor beams. Her warp engines were online in standby mode. Picard again spoke. "I must warn you, sir, that as yet I fail to understand the logic of your actions."

The Vulcan's gaze was unwavering as he held up two fingers. "Attend me," he said.

A young human female, also in a Starfleet uniform with lieutenant-commander pips, stepped into the image area. She touched her two fingers to Stron's in a ritual Vulcan embrace between husband and wife. Picard estimated the young woman was six months pregnant.

"There are no prospects for the future in this system," Stron said, as if that explained everything.

"That can be corrected," Picard answered, hoping that what he said might someday be true. "But in the meantime, I must insist you and your family return to quarantine. We will escort you back to Gamow Station."

The Vulcan's mouth tensed in what Picard recognized from experience as a powerful display of emotion.

17

"The replicators are failing, Captain Picard. Gamow Station was designed to support fifty scientists for the study of solar inversions. It cannot support fourteen hundred refugees."

"We will provide additional supplies," Picard promised.

"How?" There was almost bitterness in Stron's tone. "You already off-loaded all your emergency supplies when you joined the blockade. You have not been resupplied since. No Starfleet vessel in this sector has."

Picard sighed. He hated arguing with Vulcans. "Stron, return to the outpost, submit to quarantine. It is the only way to survive."

"To return is to face certain death."

Picard spoke sharply. "If I let you go, you will spread death to whichever world you visit next."

"No!" Stron's eyes flashed with most un-Vulcanlike anger. "My mate and I have been through the transporter six times—each time with the biofilters set to finer resolution."

"The biofilters are ineffective," Picard said. "The virogen cannot be screened out by the transporter."

Onscreen, Stron and his mate appeared to exchange a worried look.

"Listen to reason, Stron. The finest minds in the Federation are working on this. There will be a solution soon. But we cannot risk spreading the contagion any further."

Stron's mate took Stron's hand in hers, squeezed tightly. It seemed to Picard that some unspoken signal had passed between them.

"I was a communications officer," Stron said, with full Vulcan reserve now returned to him. "I have intercepted and decoded every message Starfleet has sent to you in the past month."

"No. . . ." Picard knew the terrible projections the Vulcan had seen. Knew why they must still be kept classified.

18

"If we return to quarantine, we will die, Captain. Along with the rest of this sector."

"Stron! There *will* be a solution!"

Stron's mate placed her hand on her swollen stomach, closed her eyes.

"To return to quarantine is to give ourselves over to a painful death," Stron said evenly. "You will release us from your tractor beam, or we will die quickly. Either way, we will be free."

Picard knew conviction when he heard it. He turned to Deanna Troi. Eyes wide with concern, she nodded once, confirming his unspoken question. She could sense the Vulcan's emotional mood, and it was what Picard feared.

"I cannot release you," Picard said slowly, surprised by the strain betrayed in his voice.

"I am now preparing to go to warp," Stron replied.

"No," Picard said. "For the sake of your child, you must have hope for the future!"

Stron's eyes burned from the viewscreen.

"I have seen the future in your Starfleet communiqués. The Federation cannot hold. Hope is not logical."

Picard raised his hand as if he could reach through the viewscreen and save the—

Picard's bridge was caught in blinding light as the image on the screen instantly flicked to an exterior view of the *Bennett*'s destruction.

The *Enterprise* lurched violently forward as the mass she had been holding suddenly vanished, transformed into pure energy.

Red-alert sirens roared and sparks flew from an environmental station as a subspace concussion wave from the *Bennett*'s imploding warp drive slammed against the *Enterprise*'s shields along with the escort's debris.

Riker braced Picard as both stumbled.

"Stron attempted to go to warp," Data stated, quite unnecessarily.

Picard felt himself slip from the precipice as he heard Stron's calm voice whisper in his ear.

The Federation cannot hold.

Hope is not logical.

Picard knew it was not supposed to be this way.

But Stron had spoken the truth. The Federation was dying.

After more than two hundred years, that unprecedented assemblage of united worlds had finally met an enemy it could not overcome.

The Federation itself.

THREE

───────────── ☆ ─────────────

Eden was dying.

The stranger's boots trod through its ashes, following a path through the destruction and decay that had once been a city, when this world had been alive and the Federation had been secure.

The planet's name was Chal, a Klingon term for Heaven. Once, long ago, that was what this world had been.

It was a water world, on the farthest reaches of the long-disputed border between the Klingon and Romulan Empires. The children of those empires had settled this world. The *chalchaj 'qmey,* the Klingons had called them, the sky's offspring, the Children of Heaven.

For that is what they had been.

Descendants of the Klingons and the Romulans, genetically engineered for youth, and strength, and vigor, possessing the best attributes of both species, then enhanced further with transplanted tissue barbarically removed from living human captives.

They had been created at a time when interstellar war was thought to be inevitable. When the Klingon and Romulan leaders had feared the warmongering barbarians of the Federation would lay waste the worlds of the empires.

The Children of Heaven had been created to live on those war-ravaged planets, so that even if the empires should fall, their offspring could rise up against the Federation monsters and restore peace to the galaxy.

But as diplomatic relations improved between the Federation and the empires, the old stereotypes faded. Surprisingly, the soldiers of Starfleet turned out to be explorers, not babykillers. The warriors of *Qo'noS* placed honor above treachery. The Romulan senate did engage in public debate and comprehended the principles of compromise and cooperation.

Peace flourished—unsteady, uncertain, not always understood. But the arms-race mentality that had created the Children of Heaven faded from history. And left behind a paradise.

Eighty years ago, the stranger knew, the inhabitants of Chal had applied for membership in the Federation. Their world had been forgotten by the empires. They wished to chart their own future.

Though the Federation had responded favorably, certain rumors had to be dispelled. Chal was not a fountain of youth. The genetic vigor of her engineered inhabitants was solely theirs. It could not be shared by breathing the atmosphere or drinking the water.

Still, Chal prospered in the Federation's embrace.

Her legendary isles became a sought-after destination for those desiring respite from the pressures of interplanetary commerce. Cerulean blue waves lapped peacefully at sandy beaches. Soft breezes stirred tropical plants that blossomed with explosions of colors unknown on other worlds. The warmth of twin suns enriched its life. Her children thrived.

But that had been eighty years ago.

Now putrescent waves were choked with massive blooms of

algae. Dying sea creatures littered sand dunes stained by sludge and rotting alien kelp.

The verdant jungles of Chal had withered. Surviving leaves were stunted, obscured by the yellow and brown of decaying vegetation.

It had been more than a year since a flower had blossomed.

And what the collapse of nature had begun, human fear had accelerated.

Hundreds of light-years away, in the security of the Federation's Bureau of Disaster Relief, what had happened on Chal was now called the "evacuation difficulties."

The stranger walked through the aftermath of those difficulties.

Destroyed buildings. Torched hovercraft. The central transporter station little more than a blackened pit.

The only structures that appeared untouched in Chal's main city were those most recently erected by Starfleet's relief mission.

So it was to those structures the stranger went. To find the records of the past. To sift through the ashes of what once had been Eden.

Commander Christine MacDonald swore as the replicator control pad shorted out for the fifth time. The emitter of her molecular welding probe sparked an instant later, its nanotip exploding with a miniature sonic boom that echoed crisply against the stone walls of the supply depot.

"And that was the last isolinear on the planet," Engineer Barc grunted beside her. He snapped his tricorder shut and sat back on the floor, frowning at the smoke that curled up from the replicator's inner workings. His snout twitched in obvious displeasure at the acrid odor of burning insulation.

Christine pushed a lock of curly blond hair off her forehead, unaware of the soot streak her blackened fingers left behind. "That was probably the last isolinear in the sector," she sighed. Chal hadn't had a supply ship visit for almost two months. Overall, Starfleet was six months behind in her relief team's requisition requests.

"So what now?" Barc asked. He was a Tellarite, and Christine could tell from the way his fur was plastered to his snout that the oppressive heat of the main city was gaining on him.

"Why don't you go take a mud bath," she suggested.

Barc's beady black eyes widened for a moment; then he snuffled disconsolately. "Not enough water rations."

Christine pulled back and forth on her uniform tunic, trying to generate some sort of local breeze. Like most of the other Starfleet personnel on this mission, she had long ago given away almost all of her standard-issue clothing to the stricken citizens of Chal, including her sleeveless vests. To face the unrelenting heat of Chal's summer, she had then cut the arms off her uniform tunic. It wasn't regulation, but it helped. "Can't use seawater?" she asked.

Barc tapped a stubby hand against the side of his snout. "As bad as it smells to you humans, it's a hundred times worse to me."

Christine held out her hand and helped Barc to his feet. "If we can get this replicator working, we'll be able to turn out a hundred liters of fresh water a day."

"*Rrr,*" Barc snarled. "And if my grandmother had *snargs* she'd be a *trasnik*. There're just no more parts."

"There're no more isolinear control chips," Christine corrected. She gazed up at the wooden beams of the tall ceiling, trying to reformulate the problem, to see it from a different point of view. "But what if we take two engineering tricorders and set them up to *simulate* a replicator control chip, as if we were running a diagnostic?"

Barc's snout twitched questioningly. "Tricorders aren't made to do that."

"What's that got to do with anything?"

24

The engineer sniffed the stale air thoughtfully. "I suppose if I increased the power supply . . . ran it through a type-two inverter . . ."

Christine smiled at the engineer. "You're a miracle worker, Barcs."

The Tellarite snorted in derision. "That's what you keep telling me." He waddled for the depot door—no more than a curtain of cloth to block the sun. "I'll be over at the shuttle pads, trying to talk someone out of a tricorder."

Christine smiled to herself. It was amazing what a little inspiration could do for her engineer. And without supplies, inspiration was just about all she had left to offer as commander of Starfleet's relief mission to Chal.

She turned back to the replicator, took a deep breath, then exhaled sharply, straight up, to keep her unruly hair off her forehead. There had to be something more she hadn't thought of. Some way to get the recalcitrant machine to work. She refused to accept defeat. She . . . realized the shuffle of Barc's boots had been replaced by a different set of footsteps.

Christine turned to see the stranger, surprised that he was so close. She decided he must have entered the depot just as Barc left. Either that, or he had walked in as silently as a ghost.

"This isn't a distribution center," she said, adopting a more formal, Starfleet manner. But even as she spoke she realized the stranger hadn't come for food or water. He didn't walk with the round-shouldered stoop of the people of Chal— people who had lived for a year in demoralizing despair. And he didn't wear local clothes. Instead, he was garbed in the simple tunic and cloak of a Vulcan trader—austere, unassuming, the garb of a pilgrim.

"I only want information," the stranger said.

Christine stopped thinking about the replicator and paid closer attention to the stranger. Everyone on Chal was exhausted. It was odd to hear such a measured, forceful voice

25

again, especially coming from a human. If this had been the Academy and she had been an ensign, she would have been inspired to salute such a voice.

"What kind of information, Mister . . . ?"

Other than his beard, she couldn't discern his features, hidden as they were in his cloak's hood. Christine decided that under all those clothes, in this heat, he must be sweating like a . . . a Tellarite.

"There is a graveyard at the outskirts of town. At least, there used to be."

Christine folded her arms, fully aware that the stranger had sidestepped her question about his name. She was intrigued, and on guard. The last thing the people of Chal needed was some smooth-talking swindler offering a way off the planet.

"What about it?" she asked.

"At city hall, they said the maps were kept here."

"Maps? Of the graveyard?"

"A . . . friend lived here," the stranger said, and his voice, for a moment, lost its strength. "A long time ago."

Now Christine understood. Another victim of Chal's misfortunes, in search of his past. She nodded to a wide doorway in the stone wall behind her. "We've got a central library terminal still running in there. That should have what you need. Follow me."

She started toward the doorway, then paused as she saw the stranger apparently transfixed by the open access panel on the replicator. He was staring into its intricate jumble of wires, conduits, and circuitry.

It was such an unusual reaction that she suddenly had an idea.

"You wouldn't know anything about replicators, would you?" she asked.

The stranger snapped his head up, as if taken unawares. "No. Machines and I . . .." He started forward. "No. Nothing about replicators, I'm afraid."

Christine filed his reaction. She never wasted anything. But she decided the replicator's innards must have reminded him of something else. Something important, judging from his reaction.

The room in which the library terminal had been installed was windowless. It was one of the coolest locations in the depot. Christine enjoyed the sensation of the chilled air on her bare arms. She gestured to the chair in front of the terminal.

But the stranger held back. "Please," he said, motioning to the chair. "If you could."

Christine frowned at the stranger. A grown human uncertain about how to operate a computer? What planet had he come from? Literally.

But sensing his extreme reluctance, she set aside her curiosity and took her place in front of the terminal. "You can do most everything by talking to it."

"Thank you," the stranger said, leaving no doubt that he still wanted Christine to do the talking.

She cleared her throat. "Computer: Access burial records for Chal, main city . . . time period . . ." She looked back at the stranger. "When did your friend . . . you know?"

"I don't," the stranger said. "Sometime in the past . . . eighty years."

Christine passed the information on to the terminal. A stream of names flew by. She glanced over her shoulder. "The records are online. What was your friend's name?"

"Teilani," the stranger said, and instantly Christine knew his story.

Whoever the stranger was, whoever Teilani had been, they had been in love. Deeply. And then they had been separated by some tragedy that had kept him from her for almost a century. It was all there, all in the way he had said her name.

Christine turned back to the computer, overwhelmed by the emotions this traveler had nurtured for so long.

She called up a keyboard on a control surface and entered the name in multiple listings, spelling it phonetically in Romulan and Klingon script.

"Teilani," the computer said. "Searching."

Christine thought it odd that the computer even had time to add that statement. Fewer than a million people had lived on Chal in the past century. The search should have been instantaneous.

"Record not found," the computer announced.

"Are you sure she was from Chal?" Christine asked.

The stranger nodded.

"Search all population records for designated name," Christine said. Some Chal would have migrated. Perhaps the grave the stranger sought was on another world.

"Teilani: Speaker to the second Chal assembly. Federation delegate, 2293 to 2314."

The stranger stepped forward. Christine could sense his grief. "Yes," he said.

"Display location of grave."

"Speaker Teilani is not listed as deceased," the computer replied.

"Present location?" the stranger asked, his voice hesitant, as if not quite believing what he had just heard.

"Speaker Teilani is in Starfleet medical facility three, Chal, main city."

Christine caught her breath.

"She's alive . . ." the stranger whispered.

Christine reached out to take the stranger's hand, not knowing how to say what she knew she must.

Medical facility three was a hospice for the terminally ill.

If this Teilani, the love of this man's life, still lived, she was not expected to live for long.

FOUR

Babel had changed in the century since Spock had first come to it.

The neutral planetoid was now almost completely terra-formed. Where once beneath oppressive metal domes the warmongers and peacemakers of an earlier age had met to shape the history of this small quadrant of the galaxy, now the diplomats and ambassadors who were their heirs could walk beneath open skies.

Spock wondered if the less fettered environment had an accompanying liberating effect on the treaties and the issues decided here. There was no logic to that concept. But then, in his 143 years of life, he had learned that logic seldom applied in politics.

It seldom applied to anything in which humans were concerned.

But as a long-lost friend had eventually taught him, that wasn't necessarily wrong.

Thus Spock turned his mind away from logic, and concentrated on the songs of the birds in the park before him. He stood on a sweeping, white stone balcony of the assembly hall, framed by fluted pillars, looking over the green, wind-riffled leaves of the arcadia trees. Some had been planted long ago, before artificial-gravity generators had been installed throughout the planetoid, and now towered tens of meters into the air. But their younger seedlings barely topped five meters, though their trunks were nearly twice as thick.

That adaptation pleased Spock's sense of aesthetics.

Both the younger and the older trees were of the same species, yet each had altered itself according to the conditions of its germination. The two generations were different, but apart from their exteriors, they were the same within.

Spock fingered the IDIC medallion he wore, meditating on Infinite Diversity in Infinite Combinations and on the sameness of things. The trees of Babel were a worthy lesson.

In time, he heard Srell's footsteps approach.

A century ago, awaiting someone who might be bringing news of such importance, Spock might have tried to judge that person's mood by the length and strength of his stride, and thereby deduce the information he brought.

But even at the age of thirty, Srell was an adept of the *Kolinahr.* Though it would be years before the young Vulcan would be permitted to undergo the final rituals of that discipline, in which his emotions would be purged in the pursuit of pure logic, Spock had no doubt of Srell's success. Whatever Surak, the father of Vulcan logic, had envisioned as the end result of his dream for his people, young Srell had surely achieved it. It was why Sarek, Spock's father, had chosen the promising student as his aide seven years ago, and why Srell continued in that role for Sarek's son. Spock knew of no finer mind on Vulcan. Therefore he made no attempt to interpret Srell's mood.

As the elder ambassador finished his meditation, Srell waited patiently at his side. Only when Spock had slipped his IDIC back into his robes did he address his young aide, still keeping his gaze on the colonnade of trees stretching out before him.

"I once stood on this balcony with my father."

"Indeed," Srell replied. Admirably, the young Vulcan did not seek to question Spock further.

"A Babel Conference had been held to consider the matter of Coridan's admission into the Federation."

"One hundred and six standard years ago," Srell said instantly. He was an excellent student of history. "I have studied Ambassador Sarek's speech from that session. It was most . . . unexpected."

Spock nodded. He had observed that session himself, heard his father hold forth on the fundamental nature of the Federation, the quest for peace in the face of war, the pursuit of perfection in the knowledge that perfection was never possible.

To hear a Vulcan speak in such illogical terms, soar so close to poetry in his oration, had electrified the assembled diplomats of that conference.

Tellarites had pounded their hairy fists on their tables.

Andorians had hissed with excitement, blue antennae quivering.

Sarek's speech indeed had been most unexpected.

Spock knew that his father had held each of his listeners captive by the power of his words, not emotions, raising his voice only to remind them all of the power of the universal ideals each representative held dear.

That day, Sarek had made Coridan the most important world in the galaxy, because it came to represent the Federation itself.

"This is the moment we have come to," Sarek had concluded that day. "Not to vote on the admission of one small world, worth nothing in the vastness of the space and the stars that surround us. But to say we do this thing not because it

31

will make us stronger, not because it will diminish our foes, but because there is nothing else we can do if we are to be true to those great beings whose words have brought us here today."

Then Sarek had recited the preamble to the great charter of the Federation, and to all in that chamber on that day, it was as though they heard those stirring words for the first time.

Srell politely turned his gaze away from Spock as he said, "I have always been curious about Sarek's strategy in constructing that speech."

"In what way?"

Srell dipped his head a fraction of a millimeter in a perfectly crafted show of Vulcan emotion, letting Spock know that he apologized in advance for any unintentional offense he might cause with his next words. "It seemed so . . . emotional."

Spock straightened his robes. "Some of those who attended that session believed my father to be a passionate man."

Srell nodded thoughtfully. "Then his speech was not born of cynicism."

"I believe not," Spock said. "Though since his passing, we shall never know."

Srell regarded Spock with almost imperceptible puzzlement. "I would have thought that on this matter, he would have shared his mind with you."

Spock sighed, a human affectation that in his latter years he no longer strove to hide. The battle between his Vulcan and his human heritage had ended long ago. "I never melded with my father."

Though the young Vulcan's expression did not change, Spock could see that Srell was shocked speechless. For a father and son not to share a mindmeld was almost unheard of in Vulcan society. Though there was no logic to it, Spock did regret those missed opportunities to know his father's heart and mind.

True, he had shared fleeting glimpses into Sarek's thoughts. The legendary starship captain Jean-Luc Picard had once melded with Sarek when the *Enterprise* had conveyed the ambassador to Legara IV. Two years later, shortly after Sarek's death, Picard had invited Spock to meld with him and experience what Sarek had shared.

Spock had accepted the invitation. The encounter had been appreciated, but frustratingly incomplete. He had felt enmeshed in shadows, seeing only brief glimpses of his father's life. At the time, he had almost felt that Sarek had deliberately masked his thoughts from him, though that was, of course, completely illogical.

Still, the lingering doubts about Sarek's neglect to meld with his own son continued to gnaw at Spock, even to this day, five years after his father's death.

Srell seemed to sense Spock's discomfort in thinking about the past.

"Whatever the ambassador's motives, the speech was a success," the younger Vulcan said politely. "Coridan was admitted."

Spock allowed an edge of irony to color his tone. "To protect the planet's extensive dilithium reserves."

"It was a different time," Srell allowed. Dilithium crystals, so necessary for warp propulsion, had once been the fragile lifeblood of the interstellar community. But now they were easily recrystallized and thus abundant. Today, to start a war over dilithium would make no more sense than to fight over cometary ice. "Coridan's admission set a course for peace in its sector that still continues. The ambassador's accomplishment was most satisfactory."

In Vulcan terms, Srell's comments were gushing, almost fawning praise. But Spock allowed his aide the enthusiasm of youth. He almost found it refreshing.

"I regret I was not able to extend my father's legacy of reconciliation," Spock said.

Srell clearly understood Spock's comment, and that Spock's attention had returned to what had brought them both to Babel. "I suspected you would not need me to deliver the news."

"No," Spock agreed. "The result of the vote was that obvious." That was the curse of logic. Spock had always known that the first attempt to initiate official contact between Vulcans and Romulans would end in defeat. But at least the groundwork had been laid for further attempts. One of them would inevitably be successful. Eventually, Spock knew, even he would be permitted to take his place in the official negotiations, instead of having to rely on the presence of his aide, in order to spare the Federation official embarrassment caused by Spock's unsanctioned attempts to broker peace.

But Srell's next comment exploded Spock's line of reasoning. "Actually, Ambassador, there was no vote."

Spock put a steadying hand on the cool white stone of the balcony railing. "Is the advisory group aware of the danger the Romulan delegation has risked to come to Babel?" The Romulan Star Empire had few official contacts with the Federation. Even fewer with Vulcan. But for more than eighty years, Spock had been working unceasingly to bring the Romulans and the Vulcans together—*back* together. For the Romulans were an offshoot from the Vulcan race. The unification of Romulans and Vulcans had become Spock's greatest dream, and, he was convinced, a political necessity, if lasting peace was to be possible in this quadrant.

"Ambassador, the advisory group is well aware of the extraordinary efforts you have made to bring an unofficial Romulan delegation to Babel. On the surface, it is a historic accomplishment."

Spock heard the qualification. "On the surface?"

Srell adopted an even more formal posture to indicate he

was merely passing on information he had been given, without necessarily believing it himself.

"I have been informed that there are those on the Council who believe the stated reason for the Romulans' presence here is misdirection. They do not believe Romulus wishes to pursue either unification with Vulcan or membership in the Federation."

Spock tightened his grip on the balcony railing. What did the Federation Council believe he had been doing on Romulus for the past eight decades? Everything he had worked for had been aimed at this moment—to finally have representatives of Vulcan, Romulus, and the Federation sit down at the same table, however unofficially, to openly discuss their joint future.

"What other reason could there be?" Spock asked.

"The virogen."

Spock turned away. He placed *both* hands on the balcony railing. "That is"—a dozen Earth terms sprang to mind, but Spock restrained himself in order to be a proper role model for Srell—"most illogical."

"Though the news is being withheld from the public updates, I have been reliably informed that the virogen has now spread to a seventh system," Srell said. "Fully one-third of the most densely populated sectors of the Federation have been cut off from regular food shipments. Starfleet relief efforts are undeniably strained."

"One-third," Spock said, almost in disbelief.

"The advisory group believes that the Romulan delegation's sole purpose in being here is to obtain aid guarantees in the event the Empire's own food-production centers become infected. Indeed, Starfleet intelligence suggests that the virogen has already established itself in the Core sectors, and even in the Klingon Empire."

"How is that possible?"

35

Srell ignored the question. The details of the virogen's spread from system to system were the target of the greatest scientific research effort in the Federation's history. "For whatever reason, I have been informed that the Federation is unwilling to support Vulcan trade and development guarantees for the Romulan Star Empire at a time when its own resources are so taxed."

Spock turned back to Srell, using all his discipline to keep an appropriate Vulcan demeanor. "Can they not see that it is precisely because of the threat of the virogen to the food supply that we *must* enlarge the scope of the Federation? That we are *all* threatened and must share resources and knowledge to survive?"

"Ambassador, you ask that question as if you expect the Federation Council to be guided by logic. They are not. At this time, their guiding principle is fear."

Spock felt unjustly chastised by his young assistant. Had he not just been contemplating the fact that politics and logic seldom agreed? Had he not achieved a balance between his human and his Vulcan halves, so that he was uniquely placed to understand the motivations of both Vulcans and humans? And yet, he had been completely unprepared for this turn of events.

"Fear," was all Spock could say. More than three centuries had passed since Vulcans had first joined with humans in an unprecedented partnership to explore strange new worlds, to seek out new life and new civilizations. But that insidious monster of the past—fear of the unknown—still threatened to push all that they had accomplished back into the planetary mud.

Then Srell added to Spock's sense of disorientation. "For humans, it is a logical reaction."

"Fear . . . is logical?" Spock asked.

"If quarantine fails, if one more system becomes exposed to the virogen, Starfleet will not be able to respond. History suggests that if Starfleet fails in its mission to protect our food supply from contamination, some beleaguered worlds will secede from the Federation. In some systems, local resource wars will inevitably result. Any one of a dozen local conflicts could escalate dangerously."

The human half of Spock could not comprehend Srell's equanimity as the young Vulcan blandly recited the events that would lead to galactic anarchy. Even a Vulcan should have been appalled at some level by this terrible scenario.

"Multisector civil war is not out of the question," Srell continued. "Especially if any of the Federation's rivals, such as the Romulans, decide to encourage dissent through covert means."

Spock turned his mind back to the calming practices he had learned during his own study of the *Kolinahr*. "You realize you are describing the collapse of the Federation," Spock said.

Completely without emotion, Srell replied, "Unless a cure for the virogen is found and the food supply protected, the collapse of the Federation is a certainty."

Spock reached into his robes for his medallion. But it brought no comfort to him.

Here where he had once shared his father's greatest success, he was poised on the brink of his own greatest failure.

Logic was no guide. Emotion only paralyzed him.

He needed to take action.

But he missed the long-lost friend who could tell him what that action should be.

FIVE

☆

Christine MacDonald stood in the doorway of the hospice, watching the reaction of the stranger beside her. He had seen death before, Christine concluded. Too much of it. Or else he was like Christine, and even one death was too much.

Christine led the stranger along the narrow pathway that ran between the cots on which the dying patients lay. The smell of disinfectant was strong, because there were not enough medical exclusion field generators to go around. The few the mission had that still worked were being used in the nursery. If a child of Chal could survive the first round of virogen poisoning, there was a chance he or she could recover. But once the poisoning had progressed to the secondary stage, as it had in the patients in the hospice, little could be done.

Christine looked to both sides of the pathway as she headed for the doctor's office—a curtained corner in the large room. Before the evacuation, this building had been an art gallery—a large open space with spectacular skylights with holographic windows that kept the sunlight always focused in the center of the gallery. But the skylights had been shuttered to spare the sensitive eyes of the dying. Glow strips hung on the walls now, leaving the gallery's interior in a perpetual twilight, like the fading lives it contained.

Christine rapped her knuckles against the wooden beam that formed a corner of the doctor's office. "Hey, Bones—you in there?"

Christine caught the stranger's reaction of surprise—something to do with her affectionate nickname for the doctor, she decided.

"Keep your shirt on," M'Benga testily replied.

The curtain tugged back and Dr. Andrea M'Benga stepped out, medical tricorder in hand. The sleeves were cut from her blue-shouldered jumpsuit as well, and she wore a bandana of fragile white Chal fabric tied firmly around her broad forehead. The pale cloth contrasted strikingly with her dark skin and close-cropped black hair. She looked sharply at the stranger, then seemed to relax. "Well, you're not a patient, at least." Christine was unable to interpret the expression on the stranger's face as he scrutinized the doctor in turn.

Christine smiled encouragingly at the stranger. "Dr. Andrea M'Benga, this is . . ."

"Dr. . . . M'Benga." A quizzical smile flickered on the stranger's lips. "I'm looking for a patient. Her name is Teilani."

Christine's eyes narrowed. The stranger seemed determined not to give his name.

"Teilani," M'Benga said as she wearily scratched her head. "Yeah. Over in the far corner. You a relative?"

"A friend," the stranger said. "I'd like to see her."

"You understand what's happening here, do you?" the doctor asked.

The stranger gazed into the darkened corner M'Benga had pointed to. "Something's gone wrong."

Christine didn't know if the stranger was being profound or was simple.

M'Benga exchanged a look with Christine. Christine

shrugged. "I'll say something's gone wrong," the doctor muttered. "That damned virogen hit. Went clear through the food chain in less than a month. Humans, Tellarites, most carbon-based life-forms, they get a taste of it and they double over for a week. Intestinal flora shot to hell. But recovery's just a matter of plenty of liquids, salt and sugar to restore electrolyte balance, and—"

"I'd like to see her," the stranger said again, obviously not interested in the doctor's lecture.

"Look, the point is, the Chal aren't like most people. Their genetic structure is artificial in places. Most common medical therapies don't work on them. Protoplasers can't rearrange their tissue, they metabolize drugs before the drugs can help them . . ." Christine could see that M'Benga realized she wasn't getting through to the stranger. "The thing is, your friend's dying, and there's nothing I can do to save her. Understand?"

"Which bed?" the stranger asked.

M'Benga gave up. "This way." She led Christine and the stranger away from her office, along the back wall.

Teilani was in the far corner. Christine had seen enough Chal succumb to the virogen that she could tell the woman had less than a day to live. Once, she had undoubtedly had great beauty, with elegant, pointed Romulan ears and aristocratic Klingon ridges furrowing her brow, but now disease and age had blurred and diminished her.

In human terms, judging strictly by appearance, Christine would place her age at fifty, which for a Chal could make her almost one hundred and twenty-five. But the wasting of the virogen had reduced her honey-golden skin to a patchwork of broken capillaries and purple bruises, shrunken tight to her fine-boned skull. A sterile pad was taped to her sunken cheek, no doubt to cover an open sore, common in the final stages of the virogen reaction. It extended over one eye and Christine guessed she had probably lost some of her sight already.

She knew that she was looking at what had once been a vibrant being, and at the future of every human who would someday succumb to the inevitable destruction of time and fortune. But in the stranger's eyes, there was no revulsion, no pity, and no fear.

Christine watched as the stranger knelt by Teilani's cot and softly stroked her brow, as if this place were still an art gallery and Teilani was the most precious and most beautiful work in it.

The woman's eyes fluttered at the touch, but she did not awaken.

Beside Christine, M'Benga surreptitiously checked her tricorder. Christine's eyes met hers. The doctor shook her head. Time was running out.

"I need hot water," the stranger said, never taking his eyes off Teilani.

"Her liquid balance is fine," M'Benga said gruffly. "We're on strict rations."

The stranger turned to look up at the doctor. "Hot water. Boiling. A single cup."

Christine blinked at the intensity of the stranger's tone.

M'Benga started to protest.

But Christine put a hand on the doctor's shoulder. "It's all right, Bones. Take it from my allotment."

M'Benga's eyes flashed at Christine. The doctor's temper did not welcome opposition. "I hope you know what you're doing."

Christine nodded. M'Benga went to the supply room.

The stranger smoothed out the woman's blanket, adjusted her pillow. Then carefully and deliberately touched several points on her neck, forehead, and exposed cheek.

Christine's attention sharpened. Some of the locations corresponded to Vulcan *katra* points. If she hadn't heard the emotion in his voice, she'd suspect the stranger had pointed ears hidden beneath the hood of his cloak.

41

"Are you a healer?" she asked.

But the stranger shook his head, as if to dismiss her continued presence as well as her question. He was intent only on the woman who lay dying on the cot.

"Is there anything else I can do?"

The stranger spoke without looking at Christine. "You've done enough."

"No," she said, and she knelt beside him. "Let me help."

The stranger paused, as if she had said something remarkable. Then he looked around, spotted something under the cot, and pulled it out.

Whatever it was, it was heavy, wrapped in Chal fabric. The stranger handed it to Christine, having her hold it as if it were a tray.

Beneath the fabric, Christine could feel a metal plaque of some sort, thirty-five centimeters by twenty-five, a centimeter thick. It was most likely a decorative plate or something similar that had held special meaning for the woman.

The stranger produced a small earthen cup from within his cloak, then a small packet made of some type of . . . paper, Christine reasoned. It crackled like paper, at least.

The stranger unfolded it. Within was a small pile of crumbled brown leaves.

"Is that tea?" Christine asked.

"Of a sort," the stranger replied.

M'Benga returned with a flask of water. The stranger held out the cup to her. The doctor twisted the heater collar on the flask and poured out a stream of boiling water.

The stranger powdered the leaves between his fingers as he dropped them into the water, rocking the cup gently to stir its contents.

Instantly the air filled with a rich green scent. Christine was almost overwhelmed by its fragrance. She had smelled the decay of Chal for so long, she had almost forgotten there were any other scents in the universe.

"Could you at least tell me what that is before you give it to my patient?" M'Benga asked in exasperation.

"What's your prognosis for her?"

M'Benga spoke plainly. "Terminal."

"Then what does it matter?"

He turned to the woman on the cot, gently lifted her head, and carefully let the tea he had brewed trickle onto her lips.

M'Benga sighed heavily and brought out her tricorder again. She waved it over the remnants of the paper packet on the tray Christine held. Then blinked at the readings on the device as if she couldn't interpret them.

"What is it, Bones?" Christine whispered.

"Damned if I know."

M'Benga aimed her tricorder at Teilani. Shook her head again at Christine.

"I'd like to take her from this place," the stranger said.

But M'Benga would have no part of it. "No. I will not have you disturbing my patient."

Teilani moaned. The first sound she had made. Her eyes fluttered again.

The stranger leaned closer to her, touched her *katra* points again.

M'Benga activated her tricorder. Christine saw the doctor's eyes widen. "I don't believe it. . . ."

The stranger stood up by the cot, nodded at the doctor. "I believe she's my patient now." Then he gathered Teilani in his arms, and lifted her from the cot as if she were sweeter to him than life itself.

Christine got to her feet in time to see Teilani's eyes open and turn to focus on the stranger.

Then Teilani smiled, in wonder and in disbelief. Her voice was faint. "James . . . you came back. . . ."

The stranger walked from the hospice, carrying Teilani in his arms. Christine and M'Benga watched him go. The doctor tapped the side of her tricorder to be sure it was working

43

properly. "Her pulse rate is strengthening. Her fever is dropping." She lifted the packet from the fabric-wrapped tray Christine carried and sniffed at it suspiciously.

"James," Christine repeated thoughtfully. At least the stranger had a name now. A human one at that.

She looked down at the makeshift, shrouded tray, then began to unwrap the fabric from it. As she got to the last layer, she could feel that there were letters on the metal object inside. It was some type of plaque.

"Well," M'Benga complained beside her. "What the devil is that thing?"

The fabric slipped to the floor as Christine turned the plaque over to read what was written on it.

She gasped.

In raised and polished letters of bronze, almost glowing in the pale light, were the words

USS ENTERPRISE

STARFLEET REGISTRY NCC-1701-A
SAN FRANCISCO FLEET YARDS, EARTH
COMMISSIONED: STARDATE 8442.5
SECOND STARSHIP TO BEAR THE NAME

". . . to boldly go where no man has gone before."

Christine and M'Benga both turned to stare at the distant entrance to the hospice, just as the stranger disappeared through it, with Teilani in his arms.

"James . . ." Christine said again. For the second time that day, she felt goose bumps rise up on the skin of her bare arms. And not because the air was cool.

It was impossible.

But then, that's just what *he* was known for.

SIX

─────────── ☆ ───────────

Picard stared at the empty corner of his ready room.

The original plans for the *Enterprise*-E had called for an environmental unit to be placed there. Some captains chose to install a sleeping perch for a cat, some a terrarium for more exotic life-forms. The designers responsible for the life-support sections of the starship had checked Picard's service records and had specified a cylindrical aquarium, with an Earth-normal saltwater environment that would support an Australian lionfish.

But when Picard had first stepped into the ready room, after the bridge module had been installed, he had immediately asked for the aquarium's removal.

He had come to the realization that space was too unforgiving an environment for innocent life-forms.

Picard had reviewed the sensor logs of the evacuation of the *Enterprise*-D over Veridian III. He had heard the children cry out as they had been herded along, separated from their parents, only minutes away from being engulfed by the explosive fury of a warp-core breach, and still to face the harrowing descent of the saucer through the atmosphere.

Those cries of terror were not what Starfleet's mission

planners had had in mind when the *Galaxy*-class ship had been commissioned.

Picard had no complaint about families being assigned to deep space together. But children and nonprofessionals must always remain out of harm's way.

So he felt reassured that this *Enterprise* had no children aboard her. And though he missed the relaxing comfort of watching the fins of a lionfish undulate in an aquarium's slow current, he was glad that on this ship there was one life-form fewer for which he was responsible.

When he had first gone into space, it seemed to him he had seen only the brilliance of the stars. But now, more than ever, he saw the dark and endless void between them.

The door announcer chimed. "Come," Picard said.

His first officer entered, frowning, a padd in his hand. "Yes, Number One?"

Riker didn't waste any time. He didn't like the *Enterprise's* current assignment any more than Picard did. That tension was becoming more apparent in all the crew.

"There was no Lieutenant Commander Stron assigned to Gamow Station."

It took a moment for the importance of that statement to register with Picard.

"Was he from one of the other blockade ships?" Picard asked.

Riker shook his head. "I checked every personnel log remotely connected to Alta Vista. There was no Stron assigned to any of the earlier relief missions. No Stron assigned to communications since the station was brought online three years ago." Riker passed the padd across the table to Picard. "In all of Starfleet, there are nine Vulcans with Stron as a given name. The only one within three hundred light-years of this sector is a Captain Stron of the survey ship *Sloane*. And he's one hundred and sixty years old."

"Are the remaining eight Strons accounted for?"

Riker nodded at the padd. Picard scanned it. The duty rosters for all nine Vulcans were complete.

"I confess I'm not certain which surprises me more. The fact that a Vulcan chose to commit suicide, or the fact that a Vulcan lied."

"Given either possibility, sir, we really can't be sure if he was a Vulcan in the first place."

"Is there any record of a pregnant lieutenant commander?"

"Several. But again, none near this sector. None missing. And none matching our sensor-log recording."

Picard stood up and walked to an observation window, staring past his reflection. Almost half a million kilometers away, Alta Vista III was a small, faded yellow sphere, streaked by indigo clouds. A year ago, the clouds had been spectacularly green—fine, airborne colonies of alta mist, a unique epiphytic single-cell plant. But the deadly virogen had taken hold here, as it had in six other systems.

Wherever it had evolved, however it had come to the worlds of the Federation, seen in microscan images the virogen was deceptively simple, even beautiful. Physically, it was a strand of ribonucleic acids, coiled into a single-helix structure, only a few thousand amino-acid base pairs long. By most traditional definitions, it was rightly considered a mere molecule, with far too little material to qualify as living matter. On its own, it was inert, its fragile RNA chain protected by a unique and rigid matching strand of silicon. Though the genetic structure of the virogen was technically exposed in this configuration, without the benefit of a protective wall or capsule, the rigid silicon served as a molecular spine to maintain the virogen's shape and lethality.

In an animal, the virogen's genetic material curiously bonded only to the membranes of reproducing cells, and multiplied as affected cells multiplied, without ever interfering with the cells' own interior genetic structure. Thus, animals served only as factories for the virogen's production, shedding it through exhalations and secretions, all without long-lasting physical impairment in most species.

But in chlorophyll-producing plants, the virogen bonded with the chloroplasts themselves, taking over the plants' own energy-producing mechanisms to fuel its reproduction. Unlike its effects on animals, the virogen's reproduction strategy led to a slow death for each affected plant, as it gradually lost the ability to convert sunlight into energy.

Thus the virogen's effect on Alta Vista III had been no different than it had been in all the other systems it had pervaded. Every form of plant life had been poisoned— become useless as a source of food. Every form of animal life, though largely unaffected by disease, was a carrier. The repercussions for the centers of food production were staggering.

"Why would a Vulcan—or someone altered to appear Vulcan—take on the identity of a Starfleet officer to escape from a quarantined system?"

"And then kill himself and his mate when we cornered him?" Riker added.

Picard turned to face Riker. Riker looked puzzled by the slight smile his captain wore. "Number One, this almost feels like a Dixon Hill mystery."

"Except this isn't the holodeck. Two people are dead."

"Dix would be the first to say appearances can be deceiving."

Riker waited expectantly, if doubtfully.

"If everything Stron told us was a lie, then logically we should not assume that any of his actions were what they appeared to be, either."

"Sir, the *Bennett* took off from Gamow Station without authorization. Stron and his mate were down there. They were clearly attempting to leave the system."

"No. They were attempting to leave the planet and *evade*

us. That's all we can know for fact. What their ultimate destination was, we cannot say."

"Except we know they didn't achieve it."

But Picard shook his head. "Stron and his mate somehow arrived at Gamow Station without anyone discovering they weren't what they claimed to be. In the confusion of the overcrowding down there, that is an understandable, even unavoidable breach of security. But however they managed it, I think we can presume our two fugitives had an equally effective escape route planned."

"Sir, we saw them blow up. That is not what I would call effective."

"What we saw was a warp-core explosion at the same apparent coordinates as the *Bennett*. Then we left the asteroid and returned to our blockade position."

Picard could see that Riker understood where his chain of reasoning was leading.

"Shall I lay in a course back to Alta Vista two five seven?" Riker asked.

Picard nodded. "And prepare an away team," he added.

Riker returned to the bridge. Picard looked back through the observation port again. Less than a minute later, Alta Vista III shrank to a pinpoint as the *Enterprise*-E returned to the system's asteroid belt at warp.

Unfounded suspicions aside, Picard had no idea what they would find there. But the act of looking was far preferable to standing guard over a dying colony.

If the Federation were going to fall, then the captain of the *Enterprise* was determined to go down doing something more than just watching.

Riker felt a wash of vertigo sweep through him as he materialized on the surface of Alta Vista 257. Transporting from the *Enterprise*'s artificial gravity to the almost nonexistent pull of the asteroid was more disorienting than simply stepping through an airlock.

The clear visor of his environment suit sparkled with reflected energy as La Forge and Data took form beside him. Simply turning his head to check on their status was enough to set Riker drifting up from the asteroid's space-black surface.

Riker canceled his momentum by giving a momentary tap to the joystick on the control arm of the maneuvering unit he wore. He saw La Forge do the same, with small, precisely controlled puffs of stabiline gas venting from the tiny thrusters on the engineer's own maneuvering unit backpack.

Data, though deceptively slight in appearance, was much more massive than a human, and capable of controlling his movements more exactly. Thus, he alone remained fixed in position on the asteroid's surface. At least, at first. The android reached down to the leg controls for his magnetic boots, and though Riker saw the activation lights switch on, even Data began to float away from the surface.

Data's boot soles, however, bristled with nickel-iron dust.

"There are too many impurities for our boots to function properly," Data said over his suit's communicator as he repositioned himself with his own maneuvering unit. Technically, the android did not need an environmental suit to function in the vacuum of space. But he did have a number of organic components in his system whose chemistry could be temporarily disrupted by prolonged outgassing, and it was more convenient for his coworkers if he could communicate by voice.

"Well, it's not as if we can drift too far off target," Riker said. He glanced through the upper plane of his visor and saw a magnificent view of the *Enterprise* stationkeeping only a few kilometers above him, relatively speaking. "Riker to *Enterprise*. We've arrived at the center of the blast zone."

Picard's voice answered from Riker's helmet speakers. "Do the blast marks appear legitimate?"

Riker glanced around. The *Bennett* had exploded directly overhead, approximately one kilometer above the asteroid's surface. The surface around the away team was striated with raised silvery streaks, all radiating out from a central point. Riker knew the markings were the result of microscopic pieces of wreckage from the *Bennett* hitting the nickel-iron asteroid at close to lightspeed. The kinetic energy of the tiny particles had been sufficient to gouge molten tracks in the raw metal of which the asteroid was formed.

To Riker's trained eye, just as the *Enterprise's* sensors and viewscreen had initially confirmed, the blast marks did appear to be recent, and consistent with the *Bennett's* destruction. But despite all the *Enterprise's* sophisticated equipment, in some cases there was still no replacement for the human presence in space as skilled observer. Or, in the case of Geordi La Forge, a more than human presence.

La Forge manipulated his maneuvering unit controls so that he floated horizontally, only centimeters above the asteroid's surface. Riker knew the engineer's new ocular implants were scanning the blast damage with much finer resolution than the *Enterprise's* more powerful sensors could be tuned to at a distance.

"Commander," La Forge said. "I'm detecting no trace of space-dust precipitate on the melted impact streaks. These scorches *are* less than a day old. I'm certain of it."

Riker refrained from shrugging. In his suit, it would only disturb his orientation again. "Captain Picard," he reported, being careful to keep his tone neutral. "The *Bennett* does appear to have exploded as we witnessed."

Picard had proposed that the *Bennett* might have used a phase inhibitor to escape the tractor beam, then gone to warp, leaving a second, separate warp core behind, rigged to explode. There was an unexplained subspace burst in the sensor log, followed by a recording gap as the *Enterprise's* sensors had been overloaded by the warp explosion. It was possible that the deception might have been completed before the sensors had automatically realigned themselves. But being possible and being likely were two different things.

Privately, Riker suspected that Picard was looking for any excuse to relieve the monotony of and his distaste for maintaining a blockade on a Starfleet facility. In fact, he was almost sorry his captain's theory had been proven false. Riker agreed with Picard that the *Enterprise* and her crew were meant for more challenging missions.

"What about organic residue?" Picard asked. If the *Bennett* had exploded, Stron and his mate would have been vaporized, and traces of the carbon isotopes from their bodies should be spread evenly throughout the blast site. Detecting that grisly residue was Data's task.

Like La Forge, Data floated near the asteroid's surface, lightly tapping a molecular probe to likely areas and reading the results from the tricorder display screen built into the bottom of his helmet. "The isotope traces I'm detecting are consistent with machinery only," the android said. "I see no sign of organic remains."

That surprised Riker. "Are you certain?" he asked, forgetting for the moment to whom he was speaking.

"To four decimal places, sir. Which leaves room for some doubt, though not an appreciable amount. In fact, it might be said that—"

"Data," Riker interrupted, as he suddenly recollected another of Picard's speculations. "What if Stron wasn't Vulcan and his mate wasn't human? What if they were altered Klingons or Romulans?"

Data slowly rotated into a perpendicular orientation. "In that case," the android said, "the carbon isotopes of their bodies would indeed yield different fractions, according to the signature chemistries of the worlds each species evolved on. But almost any carbon-based life-form would leave a detectable trace as the captain has theorized."

Over the comm link, Picard joined the conversation again.

"In other words, Mr. Data, though the *Bennett* might have exploded as we saw, Stron and his mate were not on it."

"Yes, sir. That is the most likely explanation."

More than anything, Riker wanted to scratch at his beard. But he had to content himself with gazing over the irregular horizon of the asteroid. On the axis length, the horizon was about eight kilometers distant. On the equatorial length, only about three. But aside from the gentle rise and fall of a surface pitted with millennia of deeply shadowed impact craters, there was no sign of a pressure dome or launch facility. Besides, if there had been, the *Enterprise* could have detected either from thousands of kilometers away, along with the machines associated with any underground base.

"Comments, Number One?" Picard asked.

Riker knew he had no choice but to support his captain. Picard had put his suppositions to the test and they had been confirmed. "No doubt about it. We definitely have a mystery here, sir."

"Actually, Commander," Picard replied, "we have two."

For a moment, the implications of Picard's words were like the chill of space moving through the insulating layers of Riker's suit. Could Picard be serious? "Are you suggesting that what happened here is connected to the spread of the virogen?"

In his mind's eye, Riker could almost see Picard settle back into the command chair on the *Enterprise*'s bridge as he contemplated the challenge of a new mission. "Two mysteries in one area of space, Number One? Every instinct I have tells me that the relationship between them is not coincidental."

Riker was aware of La Forge and Data adjusting their positions so they could make eye contact with him. Even in

Data's android features, the emotion of surprise was easy to read.

Picard was not the only one in Starfleet who had theorized that the sudden appearance and spread of the virogen might be deliberate.

But it appeared he might be the first to uncover evidence to prove it.

And if Picard was right again, then the greatest natural disaster facing the Federation might not be natural at all.

SEVEN

☆

Dawn came to Chal. A lone bird sang in the dying jungle. Faintly, plaintively. Alone.

It was the last of its species. The generation to come lost to weakened eggshells that exposed the nestlings to the air before their lungs had fully formed.

The pitiful chicks had perished in their nests, suffocating within an hour of birth, watched passively by their parents, who had never evolved behaviors necessary to cope with the interference of so-called intelligent beings.

When the virogen had first appeared on this world, the first response by the guardians of the environment had been to clear-cut the affected foliage and spray broad-spectrum anti-viral agents on the surrounding areas. The results were catastrophic.

The antiviral agents had unpredictably inserted five engineered genes into an amino-acid sequence peculiar to a common flowering bush indigenous to Chal. The combination accelerated the flowering cycle, making whole fields of the plant bloom months before the insect responsible for its pollination had awakened from its dormant cycle.

Three months later, the berry yield on Chal's primary

islands was less than twenty-two percent of normal. Entire populations of birds and insects starved to death. With their passing, the absence of food rippled exponentially through the food chain, becoming more pronounced at every level.

One species of bird resorted to cannibalism of its young. Another was driven to forage among mountain plants far out of its local habitat. That change in behavior exposed the species to a high-altitude, parasitic mite that infested its plumage. Mating levels plummeted. Federation ecologists saw the multiple disasters propagating through Chal's ecosystems and reacted again with well-intentioned alarm to restore the natural order. In order to keep the mountain mite from spreading, terraforming runabouts were seconded on a priority basis to spray insecticides in the traditional habitats of the displaced birds.

The mites died as planned, but the insecticides, developed for conditions on another world, were anything but natural on Chal. They also entered the food chain, where they unexpectedly interfered with calcium absorption by Chal's indigenous animal species.

Within another three months, almost all Chal mammals were delivered stillborn, their fragile, incompletely formed bones crushed by the contractions of birth. Like the shells of birds' eggs, now mammal skulls were paper thin.

This was how a world died.

Doomed by humanity's simple intention to do good, against the realities of an ecosystem more complex than any human mind could comprehend, more dynamic than any computer simulation could model.

One bird singing. Faintly, plaintively. Alone.

Eighty years after history reported him dead for the first time, James T. Kirk heard that last bird sing as the twin suns of Chal broke through the dull gray haze of morning.

He understood the plaintiveness of its cry.

Just as he understood the unquenchable drive that made it sing, even in the face of sure and certain destruction.

Kirk had seen destruction. He had walked the ruins of civilizations that had been old before Earth's sun was born. Seen friends sacrifice themselves for love and duty. Lost loved ones to capriciousness and hate. Watched strangers die for no reason other than ignorance and greed.

Once he had thought he might change that.

In time, he had become bitter as he had learned how little one man could actually do.

Then he had faced death himself. And against all odds, for reasons which he still did not fully grasp, the end had not come.

Sometimes it seemed to him as if all his life was one endless series of second chances. But this time, he knew he had been given more than just another opportunity.

Kirk had come to Chal renewed, reborn.

He had finally learned the one secret that must be treasured above all else in a universe that had never cared about him and his kind, and never would.

He sat by Teilani's side, warmed by the fire he had built near the bare stone foundations and fire-blackened timbers of the building that had once been her home.

She stirred there, on her bed of blankets, smiling as she woke to feel the warmth of the sunslight on her face for the first time in weeks.

Kirk gently stroked her uninjured cheek.

She looked up at him, her one uncovered eye alight with awe. She reached for his hand.

"It wasn't a dream . . . ?" she asked.

"I love you," Kirk said, and it was as if he truly said those words for the first time, at last understanding their meaning. Knowing they were the only words in the universe that meant anything at all.

Tears formed in Teilani's eyes, gleaming as they slowly rolled down to her gray-flecked hair.

"You came back," she said.

Kirk smiled, and it was as if he smiled for the first time as well.

"For you," he said. "For us."

"James T. Kirk?" Barc grunted.

Christine MacDonald showed the Tellarite the padd to which she had downloaded the historical files from her ship's main computer. The display screen showed an image of Kirk recorded eighty years ago, on the occasion of the ill-fated launch of the *Enterprise*-B. "Look at this," the young commander said. "It's him."

Dr. M'Benga peered over Barc's shoulder. The morning sunlight streaming through the window of the Starfleet general-issue emergency shelter tent was bright enough to make the display look washed out. M'Benga held up a hand to cast a shadow on the padd and scowled in disagreement. "He's dead, Chris."

"That's what they said eighty years ago," Christine said triumphantly. "And then guess who showed up on Veridian Three?"

"They didn't have a body eighty years ago," Barc complained. "But two years ago at Veridian, with Picard, definitely a body. Picard buried him. End of story."

Christine flashed a triumphant smile at the taciturn engineer, pulled back the padd, called up another screen, this time of text. She held it for Barc and M'Benga to read.

The Tellarite's snout twitched in curiosity. M'Benga's scowl became a puzzled grimace.

"They left him there?" Barc said.

"With the *Enterprise?*" M'Benga added.

"Do you honestly believe Starfleet would just forget James T. Kirk?" Christine asked.

"*Rrr,* nothing the admiralty did would surprise me," Barc huffed. "But they couldn't leave the D on Veridian Three. Too many Prime Directive problems if the inhabitants of Veridian Four ever found the wreckage."

M'Benga looked thoughtful. "Or the body of an alien. Kirk's remains would have to be removed from the planet. I'm surprised they didn't bring him back to Earth for burial."

Christine gestured with the padd. "But Starfleet general records hold no information on the disposition of the *Enterprise*'s wreckage, or of Kirk's body. As far as I'm concerned, that means they didn't have a body after Veridian Three, either. And the story of whatever happened there after the crash is being covered up."

Barc grunted, unconvinced. "If it's not in the general records, then it didn't happen."

Christine knew better than to argue with the obstinate Tellarite. But M'Benga could be counted upon to see past the facts of a situation, into its heart.

"Your grandfather served with Kirk, didn't he?" Christine asked the doctor.

"Great-grandfather," M'Benga corrected. "And not for long."

"But you know the stories about Kirk."

M'Benga rolled her eyes. "Everyone knows the stories. And if even a tenth of them were true, Kirk's first five-year mission would have lasted *fifty* years."

Christine was becoming annoyed. How could she make her friends see how obvious the situation was? "All I'm suggesting is that given what we know of the man, we shouldn't be surprised that he of all people is someone who managed to cheat death yet again. I mean, come on, Bones—you analyzed the dried leaves he used for that Teilani woman. You've got your lab up on the *Tobias* churning out clone cultures, and the computer says that that tea, or whatever it is, *will* inhibit the virogen's reproduction in the people of Chal. Even you have to admit that's a medical miracle. So why can't Kirk be using some other miracle compound to keep himself alive?"

M'Benga shook her head. "Chris, all I'm hearing is hero worship. If James T. Kirk *had* survived Veridian Three, don't you think Starfleet would have hauled him back to Earth for a hero's welcome? Don't you think he'd be on every update, writing his memoirs, teaching history at the Academy?"

"Except," Christine said, pointing to the padd, "we don't *know* what happened on Veridian Three after the *Enterprise* crashed. The gaps in the general records tell me that Starfleet's covering up something."

"What?" Barc asked with exasperation.

Christine sighed. "Barcs, if I knew, then it wouldn't be a cover-up, would it?"

The engineer paused a moment to consider that insight. In her usual blunt fashion, the doctor went for the bottom line. "Why don't you just *ask* him if he's Kirk?"

"He doesn't want to tell me his name."

"Chris, you're the commander of Starfleet's relief mission to this world. It's under martial law. You have the authority to ask anyone anything." M'Benga allowed herself a small, dry smile. "Then again, maybe he's tired of people telling him he looks like Kirk."

"Or maybe he's got a good reason to want to hide."

M'Benga glanced sharply at Christine. No longer a ship's doctor, but a friend who had shared enough Academy courses to know her commander well. "Oh, no, I've seen that look before."

Christine drew herself up defensively. "What look?"

"You're falling in love with him."

"After five minutes with him? Don't be ridiculous."

Barc threw up his hands as his ear fur bristled in embarrassment. "That's it. I'm leaving. Feel free to keep all the sordid details of human mating habits to yourselves."

But Christine placed a restraining hand on the engineer's

broad shoulder. "Barc, wait. If you see Kirk—the stranger, whatever you want to call him—don't tell him about . . . any of this."

"Don't worry. I wouldn't want him to think I'm crazy, too." The Tellarite pulled back the flap of fabric that was the tent's makeshift door. "I'll be back at the replicators. For all the good it will do." He snorted in disgust as he ducked outside.

M'Benga took a long look at Christine. "Your problem is, you're bored with the mission."

Christine frowned. "How could I be? We're saving a world here. That's why we signed on."

"We're not saving anything."

M'Benga's glum words hung in the silence of the tent.

"I received an alert from Starfleet Medical an hour ago. Two more systems are affected. It's confirmed."

"Dear God, Bones, why didn't you tell me?"

M'Benga shrugged. "Barc's ready to quit as it is. In case you haven't noticed, morale among the other personnel is the lowest I've ever seen in any Starfleet operation. And whatever hope we were holding out for supplies, well, that's pretty well out the airlock. All we've got is whatever's down here now, and whatever's left to cannibalize from the *Tobias*. That's it. We're on our own."

Christine felt as if M'Benga had punched her. The promise of resupply, of new personnel for the relief mission, was all that was keeping her people going. "Does anyone else know?"

M'Benga shook her head. "It was medical eyes only. Starfleet knows how precarious the situation is. The last thing we need is more panic."

"But Kirk's leaves will work, won't they?"

"For the original inhabitants of Chal with their peculiar Klingon-Romulan metabolism, yes. I'm about as certain as I can be."

"That'll be good for morale, then. No more deaths."

M'Benga gazed down at the padd, as if she didn't have the strength to look her commander in the eyes. Christine had never seen her friend so serious. "Chris, a higher survival rate also means more mouths to feed. We're down to less than thirty days' supply of food as it is."

"The replicators . . . ?"

"Barc says your idea about using the tricorders is brilliant, and should last about ten operational hours. That'll give us what? A few hundred liters of fresh water for the children? Maybe buy us a day or two overall?"

Christine yanked the padd back from M'Benga. "I will not accept defeat."

"This isn't personal, Chris. You're the commander of a science vessel, not captain of a starship. The only reason we got this assignment is because the Fleet is stretched too thin to begin with. We weren't expected to win here. Only to hold the line."

"But you're telling me there is no line to hold."

M'Benga seemed to age before Christine's eyes. She pulled a small chair out from a folding table. Sat down, slumping wearily against the table. "I'm a doctor, not a soldier. I will care for these people as long as I am able. But the enemy we're facing here isn't personal, and isn't out to get *you* or me."

Christine leaned forward, trying to energize her friend. "But it *is* personal. It has to be. Otherwise, what's the point of trying to fight this damned virogen?"

M'Benga pressed a control on the padd and slid it across the table to Chris. Its display showed that old image of Kirk again, on the brink of another great adventure.

"You sound like you've been spending too much time reading those books about Kirk."

"He never gave up."

"He lived a hundred years ago. Life was simpler in the twenty-third century. Things were easier."

Christine picked up the padd and brandished it as if it were a talisman to ward off the evil that surrounded her and infused this world. "Don't you think Kirk said the same thing about life in the twenty-second century? Don't you think the people then said the same about Cochrane's era? Don't you think Cochrane was envious of the twentieth century?" Christine felt the surface of the padd deform under the pressure of her grip. "We all say things were different in the past, but they weren't. Every time's the same. And what worked a century ago *can* work today."

M'Benga repeated Christine's words almost with pity. "Honestly, Chris, just listen to yourself—'What worked a century ago'?"

Christine thumped the padd against the table for emphasis. "He *never* gave up. Never."

From behind her, the stranger said, "Who never gave up?"

M'Benga started in her chair, staring toward the tent's entrance. Christine whirled around.

Kirk stood there, still in his Vulcan trader's garb, though with his hood pushed back to lie around his shoulders.

His face held an inquiring expression, as if to tell them that he knew he had interrupted their conversation and wished it to continue.

Christine glanced down at the image on the padd, then looked again at the man before her. He had longer hair than in the image, tied back. There was no trace of pointed Academy sideburns. Instead he wore a neat beard, flecked with white. But the eyes were the same, Christine swore to herself. However he had managed it, she was certain James T. Kirk stood before her.

But why wouldn't he admit it?

"You were saying?" Kirk prompted again.

Christine flicked off the padd and the image of Kirk faded. "Nothing," she said, placing the padd on the table. "How is your friend? Teilani?"

"Much better."

"The leaves," M'Benga began as she rose, "can you tell me where they're from?"

"No, I can't," Kirk said, then paused, correcting himself. "They were given to me by . . . a teacher. I don't know what planet they're from."

"Do you know what they're called? They're working miracles on the Chal."

"I'm glad," Kirk said simply. "It's what I hoped. I can tell you they're called *trannin* leaves, if that helps." He pronounced the word with a guttural harshness.

Christine glanced at M'Benga. "Klingon?"

M'Benga pursed her lips. "I'll have the computer search for references." Then the doctor fixed Kirk with one of her brightest smiles. "Say, has anyone ever told you how much you resemble—"

"Dr. M'Benga," Christine interrupted with the full authority of her rank. "I believe you have morning rounds to make."

M'Benga locked eyes with Christine. Christine did not have to add the words "That's an order" for her intent to be known.

"Whatever you say, Commander." M'Benga picked up her medical kit from a cot, started out, then turned to Kirk. "Good-bye, Mr. . . . ?"

"Good-bye, Doctor," Kirk said, deflecting the unstated request.

Then Christine was alone with James Tiberius Kirk.

A pioneer whose exploits would live as long as there was a Starfleet and a Federation to guide it.

An improbable survivor from another age.

Her personal hero. Perhaps more.

"What can I do for you?" she asked.

Kirk hesitated, as if he had just thought of a topic to discuss at Christine's suggestion. "Teilani . . ." he began.

"Your 'friend'?" Christine interrupted, before she could stop herself.

"Yes, Teilani." Kirk offered no other explanation for his relationship to the Chal woman, though the way he spoke her name revealed his intimate connection to her. "She tells me that what has happened here, to Chal, is happening on other worlds."

"You didn't know?" Christine asked.

"I've been . . . away. On the frontier."

I'll bet you have, Christine thought.

"Officially," she said, "six other systems have been infected."

"Which means that unofficially, the count is higher."

"I'm afraid so."

Kirk glanced around the tent. Christine got the impression he was recording everything he saw, wasting nothing. "It was bound to happen sooner or later, don't you think?" he asked.

"What?"

"Do you have records of how it began?"

Christine felt she was missing something. As if Kirk were making leaps in the conversation she couldn't follow. "You mean the virogen plague?"

"I want to know how it came to Chal."

"You and half of Starfleet."

"Do you have records?"

Christine tugged down on her tunic to smooth it. If Kirk had some agenda he preferred to keep from her, then at least she could choose the arena.

"To thank you for the leaves you've brought, I'd be honored to have you visit my ship," she said. "We receive constant updates from Starfleet on the state of our efforts to track and contain the virogen, and I'd be happy to share them with you."

"You have a ship?" Kirk asked.

"The *U.S.S. Tobias.* A science vessel." Christine didn't understand the blank look in Kirk's eyes. "In orbit," she explained. Maybe the stranger wasn't Kirk after all.

"I'm familiar with the concept," Kirk said gently.

Christine tapped her comm badge, heard it chirp. "Mac-Donald to *Tobias.* Two to beam up."

The disembodied voice of the transporter chief replied from the comm badge. "Locking on . . ."

Christine glanced hopefully at Kirk. "You know, it would be a lot easier to give you a tour if I knew your name."

Kirk shrugged, as if his name were no longer of importance. "Call me Jim," he said.

Christine allowed herself a brief smile, and was sorry M'Benga hadn't been there to hear that name.

And then the transporter took them.

EIGHT

☆

Throughout his life, Spock had been accepting of defeat. In most cases, it could provide a valuable lesson. Properly understood, defeat in one instance could enhance the prospects for prevailing in a new encounter. Thus, logic dictated that defeat should be experienced without emotion. It was merely a tool that ultimately, if used correctly, would bring victory.

Yet knowing all that, believing all that, Spock still felt angry at what had happened on Babel. Sifting through the reasons for his feelings in his subsequent meditations, he was intrigued, though not surprised, to discover the cause of his anger.

He did not feel betrayed by the Federation advisors.

He did not feel embarrassed by the Romulan delegation's reaction to the cancellation of the vote.

He was just growing older.

The cause of his discomfort was that simple.

For almost a century and a half, he had fought the good fight, and now he was becoming impatient with the struggle. His tolerance for diplomatic niceties was fading. He understood problems more rapidly than he had in the past. He saw solutions clearly ahead of him. There was no logic in waiting to achieve them.

But the absolute key to his emotional state on this day was that he *knew* beyond any doubt that one day the Romulan and Vulcan people would be united, and that he now doubted he would be alive to see that day.

To anyone who watched the ambassador pack his few personal items into a carryall in his austere diplomatic quarters on the Babel planetoid, no trace of his emotional distress would be noticeable.

Displaying all the calm deliberation of a lifetime of discipline, Spock went about his inconsequential tasks without betraying the turmoil that raged within. Though it was his way, recently he had begun to question why it must remain so.

For a moment, Spock paused before pressing the closure tab on the small fabric case on the writing table before him. Any witness might have suspected he was merely reviewing the contents—a personal terminal padd, tricorder, formal robes, toiletries, and two physical books: Surak's *The Art of Peace,* and, for diversion, the timeless Earth classic, Harold Robbins's *The Carpetbaggers.* But the ambassador was in fact caught up in an ancient memory.

Once, more than a century ago on the *Enterprise,* when he had entered the *Pon farr,* he had allowed his discipline to break down to the extent that he had thrown—actually thrown in rage—a bowl of soup across his quarters to smash against a corridor wall.

Spock thought about that irrational act now, and reflected on how unusually satisfying it had been. He wondered if perhaps he should try such an act again. He certainly felt as if he should.

His door announcer chimed. Srell was early, but that was typical of his young aide.

"Come," Spock said.

The door slid open.

But it was not Srell who called upon him.

It was a young Klingon officer in full battle garb.

Spock raised an eyebrow. There were several Klingon delegations currently on Babel, he knew. Though relations between the Empire and the Federation were improving since the Cardassian incident, full diplomatic contact was still to be completely restored. But Spock could think of no reason why a Klingon would wish to seek him out privately.

"What do you want?" Spock demanded. It was the polite thing to say under the circumstances.

The Klingon bowed his head for a moment, then entered Spock's quarters without waiting for Spock's permission to do so. Spock noted that he carried a small diplomatic courier's pouch on his belt.

"Ambassador," the Klingon began. "I have been asked to deliver this to you."

The Klingon took a small holoprojector from the pouch and handed it to Spock. Spock recognized it as a civilian unit which could be used to record a personal message. Its most common function was to serve as a memento of the dead.

"To whom should I offer my thanks?" Spock asked.

"I have fulfilled my duty," the Klingon stated.

"Am I to receive no information about its source?"

The Klingon looked as annoyed as Spock felt. This duty had undoubtedly been forced upon him and he resented being a mere messenger.

"I cannot tell you what I do not know. I will leave now."

In a most Klingon fashion, the Klingon stalked out. The door slid shut behind him.

Spock examined the holoprojector visually. It was little more than a small black base with an activation stud. He placed the unit on the writing desk, then checked it with the small tricorder he removed from his carryall.

There were no traces of explosives. The holoprojector was exactly what it appeared to be.

Spock constructed a mental web of logic to predict the information the projector might contain. Because it was being given to him under covert conditions on the Babel planetoid, he concluded it most likely had something to do with his father. Perhaps an unofficial recording Sarek had once made, which a fellow ambassador had decided should be given to Sarek's son. He activated the projector and a pillar of light formed over the base, resolving into a humanoid form about twenty centimeters tall.

Spock cocked his head, intrigued, as he recognized the figure. Ki Mendrossen. The diplomat who had served as his father's chief of staff in the final years of Sarek's career. He was an officious human, totally devoted to Sarek's well-being, and possessed of an almost Vulcanlike capacity to focus on details. Though Sarek had never commented upon Mendrossen's abilities, the fact that the man had served so long was testament enough to his competence.

Mendrossen's appearance on this projector was unexpected, but Spock felt satisfaction that the message he was about to hear did in some way connect to his father. In some matters, it seemed, his logic remained robust.

As the holographic figure began to speak, Mendrossen seemed much older than Spock remembered him. His shoulders were stooped, as if he had recorded this message while fatigued. Visual static disrupted the projected image as well, as if the recording sensors had not been properly aligned—a sign of haste or ill-preparation, both qualities quite unlike Mendrossen.

"My name is Ki Aloysius Mendrossen, former chief of staff to the office of Ambassador Sarek of Vulcan. I make this confession of my own free will."

The word "confession" startled Spock.

"During my tenure with the ambassador, I reported on a

70

regular basis to the prefect of Gonthar District. The nature of my reports was to keep Gonthar apprised of the ambassador's work on the following matters: the Amtara reparations, the redrafting of Starfleet's First Contact protocols, the repatriation of the Andorian drallstone, and all discussions relating to the Romulan unification."

Spock absently touched his IDIC medallion. He was stunned. Mendrossen was confessing to having been a spy in an organization that routinely relied on mindmelds to maintain security and unanimity. How could such actions be possible?

"I offer no excuse for this betrayal," Mendrossen's projection continued. "For the good of the cause, of the revolution, I believed it was, at the time, a necessity. It is only now, as I see the purposes for which my information was used, that I realize the error in judgment I have made."

Mendrossen bowed his head in a human expression of shame. He did it awkwardly, as if his years on Vulcan had made him lose touch with his own human heritage.

"For all that I believed I followed in the path of Surak, my logic was uncertain and I do regret my actions."

His image shimmering erratically over the display base, Mendrossen squared his shoulders. Now his voice took on a more measured tone, as if he were reciting memorized lines. "Some remnant of the Federation will survive these dark days, and it is my wish that what rises from the ashes will be a more evolved association, devoted to the preservation of each world's distinctive nature.

"That the Federation must end, I have no doubt. That it will end in this particular way, is, I believe, more humane than if matters were left to the inevitable currents of history."

Here, the formality of Mendrossen's words seemed to fade, as if he had abandoned his script and now spoke from his heart. "But I do bitterly regret my role in the death of Ambassador Sarek. Of all the actions of which history might judge me guilty, his murder is the one for which I truly beg forgiveness." The small figure held up his hand in the traditional salute. "Peace and long life."

Spock stared with incomprehension as the holographic image of Sarek's chief of staff reached within the loose gray jacket he wore and withdrew a small, green-finished phaser of Vulcan design. Mendrossen twisted the setting ring, then clutched it to his chest, lowered his head a final time, and transformed himself into a quantum mist.

For twenty silent seconds, all the holoprojector displayed was a flickering patch of stone flooring. Then the recording ended and the shaft of projection winked out.

Spock stepped back from the projector until he bumped into the simple bed and sat down upon it, almost falling as he did so.

His mind struggled to find some logical way of dealing with what he had just witnessed. It was absurd. His father had died of Bendii Syndrome. It was a rare illness, to be sure, most often afflicting Vulcans over the age of two hundred. But the way it had ravaged his father's intellect was well documented. There could be no question that Sarek had died a natural death.

But then, there could be no question that the Vulcan diplomatic corps had never harbored a spy. Such a deception was not only unthinkable, it was impossible.

As impossible as Ki Mendrossen's confession to—Spock could barely bring himself to even think the words—Sarek's murder.

Two impossibilities. Reducing the chance of coincidence.

Spock felt his heart race. He knew he was on emotional edge, but this unexpected message from the past was having more of an effect on him than his control could suppress.

It was one thing to have lost a chance to bring Romulans and Vulcans together.

It was one thing to have lost his father to the inescapable ravages of age and time.

But if his father had been *murdered*. If Spock had knowingly abandoned Sarek to the machinations of a criminal who had worked on his staff, without recognizing the danger his father faced. The failure of son to father was more profound than any mere disturbance in diplomacy.

How could such a thing have happened?

How could he have left his father to such a fate?

Without even realizing what he was doing, Spock squeezed on his IDIC medallion until the heavy chain dug into the flesh of his neck, then snapped.

In one quick motion, Spock hurled the metal disk across the room to smash against the far wall.

His cry of outrage, of shame, echoed in the room.

There was no more room in his life for failure.

Or for logic.

It was time things changed.

NINE

─────────── ☆ ───────────

The *Tobias* was an *Oberth*-class science vessel with a total volume, including warp nacelles, less than two-thirds of the saucer section of a *Galaxy*-class starship. It was one of the workhorses of Starfleet, with a small engineering hull that sat directly beneath its command saucer. The command saucer itself was attached at both sides to the warp nacelles, with the total effect being as if a more standard starship design had been squashed together, fore and aft. The ungainly though sturdy configuration of the *Oberth* class had changed little in almost a century.

Yet Christine MacDonald was proud to be her commander. Many of the officers whose careers she studied, including Kathryn Janeway, had begun as science specialists, then risen to starship command. Christine viewed the *Tobias* as a way station on her path to taking the center chair of one of the new *Sovereign* ships herself.

Presuming, of course, that Starfleet and the Federation survived.

But Christine was willing to make that presumption.

Like the man who materialized beside her on the ship's

transporter pad, she would never give up, and neither would the Federation.

Christine stepped down from the elevated platform, nodded to the transporter tech behind his console, and started for the door. Only when the doors puffed open did she realize that Kirk was no longer at her side. She turned back to find him still standing on the pad.

"Jim?" she asked. "Are you all right?"

Kirk hesitated before answering, as if clearing his head. "It was . . . an unusual experience," he said. "Transportation."

Christine was mystified by his reaction. Even if Jim weren't the legendary starship captain James T. Kirk, though she was still sure he was, who went into space these days who had not, at least once, been transported?

"Have you never been beamed before?" she asked incredulously.

Kirk stepped lightly from the pad. "It's just been a long time since I concentrated on what the sensations of the process actually are." He smiled reflectively. "Quite remarkable when you think about it."

Christine almost said, "It's just simple matter dematerialization," but didn't, afraid she'd sound rude. However, her desire to confront Kirk about how he had managed to survive the events of Veridian III grew even stronger and harder to suppress.

"Let's go to the bridge," she said. "That's where the most efficient library consoles are."

This time, Kirk followed.

The corridors of the *Tobias* were almost deserted. The ship had been in standard orbit of Chal for almost eight months, with stationkeeping procedures fully automated, and most of her crew of ninety-eight aiding the relief effort on the surface.

The only other time her ship had felt so empty to Christine was when she had toured it in spacedock at Vulcan, during its last refit. Then, it slept like a bulky dragon, full of brute power and potential, waiting to be awakened. But now, it felt infirm to her. Passive, waiting, on hold.

If the Federation fell, she wondered, what would be the fate of the thousands of other ships that served it? Would they end their days in lonely orbits, slowly decaying until inevitable reentry, leaving fiery trails to be incorporated into the myths of the primitives living among the ruins of once great civilizations? Or, would they, centuries hence, be rediscovered in abandoned spaceports, restored, and given a second chance to become the driving force behind a second Federation?

Christine stopped for a moment by the turbolift doors. Unconsciously, she reached out to touch the corridor wall, searching for the vibration of the generators that kept her ship in standby mode.

She became aware of Kirk watching her.

"The ship is quiet," he said.

"She's old," Christine answered, though she knew that wasn't what Kirk had meant. "Refit at least five times."

"You wonder how she'll end."

Unnerved, Christine nodded as the lift doors slipped open. It was like having a conversation with a Betazoid, as if he could read her thoughts.

She stepped into the lift with Kirk. "Bridge," she said. The car hummed to life.

"The ships aren't important," Kirk said.

Christine turned to Kirk, surprised. That's not what a starship captain was supposed to believe. "The ships have to be important," she protested. "They're what keep the Federation alive and growing. They're the lifeblood of our civilization, our growth as a species, our acquisition of knowledge." She flushed, embarrassed at her outburst. She had spoken without thought, only with passion.

Kirk looked at her as if he were a parent humoring a child. Christine was annoyed to feel so foolish, so exposed.

"It's just machinery," Kirk said mildly. "And sometimes, it

can blind us to the minds that conceived it, and the souls who serve it."

Now Christine was sure that that was not anything the James T. Kirk she had worshipped might have said. Perhaps it was time to confront Kirk directly as M'Benga had urged her to do. She had to know what could have changed her childhood idol so dramatically from the way history had recorded him.

But he continued before she could begin.

"It's your crew, Commander. That's what's important. The *Tobias* is only a shell that can take you from world to world. In time, it will wear out, or be destroyed. . . ." Kirk paused, looking away, as if caught up in a memory. "There always will be another machine to replace it. Faster, sleeker, more powerful. But even the newest ship in the fleet means nothing without her crew."

"And her captain," Christine said pointedly.

The lift doors opened on the bridge. Half the stations were dark. Kirk put his hand on Christine's shoulder, to stop her from stepping forward.

She felt the heat of him where he touched the bare skin of her shoulder, exposed by the cut-out sleeves of her tunic. She turned to him, drawn by his close presence.

"I once knew someone who thought being captain of a starship was the highest goal anyone could achieve. But the position is a sentence, not a job."

"I don't understand," Christine said. The air in the turbo-lift car felt charged. His gaze still held her. His hand was still on her shoulder.

"The captain is the one trapped in the middle, caught between the machine and the crew, unable to be one or the other. It's . . . very lonely."

"Everything demands a price," Christine said, and believed every word. "If I'm willing to pay it, then nothing else should matter."

Kirk slowly took his hand away, as if understanding that he could not change her mind.

"The person I knew, he thought just like that. Believed what you believe."

"What happened to him?" Christine asked, no doubt in her mind as to the identity of the person they discussed. "Did he get what he wanted?"

"He became a starship captain."

"And what price did he pay?"

Kirk studied her, seeming to search through all the words he knew, unable to find any that could answer her question, until: "He couldn't be anything else."

It was the one answer Christine hadn't expected. She stood in awkward silence; then Kirk gestured to the bridge, as if this were his ship and she were the guest.

"This way," she said, and they left the turbolift together.

An hour later, Kirk's briefing had ended.

Christine had placed herself at the computer terminal as before, but this time Kirk asked the questions and read the screens above the science station—the largest bridge position on the science vessel. He assimilated the data in a way that required Christine to struggle to keep up.

When he had exhausted the information available, Kirk sat down in the operator's chair beside Christine. Deep in thought, he leaned back, steepling his fingers.

Christine ignored the questioning glances from the only other crew on the bridge of her ship—Pini at communications, and Changdrapnor at operations. She was intent on hearing what Kirk's pronouncement would be.

"You look like someone who's seen this before," she said.

An expression of anger darkened Kirk's eyes. "Ecological disaster? Breakdown in the food supply? What else is history made from?"

"I meant, personally," Christine explained.

Kirk seemed to think about his answer for a moment. "Yes," he said. "I have." It was the first piece of real information he had given her about his background.

"Where?" Christine pressed him. When Kirk didn't answer at once, she persisted, "Your homeworld? A colony planet?"

"A colony world," Kirk finally acknowledged. "A long time ago." He looked back at the science-station screen, where the sector's main trade routes were displayed. "This shouldn't have happened," he said.

Christine straightened up in her chair. "Hold on, weren't you the one who just told me something like the virogen plague was bound to happen? That it was only a question of when?"

Kirk tapped the display screen. "On those key trading worlds, yes. We've introduced too many different life-forms into too many different environments. We've tried to create uniform ecologies on worlds with different suns, different biological histories. Half the grain-producing planets in the Federation now use the same strain of wheat. That means one disease could wipe out half the agricultural base of the quadrant. The diversity of a thousand worlds is being eradicated more and more every day. We call it efficiency. But it's an act of strangulation. Of suicide."

It was the first time Kirk had spoken with something other than quiet deliberation and careful choice of words. She heard a passion in his tone that was as surprising to her as if a Vulcan had suddenly shouted in anger.

She probed his reasoning. "But hasn't the virogen done more than a single grain disease would ever be capable of? It affects all chlorophyll-producing plants, not just grains."

"That's my point," Kirk said, frustration evident in his voice. "Chlorophyll is only one of nature's solutions to transforming solar energy into plant growth. But the Federation has systematically spread chlorophyll-producing plants to every planet in its boundaries. If native ecosystems had been left intact, this virogen would have affected Earth, Mars, a handful of other worlds with similar plant stocks. Any disruption on those planets could have easily been dealt with, by relief efforts from non-chlorophyll-based worlds. But look what's happened because we wiped out diversity. All we cared about was growth, not stability. And now we're paying the price."

Christine had heard these arguments before, though she was surprised to hear them coming from a man of action like Kirk. And she knew the Federation's terraforming bureaus were quick with counterarguments.

Uncontrolled ecosystems were precisely those in which unexpected mutations and disease organisms arose. By establishing an artificial interplanetary ecology, one that was uniform and understood in near-molecular detail from decades of study and refinement, the Federation's experts maintained that change could be averted and biological security guaranteed. But somehow Christine was certain that even this Kirk would not be swayed by the opinions of the Federation's experts. He would never change that much.

There was another question she did want answered, though.

"If all that you say is true, then why is what happened on Chal different?"

Kirk's eyes flashed with an intensity that Christine could not identify—pain, outrage, despair . . . whatever its source, it had reached the point at which Kirk had lost all patience.

"Chal was a paradise," he said. "Its biosphere was engineered by Romulan and Klingon ecologists."

"Engineered?" Christine said in surprise. "I never read that in the briefings. The background logs say this was just a colony world."

"Then the background logs have been sanitized. Chal was established as a military outpost. Very few of the land-based plants and animals are native." Kirk's tone became scathing. "It is ridiculous to believe that a virogen that affects an artificial ecosystem created with native Earth life-forms could also affect a Klingon/Romulan ecosystem at the same time. One way or another, there has to be time for adaptation and evolution."

Christine's training came to the fore and without thought she pushed away all consideration of her hero's personal mystery. Kirk had just brought a new piece of the puzzle to the equation that affected her job, new information which she was certain even Starfleet didn't know.

"But you saw the latest report from Starfleet," she reminded Kirk. "No one believes that the virogen arose overnight. They believe it existed in a benign or dormant form for years, spread along the trade routes, and only then became active. That accounts for it striking so many different worlds in so short a time."

"They're wrong," Kirk said. "Chal is not on any major trade routes. It is not a net importer of food products. Its ecosystem is artificial. The virogen could never have arisen here by natural contamination processes."

Christine opened her mouth but nothing came out. From the corner of her eyes, she saw Pini and Changdrapnor turn to look at Kirk.

Christine kept her eyes locked on Kirk as well. The conclusion he was advancing was terrifying. She had to be sure he knew what he was talking about.

"Why do you know things about Chal's ecosystem that Starfleet doesn't?"

"Ask the Chal who live in the main city," Kirk answered. "There used to be a . . . museum in the center of town, disguised as a power-generating station. It told the history of the colony in great detail."

Christine turned to the science terminal, called up a map of the main city, and cycled back through the years until she saw a major structure in the town's center. She called up the data on it.

"Power station. Says here the Starfleet Corps of Engineers tore it down about seventy-five years ago, just before Chal joined the Federation."

"It was a military museum," Kirk said. "I was in it."

Christine turned back to him. "Seventy-five years ago?"

"Eighty years ago."

Christine let the improbability of that statement pass. Eventually Kirk would have to confirm his identity and explain how he had survived. Right now, his theory about the virogen was more important to establish.

"You're actually suggesting that the military branches of Starfleet have information which could help the science sections understand the virogen, but which they aren't sharing? I find that difficult to believe."

"Whatever else Starfleet is," Kirk said, "it's a bureaucracy. You work for it. You know how information can become compartmentalized and lost."

"Maybe that's how they did things in the past," Christine said. "But I have more faith in Starfleet than you apparently do."

"It was a long time ago," Kirk allowed. "But it's still Starfleet."

Christine turned back to the terminal, rapidly typed in more commands, then read the resulting text with a shock of understanding.

"Eighty years ago," she read out to Kirk in a low voice that would not be heard by her curious bridge staff, "Chal applied to the Federation for membership. It says here there was an incident of sorts. Klingon vessels were destroyed. The result of the last gasp of the Cartwright conspiracy in Starfleet Command." She narrowed her eyes, looking for any hint of reaction. "Starfleet's C-in-C, Androvar Drake, died in a space battle here."

Kirk gave away nothing.

"The logs say that the person responsible was James T. Kirk."

Kirk's expression was so impassive that Christine was certain he had studied on Vulcan.

"Did you ever meet him back then? Eighty years ago? Jim?"

Kirk stood up, completely unreadable. "James T. Kirk died a long time ago. I don't believe in dwelling on the past."

"I'm going to have to tell Starfleet what you've told me," Christine warned him.

"It's too late to do any good. But when you do, tell them to activate all sealed files on the *chalchaj 'qmey*. The Children of Heaven. That'll bring up the data they need on Chal's ecosystem." Kirk started for the turbolift. "I have to get back to Teilani."

"Jim, wait," Christine said. "I'm going to have to tell Starfleet how I got this information. Why won't you tell me who you are? For the record."

For a moment, Kirk hesitated, as if caught in an inner struggle. "I'm no one," he said at last. "Let it go at that."

Christine wanted to protest that he was wrong, that it was time he step out of the shadows of the past. But something in his face stopped her.

"Please," Kirk said.

Christine nodded, wondering what it would be like to find herself in a new century, with all the old familiar touchstones gone. "But if you remember anything else that might help us. . . ."

"I'm not going anywhere," Kirk said, and this time found an almost wistful smile. "Chal is my home, now. I'd like to keep it that way."

Christine nodded. However Kirk had come to this place and this time, he had clearly decided his days of adventure were over. She could respect that decision, even if she couldn't understand it.

She watched him walk to the turbolift. Once inside, he paused, keeping the doors from closing as he glanced around the bridge.

"It's a fine ship," he told Christine. He met her eyes. "But just a ship."

He stepped back. The doors closed. And he was gone.

Instantly Pini and Changdrapnor got to their feet and joined their commander.

"Who was that?" the diminutive communications officer asked.

"No one," Christine said.

Changdrapnor scratched at the iridescent scales that grew at the edge of his beak. "He looked familiar. Almost like—"

"No speculation," Christine said firmly. "We owe him that much."

Both Pini and Changdrapnor reacted with unquestioning acceptance.

Christine regarded her crew with pride. Kirk had been partially right. A ship was nothing but a shell without a good crew to go with her. And her crew was one of the best.

"Lieutenant Pini," she said crisply, "get me Starfleet Command emergency relief headquarters, priority channel. I want to speak with Admiral Goddard personally."

The communications officer looked wide-eyed in concern. "Commander . . . I'm not sure I can do that. We're just a science vessel."

"Tell his office that we have uncovered evidence that may indicate the virogen plague is artificial."

"We have?" Changdrapnor hissed in surprise.

"Maybe, maybe not," Christine said as she looked over at the closed turbolift doors. "But at least we'll get someone's attention."

TEN

☆

Will Riker's protestations were still ringing in Picard's ears as he materialized in the cramped manager's office of Gamow Station on Alta Vista III. As first officer, it was Riker's duty to take on all hazardous away missions. The captain was too valuable a resource to risk.

But Picard had argued that he was merely beaming into a Federation science station. How hazardous could that be?

Riker had muttered that he hoped they wouldn't find out, and then Picard had dissolved in the transporter's beam, and reappeared here.

The manager, Chiton Kincaid, was an extraordinarily tall and slender woman, almost two and a half meters in height, from a low-gravity Earth colony world. As she rose to greet her visitor, Picard had to look up through his helmet visor to meet her eyes. He hoped he was able to control his expression of surprise at her size as easily as she controlled her reaction to his wearing a hard-vacuum environmental suit. His communications with her by viewscreen had not prepared him for the total impact of her height.

Chiton lightly shook Picard's gloved hand. "I take it Starfleet still hasn't been able to isolate the virogen?"

Picard adjusted his interior comm-link control so he could speak to the station manager through the comm badge she wore on her Starfleet uniform. "Not yet," he said. "Though Dr. Crusher remains hopeful."

Chiton appeared to believe Picard's assessment of the situation as much as he did—not at all. She gestured to a chair by her piled-high desk. "Sit, if you can."

Picard declined. Chiton pushed a stack of diagnostic kits to the side and sat back on the corner of her desk, her thin arms folded against her chest. The movement made Picard think of insect limbs. He suppressed the unsettling thought quickly.

"Forgive me if I don't offer you something to drink," Chiton said.

Picard admired the station manager's ability to find humor under present conditions. The only way her science outpost could support the fourteen hundred refugees who had been brought to it was by abandoning all pretense as to her original mission. The domes in which solar sensors had been deployed to study the inversions of the Alta Vista sun had been emptied of all scientific apparatus. The rocky scrubland that surrounded Gamow Station's pressure domes was littered with hurriedly disassembled machinery and unnecessary equipment. Even so, there was barely room inside the domes for the cots and replicators the *Enterprise* and other relief vessels had beamed down.

But in no way could any of Gamow Station's refugees or science staff be beamed up. Everyone on the station had been exposed to the virogen, and only the strictest quarantine measures could keep it contained. *If it* can *be contained,* Picard thought.

Chiton seemed sensitive to Picard's reluctance to begin. "I'm assuming you beamed down to tell me something in person you can't risk transmitting so that others might hear," she prompted.

Picard appreciated the station manager's effort to make

this easier for him. "Two people from this station may have escaped the blockade."

Chiton frowned. "My staff tracked the chase with our deep-space sensors. The *Enterprise* was the only ship to come back."

"Our sensors might have been fooled as well," Picard said.

"Fooled?"

Picard told Chiton how the *Enterprise*'s chase of the *Bennett* had ended.

"A Vulcan and his pregnant, human mate?" she asked incredulously. "And they killed themselves?"

"Perhaps not. We checked the blast zone and there were no traces of organic residue. I believe Stron and his wife beamed to another location. A second ship, perhaps."

Chiton put a hand on her jaw and sharply twisted her head to one side as she thought over the implications. "Then it was a very well organized escape."

Picard winced as he heard a ripple of cracks come from her elongated neck. His helmet's speakers amplified the sound alarmingly.

"What I am trying to determine," Picard said, "is who among your staff would have had clearance and opportunity, first to keep Stron's presence at the station hidden, and then to allow him access to the *Bennett*."

"Me," the station manager said at once, clearly untroubled that she might be drawing suspicion to herself. "A couple of others in operations."

"Who, specifically?"

Chiton rose to her full height and walked around her desk to the computer terminal half-hidden in the clutter on the surface of the desk. She began typing in commands. "Anyone who maintained individual quarters. In the dormitories, someone definitely would have noticed a Vulcan and his pregnant human mate." Chiton turned the display screen around so that Picard could read it. "These are current medical logs for the station, including all refugees. No pregnancies. Twenty-two Vulcans. No one missing."

"You're certain that all the refugees would have been included in this list?"

"S.O.P., Captain. When the refugees arrived, we still weren't sure what we were dealing with. So everyone was inoculated with broad-spectrum antiviral serum at the transporter pads as they beamed in, or at the airlocks as they transferred from shuttles."

Picard reached for the terminal control surface, then realized he wouldn't be able to input properly with his gloves. "Are all the shuttles accounted for?" he asked.

Chiton typed in the query. "Yes," she said.

"When did the *Bennett* arrive?"

This time, the station manager didn't enter Picard's question. "The *Bennett's* been here from the beginning. It was part of the original equipment allotment for the station."

Picard stared at Chiton Kincaid, his surprise obvious. "The *Bennett* was a cruiser escort. Why was it assigned to a planet-based solar observatory like Gamow Station?"

Chiton appeared to be equally surprised by his lack of knowledge. "The ship wasn't part of our solar mission. She was part of a terraforming study group."

Picard's puzzlement deepened. "I wasn't aware that Alta Vista Three was a candidate for terraforming. It already has a native ecosystem." Picard was aware that the planet's plant and animal species thrived in an atmosphere with more sulphur and less oxygen than humans could survive in, but he also knew that Federation regulations strictly prohibited the alteration of an existing alien biosphere unless it closely matched Earth norms.

"Most assuredly," Chiton agreed.

"Then what exactly *was* the *Bennett's* mission?"

The station manager gestured up past the ceiling of her office. "The alta mist, Captain. Those colored clouds are giant colonies of what's virtually an airborne algae. They're epiphytic—absorb all their nutrients from the air. The Federation's terraforming bureaus were interested in engineering the epiphytes to help in seeding other planets with oxygen. The *Bennett* was modified to scoop samples from the atmosphere and transfer them to terraforming pilot projects."

Picard felt as if he had been struck by a phaser. "Could that be how the virogen was spread?" he asked. Could the answer to the greatest disaster that had ever threatened the Federation be so easily found?

Chiton shook her head. "We thought of that, too. But the *Bennett* never left the system. Once the virogen established itself in the alta mist, that's when the quarantine began."

Picard sighed, briefly fogging his visor. It would have been too simple a solution to connect the *Bennett* and the alta mist with the virogen. But still . . . there was one detail that nagged at him.

"What precisely was the nature of the *Bennett*'s modifications?"

Chiton called up a schematic of the ship. It was a simple warp design, sleek enough for impulse-powered atmospheric flight. The outlines of two large pods mounted on its undercarriage began to flash. "Sampling tanks," Chiton explained. "Pressurized nozzles, venting chambers, built-in transporter links for transfer to holding tanks at the pilot projects. It's a standard modification for biological assay missions."

The pods were like a red-alert beacon to Picard. "Did the *Bennett* fulfill any of its mission objectives?"

Chiton looked annoyed. "As I said, it never left the system."

"But did it ever undertake sampling runs?"

Chiton checked her computer. "Several," she said. "We were using it to track the spread of the virogen around the planet. All the data have been forwarded to Starfleet Medical."

"Then those sampling tanks must have been full," Picard said.

"What's your point, Captain?"

"There was *no* organic residue at the blast site. Even if Stron and his wife had beamed off the ship, the blast site should have been covered with the residue of the alta mist from the sampling tanks. Thus, it must have been beamed off, as well."

"You're saying someone *stole* the alta mist?"

"Under our noses." Picard wanted to contact his ship at once, assemble his team, get Data and Geordi and Will at work on this right away. But he still didn't dare transmit his suspicions over subspace. Who knew who might be listening in?

"But why would anyone do that?" the station manager asked.

"I can't be certain," Picard admitted. "But it must have something to do with the atmospheric spread of the virogen."

Chiton straightened up and put her hands on her hips. Picard could see the skepticism in her eyes and her posture.

"Unfortunately, the virogen arose on several other systems before it appeared here," she said. "That would seem to leave a rather large hole in your theory."

But Picard was certain he was on to something that no one had yet suspected. His voice rose with his urgency. "Starfleet believes the virogen might have been spreading through the sector in a dormant phase, and only last year did it become virulent. But what if it were *engineered* here in the first place? Spread by colonies of alta mist which were released into the atmosphere of a dozen worlds?"

Chiton's angular face tightened. "Captain Picard, I told you: The *Bennett* never left the system."

"But surely other ships might have come and gone before it. And the *Bennett*'s cargo and crew did break quarantine when we chased it. It could be part of an ongoing operation."

The station manager moved around her desk to face Picard directly, towering over him. "You do realize what you're suggesting?"

Picard almost trembled at the thought that this might be the breakthrough all of Starfleet had been waiting for. "Yes. That the virogen is artificial and deliberately spread. A hideous act of biological warfare against the Federation!"

Picard looked up at the manager in excitement and was surprised to see she didn't share his outrage.

"Captain," she said quietly, "I think you're very wise to keep this off the subspace channels."

"But not for long," Picard replied. He felt invigorated, charged with energy. After months of doing nothing, he had an enemy to focus on, a goal to achieve. His findings here could rally Starfleet in its darkest hour. Give the Federation hope.

Then Chiton grabbed his arm so suddenly, he didn't even think to pull away. For a moment, he wondered if he appeared too agitated, if she were going to suggest he compose himself.

He reached for the comm-link control on his forearm. "Manager Kincaid, please . . . I must beam back to the *Enterprise.*"

But from behind her back, Chiton produced a medical protoplaser.

"My regrets, Captain," she said. Then she slashed the protoplaser's cutting beam across Picard's helmet, fusing the built-in communicator circuits in a spray of sparks, and slicing open Picard's clear visor. He felt the rush of Alta Vista air strike his skin an instant before the sizzling heat of a spray of molten transparent aluminum.

Picard collapsed to his knees, gasping in agony, clawing at his helmet, futilely trying to wipe the burning metal from his face.

Then the pain seemed to disappear as he felt the manager's

boot kick him sharply beneath the ribs, driving the air from his lungs, making his vision sparkle with black stars.

He fell back on the floor of the office, his vision swimming as Chiton knelt beside him, still a giant, like a storm cloud above him as he kept falling back into a dark place where all pain would end.

The last image he remembered was the tip of the proto-plaser moving closer, glowing, whiting out the manager's face. Her voice echoed in his helmet. "You're not going anywhere."

Then the pain vanished, along with everything else.

ELEVEN

Kirk's hands were raw where blisters had burst. His muscles protested. His knee twinged where he had twisted the wrong way while hefting one of the collapsed beams from the ruins of Teilani's home.

But he had never felt better.

And looking at the small cabin he had constructed and braced between two existing stone walls, he had never felt more satisfied.

He did not know how these feelings had come to be. Over his career, he had never stopped learning. There had always been more capable teachers to follow, more experienced specialists whose examples he could profit by. As the years had progressed, so had his store of knowledge and skills, sometimes in spite of himself.

If anything, he reflected, at his age he should be capable of great and complex accomplishments, using the sum total of his knowledge and experience.

Yet more than ever, it was the simple things that drew him now. Building a cabin instead of exploring a galaxy.

Youth had been for him an explosion of opportunity and

possibilities—a thousand worlds to experience, an infinite number of directions to pursue.

Each direction he had chosen, each challenge he had accepted, had narrowed the focus of his life, until he had come to this time and this place—the crossroads of his existence.

He would not have it any other way.

One home. One dream. One love.

He felt Teilani's arms slip around him as she stood to admire his work.

"It's beautiful," she said.

Kirk tilted his head at his creation. "The door's crooked," he said.

"I understand it's a very popular architectural feature on *Qo'noS.*"

"There're only two rooms."

Teilani leaned her head against his shoulder. He ignored the flash of pain her movement caused his strained muscles. He wanted to feel her head resting against him.

"Who needs more than two?" she asked.

"And without plumbing, I had to dig a ditch out behind the far wall."

Teilani smiled up at him. "That's different. Tomorrow I'll help you find some pipes."

But whatever she said made no impression on him. He saw only her eyes, her lips, the passion they had shared once and which he knew they would share again.

There was nothing he could do but kiss her. Nothing she could do but return that kiss, as if no time had passed in all the years they had been apart.

Kirk lifted her and felt only the fire of youth in his arms. If his knee twinged, it had the good sense to keep its complaints to itself.

He carried her across the threshold he had built, leaving the nightmare of Chal behind.

The second, smaller room held their bed—a mattress made of scavenged blankets, pillows of rolled-up food sacks, a shuttered window casting bars of light and shadow as if it were summer outside and the world and the Federation weren't dying all around them.

He placed her gently on that bed and she did not take her arms from around him.

For a moment, he felt a sense of nervousness. He had been gone so long.

But she whispered in his ear to tell him that no time had passed at all. That in this bed he had made, in this home he had built, the years held no dominion.

He kissed the scar that ravaged her face, touched her hair embroidered with gray, and knew she was right.

Time meant nothing.

All his life meant nothing.

Except for this one perfect moment in the arms of this one woman.

They made love then.

For the first time, for the hundredth. It didn't matter.

After all the years and the light-years he had traveled, all the worlds he had seen, James T. Kirk had finally found what he had sought.

In Teilani's embrace, he was home.

They lay together, letting the breeze cool the sweat from their bodies, watching dust motes spiral in the thin shafts of light that pierced the wooden wall.

Teilani stretched against him. Kirk held her hand, kissed her fingers, felt the tension inside her.

He rolled onto his side, traced the frown she wore. "What?" he asked.

"Spock told me you were gone."

"Shhh," Kirk whispered. He kissed her eye, kissed the

Klingon furrows of her brow, the Romulan tips of her ears. "I didn't die. I was only lost."

"Spock came to Chal to tell me in person. Less than a year after . . . after you left. He didn't say you were dead. I don't think he believed it. But he said you were gone. And I could tell he meant forever."

She turned to touch his chest, stare into his eyes. "I read about what happened on Veridian Three." She gazed at him questioningly, waiting for him to answer next what he must.

"I didn't die," Kirk said, smiling.

"But how . . . ?" Teilani asked.

He held a finger to her lips. Saw her react to the shadows in his eyes. He had wondered how much Starfleet would make public about his rescue by the Borg. About the Borg and renegade Romulan alliance to invade the Federation. Some secrets were best left to history.

"I came back," Kirk said. "Isn't that enough?"

Teilani pressed her head against his chest, held him tight. He was flooded with the memory of where he had gone after the near-destruction of the Borg homeworld. The teachers he had found. The mysteries revealed.

"I'm so afraid you'll leave again."

"Not today," Kirk said.

They made love again. For the first time. For the hundredth . . .

. . . and awoke to the screams of the dying, as Orion fighters blazed through the night sky, raining death and destruction on the last of Kirk's Eden.

TWELVE

For the fifth time that day, Sarek's chief of staff transformed himself into the mist of quantum dissolution.

In the privacy of a Babel conference room, Spock studied his young aide, Srell, for his reaction to the holoprojector's recording.

Predictably, Srell betrayed no emotional response at all.

"It is an obvious forgery," the young Vulcan said.

"Explain."

"Ki Mendrossen is not dead."

"How do you know?"

In the clipped, efficient exchange that passed for conversation among Vulcans, Srell did not hesitate. "Before our arrival at Babel, I reviewed personnel files at the diplomatic corps. Mendrossen's was current."

Intrigued by Srell's comment, Spock reached out and shut off the holoprojector before the recording of the empty floor ended on its own. "Why did you review Ki Mendrossen's personnel file?"

"I anticipated a positive result to the vote on expanding negotiations with Romulus. To fully exploit the opportunity would have required additional workers with expertise in delicate diplomatic matters. Mendrossen's work for your father was most satisfactory. I wished to see if he were available for reassignment."

"Was he?"

"Ki Mendrossen is on leave. I presume he will be available for reassignment upon his return."

Spock nodded, placed his hands behind his back, and began to walk the length of the conference room. The walls of the simple chamber were adorned with the banners of Federation members. Many of them were battle flags—the lesson being that even onetime enemies could eventually sit at the same table in peaceful negotiation.

"What is the current status of Sakkath?" Spock asked as he paced. At the same time Mendrossen had been Spock's father's chief of staff, Sakkath had been Sarek's personal assistant. The Vulcan aide had used his telepathic skills to help stabilize Sarek's emotional control during the final negotiations to complete the Legaran treaty.

This time, Srell did hesitate before answering. "I do not know."

Spock found that a curious response. "Would it not have been logical to ascertain Sakkath's status at the same time you reviewed Mendrossen's?"

Srell remained seated at the table, hands folded before him. Spock now stood behind his assistant's chair. Their different positions and attitudes properly reflected their relation as teacher and student.

"Sakkath is Vulcan," Srell explained. "I did not believe the Romulans would deem him a suitable neutral observer. Mendrossen is human. The Romulans would complain about his connection to the Vulcan diplomatic corps, but in the end, he would be suitable."

"Sakkath is also on leave," Spock said.

Srell turned in his chair to face the elder ambassador. "Then you have checked the personnel files as well."

"No," Spock said. "I contacted a colleague at the corps. My inquiries were unofficial. No data trail exists which possibly might alert remaining spies."

"A spy in the Vulcan diplomatic corps is a logical impossibility."

"Yet Ki Mendrossen has disappeared."

A human might have questioned Spock's assertion. Srell knew better. He simply asked for more information. "Are there indications of suicide?"

Spock leaned past Srell to pick up the holoprojector which still sat on the conference table before the young Vulcan. "This unit contains power cells manufactured on New Malta. Mendrossen's last known communiqué with the corps was from New Malta. He arrived at New Malta on the passenger liner *Olaf Stapledon*. He had further booked diplomatic courtesy passage on the Starfleet survey vessel *Sloane,* to depart ten standard days later. Yet he was not aboard the *Sloane* when it departed New Malta. He is no longer known to be on New Malta. Logic, and this recording, suggest he died on New Malta."

"There are many arguments I could construct," Srell said calmly. "Perhaps Mendrossen went into hiding after creating this fraudulent recording. Perhaps Mendrossen was kidnapped or murdered by an unknown assailant who subsequently manufactured this recording."

"For what purpose?" Spock asked.

"There are insufficient data." The young Vulcan stood up beside Spock. "The most important fact is that Sarek was not murdered. He died of Bendii Syndrome. Thus, however it was made, Mendrossen's confession to participating in your father's murder is also a fabrication."

Spock took a moment to prepare himself before he stated his most shocking discovery of the day. "Srell, I have ascertained that my father was never clinically diagnosed."

For a moment, Srell's emotional control faltered. "Ambassador . . . I assure you I was at his side day and night. His wife attended him. The best healers from Vulcan attended him. You yourself have read the reports of the events at Legara Four when Sarek's emotional turmoil bled through to the crew of the starship he traveled on. Everything unequivocally pointed to Bendii."

But Spock was unswayed. "Observation of symptoms aside, the only definitive diagnosis of Bendii Syndrome is obtained by culturing tissue from the metathalamus. I have determined that procedure was never undertaken."

Spock's young assistant looked stricken. "But . . . that is illogical. How could healers treat a patient without confirming their diagnosis?"

Spock sighed for the many lessons of age that the years still held for Srell. "Even on Vulcan, logic does not always obtain. My father was old, revered, dying. I find it most logical that given the apparent definitive nature of his symptoms, no healer felt it necessary to subject him to the discomfort of a biopsy of his metathalamus."

Srell sat down abruptly, rigidly staring across the chamber at the flag of the Martian Colonies that hung directly opposite him. The flag was stitched with laser holes from the War of Declaration. "I was on your father's staff. I should have known. I might have done something."

"Regrets are illogical," Spock said, though he knew he was not convincing.

In any event, Srell did not appear interested in any wisdom Spock might dispense. "Why would anyone want to kill Sarek?"

Spock sat down beside Srell, no longer a teacher instructing his student. Instead, they were two colleagues mourning a revered mentor. "My father's career spanned more than a century and a half. That is ample time to make enemies.

Perhaps members of the cause or revolution to which Ki Mendrossen referred."

"But to kill him in such a manner," Srell said.

"In what manner?"

Srell glanced at Spock. "To make it appear as if he had Bendii Syndrome, of course."

"Of course. But how could his murderer accomplish that?" Spock asked.

Srell looked around the room at the flags, then down at the table. He found no answer. "I . . . do not know."

"There are three possible techniques," Spock said.

"You conferred with yet another colleague?"

"With a holographic representation of an expert in Vulcan criminal investigations. I availed myself of the holodeck in the health center."

Srell made no pretense of hiding his bewilderment. "How can there be an expert in Vulcan criminal investigations? There is no crime on Vulcan."

"Other than the murder of my father," Spock agreed dryly, "there is very little. Nonetheless, I reconfigured several Vulcan expert systems in sociology and medicine to interface with a fictional human detective. He was quite illuminating in his understanding of motive, opportunity, and technique. Though his violin skills are rudimentary, at best."

"You conferred with a fictional human detective on a holodeck?" Srell said in the Vulcan equivalent of shock. "That is not a technique they teach at the Academy."

"I have learned to be adaptable."

"Indeed." Srell visibly struggled to compose himself, then sat forward in his chair, holding his hands together on the tabletop again, preparing to be enlightened. "What are the three techniques by which Bendii Syndrome might be duplicated?"

"First, telepathic induction," Spock said. "It would require a series of progressively intrusive mindmelds between murderer and victim, with the memories of those mindmelds continually erased. Second, gradual exposure to deuterium, in food and drink, which would build up in Vulcan neural tissue and degrade its function, and which could be detected at autopsy. And third, deliberate exposure to the Bendii Syndrome pathogen."

Srell blinked. "Bendii is not communicable."

"Almost any disease is communicable if extraordinary measures are taken to introduce the pathogen into the body of the victim."

Srell sat in silent contemplation for long moments. "Why was your father simply not shot? Lost in a transporter malfunction? Poisoned in one dose?" Srell looked beseechingly at Spock. "He died almost three years after he was thought to exhibit Bendii symptoms. Why so long?"

"Clearly, it was important to the murderer that no one suspect Sarek was murdered. Perhaps it was enough that his abilities were impaired."

"His stamina grew steadily worse," Srell admitted. "But his abilities, when he commanded them, were as formidable as ever."

"However, as my father's stamina declined, he undoubtedly had to relinquish involvement in many ongoing missions."

"That is true," Srell conceded.

"But not," Spock said, quoting the subjects on which Ki Mendrossen, Sarek's chief of staff, had reported to the mysterious prefect of Gonthar District, "his involvement in the Amtara reparations, the redrafting of Starfleet's First Contact protocols, the repatriation of the Andorian drallstone, and all discussions relating to the Romulan unification."

Srell nodded slowly. "That is also true."

"Thus, logic dictates that the reason for my father's murder is connected to one or more of those ongoing negotiations."

"Sarek was not involved in Romulan unification. He followed that topic only because of your involvement in it."

"Indeed."

"He was . . . pleased with your progress, if not your tactics."

Spock lifted an eyebrow. It was most inappropriate for young Srell to discuss Sarek's feelings with Sarek's son. "My fictional expert pointed out a common element to all three methods of murder," Spock said, changing the subject.

"Ongoing personal contact," Srell said.

Spock noted with approval his assistant's quick and logical response. He decided the youth's earlier, inappropriate comments had merely been the natural result of shock.

"Thus, there are many suspects," Spock suggested.

"His wife, Perrin. Sakkath. Ki Mendrossen, who has confessed—"

"Who might have assisted in the murder," Spock amended, "implying there may have been other conspirators—from the so-called cause or revolution."

"Myself," Srell continued matter-of-factly. "The staff of healers who attended him." The young Vulcan paused. "It will be necessary to obtain a list of his visitors and appointments for the years preceding his death."

"They are being prepared for me on Vulcan," Spock said. Again, he had made the request of the Vulcan archives through a third party—a scholar claiming to be researching Sarek's life for a thesis.

"When will the lists be available to us?" Srell asked.

"When we arrive on Vulcan."

Srell blinked. "I had assumed we would be returning to the Romulan border."

"The Empire will wait. There is no trace of the Klingon

who delivered the holoprojector to me. There is no library correlation to a prefect of the Gonthar District. There is nothing more we can do by subspace. Therefore, whatever answers are to be found are waiting on Vulcan. The scene of the crime, as it were." He stood up, signaling to Srell that their meeting had ended.

Srell immediately stood and smoothed the long, black tunic he wore. "I will make new travel arrangements."

Spock nodded.

Srell went to the door, turned back with a sudden thought. "Ambassador, given the unusual circumstances by which you obtained Ki Mendrossen's confession, have you considered that you yourself are being manipulated into returning to Vulcan to investigate your father's murder?"

"Of course I am being manipulated," Spock said. "It is merely a question of discovering who the manipulator is: Ki Mendrossen, seeking absolution after his death, or a person or persons unknown, for reasons which for now still remain unclear to me."

Srell spoke cautiously. "In regard to those reasons, Ambassador, it could well be that having killed your father, the person or persons responsible might not hesitate to kill again if they fear their crime will be uncovered."

"They are right to be afraid," Spock said.

Srell didn't understand.

"I am only half Vulcan," Spock explained. "Whoever killed my father will have to answer to my human side."

Spock noted with interest the manner in which Srell raised both his eyebrows.

In Vulcan terms, Spock's vow of revenge was obscenely emotional.

But it felt right. And at this moment in his life, that was all that Spock cared about.

Logic and Surak be damned.

THIRTEEN

☆

Kirk leapt from his bed, propelled by instinct, not conscious thought. The whine of phaser hits was that ingrained in his mind.

He ran from the bedroom, pulling his Vulcan cloak around his shoulders. Outside, the low clouds of Chal's night sky flickered and flared with lances of phaser energy from the air, and explosions and fire from the ground.

Teilani was suddenly at Kirk's side, holding his arm, standing unafraid as the scream of impulse engines echoed around them.

"Atmospheric fighters," she said. She pointed up to a sudden streak of blue light high above them. "They're coming in from high orbit."

Kirk calculated the flight path of the attacking ships. "They're headed for the relief headquarters." He turned and ran back inside the cabin, emerged a minute later, fully clothed.

He paused to see that Teilani was already dressed.

"You have to stay here," he said automatically as the ground rocked with distant explosions.

Teilani merely smiled at him. "This is my world, James.

We'll fight for it today the way we fought for it before. Together."

Kirk caught her up in a fierce embrace. Then they ran for the center of the city, the sky on fire around them.

Christine MacDonald dug her way out from beneath her cot and crawled across the floor of the tent, blindly fumbling for her tunic and the comm badge pinned to it.

Her ears rang with the explosion that had thrown her from her sleep. She squinted as blinding phaser flashes struck a nearby building. The midrange orange hue told her she was seeing phaser bursts originating in the atmosphere, not from orbit. If the *Tobias* had not already been taken out by a mothership, then her crew should be able to handle a few fighters.

Another blast slammed into her, flattening the Starfleet tent all around her. She fought against the constricting folds of heavy fabric that pinned her arms to her sides. She gasped for air as the collapsing tent pressed ever more tightly against her face.

Then she smelled smoke. Recognized the acrid odor of the tent's insulation.

I refuse to die out of uniform, she told herself.

She stopped struggling. Forced her arms to relax at her side.

She refused to die at all.

She turned her head in the suffocating fabric.

In one direction, she could feel a breeze along her right cheek. That meant she wasn't completely entangled. There was an opening somewhere.

She rotated her right shoulder, felt the heavy fabric ease up a few centimeters up on her right side.

She ignored the roar of fighters streaking overhead. Did not react to the thunder of the shock waves they left behind, or the growing heat she felt on her left side.

First solve the problem of being trapped, she told herself firmly. Then she could worry about fighting back.

Her bare foot made contact with a blast of hot air.

She bent her leg, kicked, twisted sideways until her right hand was free at her waist. She wriggled down, bracing herself against the ground, straining her neck, her shoulders, until . . .

. . . she broke free of the tent and found herself surrounded by flames.

The relief camp was a war zone. The hospice across the town square was an inferno.

Christine stood in the middle of the destruction, in nothing more than Starfleet-issue T-shirt and shorts, and instantly assessed the situation.

Whoever was flying those fighters, no one on the ground was getting out alive.

She pushed her hair out of her face and looked around. About five meters away, there was a gap in the flames from the ruined tent. If she ran for it, didn't mind stepping on coals with her bare feet, she could make it. Might make it.

But then what?

She directed her attention to the tented landscape that surrounded her. Peered through the billowing smoke and flickers of flame until she made out what had to be the enshrouded outline of a folding chair on its side. It was where she had thrown her uniform when she had gone to bed only an hour ago.

Ignoring the flames rushing closer, she stumbled over the mounds of tent fabric until she stood beside the chair's outline. She felt around for the leg of the chair and rubbed it back and forth against the fabric until the chair leg gashed a hole in the tent. She ripped the gash wider. Reached through the opening. Felt her uniform tunic. Yanked it out. Hit the comm badge.

"MacDonald to *Tobias*—one to beam up *now!"*

And just as an explosion lifted a wall of blazing tentcloth toward her, Christine dissolved in a different fire . . .

. . . and found herself kneeling on the transporter pad of her ship.

She leapt to her feet, tunic still clutched in one hand. Battle stations sounded. Alert lamps flashed.

"How bad?" she shouted at the transporter tech.

Two more transporter columns blossomed beside her. One was M'Benga, brushing out sparks on her pant leg. The other was a young Chal male, still half asleep.

"They're jamming our sensors," the transporter tech shouted back. "But we're punching through to beam up everyone we can lock on to."

Christine grabbed M'Benga and the young Chal by their arms and hauled them off the pad. Another column of energy appeared—another crew member rescued from the carnage below.

"Is the ship under attack?" Christine asked.

The deck lurched with the shudder of buckling shields.

"They're hammering us," the tech said as his hands flew over the controls. "Barc has the conn. He wants to hold orbit as long as we can beam between shield cycles."

Christine ran for the transporter controls. "Set your sensors for human-only readings—no Chal, exclude anyone with a comm badge."

The transporter tech looked at his half-dressed commander in horror. "Commander—we've got to take 'em as we find 'em. They're being slaughtered down there!"

Christine slammed down on the controls and wiped every comm-badge trace off the board. "You're scanning for a human male. He'll be running for the center of the attack."

The tech screwed up his face in incomprehension. "What? Everyone else is running away."

"Then it should be easy to find him"—the deck lurched

again, the lights flickered as auxiliary life-support kicked in—
"right, Ensign?"

"Yes, ma'am," the tech said. Sweat dripped from his brow
to the console. "Got someone on the move, heading into
town. . . ."

"Lock on, mister," Christine said.

"Have to wait for the shields to cycle." The ship seemed to
fall a foot beneath them as the artificial-gravity field stuttered.
"Barc's not dropping the shields. He's not cycling. . . ."

Christine hit the comm control on the console. "MacDonald to bridge! Lieutenant Barc—drop shields over the transporter waveguides! Now!"

Barc growled back over the speakers. "Commander, we
won't last a Klingon second!"

"Now, Barcs! That's an order!"

The engineer's only reply was a Tellarite snarl, but the
transporter tech announced that he had an opening.

"Energize!" Christine shouted, and a moment later James
T. Kirk charged off the pad, transported in midstride.

He looked at Christine without an instant of disorientation,
as if he were transported on the run every day. It was a
startling change from his last transport—now he was the
Kirk of her history books, and dreams. "There're people
down there who need my help!"

Christine ran to him. "I need you on this ship!" Another hit
echoed through the transporter room. "We're under attack
and my only combat experience is in the Academy simulator!"

Kirk was enraged. "What makes you think I could do any
better?!"

She grabbed his shirtfront, refusing to accept any outcome
but the one she wanted.

"Because I know who you are, *Captain*. And right now,
you're our only way out of whatever the hell is happening

here!" She released his shirt. "Report to the bridge! That's an order!"

Kirk's jaw clenched. His eyes blazed into hers. But neither one would give.

Then Kirk looked at the tech. "There was a woman beside me, running in the same direction." He looked back at Christine. "And if she's not on this ship by the time I get to the bridge, so help me I'll fly us all into the suns."

Christine snapped her fingers at the tech. "You heard him! Lock on and energize!"

She stared at Kirk. "Anything else?"

"No. But when this is over, we're going to have a long talk." Then he ran for the doors and they parted before him.

Kirk was awake in a nightmare. He knew it was the *Tobias* that lurched and trembled around him. But he kept seeing the corridors of the *Enterprise*-B as he ran for the deflector relay room. Captain Harriman on the bridge. Scotty at ops, holding her together. And the Nexus a wild beast, tearing at the ship and her shields, clawing through the bulkheads to rip Kirk from his time and—

The lift doors opened and Kirk erupted onto the bridge. A Tellarite jumped up from the center chair. "Chief Engineer Barc, sir. The commander said you have the conn, sir!"

Kirk made his way to the chair, eyes fixed on the main screen. A shaft of phaser energy flashed from an invisible point among the stars and the ship trembled.

"Shield strength?" Kirk called out.

"Forty percent forward. Eighty percent aft." Kirk took a look at the helmsman. He, or she, or it was humanoid, but covered in iridescent blue and purple scales, with a mane of what appeared to be bristling, prehensile tendrils cascading from his shoulders. But one look was all Kirk had time for.

"How many attackers?" he asked the helmsman.

"Just one in orbit."

AVENGER

"Then turn the ship around!" Kirk ordered.

Instantly, the starfield on the screen twirled and the dark disk of Chal's nightside flashed by. Another impact slammed the ship, but the shields' response was stronger.

"Keep giving me readings," Kirk said.

"Aft shields seventy-seven percent, holding strong," the helmsman said.

"Who's weapons officer?" Kirk demanded.

Beside Kirk, the Tellarite nervously grunted. "Uh, this is a science vessel, sir."

The scaled helmsman didn't take his eyes off his controls, but raised a wickedly clawed hand with three jointless fingers. "I have weapons, sir."

"Then give me aft sensors on the screen," Kirk commanded. "I want range, class . . . How many fighters below us?"

"Seven, sir."

Kirk leaned back in his chair, tapped a finger against the arm, then suddenly looked down to make certain he hadn't hit any control he hadn't expected. "That's a standard Orion attack wing," Kirk said. "Any idea who our attackers are?"

A short blond officer looked over from communications. "There was no warning, sir. They refuse to respond to our hailing frequencies."

"Maximum magnification on the attacker."

The viewscreen wavered. A small point of light became a larger point of light.

"They're bleeding energy through their shields," Kirk said as he recognized the visual signature. "Keeps us from identifying their class and targeting vital areas."

Barc glanced at Kirk. "You've seen this before?"

"An old Orion trick. We're being attacked by pirates."

"There haven't been pirates in this sector for at least a century." Kirk noted the skeptical grunt that accompanied the Tellarite's observation.

111

The bridge rocked and a sensor-control station threw off an arc of sparks.

"You want the chair back?" Kirk challenged Barc.

"No. Sir."

Kirk turned back to the screen. In some small part of his mind, he was troubled that he did not have to think about the possible strategies he could follow. They were as neatly arranged in his thoughts as if they had been programmed. Is this what Starfleet had made him? Would this be the destiny he could never escape?

"That orbiting ship will have to stay in space," Kirk said, an analysis of Orion tactics coming effortlessly to him. "We have to take out those fighters. Helmsman: Weapons status for atmospheric combat?"

"None, sir."

"No torpedoes?"

"None, sir."

"Phasers?"

"Designed for clearing navigational obstructions. We could never cycle them fast enough to take on a fighter."

Kirk leaned forward in his chair. "We *can* go into the atmosphere, can't we?"

The scaled helmsman glanced over his shoulder, and his bristling mane parted so his solid green eyes could make contact with Kirk's. "We can, sir. But we'll have the maneuverability of a brick."

None of that was what Kirk wanted to hear. But there was no time to waste. "Plot a course to the main city. Take us down."

At least the crew of Christine MacDonald's *Tobias* was better than the ship's capabilities would suggest. Almost at once, the stars slipped up the viewscreen as the dark disk of Chal rushed toward them.

Kirk held on to the arms of the command chair as the *Tobias* began to vibrate with atmospheric drag.

"Structural integrity field is holding," the helmsman announced. "Two minutes to target."

Kirk was aware of everyone's eyes upon him. Two minutes to target and then what? Without useful weapons and maneuverability, the *Tobias* would be an easy target for the seven fighters laying waste to the main city. The Orions would not be able to resist attacking her.

Then Kirk saw the way out.

"Track those fighters, helmsman," Kirk ordered. He heard the turbolift doors open behind him. Teilani was now on his right. Christine on his left, back in uniform.

"Situation?" Christine asked.

"We'll know in ninety seconds," Kirk said. "Helmsman, maintain speed at Mach three. Configure shields for maximum displacement of air during sonic boom, but don't enlarge them until those fighters are coming at us."

Kirk knew the alien at the helm wouldn't understand what he was planning, but he was pleased to see the helmsman's claws race over the board, following Kirk's orders to the letter. Christine had trained her crew well.

"Fighters are banking," the helmsman said. "Coming up on intercept course."

"Do not break heading," Kirk told him. "Continue straight for them, drop at the last second, then deploy tractor beams."

The Tellarite stepped closer to Kirk and lowered his voice to a growl. "Sir, at this speed, we'll never be able to hold on to all seven of them."

"We don't have to," Kirk said. "They're atmospheric fighters, dependent on lift. Between the sonic-boom displacement and even a second or two of contact with our tractor beams, the pilots won't be able to maintain control."

"What if they have antigrav backups?"

"Then they'll be as slow as we are, and the first thing they'll want to do is get back into space."

"Fighters are converging," the helmsman reported. "Twenty seconds to intercept."

"Ready on those shields. . . ."

On the viewscreen, Kirk could see seven thin traces of fiery exhaust merging over the black silhouette of the main island. The fighters were rising to meet the *Tobias.*

Then phasers lanced out from the exhaust trails. The viewscreen flared as the forward shields, already strained by atmospheric friction, shimmered on the brink of overload.

"Forward shields at twenty-three percent," the helmsman reported. "Intercept in eight seconds . . . seventeen percent . . . five seconds . . . twelve percent . . ."

Kirk felt Teilani's hand on his. He glanced at Christine. She was grinning as she stared at the viewscreen and he knew she shared his absolute conviction that this would work.

Then the *Tobias*'s bridge angled down as the impulse engines roared and the viewscreen flared and—

—the scaled helmsman cheered!

"Four fighters down! Multiple collisions! We have midair explosions!"

Kirk leaned forward, ignoring the cheers. "Status of the other three?"

The viewscreen image shifted to show flaming debris falling from the sky. An exhaust trail traced a twisting spiral as an intact fighter spun toward the ocean.

"One fighter out of control . . . two others climbing into orbit on antigrav propulsion."

"Take them out, helmsman."

"Aye, sir," the helmsman said uncertainly, and the *Tobias* banked to follow her prey.

For the first time, Christine spoke to Kirk. "They're defenseless. Let them go."

Kirk flashed her a sharp look. She seemed so young to be in command of a ship. There was still so much she had to learn.

"If they make it back to their mothership, they can be

repaired. And I guarantee you they will not fall for this tactic again."

"We are in range," the helmsman said. "Phasers locked."

Before Kirk could give the order to fire, Christine interrupted. "Transporter room, beam the pilots to the brig."

The tech replied over the bridge speakers. "Commander, their shields are up."

Christine hesitated. Kirk turned to her. "You saw what they did to the city," he said.

Christine set her jaw. "Is this how you did things in your century? By butchery and barbarism?"

Kirk had no patience for what it would take to explain the realities of the universe to this novice. He looked back at the screen.

"Fire phasers."

The phasers whined before Christine could countermand him.

On the viewscreen, the small dots of the escaping fighters flared into miniature suns, then trailed in falling fire to the planet far below.

"Sir," the helmsman said, "the mothership is breaking orbit. Going to warp."

Christine spoke very clearly to Kirk. "We are not chasing her."

But Kirk agreed without protest. "Chal needs us." He stood up from the chair, went to Teilani as Christine reclaimed command of her ship and gave her crew the orders to return to orbit.

"Are you all right?" Teilani asked Kirk. Her gaze commanded the truth from him.

Kirk couldn't shake the feeling that he had done something wrong. The adrenaline surge of sitting in that chair, fighting that battle, left him shaken.

"I never wanted to do that again," he said to her. "I'm . . . tired."

Teilani slipped her arm around him. "I'll take you home," she said. They started toward the turbolift.

"Jim, wait," Christine called out behind him.

He paused on the upper deck.

"Barcs said you identified the attackers as Orion pirates."

Kirk nodded.

"Anything else?" Christine asked. "Any idea why they'd attack us?"

Inwardly, Kirk sighed. Sometimes he wished he could forget so many things in his past, but no one would let him.

"Put an aerial view of the main city on the screen," he said. Beside him, Teilani stiffened as the image appeared—the city scribed by precise lines of fire and destruction. "Now overlay a map schematic," Kirk said.

The schematic appeared, making it easy to identify the structures that had been hit.

Christine's chief engineer swore in Tellarite.

"They went after all the communications systems," Christine said. "Every subspace transmitter, every long-range sensor array." She turned to look back at Kirk. "They were trying to silence us. Why?"

"Did you send your inquiry to Starfleet?" Kirk asked. "About the *chalchaj 'qmey* and the chance that the virogen was deliberate?"

Christine's face went white. "Yes," she said.

"Then offhand," Kirk said as he turned back to the turbolift, "I'd say someone got the message."

FOURTEEN

─────────────── ☆ ───────────────

"We've had a bit of a revolt, Commander."

On the main screen of the *Enterprise*-E, Manager Chiton Kincaid of Gamow Station had the decency to appear embarrassed and concerned.

"Protesters broke into the office complex as I was meeting with Captain Picard," she continued. "They opened his suit with a medical protoplaser, and took him hostage."

Riker contained his anger. He had advised Picard not to beam down to meet with Chiton, precisely because the unexpected had a way of springing to life around starship captains.

"If you can drop your shields," Riker said icily, "we will be able to locate the captain and beam him up."

"You didn't hear me," the station manager replied. "Your captain's been exposed to the virogen. He's in no medical danger, but he can spread the disease to plant life-forms, just like everyone else who's infected."

Riker wanted to bellow with frustration. He didn't care if everyone on the *Enterprise* were exposed to the virogen. He wanted his captain back, and he *would* get him, despite

117

Manager Kincaid's obstructions. It was up to him to figure out how.

But his anger still disrupted his thinking. Behind the command chair, he could hear Deanna talking to Lieutenant Rolk. He turned to tell them to be quiet. He had to concentrate. He had to—

The ship's counselor made a warning gesture, the Bolian security officer hit a control, and Riker saw the viewscreen flicker out from the corner of his eye. The plain, padded wall of the bridge replaced it.

"Deanna?" Riker said, unsure why she had just cut communications with Gamow Station.

"She's lying, Will."

"About what?"

Deanna shrugged. "Almost everything. But I sense the most deception when she talks about the protesters."

Riker went to the heart of the matter. "Is the captain still 've?"

"I believe so. She is concerned about him in some way."

"Then chances are, Manager Kincaid is the one who's holding him captive."

"She is involved," Deanna said. "Absolutely."

Now Riker felt sure and composed. His voice rang out crisply. "Counselor, stand out of scanner range where I can see you. Lieutenant Rolk: screen on."

The virtual viewscreen re-formed and Chiton reappeared. "Is there a problem, Commander?"

"It's the new viewer," Riker lied smoothly. "We're still working out the bugs." He settled back in his chair. "Manager Kincaid, I am going to beam down an assault team to blow your forcefield generators from the ground." He glanced over at Deanna. She gestured imperceptibly that Chiton Kincaid was perturbed by Riker's decision.

But on the screen, the station manager conveyed only

compassionate concern. "Commander Riker, that's a valiant idea. But destroying our forcefield generators will put the whole station at risk from meteorological disturbances. And the protesters have said they will kill your captain, and their other hostages, if any rescue is attempted."

"Don't *they* want to be rescued?" Riker asked, frowning. His mind rapidly considered the possible motives of Picard's abductors. Why else would they have captured him?

"They apparently realize there is nowhere they can go. Their demands are merely for more supplies."

At the side of the bridge, Deanna mouthed the word "lie."

Riker leaned forward in the command chair. "Tell the protesters that we are willing to meet their demands for additional replicators, and whatever other matériel we can provide, on the condition that we speak with Captain Picard to ascertain he is still alive."

"I will do my best, Commander. But . . . conditions down here are . . . somewhat unstable."

"Inform the protesters that however 'unstable' conditions are now, when this ship blows holes in your pressure domes and exposes everyone inside to a poisonous sulphur atmosphere, they will discover the true meaning of the word."

Riker did not need Deanna's Betazoid abilities to register the alarm in the station manager.

"You would risk the lives of fourteen hundred innocent civilians?"

"I want my captain back, Manager. To rescue him, I am prepared to take any means necessary. *Enterprise* out."

Deanna approached Riker. "She believed your threat."

"Good," Riker said. "Only it wasn't a threat."

He could see Deanna sense the truth of what he said. "Will, what do you think is really going on down there?"

Riker stood. "The captain went down to uncover any reason which could explain how Stron managed to hijack the

119

Bennett, and who might have helped him orchestrate his escape. I believe the captain found the answers to those questions."

"You suspect Manager Kincaid was involved?"

"I'll know that when I have a chance to speak with her, face-to-face." Before Deanna could question his decision, Riker added, "Counselor: You have the conn." He strode toward the turbolift. "Data, Rolk, you're with me." He touched his comm badge. "Dr. Crusher: Report to transporter room two, combat field kit."

Deanna gave him a concerned smile. "Good luck, Will."

But Riker returned the smile with a grin as Rolk and Data joined him. "I don't need luck," he said. "I've got the *Enterprise.*"

Picard awoke in darkness. His face felt numb. He tried to touch his eyes to see if they were covered or if he were blind, but his hands were tied, as were his legs.

He strained every muscle at once.

He was in a chair. Completely immobilized.

"He's awake," a female voice said. Another deeper one, male, responded, "We'll begin."

Picard felt his head pushed from side to side. Something was being removed. Then light exploded into his eyes.

His eye.

He realized he had sight in only one.

The other half of his face was tight with bandages.

He felt groggy, couldn't focus.

"I'll hit him again," the first voice said. Though female, Picard could tell, it wasn't Chiton Kincaid's.

He braced himself for the blow.

But instead, the cool tip of a hypospray touched his neck. He heard it hiss. Felt his lungs respond reflexively as he drew in a huge gasp of air, as if they had suddenly doubled in capacity. Then everything snapped into focus and he was fully alert.

Staring directly into a face he recognized.

Stron.

The Vulcan who had lied.

But who had not, after all, killed himself.

"I am impressed," Picard said. He heard himself slur his words. Half his face was frozen, under some type of neural block, he assumed. The molten aluminum from his visor. It must have inflicted considerable damage, requiring the bandages.

"So am I," Stron said. The Vulcan no longer wore a Starfleet uniform, only a civilian jumpsuit such as a shuttle worker might wear. His was the deeper voice Picard had heard.

With some difficulty, Picard looked to one side, then the other, to find the source of the female voice he had heard.

Stron's human wife, still pregnant, though now in drab civilian clothes. She was the one who had given him the hypospray.

"So not everything you told me was a lie," Picard said.

"Vulcans never lie," Stron replied stiffly.

"Except when there is a logical reason to do so."

Stron made a show of ignoring Picard's comment. Picard's unobstructed eye scanned the room. Some type of supply storage area, he guessed. The light panels on the ceiling were too dim for a regular working area, there were no windows, and from where Picard sat, he could see no door. The unfinished walls were lined with shelves, stocked with small-part trays. From the standard Starfleet inventory stickers on the trays, and the milky smell of tetralubisol, Picard concluded they were in a storage bay attached to Gamow Station's shuttle launchpad.

Stron positioned himself on a chair in front of Picard. "I

must ask you some questions," he said. His manner was formal, as if their meeting were not that of abductor and hostage. "As a Starfleet officer, your first duty will, of course, be to refuse. However, as a reasonable being, you know that no one can resist a Vulcan interrogation."

Picard couldn't quite believe what Stron was implying. "You would mindmeld with an unwilling subject?"

"Did you discuss the *Bennett*'s modifications for gathering alta mist with any of your crew?"

Picard's pulse quickened. He felt vindicated by Stron's question. It meant there *was* a connection between the alta mist and the virogen. But he also realized the Vulcan's question was a ruse. Under other circumstances, Picard would have been tempted to say that his whole crew knew about the modifications, so that Stron would believe there would be nothing to gain by silencing Picard. But these were not other circumstances.

"Manager Kincaid was the one who informed me of the modifications," Picard began. "As you know, I have not been in contact with any of my crew since I beamed into her office."

Stron tried another trick question. "Who else among your crew are aware of your suspicions that the *Bennett* did not explode over asteroid Alta Vista two five seven?"

"But the *Bennett* did explode," Picard said calmly, matching the Vulcan's air of detachment. "The only suspicions I shared with my senior staff were that you and your mate were not aboard."

"Are you aware of how that was accomplished?"

"There are anomalous readings in our sensor logs of the explosion," Picard said. "My science department heads are analyzing them in detail."

Stron reached out and pressed two fingers into the side of Picard's neck, somehow creating a lance of pain that burned through Picard's body.

"That was a lie."

Picard's eye watered. He blinked to clear it. "If you already know the answers, you are being illogical to waste time and effort in questioning me."

"The alta mist is already en route, Captain. We have an abundance of time."

Picard strove not to react to that information. "My officers will not rest until they have found me. You have far less time than you imagine."

Stron glanced at his wife, then pulled his chair even closer to Picard. "Then we shall accelerate the process at the cost of your intellect. I have yet to meet a human with the discipline necessary to survive a forced meld unimpaired."

The Vulcan reached out to Picard's face, aligning each fingertip with a *katra* point.

Picard spit in Stron's face.

Without a hint of emotion, Stron again touched a nerve point on Picard's neck, in what was obviously not a Vulcan technique.

Picard made no effort to ignore the pain that touch created. He let it fuel his rage. Let the Vulcan deal with that if he could.

Stron's wife came to Stron's side. She had a medical kit. "Let me try the drugs first," she said.

Stron sat back in his chair. "He is a Starfleet officer. They are trained and conditioned to resist most forms of interrogation." He glanced at Picard with apparent disinterest. "Is that not correct?"

"You want answers," Picard growled, relishing the way in which Stron's wife started in surprise. "You come in and try to take them!"

Then he rocked back and forth in the chair, shouting, snarling, doing anything to keep his emotions at fever pitch. He would pit his emotions against Vulcan impassivity any day.

Stron leaned forward and locked his arm around Picard's neck, immobilizing his head. Picard struggled to bite the Vulcan's fingers.

"Hold him," Stron commanded his wife.

Picard felt inordinately pleased at the hint of exasperation he detected in Stron's voice.

Stron's wife now wrapped her arms around Picard as well, pressing on his neck, keeping his head bent forward and down, making breathing difficult.

Picard felt Stron's fingers again stab into his face, forcing the contact.

The Vulcan spoke the incantation with implacable determination. "My mind to yours, Jean-Luc Picard."

Picard thought of his brother and nephew burned alive in the fire that had swept the château. He thought of the Borg, strapping him down, drilling into his flesh, violating his identity.

He saw his ship, the *Enterprise*-D, consumed by flames as it plunged through the atmosphere of Veridian. Saw James T. Kirk die before his eyes.

Picard fought to fill his heart and his mind with hate and rage and sorrow and channeled it all at the Vulcan who dared invade his mind.

Stron's howl echoed with Picard's as those emotions shot back into the Vulcan's own mind.

Picard felt the woman's arm tighten around his neck. His breathing stopped. Blood hammered in his ears, each pulse a phaser burst of unbridled emotion.

And then, as if he had been plunged into a sea of cooling water, the hate and pain were gone.

My mind to yours, the Vulcan whispered in his mind, as he overcame Picard's defenses.

"Never," Picard croaked.

Then a sudden stream of alien words and oddly familiar

images flashed through his thoughts and he felt the assault abruptly cease as Stron pulled himself away in amazement.

Picard twisted away from the woman's grip, gasping for air. She knelt by her husband where he had fallen to the floor. "What's wrong?" she asked urgently. "What happened?"

Stron gazed up at Picard in awe, frighteningly stripped of any attempt to maintain Vulcan composure.

"He has melded before," Stron said. "With the leader."

Stron's wife stared at Picard with equal shock.

Picard trembled, still bound in the chair. He did not understand their reaction, but knew what Stron had found within him.

The echo of a long-ago mindmeld with a different Vulcan.

Ambassador Sarek.

Their leader.

FIFTEEN

☆

Smoke curled up from the fuselage of the Orion fighter, each thin tendril incandescent in the dawn's first light, dissipating only slowly into the dying yellow leaves of the jungle canopy above.

Kirk walked around the wreckage, surefootedly finding a path among the twisted roots and scattered branches outside the acrid burn zone of charred vegetation. What had crashed here was little more than the life-support and control capsule of the fighter—a battered, tapered cylinder no longer than a small shuttlecraft, and only about half its thickness.

The stubs of the fighter's forward-sloping wings trailed control linkages and ODN wires, indicating the wings had been torn off on landing, and not by phaser bursts. Judging from the orientation of the fighter, Kirk guessed the pilot had retained some sort of control until the end, struggling to bring what was left of his craft in for a landing.

Kirk checked the line of broken tree limbs and shredded foliage to the east. On other terrain, the pilot might have walked away from this one.

Christine MacDonald stumbled a few meters behind Kirk,

126

showing little interest in the wreckage, keeping her attention on her tricorder.

"This is only about half of it," she said as she caught up with Kirk.

But Kirk already knew that. "The main drive units are usually designed to explode away from the pilot's cabin. It's a safety feature."

Christine aimed her tricorder at the knot of crumpled, blackened metal ten meters distant. "Not that it did him a lot of good. We've got a body in there."

Kirk sighed. Of course there was a body in the wreckage. The *Tobias* had not detected anyone ejecting, or drifting to safety on an antigrav chute, from any of the fighters they had downed. He wondered if he had ever been as struck by death as Christine was. Or had he simply encountered it too often in his life?

For a moment, Kirk and Christine stood in silence, watching as Barc lumbered toward the wreckage in an isolation suit. Volatile lubricants and hydraulic fluids had been sprayed around the impact area. Anyone not in protective gear had to remain well back. The vapors could be corrosive, and interfered with most tricorder readings taken at a distance.

Finally, Kirk's curiosity got the better of him. "When did you know?" he asked.

"About who you were? I mean, are?"

Kirk gave her a look of skeptical forbearance. What else would he mean?

"Back at the hospice. The plaque. You gave it to Teilani, didn't you?"

Kirk nodded, remembering. He had taken the plaque from the *Enterprise*-A before he had left his ship to her fate in the fires of Chal's twin suns. Then he had given it to Teilani at a time when he had not been able to give anything of himself. When he had had to return to Earth, and the launch of the *Enterprise*-B.

"That's when I looked up the records," Christine explained. "Saw the resemblance between you and . . . you."

"And you didn't tell anyone?" Kirk asked. He felt touched that she had respected his unspoken wishes to remain anonymous in this new age.

"I tried to. But no one believed me."

Kirk nodded again. So much for respect.

"You know," Christine began, "I studied you in—"

Kirk held up a warning hand. "I do not ever want to hear those words again. Understand?"

Christine bit her lip. Looked uncomfortable. "I only meant to say you've been—"

"An inspiration," Kirk completed.

This time, Christine nodded.

Kirk had heard it all before. He sometimes wondered, with all the attention that had been paid to the *Enterprise,* if Starfleet had ever had any other starships on missions in his day. "I know," he said. "I'm what made you decide to join Starfleet."

Christine wrinkled her nose as she thought that over. "Well, joining Starfleet, that was mostly because of Captain Sulu and the *Excelsior.*"

Kirk opened his mouth to say something, then thought better of it.

"My dad used to read me stories about Sulu at bedtime." She looked at Kirk and didn't appear to know how to interpret his expression. "But once I got into the Academy, and started reading the old history tapes . . ."

"'Old' history tapes," Kirk repeated.

Christine began to falter, as if sensing how deep a hole she was digging for herself. "That's when I started reading about you . . . and the . . . old . . . days. . . . How *did* you manage to survive what happened on Veridian Three anyway?" she suddenly asked.

Kirk didn't know whether or not to be thankful for the change in subject.

"I mean, it was all over Starfleet. Captain Picard finding you, bringing you out of that temporal anomaly . . ."

"I've had quite enough of temporal anomalies, thank you," Kirk said.

"But then . . . his log did say he buried you."

"He did."

Christine stared at Kirk for a few moments. "And . . . ?" she said.

Kirk gave her a tight-lipped smile to let her know this particular topic of conversation was at an end. "He obviously didn't do a very good job of it."

"Right." Christine patted her hand against her tricorder as she studied the wreckage. By the flush on her cheeks, Kirk knew she knew she had been rebuffed. "I take it you fought Orions before. Back in the *old* days," she added pointedly.

"They've been mercenaries for as long as they've had spaceflight," Kirk said, trying to ease the sudden awkwardness that had sprung up between them. "I've had my run-ins with them."

Christine kept her eyes on the wreckage. Barc was scanning it at close range, using a tricorder modified for his bulky fingers. He seemed to keep resetting the device, as if he were getting a reading that made no sense. "Any idea why they'd respond this way to an inquiry about the virogen?" She asked the question with no hint of tension or embarrassment. Kirk approved of the professionalism it indicated. Knew it meant she'd go far.

"They were paid to respond," Kirk said. "So we wouldn't be able to connect the attack to the people who intercepted your communications with Command."

"By attacking, though, aren't they confirming what we thought? That the virogen is artificial and deliberately spread?"

"There weren't supposed to be any survivors, Commander. Whoever sent the Orions to attack Chal were expecting their only opposition to be the overworked crew of a science vessel."

"And not the legendary Captain Kirk."

"Jim," Kirk said. "The name is Jim."

Christine threw professionalism aside. "Look. Get it through your head—you're a legend, all right? You can't pretend your career never happened. So . . . move on." She slammed her tricorder shut and stared at him as if she were ready to wrestle him to the ground.

Or embrace him.

Completely unexpectedly, Kirk's first instinct was to kiss her. Fast. He knew that passion he sensed in her didn't come just from her devotion to Starfleet. He had felt the attraction spark between them from the moment he had stepped into her tent at the main city. He had seen the way she watched him when she thought he wasn't paying attention. Her response to him, physically.

He admitted to himself he had watched her the same way. Felt the same pull.

There was such energy in her. All the promise of youth, the excitement, the adventure, the universe waiting for her to reveal it. The way he had once felt.

Kirk knew that same drive and force still existed within him. He knew it would roar into renewed life with just a kiss of her soft lips, a caress of her smooth, unmarked skin. There was a part of him that knew he could be reinvigorated just being at her side, accompanying her on her grand adventure.

But it would be *her* adventure.

And his own still continued.

Teilani waited for him at the main city. She was working with M'Benga, to restore hope and order to her world. His world.

That was Kirk's adventure now. One world. One dream. One love.

He had chosen his path and he knew it was the right one. But his eyes remained fixed on Christine's.

She moved closer to him.

"Jim . . ." she said.

Kirk knew what was coming.

How wrong would it be to feel her in his arms, knowing that nothing more could come of it?

How wrong would it be to kiss her?

He knew what he should do. He also knew what he felt. Would the two ever be reconciled?

He felt her hand on his shoulder. Knew in the same instant how she would feel pressed against him.

He turned to her, to—

Barc squealed in alarm from the wreckage.

Whatever else Christine and Kirk were, they were both products of Starfleet. Without a moment's hesitation, they ran toward the Tellarite, giving no thought to their lack of protective gear. Because they were needed.

Barc was caught on something by the fighter's shattered canopy, struggling to get free.

Kirk reached him first, half-expecting to see the engineer's isolation suit snagged on a shard of metal.

But something *held* the Tellarite. Gripped his forearm.

A blackened claw of a hand.

Barc's oversized helmet visor was misted from his rapid exhalations. Even without a comm badge, Kirk could hear his husky voice.

"It's alive," the Tellarite snarled.

Kirk grabbed the engineer's shoulder for purchase, grabbed the wrist of whatever it was that held him, and pulled the two apart.

Two screams cut through the morning mist—Barc's as he

fell back from the fuselage, and the fighter pilot's as he rose from the mangled cockpit.

For an instant, Kirk was frozen by the apparition. Half the pilot's flight suit had been fused by flames to his body. Half his helmet had also melted, making his head appear misshapen, half-missing.

The visor was clouded by soot and multiple fracture lines. Kirk could see no trace of the pilot within. But he knew from the condition of the flight suit and the wreckage that the pain the pilot endured would be unbearable.

The pilot, still shrieking, jerked his charred and blackened arm away from Kirk. Kirk let it go, feeling the flakes of plastic and flesh still clinging to his hand.

The pilot's other arm emerged from the cockpit. It held a small green weapon. Too late Kirk realized what was going to happen. He had miscalculated, allowed shock to extend his reaction time.

He wasn't going to make it.

And then he felt Christine roughly shove him aside as she leapt up to plant both feet on the pilot's chest, sending the pilot flying backward from the cockpit.

As Kirk fell sideways, he saw the green weapon spiral through the air above him, its metal finish gleaming in the morning light.

He rolled once and sprang to his feet, ready at least to make the second charge if it was necessary.

But Christine stood poised on the wreckage, looking down on the other side where the pilot had fallen. She was prepared to attack again, though there was no need. She checked over her shoulder to be sure Kirk was safe, then nimbly jumped down on the far side.

Barc got to his feet beside Kirk. Together they circled the wreckage, to join Christine, who kneeled by the unmoving pilot, her fingers working the helmet locking-ring release.

Something new caught Kirk's eye. A more subtle detail

hidden in the charred pressure suit and flesh of the pilot's burned arm.

Each crack was marked by a glistening line of green.

Not the green of Orion skin.

The green of copper-based blood.

Christine grunted as she tugged the pilot's helmet free and let it roll onto the burned vegetation. It carried with it a flap of skin, fused to the melted frame of the visor. But despite the damage to the pilot's face, the missing skin, the exposed muscles and raw cheekbone, enough remained intact to reveal a pointed ear, an arching brow.

"A Romulan?" Christine asked.

But Barc answered with a growl as he played his tricorder over the pilot's body. "No. I can't detect the genetic drift. That's no Romulan," he said.

Kirk understood.

The pilot who had tried to wipe out Chal and keep the secret of the virogen from spreading was not the enemy anyone had expected.

Barc looked up from his tricorder. "He's Vulcan."

To Kirk, that meant only one thing.

This time, the Federation was under attack from within.

SIXTEEN

☆

"Any questions?" Riker asked.

On the transporter platform, Data, Crusher, and Rolk stared through their blast shield visors and shook their heads. All seemed tense in their bulky, black phaser armor. Then Data took a second look at the four hexagonal cargo containers on the opposite side of the pad and apparently reconsidered. He raised his hand. "Actually, I do have one."

Riker stepped up beside his crew and tightened the straps holding his equipment harness to his phaser armor. "Go ahead."

"Has this ever been tried before?"

"You're the one with direct access to the ship's computer," Riker said. He snapped down his blast shield and adjusted the sound level on his helmet speakers.

"That is what concerns me," Data replied. "I am unable to find any reference to this type of maneuver at all."

Riker clapped his hand against Data's shoulder. His armored glove clanged dully against Data's armored chest plate. "Then I'd say we're about to make history." He winked at the android. "Again."

Riker gave a thumbs-up signal to the transporter chief. "You know what you have to do."

The transporter chief nodded, trying to match Riker's hearty enthusiasm, though few on the ship could come close. "Stage one," the chief said. "Energizing."

Riker looked to the side and saw the cargo containers begin to dematerialize. When they had almost completely vanished, stage two began and the transporter room seemed to evaporate all around him.

A moment later, Riker's boots made contact with the solid metal dome of Gamow Station's generating complex, one hundred meters above the ground. He instantly dropped to his knees, braced his helmet with his arms, and before he could close his eyes, the dome metal flared with overhead light and an explosive concussion threw him flat against the metal.

As he rolled to his feet again, Riker saw that Data was the first one standing. The android was helping both Crusher and Rolk to their feet, as well.

Riker glanced up. About thirty meters above him, against the streaky, pale yellow sky of Alta Vista III, he could just make out the rippling blue distortions in the forcefield that protected the dome. The ripples were what was left of the explosive interference caused by his ship's attempt to beam the four cargo containers into the airspace bisected by the energy screen. For approximately three seconds, exactly as Riker had calculated, the energy of the quasi-solid containers and the dome's forcefield had been the same. The result had been four zones of zero-energy through which Riker, Rolk, Data, and Crusher had been successfully beamed.

As soon as Riker and the others had solidified, the *Enterprise* had reversed the transportation of the cargo containers. The forcefield had snapped back to full strength, simultaneously obliterating a handful of container atoms that had not been beamed out in time. Riker trusted that the explosions that had erupted on the surface of the field would be interpreted by the dome's personnel as an impact by a flock of birds, or whatever passed for birds on this planet.

Data appeared to be the most impressed by Riker's tactic. "It is unfortunate that this method of penetrating a forcefield with a transporter beam can only work on relatively low-powered meteorological screens."

"For now," Riker said. "I'm sure you and Geordi will come up with improvements."

Data's facial expression blanked as he rapidly began working on the problem.

"I meant later, Data," Riker cautioned. He unhooked a projectile gun from his harness and fired a fusion piton into the dome. The piton flared as it melted into the metal plating. Riker pulled on the carbon-fiber cable that trailed from it. The line was secure.

Riker snapped the line to the induction clip on his belt as the others did the same. He pointed to the north. "That direction to the generator conduits. Dr. Crusher, start scanning for the captain as soon as we hit ground."

Riker began running down the gently sloping curve of the immense dome, playing out the line through his induction clip until he was almost horizontal. Then he gave a push and rappelled down the rest of the dome's nearly vertical wall, pushing off every five meters until he touched down on the gravel around the dome's foundation.

As he disconnected the line, he watched with approval as Crusher and Rolk expertly rappelled behind him. Data, on the other hand, simply kept running straight down at full speed, obviously capable of maintaining a perfect balance between his own forward momentum and the rate at which his line played out.

Two meters from the gravel, Data abruptly swung upright

as if he were doing spacewalk maneuvers, and stepped onto the gravel as lightly as if he had merely stepped around the corner.

"Very smoothly done, Mr. Data," Riker said.

"Thank you, sir. According to terminology associated with the new experiences afforded by my emotion chip, I could say it was quite a rush."

Riker had no idea what Data meant. The term sounded like yet another one of the archaic slang expressions Zefram Cochrane had been so fond of using back in the twenty-first century.

"Whatever." Riker held out his hand. "Antimatter charges."

Data slapped two finger-sized tubes into Riker's glove. Riker headed for a thick conduit that snaked from the wall of the dome and disappeared beneath the gravel. It carried power to the buried forcefield generators that protected Gamow Station's exposed sensors and dome plating from Alta Vista III's sulphurous rain and acid hail. Two antimatter blasts and the forcefields would be down. Less than thirty seconds later, Captain Picard would be located and beamed to safety. *This is going to be simple,* Riker thought.

That was when the first sniper blast hit him and the ambush began.

In the storeroom, Stron's wife held the phaser on Picard. Stron seemed too upset to do much of anything. Whatever trace of Sarek's mind he had discovered in his attempt to meld with Picard, it had clearly unnerved him.

"When did you meld with Sarek?" Stron's wife demanded. Her accusing tone revealed her disbelief that the leader could ever have chosen to meld with Picard.

"Release me," Picard said. "Then we can talk."

Stron and his wife exchanged a questioning glance.

"We can't," she said.

"But he only melded with those who were part of the cause," Stron argued. He stared at Picard with an expression of near fear. "Have you been to Gonthar District?"

Picard had no idea to what the Vulcan referred, but he recognized a weakness to exploit when he saw one.

"You can ask me that when you have the temerity to tie me up like a common outsider?"

Stron looked at his wife. "He must be one of us." He started toward Picard.

"Stay back," the woman warned Stron. She raised the phaser until it was trained at Picard's head. Her death-dealing gesture seemed in cruel juxtaposition to her life-swollen belly. "These are dangerous times for the cause," she reminded her husband. "You know each cell must remain unknown to the others to avoid betrayal. We must do nothing to risk our mission."

"You risk betrayal by keeping me from my ship." Picard hoped he was playing his part correctly. "If Starfleet investigates my disappearance, I will not be able to protect any of us."

Picard could see that Stron wanted to untie him at once. But Stron's wife was not convinced.

"Give us the proper countersign," she challenged Picard. *"Have* you been to Gonthar District?"

Picard had no choice but to brazen it out. "That code is obsolete. My cell has not used it for years."

The woman studied him for a moment, then lifted the phaser in salute. "I acknowledge your courage. Farewell, Captain."

Her intent was clear. Picard did not flinch.

But Stron pushed his wife aside. The phaser beam missed. The struggle was over in seconds. Now Stron held the weapon.

"My mate is correct," the Vulcan said. "It is illogical to

believe you are part of the revolution." He spoke to his wife. "But he *has* melded with Sarek. And that we cannot ignore."

The woman wrapped her arms around her stomach, cradling their unborn child. "We have to kill him, Stron. For the sake of the future."

Stron gestured to the medical kit on a nearby shelf. "We'll use the drugs first. Then I'll meld with him again. Whatever reason Sarek had for linking with him will be easier to find."

Stron's wife pulled a hypospray from the kit. "And then we'll kill him," she said firmly.

Picard watched her approach. He was out of options. He knew that whatever dose of whatever drug she was about to give him would be too high.

"Think of your child," he said. "Don't do this."

"It is for our child that we do," she said.

She raised the hypospray.

Then the supply room was plunged into darkness.

Riker flattened himself behind one of the exterior support ribs of the dome as phaser beams whined only centimeters away from him. Fortunately, their attackers' weapons were not set high enough to risk puncturing the dome itself, so the ribs provided adequate protection.

Crusher and Rolk were five meters farther back, flattened behind another support rib. Data was beside Riker, setting his hand phaser to full stun.

"Where did they come from?" Riker muttered. He had his own phaser in one hand, the two antimatter charges in the other.

"The odds favor them not believing the power fluctuations were the result of birds flying into the forcefield," Data said pleasantly. He leaned forward and fired three precise bursts.

Riker winced as an orange beam hit Data and threw him back against the dome with a solid thud. "Are you all right?" he asked.

Data shook his head as if to clear it. "My phaser armor is operational," the android said. "However, I must warn you that our attackers' weapons are set to kill."

"How many are there?"

"There were eight. But now there are five," Data said proudly. He pantomimed blowing smoke from the barrel of his phaser. "I am a purty good shot, pardner," he drawled.

Riker rolled his eyes. Data's emotion chip could still be unsettling at times. Though the android now generally understood humor, he was still struggling with the concept of when it was appropriate.

"If I set a short timer on the antimatter," Riker asked, bringing the android back to the dangerous situation that faced them, "can you throw one at the conduit?"

"They are precision charges," Data said. "They are meant to be in contact with whatever they are to destroy. Otherwise, we might rupture the dome."

Riker fired at a figure that darted behind a small rise about twenty meters away. A puff of smoke went up from a rock, but Riker couldn't tell if he had hit the runner or not. "We've got to try, Data. Otherwise they're going to surround us and pick us off."

Data slapped his phaser against his harness. "I must estimate the distance to the conduit," he said, then leaned out for an instant and withdrew as another beam missed.

"Set the timer for one point three five seconds."

Riker twisted the dial on the charge. "I can only set it for complete seconds. Take your choice: one or two."

"Two then. I will alter the trajectory accordingly."

Riker handed Data the first charge. "Please do."

Data pressed the activation switch, leaned out again, and threw the charge like a knife.

An orange beam caught his shoulder and spun him around into Riker just as a massive concussion thundered through the air.

Riker hit the gravel beside Data. He heard running footsteps behind him, rolled to see five figures in protective gear charging at him, phaser rifles lowered.

Riker tore his own phaser from his harness, aimed it without checking its setting.

Two figures flew back as the wide beam hit them.

The three others returned fire.

Riker felt himself slammed back into Data and the dome. His armor crackled with dispersed energy, but the concentration of firepower was too intense.

A temperature alarm beeped in his helmet. "Suit destruction in three seconds," the familiar, standard Starfleet comm voice said.

In those last few seconds, Riker tried to fire again, but his phaser was blasted from his hand. He couldn't breathe. He only hoped the captain had been found alive.

Then a glittering curtain of energy filled his dimming field of vision.

He had been right about not needing luck.

Not when he had the *Enterprise.*

SEVENTEEN

─────────── ☆ ───────────

Picard jerked his body to one side so the hypospray couldn't reach his neck. But the move had been too violent and he felt his chair topple sideways.

The storeroom was without any source of light. He couldn't judge the angle of his fall. His head struck the flooring, making him gasp.

"He's right in front of you," Stron called out.

Picard felt the woman's foot hit his leg as she tried to find him in the darkness. "Open the door and get some light in here," she cried. Her hand grabbed Picard's boot. "I've got him!"

Picard tried to roll again, flopping the chair onto its back so he looked straight up.

He saw the woman looking straight down at him, encased in an indigo glow.

Picard's first thought was that Stron had found the lights.

But then the woman's eyes widened in shock as she and the storeroom were obscured by the familiar sparkle of the transporter.

A moment later, Picard was flat on his back, still tied to the chair, on the deck of a shuttlecraft.

Picard glanced around. "Hello?" he said, wincing as his movements set off a new burst of pain from his burned face. But no one answered. The shuttle was deserted. Then a shimmer of blue light reflected from the ceiling as another transporter beam materialized in the cabin.

Beverly Crusher was kneeling at his side. She wore phaser armor, blast shield pushed up, medical tricorder already open and working.

"Beverly?"

"Commander Riker shut down the station's forcefield," she explained. "You've been beamed directly to the *Galileo.*"

The *Galileo* was one of the *Enterprise's* shuttles, Picard knew. But that wasn't answer enough for his unspoken question. "Where, exactly, is the *Galileo?*"

"Shuttlebay One," Beverly said as she held a hypospray to Picard's neck. "The bay has been decompressed. We're in vacuum."

The pain in Picard's face faded instantly in response to Beverly's ministrations. "We're in quarantine, you mean."

Beverly smiled as she lightly prodded at the bandages Picard wore over half his face. "That's right. We've been exposed to the virogen."

Picard understood what the doctor had just done for him. "You mean I've been exposed to the virogen," he told her. "And you've been exposed to me."

Riker raced onto the bridge of the *Enterprise,* followed by Data and Rolk. Though he and his team had been plucked from the ground before the attackers had succeeded in overwhelming them, the beamback had been rough.

Operating under Starfleet's strictest quarantine protocols, Riker and the others had been transported to a point in space one hundred meters off the *Enterprise's* bow. Then, with precision focus, they had been beamed out of their armor and onto the ship.

The contaminated equipment they had worn was left in space. It would undergo the ultimate sterilization process as it burned up on reentry. But Riker, Data, and Rolk were free to return to the general areas of the ship, uncontaminated.

Picard and Beverly were a different matter.

"Put the *Galileo* onscreen," Riker said as he took the conn from Troi. "Then get me Manager Kincaid."

On the main screen, Crusher stood up in the cabin of the shuttlecraft, safely isolated by vacuum in the shuttlebay. Since contamination was no longer an issue with her, she had been beamed directly to Picard's side and was still in her armor.

Riker felt relief as he watched her help Picard to his feet and direct him to the copilot's chair.

"Welcome back, Captain," Riker said.

Picard lightly touched the sparkling antiseptic bandage he wore over one eye and cheek. "Well done, Will."

"Thank the chief," Riker said. "Transporter control had you located and locked on to ten seconds after the forcefield dropped." He leaned forward in his chair. "What did you find out down there?"

Picard took a breath to steady himself and Riker knew that his captain had been badly injured, more than he allowed to show. He was glad Crusher had chosen to go into quarantine with Picard. Strictly speaking, it hadn't been necessary. She could have beamed in and out in biological isolation garb. But onsite personal care was infinitely preferable.

"Stron and his wife are still alive. They are working with Chiton Kincaid as part of a . . . cause, or revolution, that is somehow connected with the virogen and the alta mist."

Riker sat back in his chair, stunned by the significance of Picard's revelation.

"By whatever means Stron used to escape from the *Bennett*, a shipment of alta mist was also transferred from the

144

vessel and is somehow already in transit to an unknown location. The blockade has been broken, Will."

"And Chiton Kincaid is in on it?" Riker asked.

"She attacked me with a protoplaser. When I regained consciousness, I was with Stron and his wife."

Riker clutched at the arms of his chair in cold fury. "I understand, sir. I'll get to the bottom of this."

On the screen, Picard forced a smile. "That would be most gratifying, Number One."

Riker turned to Troi. "Counselor, I'll want you standing by for interrogation of Kincaid, Stron, whoever else is involved. Riker to transporter room two: Stand by for—"

Rolk interrupted. "Sir, I have Manager Kincaid."

"Onscreen, and feed it to the captain in the *Galileo.*"

The main viewscreen flashed from an image of Picard to one of Chiton. Beside the station manager, Riker saw Stron and his wife, both barely as tall as Chiton's shoulders.

"Manager Kincaid," Riker began, "under the provisions of the Federation's emergency disaster relief provisions of stardate 35333, you are to consider yourself and your accomplices in custody."

"We do not recognize the Federation's authority over our actions," Chiton Kincaid responded.

"You don't have a choice."

"What do you propose to do, Commander? Beam us aboard the *Enterprise* and contaminate it and your crew?"

"There are quarantine measures that can be taken."

But Chiton shook her head. "Quarantine implies separation, Commander. And that concept does not exist. All worlds are connected. All life is one. And until the intelligent beings of the galaxy realize that, all efforts to establish an interstellar community are doomed to failure, with the lives of billions at stake."

"I suspect those lives are at stake because of actions you

yourself have taken," Riker said. "You will be held accountable for that."

"Would you be willing to sacrifice your life for the life of your crew, Commander?"

Riker didn't understand the question. "What does that have to do with—"

"I attended the Academy," Chiton said, her voice rising with emotion. "I know a commander's duty. Her life for her captain. Her life for her crew."

Riker stood, sensing he was losing control of this conversation. "I know my duty, Kincaid. You've betrayed yours."

But the station manager ignored Riker. "Where does that duty end, Commander? Your life for five hundred others? Your ship to save a world? The Federation is dying! Its end is inevitable. Would you condemn trillions of beings to hideous lingering deaths if by sacrificing only a few billion you could insure that suffering would not come to pass?"

"A few *billion?*"

Troi stepped close to Riker. "She's working up to making some kind of decision, Will. You have to get her out of there."

On the screen, Chiton continued passionately. "We know our duty, Commander, just as you know yours. The symmetry of all things must be preserved. You differ from us only in degree."

"Riker to transporter control: I want—"

"The revolution will prevail," Chiton exulted. "Those who survive will come to praise us for our sacrifice!" Then she leaned forward and touched a control.

The image winked out.

"Will—" Troi's voice faltered.

"Massive energy release on the planet's surface!" Rolk said.

"Orbital view," Riker ordered.

When the image changed again, where Gamow Station had been was only a blazing fireball, rising slowly into the superheated air above it.

146

Troi staggered back and fell into her chair, ashen. "They're
. . . all gone . . ." she whispered in empathetic agony. "I felt
them die . . . all fourteen hundred. . . ."

Riker looked at Rolk for confirmation.

"They shut off the restriction fields in their matter-
antimatter reactor," the Bolian said. "Complete annihilation.
No survivors."

Picard came back onscreen, looking as shaken as Riker felt.

"There was nothing you could do, Will. They were fanatics
of the worst kind."

Riker stared imploringly at Picard. Fourteen hundred
innocent lives lost. *Was* it because of something he had done?
Or failed to do?

"Did you hear what she said?" Picard asked. "Just before
the end? About 'the symmetry of all things'?"

Riker didn't know what he meant.

"They're Symmetrists, Will. After more than a century,
they're back."

EIGHTEEN

☆

Spock breathed deeply of the air of Vulcan. Of home.

He had played in the red-tinged desert stretched out before him on the Plains of Gol, when he had been a child and was still permitted to play. It was to the Llangon Mountains in the distance he had retreated, when he could not face his father's disapproval. But it was to this mountain villa that he had returned each time.

Even when he had been reborn on Mount Seleya, it was to this home he had come.

He closed his eyes. Smelled the faint cinnamon dust of this world. Could almost hear his mother, a fragile Earthling, doomed to age and die before even half a Vulcan lifespan had gone by.

Spock bowed his head. What would Amanda think of him, knowing he had left his father unprotected when Sarek had needed his family most? Needed his son.

"Do you recall the name Tarok?" Srell asked.

Spock was startled from his reverie. He had not heard his young aide approach. He wondered if his Vulcan senses were diminishing with each day he allowed his human emotions greater reign.

148

Spock turned to see Srell at the edge of the wide stone plaza that joined the various buildings of his family's villa. Spock still wore his ambassadorial robes, though his young assistant had opted for a more functional, long-jacketed suit.

Srell carried a small computer interface. One of Sarek's antiques. It was a thick pane of transparent crystal that had little of the capacity of a modern padd. But it served adequately to link with the villa's computer system and Sarek had seen no need to replace it.

Srell handed the crystal to Spock. Spock angled it to more easily read the Vulcan script that glowed within.

"I found the database where Perrin said it would be," Srell explained. "And I have cross-referenced it with the lists your contacts provided. Of all the visitors and guests Sarek entertained in his final months here, only one name does not have a corresponding preference file in the home system."

Spock read the name. Tarok.

"There would be no need for a file," Spock said. "He is an old family friend."

Spock remembered sitting at Tarok's knee as the Vulcan scholar had told him wholly inappropriate stories from before the time of the Vulcan Reformation. There were tales of fierce battles, jealousy and greed. Passionate romances, cruel betrayals, kingdoms lost to forbidden love, sons sacrificing all to avenge the wrongs done their fathers.

As a child, Spock had been fascinated by that earlier age in which Vulcans had not controlled their emotions. Sarek had voiced his disapproval—as he so often did—complaining that it was he, not Tarok, who had to deal with his young son's inevitable nightmares after hearing those stories. But Amanda had been a co-conspirator with Tarok, encouraging the story sessions, and keeping them secret whenever she could.

In human terms, Tarok had been Spock's uncle, though there was no kinship by blood.

"It might be possible that Tarok's file was erased," Srell suggested, "in order to divert suspicion from him."

Spock was puzzled that Srell persisted in suggesting Tarok as a suspect. "Tarok and my father were friends when they were boys. My parents knew all his preferences. A file would not be needed."

Srell was not dissuaded. *"Amanda* and Sarek would have known him well, then. But what of your stepmother, Perrin? She told me these files had all been updated after her marriage to Sarek, to help her organize the diplomatic functions held here."

Spock stopped to consider Srell's observation. His father's most recent wife, Perrin, was currently on Earth, continuing her work with the Vulcan diplomatic corps as a cultural attaché. She had been most helpful in providing Srell with the passwords and codes necessary to activate the villa's system.

"You raise an interesting point," Spock conceded. Amanda and Sarek had entertained Tarok so often, had him and his associates as guests here so frequently, that any preferences he had would be well known. But of course a new file would have to have been created for Perrin when she had taken over the villa's organizational duties.

"Tarok now resides in Gonthar District," Srell added.

"Indeed."

"And, he also is afflicted with Bendii."

Spock instantly squeezed the corner of the crystal that changed it from a data display to a communications window. "Please arrange transport to Gonthar," Spock said.

Srell folded his hands behind his back. "I have already done so."

Spock nodded, remembering when he had been as sure in his logic as Srell was now. In fact, Srell reminded him of himself at a similar age.

Spock wondered if that was why Sarek had chosen the youth as his aide. Had he also seen an echo of another time, an opportunity to replay history, to have a son who would not run off to Starfleet?

Spock thought of second chances as he placed a communications inquiry to Tarok's estate.

Of all he had been given in this life, a second chance with his father had been the one thing denied him.

The inquiry went through. An aide answered. Spock made his request.

Though he did not reveal his own reaction, Spock was amused by Srell's less than perfect attempt to control his response to his first sight of Tarok's nurse.

She was a Klingon.

Young, dressed in a tight-fitting version of pale green Vulcan healer's garb, but savage of brow, of hair, and of attitude.

"nuqneH?" she snarled as Srell and Spock stepped from the small antigrav flyer they had taken to Tarok's forest estate.

Srell was clearly at a disadvantage. His thoughts did not need to be stated. What Vulcan would entrust his well-being to a Klingon?

But Spock understood, all too well. Tarok would have hired a Klingon nursing staff for the same reason he told blood-thirsty tales of the Reformation to impressionable youngsters. Too many Vulcans believed that control of emotions meant they should have no emotions at all. But Tarok had always reveled in his, clearly understanding the difference between public comportment and private enjoyment. In its way, Tarok's unorthodox philosophy was most logical.

"I am Spock, child of Sarek, child of Skon," Spock said. "This is my aide."

The Klingon bared her teeth at Spock. Slowly she looked Srell over, coolly assessing more than his emotional detachment, apparently gratified by what she perceived to be his nervousness.

She angled her head toward the large wooden doors leading from the landing drive. "This way," she growled.

She spun around and walked away, the tightness of her uniform accentuating each taut curve of her well-exercised flesh. Despite the seriousness of their mission, Spock could not resist commenting to Srell, "I believe she likes you."

Srell kept his eyes fixed on the nurse's head and nowhere else as he followed her. Spock wondered if he himself could possibly have been as mirthless as Srell when he had been that age. He decided he probably had been. He was going to enjoy visiting with Tarok again. It might be good for Srell, as well.

As Spock and Srell were ushered into Tarok's sitting room, they found that their host awaited them, picking at a corner of the white robes he wore, his lips moving in a soundless monologue. Attending him was a second Klingon nurse, in a healer's uniform as revealing as that of their escort's.

Tarok was much smaller than Spock had remembered him. The elder Vulcan, 205 standard years old, had withered with age. His short white hair stuck up in odd tufts, his cheeks were hollow, but the lines on his face still conspired to make him appear as if he constantly smiled.

Tarok sat in a padded chair, a concession to his age and infirmity, in the low-ceilinged, wood-paneled sitting room, which was adorned with mementos of his career in interstellar commerce. Where Sarek had gone into diplomacy, Tarok had joined the Vulcan trade mission. It was Tarok's keen intellect and illuminating logic, more than any other being's in the Federation, that had formulated the current economic environment in which money was no longer necessary. Spock understood that effigies of Tarok were burned during holidays on the worlds of the Ferengi.

"Takta," the second nurse said respectfully. Spock was not surprised that she used a diminutive for Tarok's name that was by tradition reserved only for the use of children. "Your visitors are here."

Tarok looked up at the nurse, blinking as if trying to recall who she was. The first nurse leaned in closely to Spock. "You are aware of the symptoms of Bendii?"

"I am," Spock confirmed.

The nurse dropped her voice to a harsh whisper. "He is a great man. Treat him with respect, or my sister and I shall gut you and feed you to the *norsehlats*. Understood?"

Spock was not concerned by the Klingon's threat. "He is my uncle," he said. "When I was a child, I called him Takta, as well."

"That is the only reason we have allowed you to see him." The nurse snarled at her sister and they left together, though Spock had no doubt they would be watching everything that transpired on a hidden scanner.

Spock approached the elder Vulcan. "Tarok, I have come to see you." He spoke more loudly than he normally would, hoping to cut through the haze of Bendii.

Tarok peered up at him from within the enveloping billows of his robes. For a moment, his eyes seemed to clear and a childlike smile spread across his face. "Sarek?"

Spock sat in the chair the nurse had used. "I am Spock, his son."

"Ahh," Tarok said, as if everything were explained by that. He blinked at Srell. "And this young man . . . ?"

Srell carried another chair forward so he could sit at eye level with Tarok. "I am Srell, child of Staron, child of Stonn." But that association meant nothing to Tarok. "Aide to Sarek, and to Spock," Srell added.

"Sarek . . ." Tarok sighed. He reached out to take Spock's hand, a terrible breach of Vulcan etiquette because of the low-level telepathy all Vulcans possessed. Direct physical contact was rare on social occasions, and only with consent. "Is Amanda well?"

Spock automatically called on his training in the *Kolinahr* to clear his mind and keep his emotions at a level that would not upset the old one. "My mother died, many years ago."

"Ah, yes," Tarok said. "Human. Such a loss."

"I would like to talk to you about my parents," Spock said.

"Fine people. Sarek so unbending, though. At the meetings, much too serious. The humans didn't like him. Trusted him. Didn't like him."

"When did you last see Sarek?" Spock asked gently, trying to keep the old Vulcan focused. With Bendii, Tarok's recollections might well skip from one decade to another, blending all his memories into one seamless tapestry where everything happened at once.

"Tried to warn him," Tarok sighed. He squeezed Spock's hand as he studied him. His other hand reached out to touch Spock's *katra* points but Spock lightly warded off the attempt. It would be dangerous for them both to attempt a meld with Tarok's symptoms so strong.

"What did you try to warn Sarek about?" Spock asked. He had no idea if this would be a useful line of inquiry. Sarek and Tarok would have had uncountable dealings in the past. Diplomatic agreements were almost always accompanied by trade relations.

"They were coming back, you see," Tarok said.

"Who were?"

"We thought it was over. We had ended it." Tarok's voice quickened as if he were caught up in an intense memory. "At your home. You weren't there, of course. Always going off to the mountains." He took a deep and rasping breath. "Your father was so worried. But I knew why you went." He patted Spock's hand. His voice slowed, trembled. "Your Takta knew."

Spock resisted the sudden impulse to expose his emotions to Tarok. He wanted him to know how much he had appreciated the time they had spent together, the guidance he had been given.

He glanced at Srell, but the young Vulcan was correctly impassive, merely an observer.

"What did you 'end' at my home?" Spock asked.

Tarok took his hand away. Smoothed his robes. He now spoke with the energy of a younger man. "You were not to be part of it. Your father made that clear."

"Part of what?"

"He knew what it meant. No chance to meld. A terrible burden between father and son."

Spock straightened in his chair, not certain what Tarok's words meant but anxious to learn.

"We could not risk it," Tarok continued. "None of us. We could meld only with those who were in the cause."

"What cause?" Spock asked urgently, forgetting all pretense of holding his emotions in check, forgetting that Srell was a witness to his loss of control.

Tarok looked at Spock for a long time. His eyes dimmed, as if he were looking beyond Spock to a different time. "I never had a son. Sometimes, when I told you stories, I could almost imagine that you were mine. Flesh of my flesh, riding forth as in the days of old, a son to avenge his father's fate. That is what they did then, you know. Long, long ago. . . ."

"What cause?" Spock insisted.

"I was so proud of you when you went to the Academy. But that proved Sarek had been right. What if we *had* told you? Your duty would have required you to report us."

"Tarok," Spock said. "Forgive me. . . ."

Tarok's eyes cleared. Became neutral. "Forgiveness is not logical, Spock."

It might have been Sarek speaking. Spock leaned forward, disturbed, impatient. He would no longer have secrets kept from him. Impulsively, he placed his hands on Tarok's face and began to meld.

A torrent of images, emotions, experiences, chaotic in the

throes of Bendii, mixed with glimpses of his father, of his mother, an incoherent ocean of other minds, other thoughts, drowning out Tarok's cries of confusion as Spock violently burst into his mind and—

Spock felt himself fly back through the air to hit the floor. Before he could move again, one of the Klingon nurses was kneeling on his chest, holding a *d'k tahg* knife to his throat. The outrider blades sprang open as she forced it against his skin.

"Have you no honor?" she spat.

Still struggling to make sense of the images he had experienced, Spock stared past her and saw Srell in the armlock of the other nurse, another knife at his throat. Tarok had collapsed in his chair, hands fluttering at his face. His ragged sobbing tore at Spock's heart.

"You must go now," the nurse hissed in Spock's ear. Then she hauled him to his feet as if he were a sack of trillium.

Spock wrestled against the Klingon's grip. "Tarok! Who is the prefect of Gonthar?"

From across the room, Tarok looked up, tears spilling from his ancient eyes. "I told your father they would kill him if the codes were known! I told him they were back!" The old Vulcan suddenly looked to the side. He held out a shaking finger. "There! It's all there!"

Spock followed Tarok's line of sight, even as the nurse began to drag him to the door. The aged scholar was pointing to a table beside the doorway. The table held an antique IDIC medallion, a scroll, and a handful of other artifacts of great antiquity and cultural value.

But among them, the black base of an ordinary, civilian holoprojector, just like the one Spock had been given on Babel. Completely out of place.

Still in the implacable grip of the Klingon nurse, Spock shouted: "Tarok! Who killed my father?!"

Tarok staggered painfully to his feet, trembling, hands held forward in supplication. "Forgive me, my child. Surak forgive us all. . . ."

Then the room shook with the first explosion and Spock was swept once more into a maelstrom of fire and memories that were not his own.

NINETEEN

☆

Spock awoke in darkness. In the distance, he could hear phaser fire, the crackle of disruptors. Another explosion erupted nearby. He tried to get up.

But Srell pushed him down.

"The estate is under attack," Srell said.

"Where is Tarok?" Spock asked.

"The two Klingons took him. We have to get back to the flyer."

"No! It is imperative we locate Tarok!"

Spock felt Srell back away from him, no doubt alarmed by the raw emotion in Spock's voice. He sat up and looked around, eyes gradually adapting to the darkness. He was still in the sitting room. Only moments must have passed. But he could smell smoke. The estate building was on fire.

"Why is Tarok important?" Srell asked. "Did *he* kill your father? Is that what you saw in his mind?"

Spock got to his feet, slipped off his robes so he wore only simple black trousers and tunic. "I saw my parents there," he said. "As they were years ago."

Srell joined Spock as Spock moved quickly to the doorway.

"They were Symmetrists," Spock said.

"The cult?" Srell asked, faint distaste evident in his voice.

"It was never a cult. It began as a political movement. When it spread to other worlds, they called it a revolution."

The hallway beyond the doorway was also in darkness. The power lines in the estate must have been cut. Spock listened carefully. He could hear people running and tried to estimate how many attackers there might be.

"That is what Ki Mendrossen spoke of," Srell said. "In his recording. 'For the good of the cause,'" the young Vulcan quoted. "'For the revolution.'"

"The Symmetrist cause was repudiated almost two centuries ago," Spock said. The attacking force seemed to be coming from the woods at the rear of the estate. There might be a chance to get back to the antigrav flyer at the front drive. But he didn't want to leave without Tarok. He had no doubt that was who the target of this attack was.

"Then Tarok is wrong," Srell said. "He was thinking in the past."

Spock pointed down the hallway toward the main entrance of the building. "Go to the flyer. Wait for me there. I will find Tarok."

"Let me," Srell said. "You are too valuable to Vulcan. And to Romulus. You must not let your work end here."

Spock appreciated the logic of Srell's request. But what he had to do was personal.

"If I cannot save Tarok, I might have to meld with him again, so that his knowledge does not die. You go forward, Srell. You make the dream of unification a reality."

Srell seemed to recognize his place was not to argue with Spock's logic. "Peace and long life," he said. "I am honored in my work with you."

"Live long and prosper," Spock replied. "Now, go!"

Srell hurried down the hallway. Spock headed off in the opposite direction, to where the sound of fighting was loudest.

He came to a smaller hallway that, from what he recalled of seeing the estate from the air, was a connecting structure between two larger buildings. The fighting seemed concentrated around the second structure.

Spock suddenly wondered who was fighting. Tarok obviously had a staff greater than two Klingon nurses. He also wondered why anyone who wished to kill Tarok didn't just use a quantum explosive to wipe out everything within a kilometer.

Too easy to trace, Spock decided. A simpler approach would be more subtle.

But he still couldn't reconcile that strategy with the increasing sounds of all-out armed combat. Unless the attackers had been completely surprised by the size of Tarok's home security force.

Spock moved silently along the narrow connecting corridor, toward the second building. He could see flashes of orange and blue energy reflected in the tall windows. Some of the phaser fire seemed to match the wavelength of standard-issue Starfleet sidearms. He assumed Tarok had many friends in the service.

At the end of the corridor, a large atrium flickered with the firefight being waged outside. Spock judged the distance to a sizable tree in the center of the large room, and estimated he would have eight chances in nine of reaching it undetected. He had no doubt that the fighting was centered on whatever stronghold to which Tarok's Klingon nurses had taken the old trader. Perhaps he could create a diversion by attacking from behind.

Spock turned his mind to improvising a weapon as he began his sprint toward the tree.

But after he had gone a single meter, he tripped over an unseen obstacle and fell to the tile floor with a grunt.

Before he could roll over to defend himself, an attacker had leapt onto his back, then jabbed a knuckle punch under his ribs.

Spock's breath exploded from him, but he rammed his elbow upward and had the satisfaction of hearing an answering grunt as his attacker slumped to the side.

Instantly Spock was up on his hands and knees, then his feet, and then—

—down again as his assailant swept his legs out from under him.

Spock gasped for breath. It had been almost a century since his last round of intensive, hand-to-hand combat training. His stamina was down. But not his skill.

He kicked out at the approaching silhouette of his adversary and caught him in the stomach. He heard the body tumble to the floor and launched himself toward it, rolling over twice before bringing his hand down to deliver a fight-ending nerve pinch.

His fingers hit armor.

A fist hit his face.

Spock rolled again.

His attacker jumped him.

Spock's hands closed around his assailant's throat—an intemperate move, because it allowed his opponent to do the same.

Now it came down to who could hold out the longest before succumbing to suffocation.

Spock wheezed as he put all his energy into closing his fingers into fists.

His assailant wheezed just as heavily, as if he weren't a trained soldier either.

Spock felt his strength failing.

But his opponent's strength was failing just as rapidly.

Something was wrong.

A sudden phaser burst smashed through an atrium window and hit the tree behind Spock. Dried foliage burst into flames, and in the flickering light of the explosion, Spock at last saw his attacker's face.

And for one of the few times in his life, Spock screamed.

TWENTY

☆

Kirk's scream was easily a match for Spock's.

He couldn't have been more surprised if the firelight had revealed he was fighting a Gorn.

He jumped away from Spock.

Spock gaped at him.

"Jim?"

"Spock?"

Then Spock smiled broadly as he reached out to grab his friend by his shoulders. "I knew it! I knew you escaped the Borg homeworld!"

Kirk ducked as another phaser burst shattered more atrium glass.

Spock took his hands away, tried to collect himself. "What are you doing here?"

"Looking for you," Kirk said. "What are *you* doing here?"

"Trying to save the man who knows who murdered my father."

"Tarok?" Kirk asked.

Spock looked at Kirk through narrowed eyes. "Why am I not surprised."

Kirk leapt to his feet and angled a thumb toward an atrium

exit. "My crew's outside. There're at least five attackers with phasers coming out of the woods."

"Your crew?" Spock asked as he jumped up beside Kirk.

Kirk chuckled. "Listen to us trying to catch our breath."

"I am out of practice," Spock said.

"Then let's make up for lost time."

Kirk ran for the exit, Spock at his side.

That simple fact alone made Kirk feel at least a century younger. Maybe even two.

The battle outside was short and to the point.

Spock unerringly located each attacker from the angle of the phaser fire. Kirk's crew kept the attacker pinned down. Kirk unerringly slipped through the forest and surprised the attacker. Spock used the nerve pinch to end each fight. They used the attackers' own jackets to tie them up.

Kirk was troubled that all five of them were Vulcan, but he wasn't surprised. The involvement of Vulcans in the events surrounding the virogen was precisely why he had come to find Spock. He was fortunate that the Vulcan diplomatic corps kept such careful track of Spock's travel plans, and had deigned to reveal them to the commander of a Starfleet vessel.

By the time the final attacker was neutralized, both Kirk and Spock were wheezing uncontrollably, but Kirk wouldn't have it any other way.

"You know," he gasped, as he leaned over to catch his breath, hands on his knees, "if you had asked me an hour ago . . . I would have said I missed this kind of nonsense."

Spock leaned against a tree, gasping just as deeply. But he clearly had other matters on his mind. "How *did* you . . . survive the partial destruction of . . . the Borg homeworld?"

Kirk glanced toward the estate as he saw shadowy figures run toward him. "There'll be time for that later." Then Commander MacDonald, Engineer Barc, and Dr. M'Benga were upon them.

Kirk made the introductions. The two young officers and the Tellarite stared in openmouthed awe.

"Kirk *and* Spock?" Christine said.

"What did I tell you?" Kirk warned her. Then he took M'Benga's medical tricorder and fiddled with the unfamiliar controls. He pointed to a smaller building that stood alone. "C'mon, Spock. You said you were looking for Tarok."

Kirk ran off, the others at his side. He was amused to hear how both he and Spock struggled to control their breathing with an audience present.

The small building was a meditation chamber. Kirk read two life signs inside, both Vulcan, one very old. Again, not a surprise.

He eased open the ornately carved wooden door. Inside the austere chamber, candles were lit, adding a warm glow to the surreal violence frozen in place.

Two Klingon females were sprawled on the floor, pools of thick pink blood surrounding them. In the far corner, a young male Vulcan cradled an old male Vulcan.

Kirk quickly checked the tricorder's display. The old Vulcan was fading quickly. M'Benga snatched the tricorder from Kirk's hand as she rushed to the dying man.

"Anyone know the history of this man?" the doctor asked urgently.

Spock pushed past Kirk. "Bendii Syndrome," he said. "I must meld with him."

But M'Benga stood in Spock's way. "He's dying, sir. And with Bendii, not even his *katra* can be claimed at this stage."

"You don't understand," Spock said. "He is the only one who knows—"

"It is over," the young Vulcan said.

Kirk was hurt to see how his friend seemed to collapse at that pronouncement, as if the old Vulcan had been the most important thing in his life.

Kirk went to Spock's side. "It'll be all right, Spock. We're both on it now."

Spock straightened his shoulders. The young Vulcan stood up. "Srell," Spock said formally, "may I introduce James T. Kirk."

Srell stared at Kirk for several long seconds, then raised an eyebrow in an all-too-familiar expression.

Kirk smiled at Spock. "Friend of yours?"

"My aide."

"A pleasure," Kirk said, knowing better than to extend his hand. "I wish the circumstances were more agreeable, but I have the feeling we'll be working together."

Srell still said nothing.

Kirk was used to that reaction, especially since the repeated reports of his death. He turned back to the Klingons. M'Benga was kneeling by them.

"How did they die?" Kirk asked.

"Disruptor fire," the doctor said, but didn't sound convinced. "I don't often see bleeding when that happens. Could be close-range stun, but . . ." She stood up, adjusted her uniform. "We'll have to wait for the authorities to conduct an autopsy."

"I do not believe it would be wise to contact the authorities," Spock said.

Everyone in the meditation chamber stared at him.

"At this stage in my investigation," he explained, "I am not certain if we can trust them."

"Spock?" Kirk said. "We can't trust *Vulcan* authorities?"

Christine stepped up beside Kirk. "He might have a point, given who was in that fighter on Chal."

At last Srell spoke. "You were on Chal?"

"Five days ago," Kirk said.

"But," the young Vulcan came close to stammering, "that is one of the systems infected with the virogen. If you were there, you have exposed Vulcan to it."

M'Benga answered for the crew of the *Tobias*. "We're clear of it," she said. "Jim brought us a compound that removes it from animal cells."

"A cure?" Srell asked. Kirk noted that he seemed disoriented. If that was possible for a Vulcan.

But M'Benga shook her head. "A way to slow down its spread, but not a cure. At least the quarantined systems can be opened up after proper treatment."

Kirk knew the technical discussions could wait. He trusted Spock to make the right decision about what strategy they must follow right now. "It's your world, Spock. What do we do?"

"For the time being, I believe we are on our own."

"Suits me," Kirk said. *Some things never change,* he thought. Kirk looked at the bodies of the Klingons and Tarok. "Let's send down a forensics team to clean the place up and create records for the authorities for when the time comes to involve them."

"A forensics team?" Spock asked.

"From Commander MacDonald's ship. You think I flew here on my own?"

"Under the circumstances, that would not surprise me either," Spock said. With an imperceptibly slight trace of a smile, he added, "And that would explain your fatigue."

Kirk saw the look of confusion on the faces of Christine, M'Benga, and Barc.

"Did I hear right," M'Benga asked gruffly, "or did a Vulcan just make a joke?"

"You mean, tried to make a joke," Christine said with a smile.

Srell regarded them stonily, hands behind his back. "I assure you, Vulcans never joke."

"Rrrr," Barc growled, "then you haven't seen how they can translate technical manuals. They're responsible for the most confusing ones in my collection."

Kirk glanced over at Spock. "Is it just me, or do they remind you of anyone?"

Spock looked thoughtful for a moment, then raised an eyebrow and said, "It is just you."

Kirk grinned. He had forgotten just how much he had missed his old friend. He fumbled with the Starfleet comm badge on his civilian shirt.

"Kirk to *Tobias*," he said as it chirped. "Six to beam up."

Now that his team had been assembled, it was time to get to work.

TWENTY-ONE

☆

Except for the whisper of the environmental systems, the observation lounge of the *Enterprise*-E was quiet. At their chairs, La Forge, Data, Lieutenant Rolk, and Riker watched the slowly rotating surface of Alta Vista 257 beyond the large ports, or stared across the conference table at the display case of golden *Enterprise*s of the past. No one talked. They were giving Counselor Deanna Troi a moment to compose herself.

Though not a full Betazoid, Troi had been focusing her empathic ability on Chiton Kincaid, Stron, and his wife, at the moment of their deaths. And of fourteen hundred others.

The awful wave of emotion that had flashed from Gamow Station in the horror of the reactor explosion still reverberated within her, leaving her shaken and detached.

Riker did not think it was necessary for her to be present at this briefing, so soon after the disaster, but Picard had insisted. He had his reasons, he had told Riker, for wanting all his senior staff available.

The somber mood in the room was suddenly broken as the new virtual viewscreen shimmered into life in front of the far bulkhead.

Picard and Crusher appeared there, their images transmitted from the *Galileo*. The captain and the doctor were still in quarantine on the decompressed shuttlebay deck. Riker was relieved to see that Picard wore a smaller dressing on his facial wound and seemed more rested. Crusher's treatments were having some success.

"I feel awkward at having to address you in this manner," Picard said, "but Dr. Crusher has confirmed that I am now a carrier of the virogen."

"As am I," Crusher added.

"No ill effects?" Riker asked.

"Mild," Crusher said. "Slight fever. Intestinal upset. But we're both following the typical thirty-hour curve of symptoms. We'll be fine by morning, though still contagious."

Picard began the meeting. "Lieutenant Rolk: Have you had any response from Starfleet?"

As the Bolian security officer frowned, the fleshy ridge bisecting her blue face stiffened. "Sir, I've been having difficulties establishing a repeater link with Starbase Seven-eighteen." Rolk didn't wait for Picard to ask the obvious question. "All the ship's systems test out, but I'm not receiving a signal confirmation. None of the ships in the blockade can."

"Is it some type of subspace interference?" Picard asked.

The Bolian looked over at Riker. They had already discussed the situation and Riker could see she was feeling out of her depth. He took up the report.

"Captain, it could just be subspace chatter, but there have been unconfirmed reports of . . . a riot at the starbase."

Picard looked grim, yet offered no response. At any other time, such a thing would have been impossible. But for months now, the signs of growing strain in the infrastructure of the Federation had been clearly increasing. Full-scale food and resource riots were breaking out on the most badly affected worlds. But for a Starfleet installation to suffer the same fate was a serious matter, and an alarming indication of how rapidly the situation was deteriorating.

"I have not been able to confirm that report," Riker added. "But given that no ship in the immediate sector has been able to raise Starbase Seven-eighteen for the past seven days, it seems reasonable to assume that something . . . disruptive has happened there."

Riker was familiar with the stoic expression that now came to his captain. Whatever Picard's personal thoughts on this escalation of the virogen's impact, he would keep them to himself. First and foremost, he was a starship captain.

"Lieutenant Rolk, you are, of course, establishing contact with Command through other links in the subspace relay network," Picard said.

"Yes, sir," the security officer confirmed. "The fleet system is . . . suffering sporadic overloads and shutdowns because of the unusually high level of emergency traffic, but I will establish contact within the next day."

"A fast transport can travel more than five light-years in a day."

Riker knew what the captain meant.

They had finally discovered how Stron, his wife, and the alta mist samples had survived the destruction of the *Bennett*—they had beamed to the asteroid designated Alta Vista 257 during the suspicious burst of subspace static from the *Bennett's* deflector dish, only instants before the warp-core breach had begun. That static had been the source of the previously unexplained reading.

Picard had suggested the possibility of a surreptitious transport once it was determined that no organic residue of Stron and his wife could be found. But there had been no other ships within transporter range, and the *Enterprise* had been unable to detect any sign of an artificial structure or even a portable life-support shelter on the asteroid. Because there hadn't been one.

Instead, the crew and the cargo of the *Bennett* had been beamed *into* a naturally formed bubble in the nickel-iron asteroid, 2.8 kilometers below the surface, completely contained, with no physical link to the outside. Data had explored the bubble after Picard had ordered the *Enterprise* to return to the asteroid for a more thorough search.

The bubble, frozen in the metal when the asteroid had cooled from Alta Vista's planetary-accretion disk more than eight billion years ago, was one of hundreds in the object. The roughly spherical chamber was approximately twenty meters across, and had been lined with an insulating foam and outfitted with glow strips, a cargo tank for the alta mist samples, and a small life-support unit used to fill the bubble with an atmosphere and warm the contents above the asteroid's normal interior temperature of $-357°$ Celsius.

When Rolk had detected the faint though anomalous hot spot in the asteroid's interior, he had transported a remote sensor array to scan the bubble. Then Data beamed in to help recover the equipment that had been installed there.

Only now, days after the *Bennett*'s apparent destruction, was it clear to Riker and the others what had happened. Based on the replicator load Data had calculated from the life-support unit's consumables supply, the android had reported that Stron and his wife had hidden in the bubble for only a few hours. At that time, a second ship from outside the system came to the asteroid and beamed the two of them out along with the alta vista from the holding tank. Residual amounts of the one-celled, airborne plant cells still remained on the inner surfaces of the tank. The level of virogen contamination within it was exceedingly high.

How that second ship then returned Stron and his wife to Alta Vista III and left the system, Riker wasn't sure. But Rolk confirmed that while in orbit, the *Enterprise* had made no special efforts to scan for the tachyon signature sometimes associated with cloaking devices. Thus, Riker did not find it impossible that one small, fast, cloaked vessel might have successfully passed through the quarantine blockade undetected.

Which meant that that same ship could already be dozens of light-years distant, taking the contaminated alta mist to an unknown destination. And as the captain had pointed out, each hour's delay took that unknown vessel and its deadly cargo even farther away.

"With the destruction of the Gamow Station," Picard told his assembled senior officers from the viewscreen, "maintenance of the blockade in this system has become moot. In the absence of orders from Command, as senior ranking officer, I am freeing the blockade vessels to move on to other vital assignments."

Riker asked the question he knew would be on everyone else's mind. "What will our new assignment be?"

"That is where I am going to need your advice," Picard said. "It is my opinion that based on the events we have witnessed here, the virogen plague that is threatening the stability of the Federation is a deliberate terrorist attack, conducted by the organization known as the Symmetrists."

"Who, or what, are the Symmetrists?" La Forge asked. "I've never heard of them."

"Few have," Picard explained. "They grew out of an environmental movement begun on Vulcan more than two centuries ago, just after the founding of the Federation."

"In fact," Data unexpectedly continued, "the Symmetrists considered themselves a political response to the Federation's formation. They were the equivalent of the isolationist parties on Earth, which lobbied to keep that world from joining the Federation. The Symmetrists felt that logic demanded Vulcan and her colonies remain independent."

"Data, you sound as if you've studied the movement," Crusher said from the screen.

"I am endlessly fascinated by the differences of opinion

that arise among Vulcans. For a people who follow logic, they exhibit many of the same tendencies of other, more emotional races, to fragment into different political factions which—"

"I'll take that as a yes," Picard said, to stop the threatened lecture. "However, on Earth, the various isolationist groups were the last gasp of twenty-first-century regionalism, swept away in the Reconstruction that followed first contact. There was never any serious opposition to the Federation among the members of Earth's world government. But on Vulcan, those who opposed the Federation were not driven by political motives. Rather, they perceived a threat to the galactic ecology."

With that phrase, Riker abruptly remembered an obscure history course he had taken in his second year at the Academy. The idea of a galactic ecology was still widely debated among exopaleobiologists. Certainly, evidence clearly established that many worlds shared related life-forms. Some of this was due to the interplanetary exchange of bacteria and viruses fueled by violent meteoric impacts. In Earth's own system, life on Earth, the underground bacteria of Mars, the oceans of Europa, and the ice viruses of Mercury all shared common origins.

Exciting similarities between more distant worlds, such as Earth, Qo'noS, and Vulcan, were then proven, in part by this very crew, to have originated as the result of the genetic seeding of dozens of planets by the first humanoid race to evolve in the galaxy, more than four billion years ago.

But where the experts still disagreed was in accepting the existence of a natural, interplanetary web of connectedness throughout the galaxy.

The majority view held that any such theory was based on inaccurate observations and flawed reasoning. To those who controlled the scientific status quo, each life-bearing planet was a separate storehouse of biological riches to be exploited at will, with the confidence of knowing individual worlds existed in a natural quarantine enforced by the cold, radiation-filled vacuum of interstellar space.

But on Vulcan, a vocal minority said it was the majority who were mistaken. Just because a web of connection could not be rigorously demonstrated by the science of the day did not mean that the web did not exist, in a form unknown, and perhaps unknowable, to human observers.

These scientists, the forerunners of the Symmetrist movement, said that each planet was a link in a chain of life that had evolved according to the rhythms of the galaxy's natural ebb and flow of matter and energy. To those who accepted the Vulcans' postulates, the galactic ecology could be perceived as a single organism, indescribably vast, operating at a timescale in which the birth and death of stars passed in an eyeblink.

To interfere with the natural state of that galactic ecology, by traveling between the distant worlds on warp-powered ships, subjecting delicately balanced planetary biospheres indiscriminately to the shock of alien microbes, plants, and animals over the course of years and not eons, was a crime. An ecological crime.

As the newly formed Federation began to codify the rules and regulations of an organized, concerted effort to explore all the worlds of the galaxy, it was on Vulcan that the scientific opposition to this strategy became most vocal.

That opposition argued that intelligent beings must be stewards of the galactic ecology, not exploiters. Humans, Vulcans, Tellarites, Andorians . . . the citizens of all space-faring civilizations had a responsibility to recognize and preserve the symmetry of all things.

The highest ideal of that symmetry stated that the galaxy was no different from a living being.

Therefore, if the Federation accepted the sanctity of an

individual's right to exist, which it did, then the Federation must also accept the sanctity of all life, including that of the galaxy itself.

Led by some of the most noted biologists and philosophers of the day, the Symmetrists pleaded with the Federation to amend its charter so that strict quarantine protocols would be followed on each world discovered to have a native biosphere, and that colonization and terraforming would occur only on those worlds that were completely lifeless.

Logic demanded no less.

But, Riker recalled, the Federation had rejected the Symmetrists' arguments as unfounded and unproven, and perhaps, more importantly, as potentially expensive and capable of bringing galactic exploration to a standstill.

Only if the concerned scientists could return with the hard data necessary to prove their far-fetched view of the galaxy would the Federation Council deign to revisit their proposals.

But until then, the Council ruled, the Federation would continue to regard the galaxy merely as a resource that belonged to everyone.

"When the Vulcans who opposed the Federation's ambitious exploration plans were rebuffed," Picard continued, "the Symmetrist movement began. At first, they were a loosely knit academic group, committed to compiling the data necessary to prove their case to the Federation Council. Eventually, the Symmetrists became aligned with other scientific groups on other worlds, and the scope of their activities expanded."

"That was about the time of the hostage incident on Deneva," Riker said.

Picard looked pleased that another member of his staff shared his knowledge of history. "Precisely, Number One. At the time, Deneva was considered one of the most beautiful worlds in the quadrant. Its biosphere was fully developed,

Earth-normal. Exactly the kind of world the Federation sought to colonize. And exactly the kind of world the Symmetrists said must be kept isolated and untouched."

"More hostages," Deanna Troi said softly.

Everyone at the table looked at her with concern.

She kept her eyes on the tabletop. "As part of my counselor's training, I've taken part in the Deneva incident in a holosimulation. A group of radical environmentalists from Alpha Centauri said that any attempt to colonize Deneva would end in disaster. To prove their point, they took over the first colony ship, set it with explosives while it was still in orbit, and threatened to blow it up with all colonists aboard, unless the Federation withdrew."

Troi looked up at the captain on the viewscreen, and Riker could see how she was forcing herself to regain control of her emotions, to serve her ship and her fellow crew. "The radicals said it was necessary for the Federation to be taught a lesson. Rather than letting the colonists die due to environmental collapse over decades, they felt the authorities would take more notice if all the colonists died at once. So the Federation couldn't hide from the tragedy and would be forced to reevaluate their policies."

"How many colonists, Data?" Riker asked.

"Six hundred and fifty. Of which four hundred and eight died when an assault team from the *Archon* attempted to board the colonists' ship. Thirty-two Starfleet personnel were lost, as well as all of the radicals."

"The frightening thing is," Troi continued, "is that in all the simulations I tried, I couldn't get a better result. It was before subspace radio had been invented. There was no support from Command. No contact with other ships." She sighed, as if the deaths of all innocent hostages throughout all time were her personal responsibility.

"The radicals at Deneva were fanatics," Picard said sharply. "They had no intention of ever letting the colonists go. They had a point to prove. A lesson to teach. And they would let nothing stand in their way."

Riker could see what Picard was thinking. "Do you think that's what's happening today? With the virogen?"

"I do," Picard said. "The virogen and its effect on the agriculture of the Federation is precisely the type of ecological disaster the Symmetrists warned us of."

Rolk had a question. "But were the Symmetrists responsible for what happened on Deneva?"

"A radical offshoot of their organization claimed responsibility," Picard said. "For the next fifty years or so, the Symmetrists existed almost as an underground community of scientists, trying to make their concerns known, but thwarted as extreme elements among them enacted schemes of ecological terrorism."

Data clarified the timeline. "Records show that by 2248, Symmetrists had ceased to exist as an organized group, completely discredited by their more radical followers."

Riker wasn't convinced. "Captain, that's one hundred and twenty-five years ago. Are you suggesting descendants of the Symmetrist cause have been working as an underground group all this time?"

Picard's face hardened into a mask that told Riker his captain was not revealing everything he knew. He spoke his next words carefully. "You're forgetting, Number One. The Symmetrist movement came out of Vulcan. There are individuals alive today who could have been founding members of it almost *two* centuries ago. And judging from the participation of Stron, it seems likely that whole new generations as well have been drafted into the cause."

La Forge gave a low whistle. "Are you saying that this whole virogen plague is nothing more than . . . than some *lesson* the Federation is being taught? By a group of *Vulcan* terrorists?"

Riker tried to determine what it was Picard wasn't telling

178

them. Normally, when the ship was not facing immediate danger, the captain encouraged his crew to question his conclusions. Consensus was a valid operating principle for something as complex as a starship. But to Riker, it appeared as if Picard considered this time to be one of immediate danger, and La Forge's attitude was not welcome. Was it possible the captain had knowledge of an individual Vulcan who might be linked to the Symmetrists today?

Riker tried to catch La Forge's eye, to suggest the engineer ease off, but Picard responded too quickly.

"I am saying, Mr. La Forge, that the virogen plague *resembles* other acts of environmental terrorism carried out by the Symmetrists in the past, though on a vastly larger scale. And my questions to you are, *if* that is the case, then why is the alta mist an important part of that act of terrorism, and where would the Symmetrists be taking it?"

Riker could see that La Forge felt sufficiently chastised by the captain's tone. The engineer rubbed at his eyes, an unusual sight to Riker, who still hadn't completely adjusted to the replacement of La Forge's visor by eerie, blue-circuitry ocular implants. "The alta mist is how the plague is spread," La Forge said, with a tinge of desperation. "That's got to be it."

"No," Picard said. "The alta mist exists only on Alta Vista Three. Starfleet has conducted extensive bioassays of every affected system. If the alta mist had been found anywhere else, we would have known about it six months ago."

"Perhaps all the Symmetrists wish to do is measure the extent of the virogen's spread," Data suggested.

"Again," Picard said, "unlikely. When we captured the *Bennett,* Stron said he had intercepted all Starfleet communications. Certainly, that is not beyond the capabilities of any group so well prepared as the Symmetrists appear to be. And if that's the case, then they have no need to conduct their own surveys of the virogen's spread. They can simply eavesdrop on Starfleet's own findings."

Riker smiled ruefully at the captain. "In other words, we now have *three* mysteries in the same region of space."

"And all connected," Picard agreed.

Dr. Crusher appeared to have a sudden flash of inspiration. "What if we skip over the mystery of the alta mist for now, and ask ourselves the critical question—if the Symmetrists are somehow involved, where're they located?"

Just as Worf might have done, Rolk offered the most obvious answer. "Somewhere safe."

"A valid point," Picard agreed. "Though true Symmetrists would be the first to say that no place in the Federation is safe."

Troi suddenly straightened in her chair. "Fear," she said. All eyes turned to her. *"That's* what was missing!" She turned to the viewscreen. "Captain—when Kincaid destroyed the station, I felt her fear, even the fear of Stron and his wife, and . . . everyone else caught in the explosion. But . . . when we captured the *Bennett* by this asteroid, I felt only . . . tension coming from Stron. He knew he was in a difficult situation, but he did not consider it a life-threatening one.

"I assumed his emotional response was deadened because he was a Vulcan. But when we discovered the life-support bubble in the asteroid, I realized Stron's emotional response was correct. He *knew* there was a way off the *Bennett.* He *wasn't* in a life-or-death situation."

Troi paused. Though Riker knew everyone else in the room, and on the *Galileo,* was eager for her to continue, no one dared interrupt whatever chain of thought and emotion the counselor was following.

She spoke again. "I'm certain of it, sir. In all the conversations I witnessed with Stron and Kincaid, in every mention of the virogen and its effect on the Federation"—her dark eyes gleamed as she stared intently at the viewscreen—"I never felt the fear of death."

Silence ruled the lounge as the import of Troi's observation made itself known.

Then Picard stated the obvious conclusion, his face flushed with the excitement of discovery. *"They* weren't afraid of the virogen, because somewhere, somehow, the Symmetrists already have a *cure."*

For Riker, the shock of that statement brought both relief and tension. There was a chance that the virogen was not the Federation's death knell, that the disease could be controlled. But where would the Symmetrists be keeping it? With two quadrants of the galaxy to search, how could one hiding place ever be found?

Fortunately, the captain had already considered that question, and reached a decision.

"If we're to find that cure, we must first find the Symmetrists. And to do that, the best place to begin is where they themselves arose."

Riker stood at once, not even waiting for the order to be dismissed. The captain's logic was unassailable.

Less than two minutes later, the *Enterprise*-E tore open the fabric of space, and blazed through warp for where it had all begun.

And where, Riker hoped, it would all end.

The *Enterprise* flew to Vulcan.

TWENTY-TWO

☆

"Please state the nature of the medical emergency."

In the sickbay of the *Tobias,* Kirk literally jumped back into M'Benga as the ship's Emergency Medical Hologram resolved before him.

"What the hell is that?" Kirk said.

For a hologram without a personality, to Kirk the EMH looked distinctly annoyed. "I beg your pardon?"

"It's a backup medical program," M'Benga explained. "I don't have a large staff, so he comes in handy when I've got a lot to deal with."

Kirk glanced around the sickbay. It was small, even by the twenty-third-century standards of his own *Enterprise.* But it was hardly crowded. M'Benga was treating Spock for a few cuts and scrapes. Christine MacDonald was cleaning herself up at a sink that had folded out from a wall. And then there was Kirk and the holographic doctor.

It was not what Kirk would consider a medical emergency.

"What, exactly, do you have to deal with?" Kirk asked. He was winded from the fight and the chase at Tarok's estate, but the exhilaration of the physical conflict had left him feeling much better than he had after the purely mechanical confrontation in the skies of Chal.

Fighting the Orion attack wing, he had been little more than a puppet master, pressing buttons, ordering changes in vectors and velocities with all the passion of a computer.

For all that starships had opened up the galaxy to humanity, there had come a time in his career when the emphasis had seemed to shift from technology as a tool to technology for its own sake.

Perhaps more than any other person in the Federation, he knew the horror of the limits to which that worship of the machine could be taken. He could still recall the inhuman sensation of the nanites moving within him, infesting him, reworking his flesh according to their own unknowing program.

The Emergency Medical Hologram was a disturbing reminder of what had happened to him after his escape from the Borg homeworld. Especially since he could see no use for the program's presence at the moment.

But Dr. M'Benga apparently had another view of the situation.

"What I have to deal with," she said, "is you."

"Me?"

M'Benga stopped running her instruments over the cut on Spock's forearm. Green blood had crusted around the minor cut, but the flesh beneath was already being pushed together by the medical treatment field.

"Vulcans I can handle," the doctor said.

"Like great-grandfather, like great-granddaughter?" Kirk asked. He remembered the M'Benga who had served so well on his *Enterprise*. That M'Benga had been one of the first human specialists in Vulcan medicine.

"It runs in the family," the doctor agreed. "But you're another matter."

"I feel fine," Kirk said. "Never better."

M'Benga harrumphed in response, reminding Kirk of another doctor who was not inclined to have his patients talk back. "According to records, you're one hundred and forty years old. How you 'feel' and how you actually are is a bit out of my experience."

Christine joined the conversation. "Bones, there was the little matter of the temporal anomaly Picard reported."

"Thank you," Kirk said.

But M'Benga held her ground. "There was also the 'little matter' of you dying."

Kirk didn't know where to begin. So he did what he had found always worked best in these awkward situations. "Spock, explain it to them."

Spock carefully brushed off the last of the dried blood on his treated arm. "I cannot," he said.

"Spock?"

"Captain . . ." Spock paused. "Admiral . . ." That still wasn't right. Then he had it. *"Jim*—we last met two years ago on a mission that to my knowledge has remained classified at the highest levels of Starfleet. Even if we were at liberty to discuss it among present company, I have no idea what has happened to you in the ensuing two years."

Kirk realized there was only one way out—fight back. "Dr. M'Benga, classified matters aside, I am not one hundred and forty years old. When the *Enterprise*-B was launched, I was sixty, and that's how old I was when I helped out Captain Picard on Veridian. It's two years later. I'm sixty-two." He stared belligerently at the EMH. "And I don't need a hologram to give me a physical."

M'Benga shrugged. "All right. Sixty-two I can handle. Take off your clothes."

Kirk didn't like the sound of that. "Don't you people have . . . scanners? A medical tricorder?"

"Think of me as an old country doctor," M'Benga said with

a predatory smile. She pulled a pair of isolation gloves from a supply drawer, giving them an alarming snap. "I prefer the hands-on approach."

Kirk knew when he had been outmaneuvered. For whatever reason, the doctor of this vessel wanted a medical report on him, and he had long ago learned that not even a starship captain could fight a ship's doctor and win. "On second thought, I'll go with the hologram."

"How nice to be wanted," the EMH said.

M'Benga knew she had won and let Kirk know she knew with a sarcastic smile. "Thank you for your cooperation." She gestured to the others. "Why don't we give our guest some privacy."

M'Benga, Christine, and Spock began to leave. But Kirk called Spock back.

"We should talk," Kirk said. "About what happened."

Spock remained as the sickbay doors slipped shut. Kirk saw Christine turn to glance back at him, and he held her gaze for just an instant before he and Spock were alone.

The EMH came at him with a medical probe. "Say 'ahhh,'" the hologram told him.

"Is there any way to turn you off?" Kirk asked.

"Several."

"I don't suppose you could tell me the best one."

"Not a chance."

Kirk opened his mouth and said "ahhh." Then, as the hologram busied himself with other readings, Kirk turned his attention to Spock, apprehensive about the answer to the question he knew he must ask.

"How's . . . McCoy?"

For a moment, Spock looked uncomfortable, and Kirk feared the worst. But the answer was not what he had expected. "I attended the doctor's one hundred and forty-sixth birthday party on Wrigley's Pleasure Planet."

"Wrigley's? What was the doctor's . . . pleasure?"

185

Spock seemed even more uncomfortable. "Dancing girls. I told the doctor it was most unseemly for a man of his years to be comporting himself in such a manner."

"And . . . ?"

"The good doctor informed me that in his considered opinion, the mere fact that a man of his years could comport himself in any manner, let alone still draw breath, was reason enough to celebrate in whatever fashion he chose."

Kirk grinned as he thought of his friends still bickering after all these years, knowing that each argument served only to bind their friendship closer. "I'm sorry I missed the party," Kirk said, and he meant it.

"He has something special planned for his one hundred and fiftieth birthday," Spock said. "He will not tell me what it is, but no doubt we will both be invited."

Kirk winced as the hologram pushed his arm through a series of twisting bends. "Do people really live that long in this time?"

"In Dr. McCoy's case, he tells me he does it to spite me."

"Oww!" Kirk said as he felt his shoulder blade click painfully. He pulled his arm from the hologram's grip. "You're supposed to make people feel better."

"I see, you're telling me how I should do my job? And how many years of medical training have you had?"

"You're a hologram," Kirk said. "How many have *you* had?"

"Combining the years of training of all the medical experts who contributed to my programming, one thousand seven hundred and eight." The hologram sounded far too pleased with himself for Kirk's liking. "What? No snappy comeback? Has the great James T. Kirk been bested by a mere machine who—"

With a flash of light, the EMH suddenly winked out.

Kirk turned to see Spock standing by a medical computer, one finger still on a button.

"Fascinating," Spock said. "An Off switch."

Kirk sighed with relief. "You've done it again."

Spock waited patiently for clarification.

"Saved me," Kirk said.

"I would not go so far as to characterize the act of switching off an emergency medical hologram as a—"

Spock stopped in response to Kirk's upheld hand.

Kirk glanced around the sickbay. "Do you suppose this place is *fully* stocked? The way McCoy would stock it?"

Spock nodded in understanding, and began opening supply cupboards with Kirk, until he found a bottle of Jack Daniel's. It was from Manozec XII, but the label said the oak casks were made with wood cloned from the original forests on Mars. At least it was the right solar system.

Kirk poured two glasses.

Spock joined him in a toast without protest.

"To absent friends," Kirk said.

"And Dr. McCoy."

For a moment, the two men stood in silence, their lives and their careers so closely aligned that it was at times as if they were one force moving through the universe. Kirk was glad to be back. He had no idea how many more second chances he might be given, so he intended to make the most of this one.

The most of every day remaining.

Kirk looked at the whisky swirling in the glass he held. "So what now?" he asked his friend.

"For now, we must wait," Spock answered. "Srell is directing the forensics team at Tarok's estate. At the same time, he will attempt to obtain data from the estate's computers that might guide us to other people linked with Tarok, my parents, and what he referred to as 'the movement.'"

"'The movement.' What's that?"

"I do not know." Spock told Kirk the story of the holographic recording of Ki Mendrossen he had received on the Babel planetoid, of how it indicated that his father had been murdered. And how Spock and Srell had followed a chain of evidence that led back to Vulcan, to Sarek's villa, and finally to Tarok's estate, looking for any clues to a possible conspiracy—what Spock took to be "the cause" that Tarok had mentioned.

"As you can see," Spock concluded, "without additional data, I am at a loss."

"'The cause,'" Kirk repeated. "Why does that sound familiar?"

"It is a generic description for any manner of undertaking," Spock said. "Little information is contained in it." Cautiously, he sipped at his whisky.

"You never used to like alcohol all that much," Kirk observed.

Spock took another sip. "You have yet to tell me how you escaped from the Borg homeworld, and rid yourself of the nanites."

Kirk found a chair, pulled it over to the desk. Spock did the same.

"I take it that Picard told you what happened in the Central Node."

"Up to the moment you 'slugged' him, was the way he put it. Then had him beamed aboard the ship. Quite against his will, he informed us."

"He's a good man," Kirk said. "Carries on the tradition well. He's just, I don't know, too . . . by-the-book."

"The 'book' says little about fellow officers slugging each other in the jaw."

"Maybe not in the twenty-fourth century."

"The Borg homeworld," Spock said, recalling Kirk's attention to the topic at hand. "You were in the Central Node. You had Picard beamed out. And then what? Did you pull the lever?"

Kirk braced himself for what was to come. As much as he

was a man who lived in the present, always traveling toward the future, there were times, he knew, when he must return to the past.

This was one of them.

"I pulled the lever," Kirk said.

It was time to tell the story.

TWENTY-THREE

☆

It was a transporter beam that had claimed him, and that had ripped him from the Node.

Kirk knew all that the instant he re-formed in darkness, felt the physical burden of reality return to him.

Then he had dropped a full two meters.

Into mud.

He opened his mouth for air and the stench of the mud choked him.

It reeked of sewage. Of death.

He struggled as the heavy, freezing sludge engulfed him. From instinct more than thought, he strained to keep his head above the suffocating grasp of whatever held him.

He had no idea where he was.

An ordinary transport lasted scant seconds at most, accompanied by a slight vertigo, a glittering spray of light, and then solidity again.

But an ordinary transport could beam matter only twenty-five thousand kilometers.

This transport had lasted longer than any he had experienced before. Long enough that he had actually been conscious of his immaterial state.

There were other technologies possible, other rules, Kirk knew. Once his ship had intercepted a transporter beam that had originated from across the galaxy.

But how far had Kirk been transported within *this* beam? And by what or whom?

Then any thoughts as to where he might be, how far from the Borg homeworld he had come, and who or what might be responsible were vanquished by the sudden incredible pain that convulsed his body, nearly submerging him in the odiferous mud.

The nanites were still at their work in Kirk's body. Submicroscopic machines of Borg and Romulan origin. The machines that renegade Romulans had used to reconstruct his body according to the template laid down in his own DNA. Once activated, the nanites could not be stopped, or removed. They would continue their work of restructuring him until they had played out their function by accelerating the genetically programmed apoptosis that brought death by aging to all living beings.

When Kirk had pulled the lever in the Borg Central Node, he had had only hours to live. And though he had escaped the explosion that devastated the Borg homeworld, he was not going to escape his fate.

Kirk contorted in agony as he felt the organs of his body shift and twist in response to the burrowing, cutting, rearranging nanites. His fingers spread into useless claws to dig against the clinging mud.

From the surrounding darkness, he could hear the groaning sounds of other struggles. And in the distance, the rumble of vast explosions and unceasing machines.

He lay back, half-buried in the muck, gulping for air.

Whatever part of Kirk that had lived in him as a child and had made him think there might be something under the bed or lurking in the closet, it whispered to him now.

He was *dead.*

This was *hell.*

And it was here he would spend *eternity.*

The nanites ate away at him as the eagle tore at the liver of Prometheus. But in the void, he chose neither the comforts of mysticism, nor the escape of desperate fantasy.

Instead, a single word emerged from Kirk's frozen, mud-caked lips.

"*. . . no . . .*"

He was *not* dead.

There was *no* hell.

But there *was* an explanation. There must *always* be an explanation.

He was somewhere in the universe. Somewhere physical. Therefore real. And he was—

"*. . . still alive . . .*" he whispered.

Then, through force of will alone, he smiled fiercely, drawing his lips back from chattering teeth.

Because high above him, the sky was growing lighter.

The *sky.*

Low gray clouds lit by a sun that rose unseen on the horizon.

He was on a planet, exactly as he had believed. The explanation had been found.

He thrust himself up to assess his surroundings.

He was in a field of mud.

Far in the distance, he could see dark shapes moving closer, like the roiling clouds of a storm front or peaks on a slow-moving wave, something within them sparking with red and blue fire. Somehow, he knew they were the source of the machine rumbling and explosions.

But he ignored them for the moment, because they were still far off. And because the mud so much closer to him . . .

—*moved.*

At first he thought it was alive. The very mud of this planet a living creature hungrily gnawing at him, as inexorable as death, drawing him deep within itself to be consumed.

But as the light continued to increase, as day broke on this new world, Kirk saw the nightmarish landscape around him. Writhing, twisting, stretching out, reaching out, caught as he was caught, dying as he was dying.

Wherever he was, however he had come there, James T. Kirk faced the last hours of his life, trapped in a field of fellow sufferers.

He was surrounded by thousands upon thousands of dying Borg. . . .

"Fascinating," Spock said.

Kirk knocked back the last of his whisky and poured himself another shot. He swallowed that as well, letting the heat of it take away the memory of that horrible place.

"Fascinating my ass," he said. "I was in a garbage dump, Spock. A Borg garbage dump."

"Then the transporter beam you leapt into . . . ?"

"Was part of the homeworld's evacuation system. Our ships have escape pods, so maybe the Borg have escape *beams*. They punch through transwarp space so their range is virtually unlimited, and they enable Borg units that are still connected to the Collective to regather and re-form whatever branch they're from."

Spock looked thoughtful. "Last year, a Borg vessel attacked Earth. It was defeated, but during the unusual events of its attack, Captain Picard encountered a most interesting Borg individual whom all records indicate had perished years earlier in the destruction of another Borg cubeship. Perhaps these escape beams offer a possible explanation for that individual's survival."

Kirk shook his head. "Individual survival isn't what the Borg system was set up for."

Spock looked at Kirk with immediate understanding. "The machines on the horizon," he said.

Kirk nodded. "They didn't stay on the horizon for long."

Whatever sun this planet circled, its glow seemed to surge through the clouds in uneven jumps.

The machines on the horizon did the same, lunging closer in manic advances each time Kirk closed his eyes.

He could see them more clearly now—moving walls of multilayered metal, propelled by treads that rose a hundred meters in the air, each monstrous machine with a deep slot at its base, large enough to swallow a runabout, filled with grinding, gnashing blades, and lit by flashing beams of fusion fire.

The mechanical beasts swept over the mud as voracious devourers of all they encountered. Borg by the thousands were swept into their jaws, to be torn apart, reclaimed, and reassembled.

Kirk located the machine that was bearing down on him, still kilometers distant. He calculated it would reach him near sundown. Though he doubted the nanites would let him last that long.

He had to laugh at the irony of his end.

On the literal garbage heap of galactic history.

But still, somehow he could not give up. He found himself wondering what the insides of those machines might look like. He set himself the goal of surviving the nanites long enough to be swallowed by the machine.

Hadn't that, in fact, been what had happened to him ages ago, when he had taken the center chair for the very first time? When the starships had swallowed him, making him little more than another plug-in component in a cosmic machine?

"I'm ready for you," Kirk whispered to the monster that drove for him. And time and again, the sun jumped in the sky as the monster leapt forward.

In his lucid moments, Kirk realized the strobing effect meant he was lapsing in and out of consciousness. He forced himself to concentrate, to keep himself alert until the end. Determined not to waste a moment of life.

But all that came to him was a scattered vision of the bridge on Veridian III. Then, like now, he had been certain that death had claimed him, inescapably.

That day beneath the Veridian sun, after his fall, after the Nexus had passed, he had seen again the dark shape that had chased him all his life . . . felt that he was finally alone, how he had always known he would die. He had stared up into that mystery for what, in his final thoughts, he had believed would be his last moment of awareness . . .

. . . and seen Sarek?

Reliving that moment, Kirk muttered to the mud and the Borg that lay round him. As little more than an observer of his own fate, shut off from the horror around him, some still-rational part of his being decided that this must be how the human brain died. Cut off from oxygen. Brain cells making up hallucinations to hide the face of impending extinction. Floods of endorphins released to ease the suffering. Creating a white light that drew him forward.

But in that light . . .

. . . he saw Sarek once again.

For a time, it seemed to Kirk that he now stood beside himself in that field of mud, Sarek next to him, silent.

Only they weren't in the field of mud.

They were in a forest. At night. Beneath a sea of stars. Kirk recognized the setting.

Yosemite. Fragrant smoke from a crackling fire mingling with the green scent of pine and the richness of earth.

"We've been here before," Kirk said. He looked around and saw three people in sleeping bags, resting by the fire. Spock, and McCoy, and . . . himself.

Then Kirk recognized the time.

It was the day he had fallen from El Capitan. Plunged to certain death. The day when, against all reason, he had felt no fear.

That night by the fire, after Spock had rescued him, after McCoy had scolded him, he had revealed to his friends what he had never told another soul.

I've always known . . . that I'll die alone.

"Yes, Kirk. That is the key," Sarek now told him.

Kirk closed his eyes and heard the rumbling of the machines, the cries of dying Borg. He opened his eyes, and saw the forest, Sarek beckoning to him from within the trees.

"You must leave them behind," Sarek called out. "They cannot be with you."

Kirk wasn't ready. He needed to know why. "I've had this dream before," he said.

But Sarek gave no answer. His robes seemed to glow, billowing about him as if caught in a breeze that Kirk couldn't feel.

Memories flooded into Kirk then, each one about this dream, this hidden knowledge of his death.

And as always happened when this occurred, he was filled with the knowledge that he had had this dream before.

As long ago as he could remember.

And always it was the same.

Always it came with . . .

"Sarek . . ." Kirk pleaded, "why has it always been you in my dreams? Even before we met. Before I met your son. Before I left Earth . . . it has *always* been you who comes to take me from my friends and to my death."

Sarek now was only a light in the forest—shafts of radiance lancing out from the dark trees and branches.

"Because of what we share," Sarek said. "Or will share."

"My dream? Or my death?" Kirk asked.

Sarek's voice came from all around him, a roll of thunder in the air. But Kirk already knew the words Sarek spoke. They were always the same.

As long as a single mind remembers, as long as a single heart still beats with passion, how can a dream die?

Kirk held his hands up to the night, imploringly. "But what of the dreamer?"

Look to the stars, James Kirk.

Kirk felt Sarek's hand on his arm.

Just as Sarek had taken his arm that first time . . .

That first time on . . .

But once again that final link in the chain would *not* come to him, no matter how hard he tried to bring it forth, as if a portion of his mind and memory were lost to him, as if hidden behind some barricade to the truth.

Long ago on Tarsus IV, here again in Yosemite, there on the field of dying Borg . . . Sarek kept his hand locked around Kirk's wrist, to keep him close.

And the words he spoke electrified Kirk.

As they always did.

Avenge me.

Kirk closed his eyes in the agony of lost knowledge, lost time, lost life.

And even as the dream evaporated and the machine loomed above him, there was still a hand holding on to his wrist.

But the dream was over. Kirk looked up into the untroubled eyes of a young female humanoid, streaked with filth, naked except for a mud-caked loincloth. Beneath the filth, her skin was a quilt of brown and white.

". . . who are . . . you . . . ?" Kirk gasped, his throat almost closed by the ravages of the nanites.

The youth looked over at something Kirk couldn't see. "This one is operational," she shouted.

Barely conscious, Kirk felt the thunderous pulse of the approaching machine blend in his body with the unceasing waves of pain from the nanites. His death would be violent. He felt as if the end must come in mere moments, when his body could no longer take the stress and would simply explode.

A second humanoid joined the first. This time, a male, as mud-coated and as lightly clothed as the female, also with the same odd patchwork pattern of skin, this time white and pink.

The youth knelt down beside Kirk, felt his pulse, briefly touched his mud-darkened fingers to points on Kirk's face that called up the whisper of forgotten memories.

"He is not 'operational,' " the youth said to the female. "He is alive. Just as we are."

Roughly, the youth lifted Kirk's head from the mud. The towering wall of metal was visible above him, only a minute away from claiming them all.

"What is your designation?" the youth asked.

Time stopped for Kirk. He rallied himself to identify his existence before it ended forever.

". . . Kirk," he whispered. ". . . James . . . Tiberius . . ."

The youth stood and, with no sign of exertion, hoisted Kirk to his feet.

Kirk could not feel his legs. He remained upright only because the two young people supported him. Effortlessly.

"Welcome, Kirk James Tiberius," the young male said. "My name is Hugh."

"Hugh?" Spock said. "I have studied Captain Picard's detailed accounts of his encounters with the Borg. Could that have been the same Hugh who was infected with individuality? And who then was part of a revolt against the Collective?"

Kirk stretched back in the chair in sickbay. He was feeling hoarse after so much explanation. Another shot of whisky eased the irritation in his throat. "I have no idea, Spock. Half the people in the clan that found me were called Hugh. It was a common name, as if it had been passed on to them from other branches."

"The clan?"

Kirk shrugged. There were still events from those first few days on that world that weren't clear to him. "They were Borg," he said. "Or, had been Borg. Apparently, they'd renounced their implants."

"Everything we know about the Borg suggests that is impossible."

"If a Borg named Hugh can be infected with individuality and then revolt against the Collective, then I'd say the different branches of the Borg are capable of evolving their own, unique modes of organization. And the Borg who found me had access to unique forms of biotechnology."

"That would explain many inconsistencies in their behavior."

Kirk stared at his friend. "Spock, is that all you can say? That what happened to me explains Borg inconsistencies?"

"What would you have me say?"

Kirk put his glass down on the table. Despite his Vulcan heritage, Spock *had* to see the irony in what had happened.

"Don't you see? I was . . . recycled."

From Spock's expression, Kirk could see that his friend didn't see the irony at all.

"I was beamed by a Borg emergency escape transporter to a planet where damaged Borg components were sent to be broken down and reassembled. A clan of Borg who had abandoned their cybernetic implants found me, detected the nanites, and assumed I was like them. So they *processed* me, Spock. By whatever means they used to rid themselves of their machine parts, they took the nanites from me. I was . . . cleansed. Recycled. Made human again only by being treated like . . . a *product.*"

Spock regarded Kirk for long moments. "You say you had a vision of my father?"

Kirk sighed. "Why do I even bother?"

"I am trying to understand," Spock assured Kirk. "And I am fascinated that you claim to have had dreams about my father even before you met him. Though that is a common aftereffect of mindmelding, and you and I have melded often enough in the past that you undoubtedly acquired and retained early images of my father, based on my own memories of him."

Kirk thought that over. "You know, I melded with your father once myself."

Both of Spock's eyebrows shot up.

"In San Francisco," Kirk said. "After . . . after what happened with Khan. When you . . ."

"When I died."

"Your father came to me, searching for your *katra*. He didn't know you had placed it in McCoy."

Spock looked as if Kirk had just slugged him instead of Picard. "You never told me this," he said, but it was as if his words were not meant for Kirk. "It is no wonder that you have dreamt about Sarek. You have not been trained in the methods of controlling the residual effects of a meld."

Kirk was puzzled. "You mean, I *haven't* dreamt about your father since I can remember? It's all been some sort of false memory?"

Because they were friends, because they were alone, Spock spoke gently, trying to lighten the blow, Kirk knew. "Unless you melded with my father when you were a child, the dreams you experienced were merely a result of the effect of my father's more disciplined mind on yours."

"No different from the hallucinations of a near-death experience?" Kirk asked.

"An illusion," Spock agreed.

Kirk tapped his fingers against the table, considering

Spock's analysis. As always, it seemed logical. It just didn't seem right.

"But my memories of Sarek seem so clear," Kirk said.

"Then I envy you, Jim. For I never melded with my father."

Kirk was surprised by the emotion in Spock's voice. He knew that Spock had just revealed something of great importance to him. As important, perhaps, as Kirk's own feelings about coming so close to death.

What could one friend say to another after such a revelation? So much time had passed between them, yet when they were together, it was as if no time had passed at all. There must be something Kirk could say. There must be—

Every unsecured object in sickbay—including the bottle of Jack Daniel's and the two friends in their chairs—was hurled to the side as the ship's hull creaked in protest. Kirk caught the whisky bottle just before it jumped from the table.

An instant later, red alert sounded.

Kirk looked around for a wall communicator. But Spock beat him to it by pulling a comm badge from within his shirt.

"Spock to bridge. Are we in difficulty?"

Commander Christine MacDonald's young voice replied. "It depends on your definition of difficulty, Ambassador. We have just been grappled with tractor beams by Vulcan patrol ships. It seems they wish to question us about an incident at Tarok's estate. Our forensics team is already in their custody and is being beamed aboard."

"That, Commander MacDonald," Spock said, "fits my definition of 'difficulty' to perfection."

TWENTY-FOUR

─────── ☆ ───────

Vulcans were nothing if not efficient. Within an hour, the *Tobias* had been escorted to a civilian spacedock, her entire crew was in custody, and her senior officers had been assembled to face a Vulcan magistrate in the spacedock's justice facilities.

In the magistrate's antechamber, deep within the spacedock's administration levels, Kirk squirmed uncomfortably in his new uniform. Like Christine's, it was black with gray shoulders. The pips on the command-red shirt he wore under the tunic gave his rank as lieutenant. He ran his fingers behind the small metal disks, trying to stretch out the collar fabric. He glanced at Spock. "The longer I stay in Starfleet, the lower my rank gets. Think someone's trying to tell me something?"

Once more in the company of Christine, M'Benga, Barc, and Srell, Spock had reverted to his more usual stoic behavior, as well as changed back into his black robes. "If this charade is to work, 'Lieutenant,' it will be necessary for you to appear comfortable in that uniform, as if you have always worn it."

Kirk let his hands fall to his sides. "You honestly think we can fool a Vulcan magistrate?"

The doors to the magistrate's office slid open.

"There are always possibilities," Spock said quietly. Then he, Srell, and the officers of the *Tobias* followed the directional lights on the wall and, in single file, entered the office.

As the legal preliminaries were under way, Kirk took the opportunity to glance around and was surprised to see that the Vulcan style of architecture and decoration had changed little from his age to the next. An exquisitely etched glass panel was the centerpiece of the simple room, showing the IDIC symbol in the muted earth tones and deep reds so common to all of Vulcan's art.

Even the proceedings had changed little from Kirk's day. The magistrate was a middle-aged Vulcan female, dark-skinned, in a simple robe adorned by only a few polished gemstones. She had four padds on her desk, and shifted her attention easily from one to the next, each no doubt connected to a different database relating to the complex case before her.

Under normal conditions, Kirk doubted that anyone could deceive the Vulcan legal system, though he was certainly willing to give it a try. But Spock maintained that because of the virogen's impact on interstellar communications, conditions were anything but normal.

The magistrate's aide, a stern Vulcan male in an understated brown suit with a simple jeweled clasp, stood by her desk and read the names of all present for the hearing—they were not yet called prisoners. For the purposes of this appearance, Kirk had assumed the name of Lieutenant Adrian Plummer.

The real Lieutenant Plummer had served on the *Tobias* for fourteen months, and was now with the sixty crew members who had stayed on Chal with Teilani, to carry on the relief

WILLIAM SHATNER

mission. However, Christine had altered the ship's records to show that Plummer had remained aboard for the journey to Vulcan, and she had replaced all of Plummer's medical and identification files with Kirk's. Spock had felt they would have quite enough to explain, without sidetracking the space-dock inquiry by revealing Kirk's identity. No matter how disruptive the threat of the virogen, anyone, like Kirk, who had a connection with the Borg would be seen as an even more immediate concern to the Federation's security. Spock was adamant that they could not risk the extra level of scrutiny Kirk's presence would immediately bring.

After formal identification of those present, the magistrate seemed to decide that the only person in the room worth talking to was Spock. She addressed him with deference.

"Ambassador Spock, I am pleased to meet you in person. Your services to Vulcan, the Federation, and the cause of galactic peace are most remarkable, and bring honor to Vulcan and the teachings of Surak. However, I would be remiss if I allowed your reputation, and the debt which all Vulcan owes you, to influence any dealings with this office."

"Your position is most logical," Spock assured her.

"Thank you."

"You are welcome."

The magistrate's aide cleared his throat. "There are many other matters we must attend to this day," he said.

The magistrate took on a more neutral demeanor. "Ambassador Spock," she began, "current Starfleet records show that the U.S.S. Tobias is assigned to relief efforts on Chal. Yet it is in Vulcan orbital space. Is this a dereliction of duty on the part of its commander?"

Kirk would never have accepted that kind of charge, and he was glad to see that Christine wouldn't, either. She instantly stepped forward to protest. "Your Honor, I am here on a matter of utmost—"

204

"Kroykah!"

Whether Christine understood the Vulcan word or not, she recognized its intent and stopped speaking at once.

"I apologize for Commander MacDonald's interruption," Spock said sincerely. "However, I must point out that you will not find the *Tobias's* current assignment on the open Starfleet channels, as we are engaged in a classified mission."

Kirk hid his smile. Technically, Spock hadn't lied. But he had managed to convey the impression that their classified mission was somehow connected to Starfleet.

"At what level of classification?" the magistrate asked.

"Above the level of this office," Spock said firmly.

The magistrate eyed him carefully, clearly understanding that Spock was challenging her authority to hold him. "Therefore, if this office were to make further inquiries to Starfleet, we would be told nothing?"

"I believe the cover story Starfleet would be required to relate to you would state that the *Tobias* was still on duty at Chal."

The magistrate moved one padd to sit atop another, as if shuffling old-fashioned papers. "Therefore, whether the facts you present are accurate or not, the response from Starfleet will be the same. You present me with an intriguing paradox."

"That is true," Spock agreed.

The magistrate shifted the padds again. "Then there is the matter of three unnatural deaths in Gonthar District: Tarok, and two of his staff—Klingon nationals, whose involvement contributes another level of complexity. As does evidence of multiple-weapons discharge in violation of local codes."

Kirk marveled at the smoothness of Spock's reply. "We were attempting to gather evidence of those crimes to present to the authorities when the authorities arrived."

"Are you, or any of those present, responsible for the deaths?"

"We came to Vulcan attempting to stop them," Spock said.

WILLIAM SHATNER

At that admission, Kirk cringed inwardly. Spock had just given the magistrate an opening for charging them with a crime. How could he have made such a mistake?

"Therefore, you had previous knowledge of a potential crime, yet you did not report it to the proper authorities?"

Spock hesitated before answering, as if acknowledging his guilt.

"That is true, Magistrate."

"Are you aware that as a Vulcan citizen, your act of omission is considered a breach of the public good?"

"I am."

The magistrate looked at Srell. "As are you?"

"I am," Srell said contritely.

The magistrate turned her attention to the others in the room. "For the rest of you, though you are not Vulcan citizens, you are Starfleet personnel, and as such, bound to the laws of this world by the articles of Federation. Therefore, you are equally subject to charges in this matter."

Barc huffed noisily and Kirk could see the Tellarite's ear fur bristle. Fortunately, though, the engineer knew enough to control his temper. In a Vulcan court, emotional outbursts had severe consequences.

The magistrate picked up a small baton and tapped it against a tiny hanging metal plate, no larger than a hand. An electronically produced gong note sounded, and Kirk recognized the small device as a symbolic version of the larger ones used in important ceremonies on Vulcan.

"The Vulcans, Spock and Srell, the Tellarite, Barc, and the humans, MacDonald, M'Benga, and Plummer, are remanded to protective custody, pending investigation of charges to be brought, concerning violation of Vulcan laws. The prisoners will be beamed to a custodial facility on the surface, and—"

Kirk was surprised as Spock interrupted the magistrate's recitation. "Magistrate, that would not be wise."

The magistrate gestured with the small baton. "Are you

aware of the penalties involved with the obstruction of justice, Spock?"

"Please check your records," Spock said. "The crew of the *Tobias* have been on active duty on Chal. They have been exposed to the virogen."

The magistrate dropped the baton on her desk.

"Though they claim they are uninfected, it would be prudent to test them for exposure before beaming them to the surface."

Though the magistrate's expression was unchanged, even Kirk could see that her composure was no longer perfect. She turned to her aide. "This spacedock is now in quarantine. The prisoners are to be placed in detention cells in this facility. Medical workers are to be dispatched at once, to test them for exposure to the virogen." She rose, staring at Spock with all the intensity her Vulcan impassivity would allow. "You have exposed this facility and threatened our home-world, Spock."

Spock was unperturbed. "Your charge is not logical. You brought us aboard spacedock without first ascertaining the duty status of the *Tobias.*"

Kirk thought the magistrate was going to suffer apoplexy, at least in a Vulcan fashion that would be undetectable to untrained observers. "You did not warn us, Spock."

"I did not expect to have a vital Starfleet mission interrupted by so junior a functionary."

Kirk and Christine exchanged a glance. Spock had just called the magistrate an incompetent novice. In a time before the Vulcan Reformation, his head would have been cut off and on a pike before he left the magistrate's presence.

"I will conduct a full investigation into your claims," the magistrate said in a voice of iron.

"I welcome it," Spock said. "As I welcome your presence in the detention cells once our government realizes what you have done."

The magistrate fumbled for the baton, then hit the small gong once more. "Take them away," she ordered.

As Kirk and the others were shepherded away through another door, Kirk thought he heard the sound of the baton being snapped in two just as the office doors slid shut. Such an act would have been an unthinkable display of emotion for the magistrate. But then, Spock could have that effect on humans. Perhaps he did the same for some Vulcans.

The prisoners were now in a utilitarian corridor that gradually curved to match the spacedock's circumference. The lighting was distinctly redshifted, matching normal illumination on Vulcan. The magistrate's aide led the way. Two Vulcan security guards, with no obvious weapons, had emerged from another door and now marched behind the full party.

Kirk fell into step beside Spock. "Was that necessary?" he asked in a low whisper. "You just made a powerful enemy for us."

"I assure you, the animosity of a spacedock magistrate is preferable to being placed in custody in a Vulcan jail," Spock said. "Escape is not possible. At least in a spacedock detention cell, we will have a chance to get back to the *Tobias.*"

"Is that why you slipped up by admitting you didn't warn the authorities about the attempt on Tarok's life?"

"It was not a 'slipup,'" Spock explained. "If the magistrate had continued to ask us questions about our presence, she would eventually have determined that Srell and I arrived separately from you and the *Tobias.* That would imply that we were not part of a Starfleet mission, which would have raised her suspicions even more, and quite possibly have brought in a higher rank of investigator. If we are to continue our own investigation, this is by far the least difficult facility from which to extricate ourselves."

Kirk felt relieved that Spock had not made a mistake after

all. It was in matters of strategy and diplomacy that he had come to depend on his friend the most. "So, how *do* we escape from a Vulcan detention cell?" Kirk asked.

Spock looked at Kirk. "I have the utmost faith in you, Jim. It is precisely in these situations that I have come to depend upon you the most."

Before Kirk could say anything more, the magistrate's aide stopped by a forcefield frame, then placed his hand on an identity scanner. The forcefield winked out. The detention cells waited in the blind corridor beyond.

Kirk was encouraged to see that the doors of each cell were solid, not forcefields. Solid doors meant there would be locks; locks meant there were computer controls; and computers were meant to be outsmarted.

Kirk was further encouraged when Christine and Dr. M'Benga were ushered into one cell. It would be much easier for them to plan an escape with a partner. Unfortunately, Kirk saw he was going to be given the wrong one. Spock and Srell were being directed to the next cell, with Kirk and Barc obviously intended to share the last.

Kirk knew he had to be paired with Spock. Between the two of them, there was nothing they could not accomplish.

"Human, Tellarite, in here," a guard said, indicating the cell across from Spock and Srell.

Kirk looked at the Tellarite. There was only one way out.

He sneezed.

"You can't lock me up with a Tellarite. All that fur . . ." Kirk looked apologetically at the guard, rubbed his nose, squinted his eyes. "I'm allergic."

Barc snarled and Kirk guessed what he had said was considered an insult. But he couldn't turn back now.

"I'll need my medication," Kirk continued. "Otherwise, my throat swells up, I can't breathe. . . ." He sneezed again in the guard's direction.

The guard looked at Spock and Srell.

Kirk saw Spock subtly step back, knowing full well what Kirk was attempting.

The guard pointed at Srell. "You, with the Tellarite."

Srell and Kirk changed places.

Spock and Kirk walked into their detention cell together.

When the solid door slid shut, Kirk quickly examined the cell. It was surprisingly large, about four meters square, but had nothing in the way of chairs, benches, or beds. It was just an empty cube of a room.

"How Vulcan," Kirk said with a wry smile. Then he looked at the door, checking its outline to find some indication of its locking mechanism. There was a small control panel by the doorframe. It would be a good place to start. "But between the two of us, we should be out of here within the . . . Spock?"

Kirk reached out to grab Spock's arm as he felt the floor slip beneath him, angling dramatically as the outline of the door seemed to blur, then spiral away.

The sense of disorientation had been too sudden. Both Kirk and Spock stumbled to the ground. Kirk recognized part of the sensation—the artificial gravity field in the cell had cycled swiftly through multiple areas of central attraction.

When he looked up from the floor, trying to locate the door again, he recognized another trick of technology.

He and Spock now appeared to be in a garden.

The sky was Vulcan red above them. Leaves in a nearby glade of trees rustled in the gentle breeze. Birds sang. And a small plot of meditation stones to their side, artfully placed among furrows of red and brown sand, compellingly invited their contemplation of the infinite.

"It's a holodeck, isn't it?" Kirk grumbled as he stood up. The metal deck beneath him now seemed to be made of interlocked clay bricks.

"Apparently so," Spock said. "It would appear to be a re-

AVENGER

creation of the meditation gardens surrounding the Surak Memorial in ShirKahr." Spock pointed into the holographically simulated distance. "You can see the dome of the memorial through those trees."

Kirk felt all his encouragement evaporate. He knew the walls of the detention cell were no more than four meters away in any direction. But he also knew that if he started walking in what he thought was a straight line, he could probably continue for what would seem kilometers. Between the holoprojectors creating the scenery, and the forcefields and gravity control that could alter his path without him realizing it, he was trapped.

It was the ultimate prison cell because it had no walls to climb and no locks to pick.

He found it far too logical, but he had to admit that the Vulcans had known what they were doing. For the first time in his life, Kirk wondered if he was in a trap from which there could be no escape.

211

TWENTY-FIVE

─────────────── ☆ ───────────────

"Well, Spock," Kirk said as he brushed holographic dust from his uniform's trousers, "I'm certainly glad we're not in a jail on the surface. I've heard those are tough."

"This *is* what jails are like on the surface," Spock replied. "I was not aware the spacedock facilities had been upgraded."

Kirk looked around, trying to ignore the pang of desperation he felt. The illusion of being outdoors on Vulcan was staggeringly detailed. Somewhere, perhaps even within arm's reach, there was an exit that led to the spacedock's corridor. But it might as well be on another planet. "I don't suppose you have any Vulcan tricks up your sleeves."

Small specks of dirt and grit crunched under Kirk's boots. The sun gleaming off the golden dome of Surak's memorial was a pinpoint of blinding brilliance. He could scent the water from the fountain that splashed a hundred meters away.

Spock didn't grace Kirk with a reply.

Then Kirk took a second look at Spock.

In the midst of all this simulated detail, how could he know if Spock was even Spock?

"Is something wrong, 'Lieutenant'?" Spock asked.

Kirk narrowed his eyes at what might or might not be his friend. Could Vulcan logic be that devious? Would the justice authorities go so far as to make two prisoners seem to share a cell, them separate them holographically with simulated duplicates that might elicit a confession?

Technology made it possible.

But Kirk would bet on the human touch every time.

"It's all right, Spock. We're alone. You can call me by my real rank."

Spock's expression remained detached. But he idly scratched an earlobe. "Unless there is something you have not told me, as far as I know, your real rank is that of lieutenant."

Kirk had to think it through. That might have been the response of a holographic duplicate fishing for information. Or, Spock might have said that, knowing that everything they said to each other in the cell was being monitored. Is that why Spock had scratched his ear? In warning?

"Just checking," Kirk said. His mind worked furiously as he tried to figure a way around Vulcan logic—both that of his captors, and Spock's. It was worse than trying to figure out temporal anomalies. And it was giving him a headache.

"Ah," Spock said. "You believe I might be a holographic duplicate intended to elicit details of your crimes."

Kirk frowned. "Spock, we committed no crimes."

Spock, if it were Spock, spoke in a low voice. "I was speaking for the benefit of the listening devices which even now might be recording everything we say."

"Is that legal on Vulcan?" Kirk asked.

"Until we have been tested for exposure to the virogen, I think we may assume we are under the jurisdiction of one of the planetary defense bureaus. As a member of the diplomatic corps, and with you as a member of Starfleet, our civil liberties are severely constrained by the oaths of duty to which we both attested."

Kirk frowned at Spock. With conversation like that, how could he tell the difference between a computer-driven version of a Vulcan and a real Vulcan? Especially if the real Vulcan didn't want to reveal any important information that might be used against them in future legal proceedings?

It would have to be something trivial, Kirk decided. Some small detail that would be known only to Spock and himself, unavailable in any database.

Kirk scratched at the side of his jaw. He had it. "Spock, do you remember when we were on that planetoid in the Gamma Canaris region? Do you remember who we found there?"

That was a safe question, Kirk knew. In Gamma Canaris, he and Spock and McCoy unexpectedly had come upon the human inventor of the warp drive, Zefram Cochrane himself. Cochrane had survived his own era because of the influence of a mysterious alien he called the Companion. When Kirk, Spock, and McCoy were ready to leave, Cochrane had asked them to promise never to reveal his existence to anyone else. He wanted to remain with the Companion undisturbed, to live out the remainder of their lives in peace.

Kirk had kept his word. Spock and McCoy were the only two people who shared that secret with him. If this Spock was a hologram, he would have no idea to what Kirk referred.

But Spock's reply revealed a third possibility. "I am afraid you are mistaken. I was last in the Gamma Canaris region on stardate 3219.8; one hundred and six years ago. Clearly, you had not been born at that time."

Kirk stared up at the simulated sky. Of course. In this detention cell, for the benefit of their Vulcan captors, Kirk was Lieutenant Plummer. Spock's reply could have come from a holographic duplicate, or from the real Spock, determined to keep Kirk's identity a secret. Whatever question

Kirk asked, it would have to be based on more recent events. He cleared his throat.

"Ambassador Spock, when we were on Tarok's estate, I asked you if the crew of the *Tobias* reminded you of anyone."

"No," Spock said. "You asked me if the senior officers of the *Tobias* with Mr. Srell reminded me of anyone."

Kirk closed his eyes in relief. No one else had heard him ask Spock that question.

"And I told you they did not," Spock added.

"Thank you," Kirk said. "I'm convinced you're you."

Then he realized that now Spock was giving him a questioning look.

"Don't tell me," Kirk said as he understood the reason for Spock's expression. "Now you're wondering if *I'm* a hologram."

"Someone else might have overheard you ask that question, and then related it to an interrogator for inclusion in a holographic simulation," Spock said.

"So, ask me something, Spock. Something that only I would know. That would never have been input into a database or told to anyone else."

Spock looked thoughtful for a few moments. "Once, I and a mutual physician friend of ours had to access the personal safe in your quarters on . . . your vessel."

Kirk thought frantically. The mutual friend was certainly McCoy. The unnamed vessel had to be the *Enterprise.* But when had Spock and McCoy gone into his safe? It was something they would have done only if they thought he had died in the line of duty, and they required copies of his final orders. And the only time that had happened was . . . in Tholian space?

"Just a minute," Kirk said indignantly before Spock could finish. "At the time of the incident to which you're referring, I specifically asked you and . . . our friend if you had looked at the orders in my safe, and you told me you hadn't."

"We lied," Spock said blandly. "Returning to the safe. What was the combination?"

Kirk didn't have to think. "Five three four," he said. They were the birth months of his brother, Sam; himself; and his nephew, Peter—certainly not trivial. And certainly not anything he would ever forget.

Spock nodded. "I am satisfied. Only the real . . . Lieutenant Plummer would have known that code."

Kirk still couldn't get over Spock's earlier admission. "You lied to me."

"It was the doctor's idea," Spock countered.

Kirk was getting tired of standing. He took a few steps toward the low wall surrounding the meditation garden and sat on the gold-colored, metallic ledge that topped it. It was difficult to believe it was only a holographic illusion, but his feet felt better. "So what now?"

Spock joined Kirk on the ledge. "I am open to suggestions."

Kirk drew in a deep breath. The illusion of being on Vulcan was so complete that he could even detect the faint scent of cinnamon that seemed to perfume the dust of the planet. "The magistrate said we were to be tested for exposure to the virogen. Is that something that can be done by medical scanners?"

"No. The test will require blood samples."

That gave Kirk a starting point. "Then we'll have company any time now. A medical technician. Probably a guard."

"That would be logical."

And if they can get in, Kirk thought, *they'll know the way out. How's that for logic?*

"We should keep our eyes open," Kirk said. "Try and see where they come from."

Spock looked skeptical. "Though I am willing to be open-minded, it *is* a Vulcan prison. You can be sure there are countermeasures for every strategy you can devise."

216

Kirk reached behind himself and ran his fingers over the sand in the meditation garden, disturbing the precise alignment of two channels of red and brown. The deception was so perfect, he could even feel small particles of sand cling to his fingertips.

"Since we have nothing else to do at this time," Spock said, "perhaps you could continue your story."

"Story?"

"About . . . our friend," Spock said. "Who last found himself being helped by Hugh's clan."

Kirk took a handful of holographic sand and let it fall from his fist. It feathered into a wispy plume in the artificial breeze.

"Why not?" Surrounded by the artifice of technology, it seemed the perfect setting to explain how it came to be that he had freed himself from it.

Or, at least, how he had tried.

The female's name was Miko. She and Hugh had carted Kirk through the mud, past the dead and dying Borg, letting his useless feet drag behind him.

To Kirk, it was as if he floated over a war zone, the aftermath of a battle waged by demons.

Looking back on it, perhaps it was a suitable way to think of the life he had lived up to that place and time—a war of demons, out of control.

Perhaps it was time that control finally emerged.

Eventually, the rapacious monsters that cleansed that battlefield were left behind, to scoop up and dismember the remnants of whatever Borg bastions had fallen.

In time—how long, he couldn't tell—Kirk was aware that Hugh and Miko were carrying him across solid ground.

They climbed a worn path hacked out of obsidian stone, flecked with glints of red and silver, bearing him up a mountainside shrouded in the low-lying clouds of this world.

The cold, cloying mist enveloped Kirk as they climbed.

He felt the nanites burn within him. The pain now unceasing. All the peaks and surges of it joined in one continuous wave of agony.

He knew he would never live to see this journey's end.

And then, they passed through the clouds, and the sun of this world blazed down upon him.

But it was not a sun.

Kirk trembled as he saw the vision that awaited him.

Its beauty was so overwhelming that he did not know when Hugh and Miko had lowered him to the ground.

For it was not one star that shone on him.

It was thousands, *millions,* all the stars that he had ever seen in his entire life, brought together in some way to shine their light on him alone.

Long after, he would come to understand that what he saw was a galactic core—a dense collection of stars so closely packed that supernovae flared among them in a cosmic chain reaction, creating a star-strewn ball of luminescent fire that filled a quarter of the sky.

Kirk stared up at that fire and that brilliance, seeing wisps of matter and energy dance with incalculable energies, and knew he was no longer in the galaxy of his birth.

Removed beyond all reason from everything that he knew, he cried with the joy and the pain of facing death while beholding such beauty. To know such transcendence only in the final moments of his life seemed both miraculous and cruel, a gift desired but acquired too late.

Had he really come to take the universe for granted?

With all that he had been given by fate, with all that he had earned by effort, had he really grown so inured to the wonders he had encountered that he had forgotten there were wonders more, still to be discovered?

Kirk raised his hand to that vast assembly of stars, longing to reach them, to touch, to go on.

He *had* forgotten.

There was still more to do.

But his realization of that simple truth was far too late. The nanites were almost finished with their work.

Kirk's vision shifted from the infinity of stars to his own tattered flesh. Blood welled from a thousand microscopic cuts on his arm as the nanites at last reached the surface of his skin and burst through.

Blood dimmed his vision as he lost all sense of feeling and fell up to those stars . . .

. . . only to feel the gentle pressure of Miko's hands, holding him back, soothing his wounds with a smooth, fragrant salve.

Then Hugh and Miko brought him to a stream that gushed into a hollow in the slick, black rock.

They plunged him into the icy depths and it was as if his flesh froze and shattered and he was plucked from within it, new, and whole, and cleansed.

Kirk lay beside that stream as Miko wiped the mud and the salve from him. He did not know it at the time, but when she was done, the nanites were no longer within him. The salve had lured them out and neutralized them with plant-based pheromones and genetic markers that the nanites' voracious programming could not resist.

Thus had technology succumbed to its own selfish appetites.

It might have been days later. It might have been months. But when at last Kirk felt sensation return to him, all he could see on his skin was a faint pebbling of tiny scars.

"The nanites?" he asked.

Miko drew a cloth across his brow. "All that was machine has been taken from you. Just as it was taken from us."

He stared at her then, and saw the logic of the brown and white skin that covered her.

She had been Borg, but now, wherever Borg implants had been taken from her, new brown skin was in its place. White skin showed where she had remained untouched at the time of her assimilation.

"How?" Kirk asked.

Hugh took Kirk's hand as he led him from the water. "We will show you," he said.

And Kirk went with them from the mountain to the village of the clan.

"An actual village?" Spock asked.

"It's the best word for it," Kirk said. "Some of the dwellings were carved from the rock walls. Some were wood. And the whole of it was filled with . . . others who had been reclaimed from the Collective. Humanoids, aliens, skin, fur, scales . . ." Kirk shook his head at the memory of it. "Every day, that galactic core would blaze like a sun. And every night, the sky burned with transwarp transporter beams, bringing in reclaimed material from . . . from wherever a Borg installation had failed but was still in contact with the Collective's backup systems." Kirk rubbed the grains of sand between his fingers. "It gave me . . . it gave my *friend,* the feeling the Borg were everywhere. Not just this galaxy, but . . . everywhere. As if the fusion of flesh and machine were . . . inevitable."

Spock regarded Kirk intently. "It appears to have been a profound experience. For your friend."

Kirk grinned for a moment, marveling at Spock's gift for understatement. Then he gave up any pretense of trying to make possible eavesdroppers think he was relating a tale told to him by someone else. He doubted the Vulcans would know what to make of his story anyway. It was one purely of emotion, not logic.

"Spock, in the true sense of the word, I had become Borg. Not like Picard. Not with implants. I hadn't been assimilated. But figuratively, metaphorically, if you want, I had allowed myself, in the way I had lived my life, to become . . .

absorbed by the objects and the things around me." Kirk tossed the sand away, not bothering to see where it would fall. "I lost *myself.* Everything else was just trappings. My career in Starfleet. Whether I could have that chair again. Whether there'd be another mission for me. Maybe falling into the Nexus was the best thing that could have happened to me. To die on Veridian, to finally be cut off from history . . . really, it ended up freeing me in a way I'd never have expected."

"Yet," Spock said, "you have returned. You could have stayed with Teilani, out of sight, undisturbed, like our mutual friend in the Gamma Canaris region."

"I'm not who I was, Spock. For what I did in the past, I've no regrets. And maybe, if the Federation survives, somehow I'll keep on doing what I've always done. But *why* I'm doing it, and *how,* that's different now. To lose everything, and then to have a chance to get it back, that experience makes *everything* different."

"Is this what you were taught?" Spock asked.

"It's what I was shown. It's what I came to know."

Miko had stayed with him, in a shelter made of wooden beams and woven fibers that had never seen a replicator.

She took him to the fields where the clan grew the crops that fed them. She took him to the forests where the clan hewed the wood that sheltered them. She took him to her bed, where she let sensation rule him, driving out the need for thought.

When his strength had recovered, Kirk had joined Hugh in the clan's work. Moving through the reclamation fields to find those who could be saved from assimilation. Hugh showed him how to touch those precise points on a being through which the life force could be sensed.

Kirk recognized the placement. They were the same as those Vulcans used in mindmelds.

Hugh agreed. He knew about Vulcans.

The Borg had assimilated thousands of worlds, tens of thousands of cultures. Though Hugh and his clan had abandoned the machine, they retained the knowledge that had been absorbed by the Collective.

"That knowledge is the same," Hugh said. "That spark of life that fills the worlds of all the galaxies, it is the same everywhere. A necessary part of existence. As sure as the fusion of hydrogen or the orbit of a star."

Kirk took other Borg to the stream to cleanse them of their implants. Miko showed him the secrets that would free and redeem them, secrets that had been learned only here, known only to the Borg who were brought to this world.

The transwarp transporters brought everything here—Borg, and machinery, and clumps of soil from worlds throughout the universe.

Some of the clan sorted through that soil, to find green shoots and seeds. These they grew on the mountain slopes. These they used to make the salves and dried compounds that would ease the pain of those who were reclaimed.

Kirk learned well. Held the Borg down as their implants were rejected. Applied the medicines that would heal their wounds.

Since he had not been Borg himself, it was simpler for him to handle those implants, to gather them together, some still moving with a macabre machine-echo of life, and take them to the dumping grounds where they could never be recycled by the all-consuming machines.

It was there Kirk found the Borg scoutship.

Intact.

And he realized the time had come for his journey to continue once again.

TWENTY-SIX

───────── ☆ ─────────

"It was as simple as that?" Spock asked.

Kirk was irritated by the question. "Spock, it wasn't simple at all. I spent two years with Hugh and his people. My wounds healed. I lived with them. Celebrated with them. Learned from them. But they had all been Borg. The life they led there, it was what *they* needed. I had my time with them, and then it was time for me to move on with what I had to do."

"How did you know how to operate a Borg scoutship?"

"I didn't have to. The clan knew. Some of them, who weren't afraid of the machine, they operated it for me."

"And brought you where?"

Kirk smiled. "Heaven. Chal. If I were really going to have a second chance at life, I knew I had to lay my old life to rest. It didn't matter how Teilani and I had met, that we'd both been manipulated by Drake, I knew I loved her. I had to see her grave. To say good-bye."

Spock nodded. "But she hadn't died."

"A second chance," Kirk said. "After all the things this universe has taken from me, it finally gave me something back. Something I know how to treasure now."

Spock stared far away, as if this false garden really were Vulcan, as if this really were his home.

"I understand the irony now," he said. "The universe has given you a second chance at life, at love, and yet the Federation, the very thing that makes your life possible, is on the brink of ruin."

"We've saved it before," Kirk said.

"From its enemies. Hugh told you the spark of life was intrinsic to the universe. It could well be that the virogen confronting us is a natural by-product of the Federation's own unprincipled growth. I do not know how we might save the Federation from itself."

"When has not knowing stopped us before?"

Spock rose to his feet. He seemed offended by Kirk's attempt at humor. "My father was murdered. I was not there to protect him." Spock pointed at Kirk. "What *I* want from the universe is a chance to set that right."

Kirk stood up slowly, alarmed to see his friend actually begin to tremble with what could only be rage. He reached out to touch Spock's arm. "Are you all right? This isn't like you at all."

But Spock tore away from Kirk's grasp.

"I am tired of 'being like me.' I am tired of control, and denial, and the blind, Vulcan acceptance of everything that is wrong in this world!"

Kirk stared at Spock as if he were watching a transformation at work. As if some shapeshifter had taken Spock's form. Because what Spock was saying simply could never come from him.

"Spock, this isn't the time or the place for—"

"It is! It is what I feel! And I will not deny it any longer!"

For an instant, Kirk's instinct was to slap Spock, to focus his attention, to break the momentum of whatever had caused his friend's startling loss of self-control. But before he could act, a new voice called out in the cell.

"Do not move from your positions!"

At once, Kirk and Spock both turned their heads toward the direction from which the voice had come.

Two Vulcans stood two meters away, as if they had stepped out from the air. One was a spacedock guard. The other, from her pale green cloak, was a healer. She held a medical kit and had obviously come to draw blood samples.

Both Vulcans stared at Spock with disquieting intensity. They had obviously witnessed his most uncharacteristic outburst.

The healer broke the silence. "Are you well, Ambassador?"

Spock smoothed his robes. "I say again for the benefit of the magistrate, you are interfering in vital Starfleet affairs."

The healer approached Kirk. "The magistrate is attempting to contact Starfleet Command to confirm your assignment. In any event, this test is necessary in order to insure the safety of Vulcan's biosphere."

The healer took Kirk's arm and motioned for him to roll up his sleeve.

"Where is your logic?" Spock complained. "We have already been down on Vulcan. Do you really think I would allow my home to be placed in danger?"

The healer drew a sample of Kirk's blood from his inner elbow. "The magistrate is aware of that," she said calmly. "There are many aspects to your presence and your actions here that trouble her."

Kirk rolled down his sleeve as the healer deftly placed the ampule of his blood into her kit. He saw four other ampules there. One green, one purple-black, two dark red. Vulcan, Tellarite, and human. "Are our friends all right?" he asked.

The healer looked at him as if a trained monkey had addressed her. "The others are as you last saw them. Their blood will be tested for the virogen, as well." She looked away from Kirk as if he had ceased to exist. "Ambassador, please expose your arm."

Kirk watched as Spock chewed his lip, as if debating the healer's request.

"Ambassador, this is a serious matter. I am authorized to have you stunned in order to obtain a sample."

Spock wrenched his sleeve up and thrust his arm at the healer with a barely restrained expression of anger.

When the healer approached Spock with her syringe, Kirk sensed her caution. "Sir, I am a healer. Is there anything else I can do for you?"

Spock fixed his eyes on the ampule that filled with his green blood. "Release me."

Once she had obtained her sample, the healer stepped away quickly. "I am sure the magistrate is doing everything in her power to expedite your request."

She rejoined the guard. Kirk watched them closely, hoping to see them step through the doorway that was hidden by the holographic imagery.

"Good-bye, Ambassador," the healer said. "May your journey be without incident." Then she nodded at the guard, he touched a control on the belt he wore, and both Vulcans appeared to take on the colors and details of the scenery behind them, then faded from view.

Kirk fixed their exact location by counting the bricks between him and where they had last stood. He looked at Spock. "What happened to them? Don't they have to step through an arch to get in and out?"

"That is on a standard holodeck," Spock said, as if annoyed that Kirk was speaking to him. "In the event your attention has been elsewhere, this is a prison."

Kirk regarded his friend with concern, but did not move toward him. He was determined to keep his feet in exactly the same position they had been when the Vulcans had faded into the background. It was the only way he could be sure of what constituted the real volume of the holodeck.

"Spock, I don't know what's happened to you, but if you

want to get out of here, you're going to have to work with me."

"What leads you to believe you can possibly escape a Vulcan cell?"

Kirk was appalled by how much Spock sounded like a petulant child. "Because you said you had faith in me," he snapped. "Now get over here."

Reluctantly, Spock walked over to Kirk. Both their backs were to the meditation garden. Kirk maneuvered Spock into position and had him place his feet in Kirk's own footsteps, one foot after another. "All right, now don't move. You're going to give me a lesson in holosimulations."

Kirk ran a few steps to the meditation garden, leaned over the low wall, and scooped up two handfuls of sand. "First thing, where does the sand come from?"

Spock sounded totally disinterested. "It is replicator matter. Everything physical with which we can interact is some form of replicator matter combined with precision force-fields."

Kirk started a trail of sand from the toe of Spock's boots, on a direct line toward the bricks where the guard and the healer had been standing. His first handful of sand ran out as he reached that brick. He kept going, checking to make sure he was keeping the line of sand straight. When he was finished with the second handful, he had a trail of sand at least eight meters long.

Kirk stood at the end of the sand line. "We're now farther apart than the room is wide. Explain to me how it works," Kirk called back to Spock.

"It is, of course, a logical impossibility," Spock said, still irritable. "As you walked away from me, sensors in the floor tracked your footsteps. As you neared the wall, forcefields in the floor began moving like a treadmill, giving you the physical sensation of walking, even though you remained in place. The OHD panels lining the cell projected holographic images to keep the scenery moving to match your apparent physical progress."

"But you *look* as if you're eight meters away, Spock."

"What you are seeing from your vantage point is a holographic image of me in forced perspective. In actuality, I am no more than three or four meters from you, as logic demands."

"So the real you is hidden behind a holographic screen," Kirk said.

"Until you come within a logical visual range of me. Then the plane of the holographic illusion will pass over me, allowing you to see me as I really am."

Kirk walked back along the line of sand. In his mind's eye, he pictured the bare cube of the holodeck, filled with a series of virtual-projection screens that changed their position according to the position of the two people within the cell. The trick was to get behind one of those screens. And Kirk knew how to do it.

He stood on one foot and pulled off his boot. Spock watched him with a frown.

"I assure you, the tactile response works on feet as well as fingers," Spock said.

"That's not what I had in mind," Kirk told him. "Watch. And listen."

Then Kirk threw his boot as hard as he could, straight along the line of sand.

About three meters away, he heard a faint thump, as if the boot had hit something solid. But visually, the boot seemed to sail another five meters before tumbling onto the ground.

"Let *me* tell you what just happened," Kirk said. "My boot, which is not replicator matter, hit the wall of the cell somewhere between here and the end of that trail of sand. But what the holoprojectors did was to create an image of the boot continuing on its trajectory, while at the same time putting a holographic screen over the boot as it fell to the floor against the wall."

"Exactly," Spock said. "So."

Kirk looked down at the blank spot on his uniform where his comm badge had been fastened. Unfortunately, it had been removed by the guards before he had been brought before the magistrate. "So, my friend, the trick is, we need to know exactly how far the wall really is."

"I fail to see how that information could possibly be useful."

"I don't suppose they let you keep your comm badge? We need something hard."

Spock fingered his IDIC medallion. It gleamed in the artificial light of the artificial garden. "Would this suffice?"

Spock handed the medallion to Kirk.

"May I throw it?"

Spock shrugged. "I have."

Kirk didn't bother to ask for an explanation. "Close your eyes," he said. "You have to listen for the medallion hitting the wall, and then tell me how far away it is."

Spock closed his eyes.

Kirk hurled the medallion like a miniature discus.

Though it appeared to soar far away, he heard the metallic impact of it striking the wall only a second after release. A section of the background scenery even wavered for a moment, as if one or two of the OHD panels had been broken.

Kirk turned to Spock. "How far?" he asked.

"Two point six meters," Spock answered. "And you broke the medallion."

"I'll get you another. How're your arms?"

Spock instantly knew what Kirk had in mind. "You cannot be serious."

Kirk was hurt. "Did I miss something about how this holocell works?"

Spock followed the line of sand with his eyes. "Two point

six meters," he repeated. "It will have to be done with sufficient force to strike the wall before touching the floor."

Kirk nodded. "Exactly, so the forcefields on the floor will lose track of me."

Spock looked dubious.

"It worked for the boot," Kirk said, "and the medallion."

Spock took off his robe and dropped it to the holographic bricks, then cupped his hands and adjusted his stance. "You will have to do it without running, to take the program by surprise."

Kirk put his bootless foot in Spock's cupped hands and braced his hands on Spock's shoulders. "What if we're being watched?"

"Then I trust the guards will be entertained," Spock said. "On the count of three?"

Kirk counted off, setting their timing.

On "three," he pushed up and forward as Spock pivoted and threw him in the same direction.

For an instant, Kirk saw the meditation garden swirl around him, and then he felt the jarring shock of hitting an invisible wall.

He slapped his arms against it, trying to absorb some of the impact, but he had miscalculated and felt his breath explode from his lungs as his chest was momentarily paralyzed.

Fortunately, the jolt against the floor as he slid down the wall relieved the symptom. He could breathe again, almost.

"Are you all right?" Spock called out.

Kirk raised his head from the floor and looked in the direction of the sound of Spock's voice. Beneath his hands, he could feel, and more importantly, *see* the bare floor of the cell, not holographic bricks. He ran his fingers along the dark metal, confirming the texture of the miniature OHD panels that lined it. He was out of the illusion!

Spock was less than three meters away, but appeared to be

little more than a splotchy collection of coarse pixels, shimmering with out-of-phase color and motion.

"Spock! It worked!" Kirk shouted. He was *behind* the holographic screens. The program running the simulation had treated his thrown body as if it were an inanimate prop. "What do you see?"

"You appear to have rolled onto the bricks about four meters away," Spock called out. "I suggest you hurry, before the program's heuristics realize what you have done and trigger a restart."

Kirk got to his feet and turned to face the wall, keeping in as close contact with it as possible. He looked to both sides. To the left, he saw the outline of the door. He edged toward it, pressing against the wall so that he wouldn't slip back into the holographic illusion.

It was better than he had hoped. He easily found the small control panel by the door which he had noticed the first time he had looked, just before the simulation had begun. The panel had only two control surfaces. He pressed the one on the left.

The door slid open onto the corridor, no exit code needed.

Kirk could understand the simplicity of the mechanism from a Vulcan's point of view: Why bother to lock a door that the prisoner would never find?

He pressed the control on the right, confident of what the result would be. Sure enough, there was a flashing flurry of lights behind him, and when he turned again, Spock was standing in the center of the bare holocell, his robe on the metal floor beside him.

"Pick that up, would you?" Kirk pointed to his boot lying against the wall. "I'll hold the door." Then he stepped halfway through the doorway and glanced down the corridor.

Christine and M'Benga were running toward him.

Kirk stared at them. "How . . . ?"

M'Benga rotated her shoulder with a tight-lipped expression of pain. "Chris had this bright idea of throwing me against the wall."

"It worked, didn't it?" Christine said.

Spock appeared in the doorway and handed Kirk his boot. Kirk pointed across the corridor. "Barc and Srell are in that—"

They heard a dull clang of metal and a Tellarite's grunt of pain. A moment later, the cell door slid open to reveal Barc shaking his head. Srell stepped out from behind him.

"Did everyone figure out the same flaw?" Kirk asked incredulously.

Srell adjusted his jacket. Kirk realized that Srell and Spock were the only two who hadn't seen the way out. "When Vulcan prisoners are placed in a holographic re-creation of Surak's meditation garden," Srell said loftily, "they are expected to meditate and reflect on their wrongdoings. These are new facilities, and I imagine the authorities will augment the simulation to take into account the actions of non-Vulcans."

"A logical assessment," Spock said. "And now, I believe we should continue our escape."

"Of course," Srell said.

But it was a blind corridor. Kirk pointed toward the only exit. "Forcefield," he reminded everyone. He reached down for his boot.

Barc merely growled and waddled toward the forcefield frame. In seconds, he had popped a wall access panel with a powerful punch. Then, boot forgotten, Kirk watched in amazement as the Tellarite used his seemingly clumsy hands to pick the metal pips from his collar, tie them together with a thread he pulled from his tunic, and dangle them inside the access port. He pushed his head half inside, one eye closed, the tip of his broad tongue sticking out from the side of his snout in an expression of rapt concentration.

Barc grunted to himself once or twice; then he pulled back

his hand, and the forcefield frame shorted out in a gratifying display of static and sparks.

Barc shook his fingers back and forth. The fur on his knuckles was smoldering.

"Next," he said with great satisfaction.

Christine thudded him on his shoulder, making him rock. "You did it again, Barcs!"

"Rrrr, that I did."

Kirk looked up from pulling on his boot. "Am I the only one who wants to know what's keeping the guards?"

Srell gingerly passed his hand through the forcefield frame, confirming that the field was down. "Until the blood samples confirm that we are free of virogen contamination, there will be no guards assigned to this section."

Kirk walked through the frame. However the Tellarite engineer had managed to shut down the field, there wasn't even a residual static charge left. Very impressive. But the forcefield couldn't be the only security measure in use. "Why aren't they using scanners in the corridor?" he asked.

"That would not be logical," Spock said. "Since no one can escape from a holocell, there is no need to look for escapees."

Kirk saw Barc turn to Christine and M'Benga. "It's still too easy if you ask me."

Kirk agreed, but wasn't inclined to join the debate. "Why don't we just keep moving," he suggested. "After all, when on Vulcan. . . ."

He turned and began to jog down the corridor, away from the magistrate's office, in the general direction of the turbolift banks that served the spacedock's umbilical docking levels. He was gratified to hear the others quickly catch up behind him.

Kirk had long ago learned that when faced with an apparently complex problem, it was sometimes better to make a quick decision, rather than remain immobile while trying to determine the correct one.

But even with his decision made, he still wrestled with himself to determine if he was doing the right thing. Because Barc had been right. Vulcan obstinacy aside, this escape *was* too easy.

Which meant he could be leading his team into another trap, even worse than the last.

Wouldn't be the first time, he thought. And with no other options before him, Kirk did the only thing he could.

He ran faster.

TWENTY-SEVEN

─────── ☆ ───────

Picard had never felt so frustrated.

All around him, he could feel the pulse and the rhythms of his ship. Even in the vacuum of the shuttlebay, the vibrations traveled through the deck plates, through the landing skids, and brought the hull of the *Galileo* to resonant life. The life of a starship.

Yet because he was in quarantine, Picard could not be part of it.

Beverly placed a cup of Earl Grey on the work surface that folded out from the *Galileo*'s main instrument panel.

"This is quite maddening," he said.

"The tea?"

Her smile was enough to ease some of his tension. Her presence, even more. He returned the smile gratefully. The week they had spent in the close quarters of the shuttle had been a reminder of the rare treasure of time spent in each other's presence, free of the ever-present responsibilities both took so seriously.

"Certainly not the tea," Picard said as he savored the aroma. "Nor the company. But . . ." He gestured wistfully at the small navigational display on the instrument panel.

Upon it, the planet Vulcan, in all her stern and crimson majesty, was reduced to little more than a dull red disk on a ten-centimeter screen.

The flight deck of a shuttle was never meant to be the bridge of a starship.

Beverly sat on the arm of Picard's flight chair. "We won't be in here forever."

"Does that mean you have faith in my supposition that the Symmetrists' cure can be found on Vulcan?" he asked. "Or are you about to tell me you've discovered an antivirogen yourself?"

Picard had asked that last question almost in jest. He still hadn't dared share with anyone Stron's startling identification of Sarek as the Symmetrists' leader. That possibility, if true, was the key reason why Picard believed Vulcan might hold the answer to the mystery of the virogen's creation and purpose.

"As a matter of fact," Beverly said, "Starfleet Medical may be making some progress. Three days ago, they completed a simulated clinical trial using an old Klingon herbal treatment for certain types of food poisoning. Dried *trannin* leaves, of all things.

"Apparently, when the leaves dry, they exude a resin containing a compound that binds perfectly to the virogen's silicon spine, so its RNA can't cleave. That stops reproduction of the virogen, *and* tags it so antibodies can form. The simulator trials indicate that the *trannin* compound can reduce the virogen load in a typical animal model to zero within thirty hours."

"That is most encouraging. Can the treatment be applied to plants as well as animals?"

"Not yet. The compound is a macromolecule—too large to efficiently penetrate plant cell membranes the way the virogen does. But if the compound really does test out, and it can be synthesized *and* replicated, then we have a good chance of stopping all animal transmission. Which means, we can get out of this shuttlecraft."

"Are you in that much of a hurry? It's so peaceful."

"I could erase the medical logs," she teased. "We might have to stay here for years."

Picard made a show of thinking the possibility over. But one detail stopped him. "How did Medical ever come up with the idea of testing an old Klingon folk remedy for a new disease organism?"

"Well, technically, the virogen isn't an organism. And the idea came out of a medical log filed from one of the affected systems. Apparently, a doctor assigned to a relief mission reported positive results on some of her patients and recommended the leaves for further study. I only read the abstract, but I gather she got the leaves from some sort of Klingon folk healer on the planet."

"How fortunate for us all."

"I'd say it was time something fortunate happened in all of this." Beverly's smile faltered. She glanced away for a moment, looking through the shuttle's forward viewport at the deserted bay. "Jean-Luc, the latest figures from Medical put the number of affected systems at nineteen."

Picard was stunned. "That's more than double what it was a week ago."

"Between emergency transport of food supplies, relief missions . . . Starfleet no longer has enough ships to adequately maintain the quarantine. Blockades are being run everywhere. The contagion's spreading."

Picard sat forward to enter his access code into the shuttle's communications system. Instantly, all command bulletins he had received from Starfleet over the past seventy hours appeared onscreen. Picard had read them all as they had been received, but he checked their subject headings again. "Beverly, my command updates report only nine affected systems."

Beverly leaned forward to read over Picard's shoulder. She found the reason for the discrepancy at once. "Look at the stardates. These were already four to five days old when you received them."

Picard expanded the most recent update and accessed the routing information embedded in it. It was horrendously complex—a hopelessly inefficient web of starbases, subspace relay stations, and even ship-to-ship transmissions. A message which normally should have reached the *Enterprise* in less than half a day had taken five.

Picard traced the data on the screen with his finger, astounded by the revelations contained within them. "The whole subspace network is breaking down. There are missing starbases, retransmissions . . . How can Medical's communications be so far ahead of Command's?"

Beverly input her access codes to call up her own most recent medical bulletins on another display. The routing information contained in them explained part of the reason for the timing differences. "The Command bulletins are originating from Starfleet Headquarters on Earth. The medical bulletins originate from the Virogen Task Force Headquarters at Starbase Five-fifteen."

To Picard, it made perfect sense that in this emergency Starfleet would decentralize its command structure to insure a more rapid response, and he knew from personal experience that the medical facilities at 515 were superb. But according to the time delays indicated in the routing information, Starfleet Headquarters and Starfleet Medical were no longer in direct communication with each other.

"They're not coordinating their actions," Picard said. "They've lost the capability. . . ." He sat back in the flight chair, rubbing his hands over his face in exhaustion. "Beverly, even if we find the Symmetrists' cure on Vulcan . . . or even if those Klingon leaves were found to be a total cure for every expression of the virogen, animal and plant, if this communications breakdown continues to spread, Starfleet won't be able to disseminate its discoveries." Picard looked up at the doctor. "And if the virogen's range continues to double every seven days. . . ."

Beverly didn't need him to complete the calculation. "In less than three months, every home system, every colony, every world in the Federation will be contaminated."

Picard stared out the viewport, overcome by the escalation of the disaster's scope. "Why didn't you share your medical logs with me, Doctor?"

He could see Beverly stiffen defensively at his use of her title. She replied in an equally brittle tone. "Because, *Captain,* I had no reason to suspect that Medical's updates were appreciably different from Command's."

Picard immediately regretted the severity of his question. He wondered how often in the past week this same conversation had been enacted on starships and starbases throughout the Federation, as the extent of the communications breakdown became apparent.

"Beverly, forgive me," he said. "That didn't come out the way I had intended."

Beverly understood. She put a hand on his shoulder. "The Federation has faced worse, Jean-Luc."

"And so have we," he said.

She was too close, too caring, the home of too many memories.

He reached up and placed his hand around hers.

She leaned down, her lips close to his.

"Captain?" On the display beside Vulcan, Will Riker suddenly appeared.

Beverly straightened up so quickly, she almost fell from the arm of the flight chair.

Picard replied to his first officer with equanimity, as if he and Beverly had just been conferring as usual. "Yes, Number One?" At any other time, Picard would have expected to see at least a hint of a smile play over Riker's face, for having caught his captain in so human a moment.

But Riker continued seriously, as if he had seen nothing out of the ordinary, or as if he didn't have time to deal with it.

"Sir, we've arrived on orbit, but none of the Vulcan orbital authorities has a record of our arrival notice."

Because of what he had just seen in his own updates, Picard knew why. Upon leaving the Alta Vista system, he had filed the *Enterprise's* new flight plan through regular Starfleet channels. Given what he'd just learned about the state of the fleet's communications system, it was most likely the message hadn't even arrived at Earth for processing. "Have any of the support vessels we requested arrived?"

Riker shook his head. "Lieutenant Rolk has contacted all other interstellar Starfleet vessels in the Vulcan system. There are fifteen in total, none larger than *Miranda*-class. Eight are here on other Starfleet assignments, and their commanders have offered whatever support they can provide to help us search for a Symmetrist base. Six are in transit under urgent orders connected to other relief missions, and must decline."

"What about the fifteenth?" Picard asked.

"That appears to be a troubling matter, sir. The ship is currently impounded at a civilian spacedock."

Picard let his expression of surprise ask his next question.

Riker continued. "Rolk has put through a formal request for information from the civilian authorities. But, unofficially, sir, a local magistrate has forwarded a report to Starfleet recommending a possible mutiny investigation. The impounded ship is listed as being currently assigned to relief duties near the Klingon-Romulan border. She shouldn't be anywhere near here."

"What ship, Number One?"

"The *Tobias,* sir." Riker looked offscreen to check his own data display. "Commander Christine MacDonald's ship."

Picard knew of the *Tobias,* a standard Starfleet science

vessel that had been in service for decades. But he was unfamiliar with her commander.

A hundred questions came to Picard then. Why had the *Tobias* abandoned its duty? More importantly, why had an allegedly mutinous vessel come to Vulcan, instead of trying to escape to a nonaligned system? Still, Starfleet maintained considerable resources on Vulcan, and the question of the *Tobias* must properly remain with the local command. Especially if it was up to Picard alone to convince the Vulcan authorities that the Symmetrists might be behind the virogen outbreak.

"Has there been any further word on the possibility of riots at Starbase Seven-eighteen?" Picard asked. Mutiny was a virtually nonexistent crime in the fleet. But if the rumors of riots at Starfleet facilities were true, how long could it be before dissent and fear did incite mutiny on individual ships?

Riker frowned and Picard suddenly realized how haggard his senior officer looked. Locked away in the *Galileo,* Picard felt increasingly out of touch with his crew as well as his ship.

"Seven-eighteen's sector is in a complete subspace shutdown, sir." Riker's response left no doubt that there was more bad news he had to report.

"What else, Number One?"

"I've been trying to sort out all of this . . . confusion with local command. But Admiral Strak and his staff left on the *Intrepid* five days ago, and—"

"Left the Vulcan system?"

"There's an emergency situation at Bajor. It's the Cardassians and the Dominion, sir. With the fleet spread so thin, they appear to be testing our defenses and response times. Intelligence has also reported a buildup of Romulan ships just off the Neutral Zone. The alerts are coming in from everywhere."

Picard stood. "Why am I just hearing this now, Commander?"

241

Riker gestured uselessly. "As far as I can tell, sir, these alerts haven't been relayed out of Vulcan command. Rolk says Starfleet facilities here are operating with about ten percent of their normal workforce, with most replicators already shipped out for emergency duty, and no spare parts."

Picard braced himself on the work surface that still held his untouched tea. All starship captains were prepared to carry out their missions while out of contact with Command. It was the nature of the job. But those situations arose only on the farthest reaches of the frontier. To be cut off within the heart of Federation space, in the Vulcan home system itself, was unthinkable. And in this time of crisis—unacceptable.

Picard concentrated on controlling his voice. Anger had no useful role to play in what was happening. He *had* to arrange a full planetary search for a hidden Symmetrist base. And only Starfleet Command could give him the necessary influence to persuade Vulcan civilian authorities to allow such an unprecedented intrusion into the planet's security. "Will, with everything you're reporting, is there a Starfleet presence in the Vulcan system at all?"

Riker hesitated, as if recognizing the absurdity of his captain's question. His reply was cautious, but definitive. "Sir, as far as I can tell, all starbase facilities in the Vulcan system are intact and operational, staffed by skeleton crews of support and administrative personnel who have not been transferred to relief duty. But, if you mean, is there a Starfleet *command* presence here . . . sir, I'd have to say, no. Except, perhaps, for the *Enterprise,* and you."

For a moment, Picard was overwhelmed by a feeling of being completely powerless. He couldn't help thinking that if he were not confined to the *Galileo,* if he were only back in his command chair, that he could seize full control of the situation.

But control required information.

He and his ship were but tools of the Federation. They had

duties to perform, capabilities to unleash. Yet, without direction, without consensus, even the *Enterprise* could be rendered as ineffectual as if it had been hit by a quantum mine with all shields down.

The situation was intolerable.

And Picard would not—*could* not—allow it to continue.

With deliberation, he slowly sat back in his flight chair. Beverly now stood at his side.

"Commander Riker, in light of the extraordinary circumstances surrounding our presence in Vulcan space—specifically, my belief that the virogen plague is a deliberate attack on the Federation, an attack that has already crippled our lines of communication and supply—I am, under Starfleet Wartime Regulations, initiating a Code One alert."

Picard could see that Riker understood the seriousness of his decision, but the first officer showed no sign of protest.

Cut off from Command, the captain of the *Enterprise* had just issued a declaration of war.

Picard reached for his tea. "Have Rolk alert the commanders of the other Starfleet vessels standing by. I would like to have them gathered in the observation lounge within the hour, and I will brief them via viewscreen to coordinate our search of Vulcan. We'll need to contact senior members of the Vulcan government to attend as well, but their presence will be merely as observers. Stress that, Will. We will make the search as unobtrusive as possible, but we will be conducting it on a war footing."

"Aye, sir."

Picard was about to sign off, when he felt Beverly's hand on his shoulder.

"Excuse me, Captain," she said. "But if we really want to conduct high-resolution scans of Vulcan as quickly as possible, perhaps we should see about getting the *Tobias* released from impound and staffed with personnel from the other ships."

Picard didn't even have to think about the suggestion. As a science vessel, the *Tobias* would have permanently configured sensors that could be used at once.

"An excellent suggestion. Follow up on that as well, Number One."

Riker nodded. "At once, sir."

"I'll be standing by to talk to whichever Vulcan representative wishes to lodge the most serious protest to our presence here," Picard added.

At that, Riker finally smiled. "I'm certain there will be considerable competition for the honor." Then his image winked out.

Beverly sat in the second flight chair as Picard stretched back in his. He could see from the corner of his eye that she was watching him.

"Yes?" he said.

"For as long as I've known you, you've always shown respect for the system, the chain of command. I've watched you in crisis situations and seen someone who enjoys the interplay, the challenge of being part of a team."

Picard turned to face her. "Are you being a psychiatrist now, Doctor?"

Beverly smiled. "Off the record, if I didn't know better, seeing you right now, cut off from Command, with no support from Starfleet, the chain of command broken . . . I'd almost say you were enjoying yourself even more."

"Acting unilaterally can be rather exhilarating. And it certainly gets things done faster."

Beverly's smile faded. "What about acting correctly? Shouldn't that be the overriding concern?"

Picard understood what she meant, from both sides. But the key to survival was adaptability. It was a lesson he had learned only after years of unbending rigidity and devotion to rules and regulations written to serve an organization that might not exist in the next three months.

"Absolute certainty requires time, Beverly. That is a luxury we and the Federation no longer have."

She had no reply for him. Instead, she watched the tiny disk of Vulcan slowly rotate on the screen.

Picard decided to enjoy the silence. Once Riker made contact with Vulcan and the other vessels, he knew it wouldn't last.

He sipped his tea.

It was cold.

So, as he had so many other things in his life, he set it aside.

And waited for the Federation to fall.

TWENTY-EIGHT

─────────── ☆ ───────────

The problem was insoluble.

Kirk, Spock, and Srell, and Christine MacDonald, M'Benga, and Barc, were trapped in a thruster repair chamber on one side of the spacedock's cavernous cargo bay. The circular chamber was narrow, but stretched twenty meters above them—high enough for disassembling most impulse-thrusters, including the one that currently towered overhead on the central work platform.

Outside the chamber's half-open personnel doors lay the cargo bay, and the turbolift station at which Kirk and the others had arrived. The incessant thrumming that pulsed from the bay was a combination of noisily vibrating antigrav loaders, cargo containers slamming into each other and the deck, and the shouted commands of the stevedores.

A full half-kilometer distant was the bay's far wall, inset with several multilevel viewports. Through those viewports, Kirk could see the even larger expanse of the spacedock's enclosed docking area, where a handful of ships rested in webs of umbilical tunnels, and were serviced by darting maintenance shuttles.

The closest of those ships was the *Tobias*.

Which was where the problem lay.

Between the repair chamber and the far wall of the cargo bay, there were just too many customs patrol points, safety inspectors, and ID stations. The six escapees didn't have the slightest chance of reaching the airlock doors that led to the *Tobias's* umbilical. And even if they could make it that far, the two Vulcan security officers guarding the airlock were an effective last line of defense.

"We're done for," Barc growled. "There's no way through."

"There's a way through everything," Kirk said. "It's just another *Kobayashi Maru.*" Kirk knew the Academy still ran that supposedly unbeatable scenario for its students. He looked expectantly at Christine, waiting for her to argue with him. Then he'd be able to explain how he had defeated the test's no-win scenario, and enlighten her about looking at problems from a different perspective.

Christine carefully studied the layout of the bay outside. "Unfortunately, there're no computers to reprogram out there."

Kirk stared at Christine. "You know how to beat the *Kobayashi Maru?*" He had been the first cadet to do it—the first to ever win.

Christine shrugged. "Who doesn't? Figuring out new ways to change the parameters is the whole reason for the test. How else could anyone win?"

Kirk consoled himself by deciding he had blazed the path. But it appeared Christine might not need as much instruction as he had thought. He turned to the Tellarite engineer.

"Barc, you know how these docks are built. Are there any Jefferies tubes running under this chamber and the cargo bay deck?"

Barc nodded his understanding of what Kirk was after. "You're thinking we might tunnel our way out."

"It'd be a good start," Kirk said. "Provided we don't take a detour into hard vacuum."

Barc scratched at the fur around his snout, then glanced around the narrow chamber. "If I had a tricorder and an anaphasic jack for the floor plates . . ." He lumbered over to an equipment pod, still muttering to himself.

Christine caught Kirk's attention and pointed to a diagnostics display screen on a nearby section of the wall. "We might need a few other strategies to fall back on. According to the schedule up there, the next shift is due here in eight minutes."

Kirk felt a twinge of embarrassment. Christine had noticed a critical factor in the situation which he had overlooked. Quickly he glanced around, saw a row of storage lockers on the far wall. "Let's see if we can find some engineer coveralls. Maybe try a disguise." He led Christine and the others across the chamber to began the search.

"I still say we're better off talking to the Vulcans," M'Benga grumbled as she followed them around the thruster platform.

Srell dismissed her suggestion. "You are not being logical, Doctor."

M'Benga glared at the presumptuous Vulcan, but allowed him to explain himself without interruption.

"If we were to turn ourselves back in to the authorities, we would no longer be simply held for further disposition. Instead, they would deliver you and your crew to Starfleet security, and arrest Ambassador Spock and myself. Split up, our capability for action would be diminished. Additionally, we would undoubtedly be incarcerated at a greater distance from the *Tobias,* further limiting our ability to escape."

"That's where you're losing me," M'Benga said. "If we tell them the truth, it'll be clear we're not guilty of anything, and we won't have anything to escape from. Logic your way out of that one." M'Benga looked pleased with herself for having set a logical trap for her maddeningly self-assured adversary.

Kirk and Spock exchanged a glance as they arrived at the

lockers. Kirk knew the answer, but he was curious to see how well Spock's young protégé could handle himself.

"Consider the reasons which have brought the ambassador and me to Vulcan," Srell began. "We are searching for a sophisticated, likely criminal organization, which apparently is capable of infiltrating the Vulcan diplomatic corps and murdering our planet's most revered statesmen. Our search took us to another elder Vulcan who might have shed light on the circumstances of Sarek's death. Yet at the very time we visited Tarok, assassins struck and he also died. I submit that those responsible for Sarek's death therefore might also be capable of intercepting private communications and of infiltrating other Vulcan organizations. That would explain how our presence at Tarok's estate was known, as well as the relatively early arrival of the peacekeeping forces who took our forensics team into custody."

As Kirk and Spock began searching through the first pair of lockers, Kirk listened nostalgically for M'Benga's response. The doctor and the Vulcan were bringing back memories of another unlikely pairing of friends, and he wondered what the future held for these two young adversaries.

M'Benga and Srell continued their debate as they searched through a second pair of lockers. Beside them, Christine searched a third set.

"All right," M'Benga said, "I'll grant that covers you and the ambassador, but what about Commander MacDonald and the crew of the *Tobias?* We're not involved with you or your search."

"My good doctor, may I remind you that whatever brought you to Vulcan also had the misfortune of bringing you to Tarok's estate at the time of the assassins' attack."

M'Benga's eyes narrowed. "I wouldn't exactly call it misfortune. If it weren't for Jim and Christine and Barc and me, the assassins would've won."

In the first locker, Kirk had found nothing but old tools, a few water bottles, and a pair of scanner goggles. He looked up at the diagnostic display. Six minutes to shift change. In the few minutes left to them, he needed everyone working on a way out of the chamber, but Srell might be onto something.

"Mr. Srell raises an interesting point," Kirk said. "The crew of the *Tobias* came to Vulcan for virtually the same reason. We're also looking for a sophisticated, definitely criminal organization of Vulcans—one able to intercept Starfleet communications. Only the crime is different. The group we're after might be responsible for murdering millions, if not billions, of people by releasing the virogen."

From the next locker, Spock looked over at Kirk. "At Tarok's estate, you said you were looking for me."

Kirk shut the door of the locker he'd been searching. Still nothing that could be a disguise. "Who better to investigate a Vulcan terrorist group? You mention the possibility to most people, and all they'll say is that Vulcan terrorists *can't* exist."

"They cannot," Srell said.

"Yet, here we are," Kirk pointed out, "all talking about Vulcan murderers and criminals as if they're as common here as everywhere else."

M'Benga looked thoughtful. "You don't suppose we're looking for the same people, do you? I mean, it's pretty remarkable to be thinking there's even one group of Vulcans that's capable of murder. But *two* groups? The odds would have to be pretty low."

Kirk glanced at Spock, but it was Srell who gave the inevitable response. "I believe the odds would be roughly on the order of . . . 10,126,582,300 to one."

"'Roughly'?" M'Benga asked with a hint of contempt.

Kirk saw Srell stiffen, as if he didn't realize the doctor was leading him on. "The calculation is based on the total number of Vulcans who have lived on the planet since the Reformation, and assumes that any effective terrorist organization would require a minimum of ten individuals. I thereby calculated the odds that any twenty Vulcans at random from the total population would happen to be alive in the current generation, and divided by the number of Vulcans who, since Reformation, are known to have engaged in terrorist acts. Given the understandable ambiguity surrounding population figures for the first few hundred years following the establishment of Surak's peace, I do not believe I am off by more than a factor of two. Hence, the modifying descriptor, 'roughly.' "

"Are you saying that Vulcans *have* been known to participate in terrorist acts in the past?" Kirk asked his question before M'Benga could torture Srell with another provocative remark. The math didn't interest Kirk. Srell's startling revelation did. For the moment, the search of the lockers and the impending arrival of the next shift of workers could wait.

Srell looked pained, as if he had just given away a planetary secret. "Not counting those individuals whose violently antisocial actions resulted from alien mind-control, disease, or physical injury to the brain, a total of three hundred and twelve Vulcans are known to have committed terrorist acts in the past millennium."

Kirk looked at Spock for confirmation. "That is correct," Spock said.

Kirk was astounded. He had assumed that the Vulcans they were looking for were modern aberrations, perhaps unduly influenced by alien upbringing on a Vulcan colony world. Yet now it appeared that Vulcan actually might have a history of such criminal behavior. In all their many discussions of Vulcan, Spock had never admitted to Kirk that his planet had had such problems. But then, after the incident with Balok and the *Fesarius,* Spock had become quite skillful at poker.

"What could possibly make a Vulcan think it was logical to commit an act of terrorism?" Kirk asked.

Christine pointed to the display again. "Four minutes," she warned.

But Srell did not make use of her warning as a way to avoid

answering. Especially when Spock nodded at him, as if to say the teacher condoned the student's report of hidden knowledge. "Terrorist acts on Vulcan have been rare, generally limited to expressions of extreme political theory and, in the past, to sporadic attempts to return to the violent philosophies that ruled our world in the days before Surak."

Kirk could see a possible connection forming. "If the terrorism came out of politics, then that implies it was organized, correct?"

"It does," Srell conceded.

Kirk could tell that even with Spock's approval, the young Vulcan was uncomfortable to be discussing what must be, for him, an embarrassing facet of Vulcan history.

"Is there a chance," Kirk persisted, "that any of those political terrorist groups might exist in some form today?"

Srell fumbled for an answer. "Within reason, anything is possible. That is to say . . . any number of political groups . . . but if they are secret . . ."

"Good Lord," M'Benga said. "Just spit it out. Yes or no?"

"Yes," Srell said, clearly displeased.

Kirk gestured for the young Vulcan to hurry. "What groups? Their goals? Who are the most logical ones to remain active today?"

Srell glanced up at the distant ceiling of the thruster chamber. "The Adepts of T'Pel," he began, as if reading from a hidden list. "They are a guild of assassins dating from the time of Surak. Some say they continue their secret traditions among the Romulans today."

Kirk quickly looked to Spock. "What about it, Spock? Could there be a Romulan connection to all this?"

"I am doubtful. The majority of Romulans know that a strong Federation is necessary to keep the Klingon Empire in check. It is not in Romulan interests to destabilize the Federation, and certainly not with a biological weapon that could spread to their own planets."

Kirk looked back to Srell. "Who else?"

"The Kahrilites. A small group that fought for the independence of a southern district more than three centuries ago. They were given independence and the movement quickly died." Before Kirk could prompt him, Srell continued. "The Followers of the Cupric Band. Their mistaken logic led them to reject the concept that intelligence is possible in beings with non-copper-based blood. They were active at the time Vulcan's first contact protocols were formulated."

Kirk could see Spock's interest was piqued by that. "What is it, Spock?"

"In his holographic confession, Ki Mendrossen said he reported on my father's activities regarding the redrafting of Starfleet's first contact protocols. But as one of one hundred and fifty Federation member worlds, the question of first contact as it applies to Vulcan is moot. We are a fully interplanetary society. The Cupric Band is not applicable to this situation."

"The Binaries," Srell continued. "Opposed the introduction of duotronic computer circuitry. The Traxton Compound. They follow a school of logic that does not focus on Surak, believing the concentration on the individual to be in conflict with the attainment of *Kolinahr*. The Central Source. Aggressive opposition to financial policy and the abolition of money as a means of exchange." Srell paused, then unfolded his hands, ending his recitation. "In addition, a handful of other violent individuals acted on their own for reasons best described as politically unsound. To the best of my knowledge, that is the extent of terrorism on Vulcan."

Kirk felt his excitement fade as he realized his first guess must be closer to the truth; that the Vulcans who might be involved in the spread of the virogen were a relatively recent group, diverted from peaceful Vulcan ways because of alien influences. But Spock's next statement changed all that.

"Srell," Spock said, "you did not mention the Symmetrists."

Srell seemed unperturbed by the omission. "They were not politically motivated. And whatever acts of terrorism they are alleged to have committed, historians disagree as to the extent to which Vulcan Symmetrists were responsible for the actions of non-Vulcans."

As long as there was a single pathway to explore, Kirk was not ready to abandon a possible connection to an existing group. He checked the display again. They were almost out of time. But he had to know. "Tell me about the Symmetrists," he said to Spock.

Spock kept his gaze on Srell. "More than two centuries ago, they began as a group of noted scientists concerned about the ecological ramifications of the newly formed Federation's plans for exploring other worlds."

"They were environmentalists," Srell said. "Not political activists."

Kirk noted, with interest, the difference of opinion between Spock and his student.

"An interesting distinction," Spock said. "But the environmental issues they addressed were defined by the political process."

Christine raised her hands. "This is all very fascinating, but we've got precisely two minutes to come up with something here."

M'Benga looked back at the personnel doors. "Can't we seal those doors? Buy us some more time?"

Kirk and Christine both spoke at the same time.

"They'd just transport in a repair crew . . ." Kirk began.

"Not with so many transporters in this . . ." Christine said.

Kirk and Christine looked at each other, sharing a single thought. Then they looked up at the thruster assembly towering above them. It was far too large to have entered the chamber through the personnel doors.

And the doors were the only way in or out of the chamber. "Barc!" they both shouted.

The Tellarite looked out from behind the central platform with an answering growl.

"The platform!" Christine called out.

"It's a cargo transporter pad!" Kirk added.

Barc almost danced as he waved everyone over.

They ran to climb up on the platform as the Tellarite scurried to find the transporter controls.

But Kirk hadn't forgotten what had brought them this far, nor how much farther they still had to go.

"Quickly, Srell—what acts of violence did the Symmetrists commit?" he asked as he and his team reached the platform.

"Please bear in mind that at one time, they were respected scientists," Srell said as he looked for a handhold to begin climbing. Kirk marveled again at the Vulcan's emotional control, even in times of crisis. His own heart was pounding, but Srell revealed no concern. "Only later did off-planet factions take up violence in the Symmetrists' name. And the subsequent public outcry led to the cause being abandoned on Vulcan."

Kirk felt electricity shoot through him. "The 'cause,'" he repeated. "Spock—*what* did the Symmetrists do?"

Kirk could see that Spock sensed his excitement, though he couldn't know what fueled it.

Spock pulled himself up onto the platform beside the thruster, and reached down to help M'Benga complete the climb. "If memory serves, the Symmetrists would board colony ships and take hostages in order to 'save' pristine planets from ecological contamination. They poisoned water sources and food supplies to force colonies to relocate. They—"

Kirk jumped up beside Spock on the platform. "Kodos!" he said.

Srell stared at him blankly. Spock seemed intrigued.

"Kodos the Executioner? Of Tarsus Four?" Christine asked as she climbed up behind the others.

"Tarsus?" M'Benga added. "That was one of the first systems hit by the virogen."

"When Kodos was governor, the colony's grain supply was infected with . . . a fungus," Kirk said, overwhelmed by the memory of what he had seen when little more than a child. "He butchered four thousand colonists. A lesson, Mr. Spock?"

"It is an intriguing hypothesis. Subsequent to Kodos's death on the *Enterprise,* I researched the events at Tarsus Four. No cause for the fungal infection was ever found, thus sabotage could not be ruled out. As policy, emergency food supplies were maintained only to support the colony for a three-week period, which was the normal shipping time from the closest port worlds. However, at the time the colony's grain stores were infected, the Romulans constructed several outposts at the outer boundaries of the Neutral Zone. Fearing a new outbreak of hostilities, Starfleet closed all shipping lanes. Resupply of Tarsus Four was impossible, and only an unsanctioned relief mission undertaken by ships of the Earth Forces managed to avert the total loss of all colonists."

Kirk looked at Spock closely. "Earth Forces? Weren't the Vulcans involved in the rescue mission?"

Spock thought a moment, then shook his head. "There was no mention of Vulcan involvement in the records."

Kirk frowned. "That's odd. I thought I remembered . . ."

But Kirk's memories were cut short as a blue light abruptly began to flash in the thruster chamber, accompanied by the echoing of buzzers from the cargo bay beyond the doors.

"Is that a prisoner alert?" M'Benga asked with sudden worry.

But Barc flailed up onto the platform beside the others, an engineer's remote-control padd in one hand. "It's the shift change," the Tellarite grunted. "We've got sixty seconds."

Kirk eyed him. *"Is* this a transporter pad?"

Barc's tiny black eyes sparkled. *"Rrrr,* that it is." He held up the padd. "And I've set it for a one-minute delay to give me time to get up here with the rest of you."

M'Benga gave the Tellarite an inquiring look. "You *are* sending us to the *Tobias,* right?"

Barc bared his teeth. "No, Doctor, I'm beaming us back to the magistrate's office. What do you think?"

"It's a cargo transporter," M'Benga said. "And we're not cargo."

The Tellarite smiled. "If that's what you're worried about, let's just say I've made a few small adjustments to the resolution buffers."

M'Benga seemed relieved. They waited.

Christine stepped closer to Kirk. "Are you thinking Kodos was a Symmetrist? And that what happened on Tarsus Four was just . . . a trial run for what's happening across the Federation? I mean, Bones is right—that world was the first to collapse because of the virogen."

Kirk wanted to answer, but there was a memory just beyond the reach of his consciousness. Why was he so certain that Vulcans had been part of the relief mission to the colony?

"Jim was at Tarsus Four during the crisis," Spock explained. "He was one of nine eyewitnesses to the first wave of executions by the governor."

Christine put a hand on his shoulder, misunderstanding the reason for his concern. "Jim, I'm sorry. Was your family . . . ?"

Kirk brushed her question aside. "They were on Earth. My mother was, at least. My father was on his ship. Spock, it was something Kodos said."

"His notorious address to the colonists he selected for execution?"

As if he were a boy of thirteen again, Kirk heard that harsh voice in his mind. He spoke aloud the words he could never forget. "'The revolution is successful . . . but survival depends on drastic measures. . . .'"

Spock broke in. "Of course—Mendrossen referred to the revolution in his confession. 'For the good of the cause, for the revolution,' he said."

Kirk pounded a fist into his hand. "Spock! That's it! It wasn't what Kodos said on Tarsus Four—it was what he said to *me* on the *Enterprise!*"

M'Benga looked nervously around. "Didn't Barc say we were on a sixty-second delay?"

"That I did," Barc confirmed. He held up his padd. The time display on it counted down the last five seconds.

Across the chamber, the personnel doors slid open and the voices of the arriving crew of technicians became clear over the din of the cargo bay.

"You *spoke* with Kodos?" Christine asked Kirk.

Kirk heard the initiating hum of the transporter circuits start up. He took Christine's hand.

"It'll have to wait," he said as the first glimmer of golden light began to shimmer around them.

But even as Kirk vanished in the transporter beam, he knew he had found the answer to what had happened.

All that remained was to prove it.

TWENTY-NINE

─────────── ☆ ───────────

"You will forgive me, Captain Picard, if my logic is uncertain, but you have apparently had Starfleet declare war against Vulcan."

At any other time, Riker would have laughed. But the tension in the observation lounge was at a dangerous level.

He and Data shared the table with eight starship commanders and three representatives from the Vulcan planetary government. Each of the Vulcans was more than a century old, their robes resplendent with the polished gemstones of their office.

Solok, the most senior of the three, steepled his fingers as he fixed his green eyes on the virtual viewscreen on the far wall. The observation-lounge lights gleamed from his hairless, black scalp. He was framed by the crimson mass of Vulcan that filled the observation ports behind him. Somewhere over the equator, storm clouds flashed with hidden lightning.

From the viewscreen, Picard returned the Vulcan's patient stare. "With respect, Representative Solok, the time for debate is at a later date. I have merely invoked a condition of war. I have not stated who our enemy is."

Solok tapped two fingers together. "Captain, you have

issued a Code One alert. It is a declaration of war. You then inform the Vulcan government that a fleet of nine Starfleet vessels will englobe our world and subject it to a full-spectrum sensor sweep at maximum power and resolution, with the intent of locating the base from which your 'enemy' is thought to operate."

Beside Solok, Representative T'Pring continued the statement. Her stark white hair was cut short to reveal her dramatic ears, accentuating her sharp features. "Your search of Vulcan under these conditions is a violation of our sovereignty, will interfere in numerous scientific and industrial endeavors, will reveal the nature of Vulcan planetary defenses in a way that third parties might exploit, and cannot logically be expected to yield positive results."

The third representative, Stonn, concluded the statement of the Vulcans' position. Riker had escorted Stonn and T'Pring from the transporter room, and had learned they were husband and wife.

"Captain Picard," Stonn said, "all other matters of sovereignty and interplanetary law and treaty aside, the fact remains that you believe the enemy you seek is on Vulcan. Therefore, the enemy is Vulcan. Therefore, you have declared war on Vulcan."

Solok delivered the summation. "The situation is unsatisfactory. Permission to search our world in this manner is denied."

All eyes turned to the viewscreen and Picard's response.

"I agree," Picard said, and Riker could tell how the captain struggled to maintain a reasonable tone. They had expected reticence on the part of the Vulcan government, but not outright refusal. "The situation is *most* unsatisfactory. But it is your position that is without logic."

Riker checked. None of the Vulcans reacted. But the Starfleet commanders were fully on Picard's side.

AVENGER

"We are facing the gravest threat our worlds have ever known. You have seen the figures provided by my chief medical officer. The lifetime of the United Federation of Planets can be measured in *days* unless a cure to the virogen is found. Does not logic demand that every means must be undertaken in order to find that cure?"

Solok carefully folded his hands in his lap. "Your tales of the long-forgotten Symmetrists are sheer speculation, not logic. It is impossible to conceive of a group so clever, and so secretive, that they could operate on Vulcan without attracting the scrutiny of our peacekeepers."

"We submit," T'Pring continued, "that you have access to information which you are not sharing with us. That suggests that you have an ulterior motive for your desire to subject Vulcan to such an unwarranted intrusion of its fundamental rights as an independent world."

"And that," Stonn said, "suggests that for some reason, you have declared war on a sister member of the Federation. Either that or, as certain developments suggest, you and the ships you represent no longer speak for Starfleet, and have mutinied."

All the commanders began to protest at once, but Picard cut them off with an authoritative command for silence. This time when he spoke, he wasn't concerned with hiding his anger.

"I submit to you that your reluctance to participate in an operation that could save the Federation suggests that you are also in possession of information that you wish to keep secret."

Solok's steely gaze did not waver. Yet Riker noted that Solok avoided directly looking at Picard. "To use an Earth term, Captain, that statement is preposterous. And unless you can provide some evidence to support your incautious accusations, this meeting will end and you and your vessels will be served formal notice to quit our system."

261

Solok, T'Pring, and Stonn exchanged quick glances, then rose as one, their decision made.

"I know who the Symmetrist leader was," Picard said.

That stopped the Vulcans.

"Was?" Solok asked. He still looked away from the view-screen, as if Picard still offered nothing of interest or importance.

"He died five years ago. But given his renowned abilities and accomplishments, his role as leader could explain the ability of a secret organization to exist on Vulcan without detection."

Solok smoothed his robes. "You are prepared to share the name of this 'leader' with us?"

"Ambassador Sarek."

Everyone except the Vulcans reacted with stunned silence. But even Riker could see the effect that name had on them.

Solok finally stared at Picard. "Sarek . . . of ShirKahr?"

"Yes," Picard said.

Solok raised a hairless eyebrow as he considered that information.

Riker saw Stonn and T'Pring lean close to each other so that T'Pring could whisper in Stonn's ear.

"Did you know the ambassador?" Riker asked, hoping to break up their private conversation.

T'Pring addressed Riker as a queen might address a commoner. "All on Vulcan knew Sarek. That he would be involved in the Symmetrist cause is . . . absurd."

"Do you have evidence to support this accusation?" Solok asked.

Picard touched his temple. "I have the evidence of what I learned in a mindmeld on Alta Vista Three. I invite you to meld with me, and know I speak the truth."

Stonn pushed his chair back, ready to depart. "You would have us expose ourselves to the virogen based on your improbable theory?"

Beside Picard, Dr. Crusher spoke. "Representative Stonn, Starfleet continues to make progress on a treatment for animal exposure to the virogen. If you, or some other member of your party, joined us in quarantine, I feel confident you would not be confined for more than a few weeks."

"Is that not a small enough price to pay for the truth?" Picard asked.

Solok hesitated, as if prepared to seriously consider the captain's argument. But T'Pring would have no part of it.

"It is also a clever pretense for a trap," she declared. Then she turned to Solok. "The Federation is in danger. Of that there can be no doubt. But surely part of the problem is Starfleet itself. Recent developments in our own system prove that Starfleet has already been destabilized. We cannot trust them, Solok. As long as we keep our world free of contamination, Vulcan can survive the collapse of the Federation. Therefore, it serves no logical purpose for us to sacrifice our world for a spurious argument from an emotional being."

Riker saw his captain reflexively straighten his tunic, as if getting ready to issue an ultimatum. He saw that this meeting was about to fall apart. He saw a way out.

"Representative Solok," Riker said, "what if Captain Picard is correct? Even if there is the smallest chance, is that not worth a few more minutes of your time?"

"To what purpose?" Solok asked.

"Let's find out about the mutiny on the *Tobias.*" Riker looked at T'Pring and Stonn. "That is what you're concerned about, isn't it? That whatever happened on that ship might be happening on the *Enterprise,* and on all the ships represented here?"

Before T'Pring could reply, Solok said, "That is a reasonable request. How do you propose to proceed?"

"The crew was called before a magistrate on one of your spacedocks. Let's contact that magistrate, review the crew's statements. Even interview the crew if we have to. Whatever it takes for you to be confident that we are not involved with them. Then we can arrange a mindmeld with Captain Picard."

Solok nodded gravely, and sat down. "Given the stakes, I will wait." He looked up at T'Pring and Stonn. Reluctantly, they sat as well.

On the viewscreen, Picard gave Riker a small nod of approval. Then Riker tapped his comm badge and put Rolk to work on the bridge, setting up a communications link to the civilian spacedock where the *Tobias* was impounded.

It took less than a minute. The virtual viewscreen shifted so that Picard and Beverly in the *Galileo* appeared on one side, and a stern female magistrate appeared on the other. She hid her reaction well, Riker knew, but the presence of Solok, T'Pring, and Stonn surprised her.

Riker got to the point at once. "Magistrate, we are most interested in learning more about your request that the crew of the *Tobias* be investigated for possible charges of mutiny."

The magistrate cleared her throat, as if she were not used to speaking with government representatives of the rank present here. "The *Tobias* is not where orders require it to be. Her commander could not give adequate explanation for her presence here. Three people are dead, perhaps because of actions taken by her crew. And in an alarming breach of all Federation policies, her crew may have exposed our world to the virogen."

This time, Riker noted, even the Vulcans at the table reacted.

"Did the commander of the vessel give an explanation for her actions?" Riker asked.

"She did not. The explanation given was that her ship was on a classified mission at Starfleet's behest."

Solok abruptly stood. "That is all I needed to hear." He glared at the viewscreen, and at Picard. "Are you satisfied,

Captain? A classified Starfleet mission to expose this world to the virogen? Your mutinous ruse has been penetrated."

Stonn and T'Pring rose beside Solok. Riker realized that all control had been lost. He had no idea how to reclaim it.

But apparently Data did. "Representative Solok, may I ask your patience for one final question of the magistrate?" the android asked.

Solok gave no answer, but he remained where he was, giving Data tacit approval.

Data addressed the viewscreen. "Magistrate, you stated that the ship's commander did not give an explanation for her actions, but that an explanation was given, nonetheless. May I ask who gave that explanation?"

The magistrate looked uncomfortable. "This is a delicate matter." She looked to Solok for guidance.

"It is also crucial," Solok replied. "We await your answer."

Riker looked at Data. His machine memory and attention to detail might have come through for them again.

"The explanation was given by Ambassador Spock," the magistrate said.

Riker saw Solok's grip on his robes tighten. "Spock, child of Sarek?"

"The same."

"Indeed," Solok said. "Is it possible you have a recording of Spock's statement?"

The magistrate seemed relieved to be excused from assuming further responsibility in relating what had happened. "I will play it for you at once, sir." She adjusted some controls out of scanner range; then her image was replaced by a log tape of her office.

Riker watched as the time and date codes slipped by in Vulcan script. Then, onscreen, two carved wooden doors in the office slid open, and a group of six people entered the magistrate's office, four in Starfleet uniforms, one of them a Tellarite.

Spock was unmistakable, his distinctive features known to half the Federation on sight. To one side was a young Vulcan civilian, to the other a Starfleet lieutenant. Though, Riker thought, the lieutenant seemed mature for what was a relatively junior—

"Sacre merde!" Picard sputtered. "Computer—freeze frame! Enhance grid section twelve!"

On the viewscreen, the image from the magistrate's office expanded into coarse pixels, then resolved into finer detail until the Starfleet officer beside Spock filled the screen.

An instant later, Riker felt the hair on his neck bristle as he saw what Picard saw.

That was no lieutenant.

It was James T. Kirk.

THIRTY

————————— ☆ —————————

With unerring accuracy, Barc had placed them on the bridge of the *Tobias*.

Seconds after the transporter effect had faded, Kirk watched as Christine spun around, quickly assessing the status of every station. He recognized the fire in her eye, the territorial gleam.

This was her ship.

"You did it again, Barcs," she said.

The Tellarite was already making his way to the engineering station. "I always do," he growled.

"Only one problem," Kirk said.

Christine nodded. More than half the bridge stations were dark. "We've been powered down and placed on umbilical supply from the spacedock."

"And any surge of power drawn through the umbilical is going to raise someone's suspicions," Kirk said.

"Therefore, we should disconnect the umbilical," Srell suggested.

"Which would also raise suspicions," Spock said. "And would leave us in the precarious position of powering up the vessel while a security team came to investigate."

Kirk looked around the circular bridge. The basic design had changed little, even from the days of his first five-year mission. But who knew what advances hid behind the sleek control surfaces? "How long will it take to get a ship like this up to full power?"

"With a full crew," Christine said, "we've drilled at one minute, eighteen seconds."

"And under present conditions?" Kirk asked.

Christine looked over at Barc. "What do you think, Barcs? We reset the main power buses throughout the ship manually, leaving the final connections isolated to the bridge controls, then we detach the umbilical and throw all the final switches at the same time from here?"

The Tellarite rubbed his thick fingers along his snout. "Maybe thirty minutes to set up the buses. But then no more than ten seconds to bring us up to full shields and impulse."

"How long to warp capability?" Kirk asked.

Barc checked the readouts on the engineering station, and huffed approval at what he read. "At least they had the good sense to keep the core on standby. I'll get you warp three minutes after we have power."

"Sounds good," Christine said. "Here's the breakdown—"

But before she could continue, Srell interrupted. "A question. Once we are powered up and have warp capability, where, exactly, do you propose to take us?"

Christine looked at Kirk and Spock.

"If you're right about the Symmetrists, where *do* we go?" she asked.

Kirk was surprised Spock didn't respond to Christine's question, as if he didn't have the answer. But only one answer was possible. He was sure of it. "You get this ship powered up. I'll get us where we need to go."

"Good enough for me," Christine said. If she was curious about their ultimate destination, she held whatever questions she might have in check. Kirk appreciated her professional acceptance of his command of the mission, if not of her ship.

Christine began to describe the sequence by which the *Tobias* would be brought to life. Barc would begin in engineering, with M'Benga helping Christine set the power conduits in the deflector and shield control rooms.

Since Srell had no experience with ships of any kind, he would remain on the bridge with Kirk and Spock. Kirk and Spock would watch the individual station boards as internal connections were set throughout the ship. They would be responsible for placing the bridge switches on standby, so they could be activated when the umbilical joining the *Tobias* to the spacedock was disconnected.

Then Christine, Barc, and M'Benga were gone, using the interdeck ladders instead of the turbolifts to avoid drawing noticeable amounts of power.

Kirk and Spock positioned themselves by the science vessel's engineering and deflector stations. Srell studied the blank main viewer. For now, all they could do was wait.

Kirk took advantage of the few moments of respite. He closed his eyes, rubbed the bridge of his nose, and again reached back into the past. Once more he was on the *Enterprise* of old, face-to-face with the acclaimed Shakespearean actor Anton Karidian, a man whose history began only where that of Kodos the Executioner ended.

When the supply ships had finally reached Tarsus IV, Governor Kodos had disappeared. A burned body had been found in a crashed orbital transfer shuttle, a body so badly charred that not even DNA analysis could be performed. But the craft had been Kodos's personal transport and the search for him was called off, the case closed.

Twenty years later, the Karidian Company of Players had come aboard the *Enterprise,* and Kirk had learned that the actor and the executioner were one and the same.

Kirk went to the actor's quarters to confront the monster from his past, not knowing if he were searching for justice as a starship captain, or vengeance as the victimized boy he had been on Tarsus IV.

But instead of a monster, Kirk had found a confused old man whose memory had grown dim. Kodos did not hide from his past, nor deny it. He was *tired* of it.

At the time, Kirk had been a young man, and could feel nothing but contempt for Kodos. The old man's point of view was beyond Kirk's understanding.

"Here you stand, a perfect symbol of our technical society," Kodos had said. "Mechanized, electronicized, and not very human."

Kirk had had no interest in an old man's demented ramblings, but the words had somehow stayed with him, and they came back to him now with surprising clarity.

"You've done away with humanity," Kodos had said accusingly, as if Kirk and not he were the guilty one, "the striving of man to achieve greatness through his own resources."

Full of himself, his mission, and his youth, Kirk had discounted Kodos and all that he was or believed.

"We've armed man with tools," Kirk had answered. "The striving for greatness continues."

Kirk paused in his recollection, rehearing his own words of so long ago, wondering how he had survived those early years, understanding so little of what life was about.

For part of what Kodos had told him was true. Kirk himself had said as much to Christine MacDonald when he had stepped aboard her ship at Chal—that her generation placed too much emphasis on the machinery of their lives, and not enough on the spirit; paid too much attention to the starship, not to the crew.

Kirk wondered if Christine saw him as he had seen Kodos: unable to comprehend, let alone meet, the challenges of modern life; no longer relevant; old.

He wondered if Kodos had seen him as he himself now saw Christine: a distant reflection of what he had been once: headstrong; talented, though unseasoned; young.

Was this cycle of the generations bound to continue forever?

Had Kirk come all this way in his life's journey only to discover the unthinkable—that the worst monster from his past, Kodos the *Executioner,* had in some cold-blooded way been *right?*

Uneasily, Kirk now remembered being on the bridge of the *Tobias* over Chal, ordering the destruction of the Orion fighters. Ordering their pilots to their deaths to prevent more deaths in the future.

Had *he* become Kodos?

"Are you well, Jim?"

Spock's concerned voice broke Kirk from his reverie. He quickly checked the engineering board. The status lights were still out. Barc had yet to complete his tasks.

"Sorry, Spock. I was just remembering."

"What Kodos said to you on the *Enterprise?"* Spock asked. It was what they had been discussing before they had been transported from the spacedock to the *Tobias.* Spock forgot little.

" 'I was a soldier in a cause,' " Kirk said, quoting what Kodos had said in his quarters more than a century ago. "There were things to be done. Terrible things."

Spock nodded, then turned to Srell. "After consideration, I concur with Jim. It is possible Kodos was a Symmetrist and what happened on Tarsus Four can be considered a model for what's happening throughout the Federation."

Kirk saw Srell's reaction to what Spock had said.

"Objections, Mr. Srell?" Kirk asked.

"Three," Srell said promptly. "First, the Symmetrists, at least those who embraced violence, were not reserved about claiming responsibility for their actions. Yet they made no claims about actions on Tarsus Four. Second, there was no Vulcan involvement in Tarsus Four. Third, though a case can be made that the colony's grain was exposed to a fungus in order to halt a colonization program, there is no support for the theory that today's spread of the virogen is a political action. The intelligent mind searches for patterns, Mr. Kirk, with the danger that patterns are often seen where the data do not support the conclusions."

"I beg to differ," Spock said, and Kirk could see something in Spock's face that told him his old friend was about to say something that he was reluctant to share, but felt obliged to state.

"If I am in error, I would be pleased to be corrected," Srell replied stiffly. Not even Kirk was convinced the young Vulcan meant what he said.

"My parents were Symmetrists."

Both Kirk and Srell stared at Spock in surprise.

"Sarek?" Kirk said. "A Symmetrist?"

"I learned of it only recently myself," Spock explained. "In my mindmeld with Tarok, just before his death."

"I must protest," Srell said. "Sarek's belief in nonviolence formed the core of his reputation and personal beliefs. Consider the source of your information, Ambassador—the confused recollections of a diseased mind."

An expression of concern came to Spock. "Do not misunderstand, Srell. My parents were not terrorists, and as Surak and logic demand, they denounced violence as a means to any end. But it does explain much about my childhood."

Kirk could see that Spock was now retreating into long-buried memory, just as he himself had done moments earlier.

"The conversations that would stop when I entered a room," Spock said. "My father's unexplained absences when he was not on diplomatic assignment. So many inconsequential yet perplexing occurrences are now so obvious. For quite legitimate reasons, Sarek and Amanda were members of an organization the galaxy abhorred because of acts of violence committed by others in the Symmetrists' name. It is quite a profound discovery to make about one's parents after so many years."

Kirk asked the necessary question. "Spock, do you think your father's tie to the Symmetrists could be the reason he was murdered?"

Spock considered the question for long moments. "Logic suggests—"

"Logic suggests *nothing,*" Srell interrupted. "How could you even conceive that someone like Sarek, whose every move and appointment were rigorously scheduled, could have the time to consort with criminals?"

Spock looked at Srell as if the young Vulcan were a misbehaving child. "Srell, I said my parents *were* Symmetrists. Quite clearly in Tarok's mind I saw that their group disbanded, long ago, when I was a youth, when they realized that their beliefs were being distorted and their influence misused."

Something about Spock's reference to his being a youth prompted Kirk to ask, "How long ago?"

"More than a century."

"I mean, how old were you?"

"In standard years, sixteen, I would suspect."

Kirk did the conversions from stardates. "That would make it . . . 2246."

Spock angled his head as he made the same connection. "Fascinating."

Srell folded his arms in a show of Vulcan impatience. "I fail to see the significance of the date."

"Twenty-two forty-six," Kirk said. "Spock was sixteen, I was thirteen. And Kodos was governor of Tarsus Four."

"And at about the same time, my parents withdrew from the Symmetrists."

Kirk took the chain of logic to its ultimate conclusion. "Because someone had used whatever information the Symmetrists had developed about ecological disaster to deliberately engineer the events at Tarsus Four."

Srell was as close to sputtering as a Vulcan could ever get in public. "Are you seriously suggesting that Ambassador Sarek was *responsible* for the events there?"

"Not directly," Kirk said. "But it seems clear he had some connection to them. A connection that led to him withdrawing from the Symmetrist cause after what happened. And a connection that might have led to his death in this age."

Srell confronted Spock. "Ambassador, are you going to let this . . . this human besmirch your father's name?"

"He has done no such thing," Spock said. "My friend has simply pointed out a series of logical connections between uncontested historical events. You would do well to reconsider your reluctance to accept that logic."

Srell reacted as if Spock had slapped him.

Then four power-supply panels lit up on the engineering board and Kirk knew the time for reflection and discussion had passed. Somewhere in engineering, Barc had manually reconnected all the power couplings, with the final break in the circuit routed to this board.

The theory was the same as in Kirk's cadet days, and he quickly touched the standby controls on the board. "That's impulse, environmental, gravity, and internal power," he said.

Spock was already pressing the controls on the deflector board, responding to what Christine and M'Benga were doing in their sections of the ship. "We now have navigation, shields, sensors, and deflectors on standby," Spock reported.

Kirk and Spock swiftly rotated to other dark stations, placing additional systems on standby as Christine, M'Benga, and Barc ran through the ship.

Fifteen minutes after they had left, the commander, doctor,

and engineer scrambled up the ladder in the emergency alcove off the bridge.

Christine was flushed, her blond curls stuck to her forehead, but there was no sign of exhaustion in her. Kirk recognized the cause of her excitement. When her ship came to life again, so would she.

She hurried to the ops console to check the ship's status, gratified by what she saw. "Barcs did it again. We took less than half the time he thought!"

Kirk glanced at the bulky Tellarite as he stepped up to the engineering board. "Or else he thought it would take fifteen minutes to begin with, and multiplied by two," Kirk said softly.

Barc glared at Kirk and drew back his lips in a subtle warning snarl.

Kirk smiled as he relinquished the engineering station to him. "Your secret's safe with me." Then he went to join Christine.

"All we have to do now is drop the umbilical," she said as the main viewscreen switched on, showing the forward view from the leading edge of the *Tobias's* command saucer.

On the screen, Kirk could see two viewports in the cargo bay wall. Beyond them, the cargo activity was unceasing, normal. More importantly, there was no sign of security forces conducting a search.

"Can't we just back out?" M'Benga asked as she stood at Kirk's side. "Why give them any warning?"

"We might rupture the airlock," Christine explained. "Too many people could get hurt."

"In my day," Kirk said, "most spacedock umbilicals had manual release locks with physical timers, so computer error couldn't cause an accidental disconnection."

"This spacedock was built in your day," Spock said dryly.

Kirk grinned. "Then we shouldn't have a problem disconnecting, should we, Spock?"

WILLIAM SHATNER

"I take it I have volunteered, again."

"Some things never change. Let's go."

As Kirk and Spock headed for the emergency ladder, Srell joined them.

Kirk stayed out of what he thought might become a confrontation between Sarek's devoted defender and Sarek's son. But Srell wasn't looking for conflict.

"Ambassador, I would like to do something concrete to assist us in our . . . escape," the young Vulcan said.

"Your help will be most appreciated," Spock replied.

Between Vulcans, that was all it took. Kirk saw that an apology had been made and accepted. He jumped onto the ladder, hooked his feet around the outer poles, and slid from the bridge.

Only when he had reached the first full deck and swung out to the corridor did he suddenly realize he wasn't on a *Constitution*-class ship. He had no idea where the umbilical airlock was.

Spock and Srell swung out from the alcove seconds later. Spock instantly grasped Kirk's dilemma. Ever discreet, he pointed helpfully down the corridor. "Starboard, outer corridor, section four."

"Thank you, Mr. Spock." Kirk began to run, the Vulcans keeping up beside him.

When they reached the airlock, it was open. It led to a circular umbilical tunnel that extended ten meters to a matching airlock that opened onto the cargo bay. Kirk was pleased to see that the inner doors there, the ones that opened directly onto the bay, were closed. Back in the impulse repair chamber, he had looked across the cargo bay and noted the two Vulcan guards posted at those doors. But as long as the airlock remained closed, he wouldn't have to deal with them.

Kirk led Srell to the edge of the *Tobias*'s airlock. "All we have to do is go through this tunnel, keeping low so no one can see us through the umbilical's viewports. When we get to

276

the cargo-bay airlock, you close the outer doors so the cargo bay will be sealed off behind both sets of doors, then run back here. Spock and I will set the timers on the manual releases and follow."

Srell nodded, but Kirk thought his eyes were a bit too wide.

"You do know how to close an airlock, don't you?"

"I have undergone basic safety training on transport ships."

"That is adequate," Spock said.

Spock's confidence was good enough for Kirk. He started along the umbilical tunnel, crouching low to avoid the small viewports that studded both sides every two meters.

At the cargo-bay airlock, Kirk and Spock positioned themselves at the manual release levers that physically clamped the umbilical collar to the airlock. Srell continued inside.

"Press the control, then run," Kirk reminded him. "You'll have . . ." He looked at Spock.

"Fifteen seconds," Spock said.

Srell nodded. He pressed the control.

And the inner doors began to open.

"Get out!" Kirk shouted as a small gust of wind blew through the tunnel and the atmospheric pressure between the cargo bay and the *Tobias* equalized.

He ran into the airlock just as the two Vulcan guards appeared between the still opening doors. A Vulcan green warning light flashed overhead to indicate the umbilical was open at both ends.

Kirk pushed Srell back as he hit the Close controls for both sets of doors.

A Vulcan guard grabbed him.

Kirk whirled around and kicked out, hard, connecting with the guard's chest, sending him into the airlock wall. Both sets of doors began sliding shut. Fifteen seconds left.

The second guard swung at Kirk. Kirk ducked. As he came up ready to swing back, the second guard's body was already crumpling to the floor, Spock's fingers pressing on the key nerve points in his shoulder.

"I'm sorry!" Srell said, revealing far too much emotion. "I activated the incorrect controls."

"Don't apologize!" Kirk told him. Ten seconds left. He pointed toward the tunnel. *"Move!"*

Kirk and Spock rushed through the half-closed doors to the umbilical. Eight seconds. But two meters into it, Kirk realized he couldn't hear Srell behind them.

Together, Kirk and Spock turned to see—

—Srell still in the airlock, in the grip of the first guard.

And the first guard had a phaser.

Small, green gleaming metal.

Ten centimeters from Srell's chest.

Five seconds.

"No!" Spock said.

He started forward.

Kirk grabbed Spock's arm, pulled him back. "Get to the ship!"

Srell looked out at them, the doors almost closed. Three seconds.

"I'm sorry!" he cried.

And then Srell grabbed at the phaser as if to push it away and the weapon discharged. A bolt of blue phased energy blasted Srell's chest. His eyes glowed. A gout of green blood burst from his mouth and he flew back from the guard's grip against the wall as—

Zero seconds. The airlock doors shut and sealed.

"Srelllll!" Spock's shocked cry sounded human.

"Spock, no! We have to get back! We've set the timers!"

Spock looked at Kirk in crazed despair. In all their years of friendship, Kirk had never seen Spock so disturbed, even when Spock had been in the violent throes of the *Plak-tow,* the Vulcan blood fever.

Kirk heard the hiss of the first umbilical collar releasing. He yanked Spock forward by his robe. "Run!"

But it was Kirk who did the running, dragging Spock who stumbled behind him.

Five meters from the *Tobias,* the second release hissed.

At three meters, the ship's umbilical detached.

At two meters, a hurricane blasted Kirk as the *Tobias* decompressed.

He nearly fell, sucked into vacuum.

Spock nearly tumbled back and out of his grip.

But Kirk had not come this far to fail.

He defied the raging wall of wind that tore at him. Step by step he leaned against it, pulling Spock with him until he could push his friend through the outer doors of the *Tobias's* airlock and stagger through himself.

He braced himself on the airlock frame and used every ounce of strength he had to lift his arm against the howling wind to press the airlock control.

He heard the pressure sirens wailing in the *Tobias,* almost inaudible above the raging storm.

But the doors began to close.

The wind diminished.

The umbilical tunnel deflated behind him and already he could see that the *Tobias* had begun to drift away from the cargo-bay wall.

Then the airlock door thunked shut and the rush of air ended.

And beneath the mad howl of the sirens, Kirk heard a sound he had never heard before.

Spock weeping.

Kirk drew his old friend near, knowing too well the burden of guilt Spock felt, but not comprehending how it had so thoroughly shattered his Vulcan training.

He slammed his hand against the airlock comm panel.

He was tired of death. Tired of the price that had to be paid.
He was beginning to understand what Kodos had felt.
What Kodos had meant about being *tired*.
And it frightened him.
"Kirk to bridge," he said. "Get us the hell out of here. . . ."

THIRTY-ONE

————————— ☆ —————————

There was pandemonium in the observation lounge of the *Enterprise*-E. Half the starship commanders were on their feet, arguing with each other or trying to get Picard's attention. But it was Representative Solok's resonant voice that rose above the confusion.

"That cannot possibly be *the* James T. Kirk."

Again Riker resisted the urge to laugh. "Oh, yes, it can be," he said.

It had been two years since Riker had last seen Kirk, a traveler out of time. Afterward, the Borg homeworld had been devastated; at Starbase 324, the engineers responsible for devising anti-Borg weaponry were now closing in on a new understanding of the secrets of the Borg transwarp drive; and an alarmingly unexpected alliance between the Borg and renegade Romulans had been totally defeated. All because of James T. Kirk, a man who had died twice. At least, twice that history knew of.

"It appears you were right, Number One," Picard said from the virtual viewscreen.

It took a moment for Riker to understand what his captain meant. Then he remembered: Two years ago on the bridge of a *Defiant*-class starship that had unofficially been christened the *Enterprise,* he'd watched a pyre of destruction erupt from the Borg homeworld. At the time, he'd been certain that the spectacular fountain of flame was Kirk's final, fitting memorial.

But beside him on that bridge, he also remembered seeing the expression on Ambassador Spock's face. It told him that Spock did not believe that Kirk was dead.

Riker had shared his observation with Picard. Somehow, the captain had understood what Riker could only suspect. The mindmeld Picard had undergone with both Kirk and Spock at the same time had left him with a deeper sense of Kirk's fate. Something to do with an echo of Kirk's mind that told Picard that Kirk had always known how he would die.

The Borg homeworld was not the time, and not the place.

"There are always possibilities," Picard had said.

"We both were right," Riker now told Picard. He raised his voice to be heard over the other conversations in the observation lounge. "Along with Ambassador Spock."

"Captain Picard, the government of Vulcan demands an explanation," Solok said.

"I wish I had one to give you," Picard answered. "But believe me, Representative, I have no more explanation for Kirk's presence on that ship than you have for Spock's." Picard reached down to touch a control out of the scanner's view. "Magistrate," he asked, "what is the disposition of the people you took into custody?"

On the viewscreen, the unlikely image of Kirk in Starfleet's latest uniform rippled away, to be replaced by the stern magistrate.

"Spock, his aide, and the crew of the *Tobias* were placed in detention cells awaiting Starfleet's response to this office's request for investigation."

Riker looked up at Picard and saw in his captain the same amused skepticism he felt himself.

"Magistrate," Riker asked, "how long ago did you place Kirk and Spock in detention?"

"Two point three hours."

Riker gave her a smile of commiseration. "Magistrate, if you check your detention cells, I believe you'll find you've had a breakout."

"Impossible."

Riker shrugged. "Not if history is to be our guide."

A green light suddenly began flashing beneath the magistrate's face. She looked down and Riker saw the unmistakable hallmark of Vulcan surprise—a slowly raised eyebrow.

Then Riker's comm badge chirped.

"Bridge to Commander Riker." It was Lieutenant Rolk.

"Riker here."

"Sir, we've received a distress call from a civilian spacedock. The impounded Starfleet vessel . . . it seems it's being stolen."

Riker kept his eyes fixed on Solok, trying with difficulty not to gloat. "I take it you're referring to the *Tobias?*"

"Aye, sir."

Riker addressed the senior representative. "That would be the ship on which Kirk and Spock arrived." He looked at the magistrate. *"Are* your prisoners in their cells, Magistrate?"

The magistrate folded her hands inside her robes and took on an air of unnatural calm. "We appear to have suffered a systems malfunction. That is the only explanation."

"Don't bet on it," Riker said softly. "Captain Picard, should we intercept the *Tobias?*"

"Take us to the spacedock, Number One, and have Rolk open communications."

Riker got up and gestured to Data. "Mr. Data, please take over."

Data glanced around the observation deck. Noisy confusion still reigned. "Of course, sir. But take over what?"

"You'll think of something." Then Riker hurried out to the

bridge. Behind him, above the excited babble, he was glad to hear Representative Solok's sonorous voice cut off in midsentence as the observation lounge doors slid shut.

"Helm, take us to the spacedock," Riker said as he took the center chair. He touched a comm switch on its arm. "Counselor Troi, Commander La Forge, to the bridge."

On the main screen, the scarlet arc of Vulcan rolled beneath them as the *Enterprise* changed orbits. By the time the turbolift doors opened and Troi and La Forge arrived, the impressive, elongated mushroom shape of the spacedock was already coming into view.

"Where is the *Tobias?*" Riker asked.

Behind him, at the security station, Rolk said, "Still within the main enclosure, sir. Traffic control reports spacedock doors are closed and locked."

"Not for long," Riker said.

Deanna Troi slipped into the chair to Riker's left. "Are we transferring crew to the *Tobias* for the search?" she asked.

"The *Tobias* already has a crew." Riker watched for Troi's reaction to what he said next. "It includes Ambassador Spock and James T. Kirk."

Her mouth opened in shock. "Will . . . you're joking. Aren't you?"

"You should have seen the look on the Vulcan representatives' faces when they saw him."

La Forge stood beside Riker, watching the spacedock grow on the screen. "Kirk and Spock back together? Now, this I've got to see." Then he looked down at Riker. "But you didn't call me up here to watch, did you?"

Riker shook his head. "This is the situation. Almost three hours ago, Kirk, Spock, a Vulcan aide, and three members of the *Tobias*'s crew were placed in detention cells. They've escaped—"

"That's a surprise," La Forge joked.

"—reclaimed their ship," Riker continued, "and are now attempting to leave the spacedock."

"Do we have any idea what they're after?" Troi asked.

"That's what the captain would like us to find out." Riker shifted in his chair to look behind him. "Rolk, put the captain on the corner of the screen, and keep feeding our main sensor view to the *Galileo.*" He turned back to La Forge. "Geordi, the spacedock doors are closed, but I have no doubt that Kirk will get the *Tobias* out. When she's clear, I want you ready to stop her with absolutely minimal damage."

"You've got it, Commander." La Forge moved forward to replace the ensign filling in for Data at ops.

On the screen, the visual feed from the *Galileo* appeared in the upper right-hand corner. Both Picard and Beverly were there.

"I trust you've reached the same conclusion I have?" Picard asked Riker.

"Sarek was the leader of the Symmetrists, and Sarek's son is now present on Vulcan under unusual circumstances," Riker said. "I'd say that's *four* mysteries to deal with, which means they're all connected."

"The only wild card is Kirk," Picard agreed. "But if he's involved with Spock, I'm certain he can only be a benefit to what we must do."

Beside Riker, Troi leaned forward. "Captain, I think we should remember that the last time we encountered Kirk, he was infused with Borg nanites. There's no way to predict what his condition is today."

Suddenly, the bridge was sharply illuminated by a web of flickering energy discharges arcing from a section of the spacedock's outer hull. As the discharge faded, Riker saw two massive doors begin to slide open.

"Stand by, Mr. La Forge. I believe Kirk is right on schedule."

Rolk cleared her throat behind Riker. "Sir, spacedock is reporting a power surge in all their computer controls. The doors are opening in response to an outside signal."

"I'll bet they are," Riker said. "Helm, head in to block the *Tobias,* hold at five hundred meters and dip our bow. I'd like the people on that ship to know who they're dealing with."

On the viewscreen, the *Tobias* eased out from the spacedock doors, probably at the exact instant the doors were open wide enough to allow her to pass, Riker guessed. If Kirk was known for anything, it was his timing. Then the image of the small science vessel grew to fill the screen as the *Enterprise* moved into the path of the *Tobias.*

The observation lounge doors opened again. Riker was pleased to hear that the sounds of heated argument had diminished to a less-confrontational murmur. Riker saw Data leading the three Vulcan representatives to the side of the bridge. Then Data approached Riker.

"I am sorry," the android explained, "but the Vulcans are within their rights to insist on monitoring Starfleet activity in their system."

"That's all right," Riker said. "I guarantee they'll find this interesting."

"Commander," La Forge reported from ops, "the *Tobias's* warp core is powering up. She'll have warp in . . . ninety seconds."

Riker stood up from the center chair and faced the screen. "Open hailing frequencies, Lieutenant Rolk, and patch through the captain."

"Aye, sir," Rolk replied. "Going to visual."

Riker smiled with anticipation. He wished he were in a position to see the Vulcans' faces this time. Because, as the Vulcans might agree, Riker was certain the next ninety seconds should be . . . fascinating.

THIRTY-TWO

---------------------------- ☆ ----------------------------

Kirk and Spock stepped onto the bridge of the *Tobias* just as she cleared the spacedock doors.

Christine MacDonald was in the command chair, Barc at the helm, M'Benga at ops. Kirk supposed he should go to the engineering station, to make certain the warp-core power-up was proceeding correctly. But he didn't want to leave Spock. His friend looked dazed. The death of Srell clearly weighed heavily upon him.

Barc glanced back at Kirk. "I wouldn't have believed it, but that override command sequence worked," the Tellarite engineer said. "Once I updated it, of course."

"A little trick I learned from one of your colleagues," Kirk said. He helped Spock to a chair at one of the science stations.

"Ninety seconds to warp," Barc announced. "We could be using a heading sometime soon."

Kirk took a final concerned look at Spock, then went to the helm, just as a huge white disk swept up on the main screen.

A collision alert siren roared.

"Full shields!" Christine ordered. "All stop!"

Kirk grabbed the back of Barc's chair as the bridge lurched. Then he saw the name and number emblazoned on the disk.

287

"The *E?*" he said. "What's wrong? Has Starfleet run out of names?"

"It's the new one," Christine said from behind him. "The tradition continues."

Then the image of the *Enterprise* cut out, to be replaced by a familiar face.

"Jean-Luc," Kirk said with a wary grin, "what a surprise."

On the screen, Picard returned the smile, a bit too warmly. "Jim, a pleasure as always."

Kirk nudged Barc aside and slipped into the helm position. "I'd love to talk, but we are running late. I don't suppose you'd like to move out of our way?"

Kirk checked his board, saw the distance to the *Enterprise,* gave a nudge to the stationkeeping thrusters to give the *Tobias* just a few meters per second of relative forward motion.

"Talking sounds like a grand idea," Picard said. "Why don't you come aboard, and we can . . . catch up on old times?"

Kirk shot a quick glance toward M'Benga's ops board. A display of the *Enterprise'*s online defenses showed that her shields were set for low-risk orbital navigation, holding steady at ten meters from the hull. She was not expecting any trouble. Always a good sign for the other side.

The *Tobias* kept drifting forward.

"Jean-Luc, trust me. We don't have the time. The Federation doesn't have the time."

The ships were three hundred meters apart. Two ninety. Two eighty.

"I believe we can help you," Picard said.

Kirk saw with satisfaction that the *Enterprise* was now drifting back as well. The larger ship was taking measures to avoid collision, probably assuming that with only a handful of people on board, the *Tobias* was not under full control.

"Help us do what?"

Picard's polite smile vanished. Kirk saw that a line had been crossed. "You are not the only one who is running out of time. You are here because of events involving the Symmetrists. Yes? Or no?"

Kirk was aware of Spock moving to stand behind him. With the *Enterprise* backing off to match the *Tobias's* forward drift, the ships were holding at 285 meters separation.

"What do you know of the Symmetrists?" Spock asked.

Picard's expression became even more serious. "Ambassador Spock, I am truly sorry we meet again under these circumstances. I regret even more to inform you that in investigating the spread of the virogen, I am forced to conclude that its spread is the result of a deliberate attack on the Federation, and that your father was a part of the organization responsible. The Symmetrists."

Kirk felt Spock's hand tighten its grip on the back of his chair.

"That is true," Spock acknowledged. He sounded exhausted. Despairing.

Kirk could see that Picard was hesitant, as if uncertain how to deal with a Vulcan who appeared to be expressing his emotions. "Ambassador, please give careful consideration to what I am about to say. I believe the Symmetrists' base is hidden on Vulcan. I believe that at that base we will find a cure for the virogen. To find that cure, Starfleet must subject Vulcan to an intensive and intrusive sensor sweep. And to do so, we will need the permission of the Vulcan government. Three representatives of the government are on board the *Enterprise.* Will you talk to them? Will you help me do what must be done?"

Spock said nothing. Kirk checked the board. Warp power would be online in thirty more seconds.

"Put the representatives on," Kirk suggested.

Picard vanished. Three Vulcans appeared on what was

apparently the *Enterprise*'s bridge. Kirk recognized Commander Riker and Counselor Troi standing behind them. He took a closer look at the Vulcans. Two were familiar.

Spock raised his hand in the traditional greeting. "Peace and long life, Representative Solok."

The dark-skinned Vulcan returned the salute. "And to you, Ambassador."

But then Spock turned his attention to the other Vulcans. "Representative T'Pring, Representative Stonn, I bear unfortunate news."

T'Pring? Kirk thought. *Stonn?* No wonder the two Vulcans were familiar. The woman had been Spock's betrothed. Stonn had been her suitor. Kirk had almost been killed in hand-to-hand combat with Spock in the machinations that had surrounded T'Pring's new choice of husband.

"Your grandchild, Srell, has died."

Kirk half rose from the helm, then pushed himself back in position. Srell? The grandson of the woman who was to have been Spock's wife? Kirk had seen Spock treat the young Vulcan as if he were his own son. Was *that* the reason for Spock's unprecedented loss of self-control? Was Srell the son Spock felt he had never had?

Kirk suddenly thought of his own lost son, David. For all that Kirk and Spock had shared, Kirk now wished he could spare Spock the pain that would never lessen. Of a future never realized.

On the screen, both Stonn and T'Pring remained emotionless. "Do you carry his *katra?*" T'Pring asked.

"I do not," Spock said. He lowered his eyes. "His death was unanticipated."

"Regrettable," Stonn said.

That appeared to be the extent of the grandparents' mourning.

Kirk kept one eye on the screen as he entered a warp

heading for the *Tobias.* The new *Enterprise* was undoubtedly faster than Christine's ship. But if he timed his next maneuver properly, he was certain he could get an appreciable head start. And if Picard was convinced he would find the Symmetrists' base on Vulcan, then more power to him. But Kirk already knew where that base had to be, the only logical place it could be, and those were the coordinates he fed into the helm.

On the screen, Solok stepped in front of T'Pring and Stonn. Kirk noticed that in the background, Deanna Troi was whispering something into Riker's ear. Riker looked even more intent than usual, his attention fixed rigidly on Srell's grandparents.

"Ambassador," Solok said, "Captain Picard has made troubling charges in regard to your father. He uses them as justification for an unprecedented violation of Vulcan's security. Can such charges be true?"

"Regarding my father and the Symmetrists, yes," Spock said. "I believe it was for that very reason that my father was murdered."

Kirk saw the barely perceptible expression of shock on Solok's face. Stonn and T'Pring gave no reaction. But then, neither had they responded to the news of their grandson's death.

"Spock," Solok said, "that cannot be possible."

"If I had time, I could relate the logic of it. But it is true."

Solok licked his lips in what was almost a gesture of nervousness. "Is the rest of it true? Can the Symmetrists be found on Vulcan?"

"Some, undoubtedly," Spock said. "But not their base. And as for a cure for the virogen, of that I have no knowledge."

The bridge scene disappeared at once, to be replaced by Picard. Kirk suddenly wondered where exactly Picard was.

His surroundings looked more like a small flight deck than anything else. But for whatever reason, if Picard were removed from the center of the action, even longer delays in his response were likely.

"Ambassador," Picard said urgently. "Do you know where the Symmetrist base is? I guarantee you the cure will be found there!"

"Captain Picard, I know you are an honorable man." Kirk was surprised to hear Spock almost slur his words, as if overcome by a sudden exhaustion. "But the truth is, I can no longer trust the Federation. Not under present conditions."

Kirk saw the look of puzzled hesitation on Picard's face as he assessed Spock's condition. Kirk seized the advantage. The time was right.

He punched the forward impulse controls and the *Tobias* jumped forward.

Instantly, the main screen blazed with the energy discharge as the *Tobias*'s shields impinged on the *Enterprise*'s.

But Christine had ordered her ship's shields set to full power. The *Enterprise*'s were on low.

The physics of the situation were clear in any age.

David beat Goliath.

Kirk reached back to brace Spock as the *Tobias* pushed through the *Enterprise*'s navigational shields. Spock seemed disoriented and slipped from Kirk's grasp. Then the *Tobias*'s own shields made violent contact with the bare hull metal of the huge new ship, before rebounding away as the *Enterprise*'s shields finally responded automatically and cycled to full power. The impact sent shudders through the small science vessel, and Spock fell to the deck.

By then, the *Enterprise* was spiraling away from the *Tobias,* her crew obviously aware that any rapid response to correct her course might lead to a collision with the spacedock.

Onscreen, the stars, Vulcan, the *Enterprise,* and the space-dock spun rapidly around a central point as the small science vessel rolled. Adjusting for that could come later, Kirk knew. For now, he hit the warp controls and all other objects were gone in a heartbeat, replaced by the comforting passage of stars seen from warp.

As Kirk used the attitude controls to level the *Tobias's* orientation, M'Benga jumped up from her chair to attend to Spock.

"How are we doing, Mr. Barc?" Kirk asked.

"Warp five point eight and climbing," the Tellarite answered. "We'll get you nine point two and then some."

Kirk checked that M'Benga had Spock in hand, then faced Christine, who still sat in her command chair, little more than a passenger at the mercy of Kirk's maneuvers. She wore an expression that was equal parts bemused delight and apprehensive confusion.

"How fast is the new *Enterprise?"* Kirk asked.

"If she's still in one piece after that little trick, she's fast enough to catch us for breakfast."

Kirk checked the automated heading indicators. They were on course. He got up and went to Spock. "That's *if* Picard decides to chase us. He seems convinced that what he's looking for is on Vulcan."

"Let's get him to sickbay," M'Benga said as she took hold of Spock's arm and helped him up from the deck. Kirk took hold of his other arm and they guided him toward the turbolift.

Christine watched as the lift doors opened. "If the *Enterprise* were my ship and you did that to me, there's no way I'd be staying around Vulcan."

"But the *Enterprise* isn't your ship," Kirk said as he entered the lift with Spock and M'Benga. "She's Picard's. And he likes to look at the big picture." Kirk studied Spock.

The Vulcan hung his head as if unaware of his surroundings.

"Our job's to look after our own," Kirk said. "We won't be seeing Jean-Luc Picard anytime soon. Trust me."

"As if I have a choice," Christine said as the doors began to slide shut. "You haven't even told me where we're going."

Kirk looked again at his friend. "Would it make a difference?"

THIRTY-THREE

☆

As the collision alarms blared, Riker pushed himself up from the deck of the bridge and ran for the helm. "Geordi! Pursuit course! Maximum warp!"

But La Forge slammed his fist against the console in frustration. "No good, Commander! We've got physical damage to the forward saucer!" The engineer looked at Riker in amazement. "He actually *hit* us. *Through* the shields."

"Can't the structural integrity field compensate until we make repairs?" Riker asked.

"Sure, but we can't risk warp until we've done a visual inspection. We're stuck here for a couple of hours at least. He knew what he was doing, all right."

Riker threw his hands up in defeat. "He's had a hundred and forty years to practice," he complained.

Troi joined Riker at the helm. "Will, you were the one who was so positive he'd escape the spacedock."

"But from the *Enterprise?*"

Picard appeared on the screen again. "How are our passengers, Number One?"

The Vulcans were on their feet, apparently unperturbed by what had happened. Solok stepped forward.

295

"Captain Picard, in light of Ambassador Spock's confirmation of your charges linking his father to the Symmetrists, logic suggests we allow your request to search Vulcan."

"We are in agreement," Stonn added.

Picard seemed surprised by the Vulcans' acquiescence. "The emotional content of Spock's confirmation was not alarming to you?" Picard asked.

Solok looked noncommittal. "We have seen such behavior before, Captain. We prefer not to comment on it. If you could beam us to our assembly, we shall begin making preparations for your task."

Riker had Data escort the Vulcans to the transporter room. The individual Starfleet commanders still in the observation lounge had their own ships beam them directly from that part of the upper deck.

Ten minutes after the *Tobias*'s remarkable escape, Riker was reduced to sitting in the command chair, tapping his fingers, waiting for La Forge's damage-control team to certify the *Enterprise* for warp travel. The *Tobias,* whose last speed had been edging up to warp nine, was long gone from sensor range. Instead of a chase, it was now going to be a search.

Troi came over to Riker with a cup of replicator coffee. "Come into the observation lounge with me," she said.

"Are you going to show me the stars?" Riker asked.

"I believe I already have," Troi replied, then headed for the lounge.

When Riker and she entered, Picard and Beverly were back on the virtual viewscreen. Riker was still not used to dealing with the captain at such a remove.

"The counselor told me what she reported to you about the Vulcans' emotional response to Spock's revelations," Picard said.

Riker took a chair beside Troi and warmed his hands around the coffee cup. Troi's report had been little more than a whispered warning in his ear as the Vulcans and Spock had conversed by viewscreen.

"I just checked the records about that," Riker said. "There was another emotional dynamic at work. Spock used to be, I suppose the word is 'engaged,' to T'Pring. She chose Stonn, instead."

"No, there was something more present," Troi said. "I sensed no emotions relating to any previous entanglements between Spock, Stonn, and T'Pring. Instead, it was the absence of emotion I felt."

"They're Vulcans, Deanna. Of course there was an absence of emotion."

But Picard interrupted from the viewscreen. "No, Number One. That's too simple an explanation for what the counselor sensed."

"It was Solok who reacted emotionally to the news of Srell's death," Troi said. "On the surface, he showed nothing, but inside he experienced . . . sadness. Yet T'Pring and Stonn, they felt nothing, Will. And I sensed that same absence of feeling in Stron and his mate when the *Enterprise* confronted the *Bennett.* They were not afraid because they knew they had a way to escape us. And I propose that Stonn and T'Pring felt nothing about the death of their grandson because they do not believe he's dead."

"I don't know, Deanna. That's quite a leap."

"Go on, Counselor," Picard said.

"I sensed an even stronger emotional response from Solok when Ambassador Spock began . . . having difficulty speaking. Solok became alarmed, and again, very sad. But at the same time, Stonn and T'Pring seemed pleased that Spock appeared to be experiencing a problem. It was almost as if they were expecting it."

Riker took a sip of his coffee, giving himself a moment to think. "I think I see part of what you're getting at. You're suggesting that Stonn and T'Pring have information about Srell that Solok doesn't. And if they're not surprised by Spock's behavior, then perhaps . . ." He shook his head. "No. I don't see the connection. Especially since we have been given permission to search Vulcan."

"This is the connection," Beverly said.

Riker glanced up at the viewscreen and beside Picard, he saw the doctor holding up a medical padd.

"When Spock and the others from the *Tobias* were placed in detention, they were given blood tests to determine if they had been exposed to the virogen. Fortunately, the virogen tests came back negative, which means Vulcan has not been exposed, and neither has the spacedock. However, the magistrate was concerned by what she thought was Spock's overly emotional behavior at the hearing. She ordered additional tests."

"And . . . ?" Riker asked.

"Well, the only conclusive diagnostic test would be to culture tissue from his metathalamus, but Ambassador Spock's blood shows antibodies suggestive of the presence of Bendii Syndrome."

Riker went on alert. "That's the disease Sarek died of."

"Officially, yes," Picard said. "But remember what Spock told us. He said his father had been murdered because of his connection to the Symmetrists."

"Bendii is a disease of extreme old age," Riker said. "How can someone be murdered by it?"

"I'm not an expert on Vulcan medicine," Beverly answered, "but I presume that measures could be taken to introduce the pathogen directly into the victim's body."

"And in the case of Spock," Picard continued, "I think we have proof that that is exactly what happened."

"I don't understand," Riker said.

Beverly explained. "Bendii is very rare, and almost entirely limited to Vulcans over the age of two hundred. Spock is a hundred and forty-three years old. That either makes him the youngest Bendii sufferer in the entire history of Vulcan, or a potential murder victim, just like his father."

Riker stared across the table at the collection of earlier *Enterprise*s. He picked out the simple, geometrical lines of Kirk's ship. Spock's ship. Two of them, actually. The first, and the A.

"You're right. That's the connection," he said at last. "Stonn and T'Pring are Symmetrists. They're killing Spock, or they're at least aware of the attempt to kill him, for the same reason Sarek was killed."

"And," Picard concluded, "they no longer protest our proposed search of Vulcan."

Riker understood. They had been manipulated from the beginning. "Which means," he said, "that what we're looking for is obviously not on Vulcan, and they don't want us going off anywhere where we might find it."

"Precisely," Picard agreed. "And it is my order that we not reveal that conclusion to any member of the Vulcan government, or to any other member of Starfleet present in this system."

"You think the Symmetrists are that powerful?" Riker asked.

"If they have survived the centuries with the power to infiltrate the Vulcan government, to kill her most revered citizens in an indetectable manner, and to bring the Federation to its knees, I think they are more dangerous than any foe we have ever faced before."

Riker was having a hard time accepting the inescapable conclusion. As members of the Federation, Vulcans had been among its greatest and most valuable supporters. To now imagine them as enemies was to see the Federation dead.

"Kirk knows, doesn't he?" Riker asked, as he put the final pieces of the puzzle together. The final picture was appalling.

"I believe so," Picard said. "I believe he was the one

element that Vulcan logic could not predict. The Symmetrists conceived what they believed to be a perfect plan. Sarek's murder, committed without a hint of suspicion, is more than enough proof of their ability to make perfect plans that cover every eventuality."

"Except for one," Troi said.

Riker straightened his shoulders. Their next move was obvious. "Shall I lay in a pursuit course, sir?"

"Exactly, Number One. And contact Virogen Task Force Headquarters at Starbase Five-fifteen to let them know where we're going. We'll need a full medical support team when we arrive."

"Excuse me, sir," Troi asked, "but where are we going?"

"We follow Kirk," Picard said. "To the source."

THIRTY-FOUR

☆

Spock sat in silence in his quarters on the *Tobias*. He kept the lighting dim, the temperature Vulcan warm. At any other time in his life, he would have meditated.

But he could no longer see the point.

What was the sense of discovering inner peace when the universe tore itself apart in chaos all around him?

Too late he realized that chaos was the goal he should have sought. To fight the forces of existence with logic was to build a fortress of reeds. The storm did not care about aesthetics. Only about wiping the worlds clean.

Spock put a hand up to cover his eyes. He lowered his head. He wept.

For Sarek. For Srell.

And for himself.

In time, his door announcer chimed.

He looked up, unmindful of the tears that streaked his face. "Come," he said, not caring who was on the other side.

But it was Kirk.

He carried a tray of food, though Spock wasn't hungry.

Kirk seemed to sense that. He put the tray on a dresser at the side of the room, pulled up a chair, sat next to his friend.

"It wasn't your fault," Kirk said.

"Does it matter?"

"Sadness is one thing. Guilt is another. You have no cause to feel guilty."

Spock looked away. "I have no cause to feel anything. Yet I do. I always have. And I have never understood why."

"Spock . . ."

But Spock wasn't ready to listen.

"How much time have I wasted, Jim? I thought . . . I believed I had conquered this war inside me."

"It's not a war, Spock. You've told me yourself: It's a balance. Harmony. You found it once. Not the harshness of total logic. Not the . . . the madness of total emotion. But the blending of the two."

Spock looked at his friend with haunted eyes. "Have you found it? Can it ever be found?"

Kirk returned Spock's thoughtful gaze. Got up. Went to the tray of food. Returned with the black base of a commercial holoprojector.

Spock stared at it, bewildered. "Ki Mendrossen's confession?" As far as he knew, the holoprojector containing the message that had shattered his life was still on Vulcan. He had left it at his family villa.

"M'Benga found this in one of the onboard labs," Kirk explained. "When the peacekeepers at Tarok's estate took the forensics team into custody, they beamed everyone back to the *Tobias,* along with everything they'd collected. I suppose the authorities didn't want to move it again until they were certain it hadn't been contaminated."

Spock took the black base from Kirk, turned it over. It was the same model as the one that had contained Mendrossen's recording.

"The notation on this one said Srell collected it personally," Kirk added.

"I remember," Spock said. "I saw it in Tarok's sitting

room. It was on a table with . . . quite rare antiques. Objects of great value. It seemed out of place."

"Maybe not," Kirk said.

Spock didn't know what his friend meant. "You have seen it?"

"So should you."

Spock hefted the base in his hand, wondering if there was any reason he should ever care about anything again. There was nothing this projector could do to repair his past. Nothing it could do to restore his future. If he had the superhuman strength required, he would have been tempted to heave the base through the viewport and follow it gladly into the oblivion of space.

"Play it, Spock."

Spock sighed. He'd play it. If not for himself, then for his friend.

He placed the holoprojector on the low table beside him, and touched the switch.

A shaft of rose-colored light grew from its center.

Spock waited to see his father's image resolve from that light. It was the only logical explanation for Kirk's insistence that he watch the recording.

But Spock was wrong.

There was another explanation. One that had little to do with logic.

And everything to do with emotion.

The figure was Amanda.

Tears stung Spock's eyes, as once again he heard his mother speak.

"Oh, Spock," she said, her long-silent voice like magic to him, "I've waited so long to tell you this, and I know your father's right and that even after I've made this recording, it might be years before you hear it. But you must hear it. And I must say it. Because we . . . I . . . have not been honest with you.

"Just yesterday, you left for Starfleet Academy, to learn to sail the stars. How I envy you. How proud I am of you. And even your father, in his way, feels the same.

"Oh, I know you're not speaking. I know that you know why your father objects so forcefully to your joining Starfleet. And I know all about the Vulcan traditions between fathers and sons so I am not going to try to use this to bring you back together. That is something only the two of you can do.

"But there is one small part of your father's decision that you do not know. Something you have to know. And maybe it will help you understand.

"Spock, I know what's gone unspoken between you and Sarek. And I know that you especially feel that if only your father could touch your mind, he could feel what you feel, understand what you need and desire.

"And I know the Vulcan pride that keeps you from asking for that contact.

"Believe me, Spock, it is not Vulcan pride that keeps your father from offering you that joining of minds. He only wishes to protect you."

Spock looked at Kirk but Kirk pointed back to the glowing, radiant image of Amanda. She held her hands together, above her human heart, speaking to a son she didn't see, and now would never see again.

"Spock, I am going to give this recording to Uncle Tarok, and he will see that you get it . . . when he thinks that enough time has gone by." Spock understood the hesitation in his mother's voice. For some reason, she did not intend for him to hear her words until both she and Sarek were dead. "When you see this, go to Tarok. He will answer all the questions I know you'll have when you hear what I have to say."

Amanda placed her hands at her side, glanced down, as if preparing herself to make a confession, just like Ki Mendrossen. The light that formed her image sparkled through Spock's tear-misted vision.

"Years ago, when we were young, your father and I believed our worlds, Vulcan and Earth and all the other planets of the Federation, faced great danger. We were members of a group called the Symmetrists. And you must believe me when I say we intended no harm toward anyone. We only wished to gather information, to make others see the unifying symmetry of all things the way we did, and then use those insights to solve the problems we faced, together and in peace.

"But others, whose identities we do not know, took up our cause without our knowledge, and corrupted our ideals, committing hideous crimes in the name of our cause. And so we, and Tarok, and our friends have abandoned our organization.

"We have done nothing wrong, Spock. But the false Symmetrists have. And your father is fearful that if you meld with him, and see these secrets in his mind, then your duty as a Starfleet officer will force you to denounce him. And your own connection by birth to such a group could end the career that even your father knows means so much to you.

"Someday, I know he hopes to explain this to you himself. I know he longs to share his mind with you as his father did with him. But for now, he cannot. And for his sake, I ask for your understanding and forgiveness.

"I love you, Spock. And so does your father.

"Never forget that. Never."

Then, like the fading luster of a comet's tail, the rose-colored image from the past diminished, its light swallowed by the darkness of the room, and the years.

Kirk and Spock sat in the dim light and the silence together. There was no need for either to speak.

Presently, Spock straightened in his chair, wiped the tears from his face. When he spoke, his voice was stronger, more assured.

"I was eighteen when I joined the Academy," he said. "My father and I did not speak again until. . . ."

"The Babel Conference," Kirk said. "About the Coridan admission. That was when I met your . . ."

Kirk paused, looked into a far dark corner of the room.

"Jim?" Spock said.

Kirk shrugged. "That mindmeld confusion," he said. "I know I never met your father until he came on board the *Enterprise* that time. But . . . Spock, those dreams of your father seem so real."

Spock carefully took the holoprojector in his hand. "Answers sometimes lie in unexpected places," Spock said.

Kirk smiled at his friend. "Then you admit that there *are* answers?"

Spock nodded. "I am afraid I have not been myself. I have been . . . a burden to the mission."

"Never," Kirk said. He hesitated again. "That's what I told your father . . . ? Never forget . . . no! He told me to forget? I said never?" Kirk closed his eyes, grimaced in his efforts to remember. Spock grew concerned. Kirk stood up, held out his hand as if to grasp an answer from the air. "There was something your father told me, Spock. Something important. But . . . what? And when?"

Spock was glad to have something other than his own pain to focus on. "Do you remember the context?" he asked.

Kirk's comm badge chirped. Kirk touched it, gingerly, still becoming used to his new environment. "Kirk here."

It was Christine reporting from the bridge. "We're coming up on orbit, Jim."

"I'll be there," Kirk said. He looked at Spock. "What do you say? One more mission?"

Spock allowed just the hint of a smile to form, almost as if he were himself again. "At the very least."

Kirk touched his comm badge again. "We'll both be there," he said.

THIRTY-FIVE

---------------- ☆ ----------------

Kirk and Spock stepped onto the bridge of the *Tobias.*

It didn't matter that it wasn't an *Enterprise.*

It didn't matter that it wasn't even Kirk's ship.

It wasn't the machinery that was important, it was the people. And with Spock at his side, with Christine, M'Benga, and Barc, Kirk knew he was ready for what would come next.

For what he knew had been waiting for him all his life.

If only he could remember *why* he knew. And *how* . . .

He stood by Christine's chair as the small disk of their destination grew against the stars. The last time Kirk had seen this world, it had been a sweep of equatorial green and purple vegetation with milky blue seas, bordered by bands of snow in the temperate zones, and wreathed in misty clouds.

Now, except for the white of the swollen polar regions, it was black, and brown, streaked with red, its waterways clogged with eruptions of strange yellow formations that resembled spreading colonies of mold.

"Coming up on standard orbit," Barc said from the helm.

Christine leaned closer to Kirk. "You're sure about this? This planet's so far gone we didn't even have to run a Starfleet blockade."

"I'm sure," Kirk said as the dead world filled the screen and scrolled beneath them. "It's where it started."

Spock nodded. "And where it will end."

"Standard orbit," Barc growled. "Welcome to Tarsus Four."

Christine pushed herself up from her chair, nodded at Kirk. "You take the conn. I'll be more useful at the sensor stations."

Kirk looked at the empty chair. "I can't," he said. He had to put those days behind him. "I'll take the helm."

Christine didn't argue, told Barc the conn was his, then moved to the main science station to prepare for the first sensor sweep. Spock joined her there, to offer assistance. Kirk could see she was alert to Spock's change of mood.

Kirk took his place at the helm. M'Benga was beside him at ops. "Why here?" the doctor asked.

Kirk's eyes stayed on the screen. He could see the outlines of landforms and lakes and mountains he had memorized as a child, when coming to an alien world for a summer trip from Earth was to be the greatest adventure of his life.

"Logic," he said. "The Symmetrists tried an experiment here before. It worked."

M'Benga's dark eyes flashed with outrage. "Kodos executed four thousand innocent people on this world, and you say the experiment 'worked'?"

Kirk understood her reaction, but for him, the outrage of Tarsus IV had passed into history, when he had seen Kodos die to save Kirk's life. The executioner had been executed by his own daughter—the final step in the old man's efforts to forget the past of which he had grown so tired. Outrage meant nothing in the face of that. The memory of boyhood terror remained. But he had nothing left to feel about Kodos the man.

"Because of what happened here," Kirk said, "food distribution policies changed throughout the Federation. Crop diversity was mandated to prevent another case where a single disease organism could wipe out a colony's entire food supply." He glanced at the doctor. "Of course, that was when I was a teenager. By the time I graduated the Academy, those rules had all been rewritten or forgotten."

"So, you think the Symmetrists came back here to try again, but on a bigger scale?" M'Benga asked.

"I don't know," Kirk said. On the viewscreen, he saw the main continent of Tarsus Four coming up. In the central plain would be the main city, where the first colony had been founded. Where the mass graves remained as a memorial, in mute testimony to the madness that had come to this place. "Maybe they never left. Maybe they felt they could make a stronger point if this became one of the first worlds to be infected by the virogen. History repeats itself. The lesson reinforced by blood."

"That doesn't sound like logic," M'Benga said. "It sounds like emotion."

"When you get right down to it," Kirk said, "there's not a lot of difference between the two. It's just a question of finding the proper balance."

M'Benga eyed him skeptically. "You're the same Jim Kirk who stole your old starship from under Starfleet's nose, risked war with the Klingon Empire, blew up the *Enterprise,* and hijacked a Bird-of-Prey to rescue Spock? And you talk about *balance?"*

Kirk saw his control boards change configuration as Christine switched sensor control to the helm and ops. "Dr. M'Benga, all I can say is, at the time, it seemed like the logical thing to do."

M'Benga had the decency to laugh. She obviously knew when she was being set up, and understood the game.

"Coming up on main city," Kirk said.

M'Benga asked quietly, "Did it ever get a name?"

"New Haven," Kirk said. "But after Kodos, they just called it the city."

Kirk brought the sensors online and the first returns were depressing. Frequency of viable life-forms was less than eight percent of the figure given in the Starfleet database from the last planetary survey only two years ago.

"No sign of any colonists," Kirk said.

"That's probably why there was no blockade," Christine said from her station. "The evacuation was completed."

"You'd think they'd keep at least one ship on station," Kirk said as he kept scanning the sensor returns. "If only to keep Orion pirates from looting the place."

"Acquiring main city," Spock announced.

Kirk reassigned sensor sensitivity to search for humanoid life and industrial installations. Both should be present if his theory was correct.

"Picking up sensor scatter," Spock said.

Kirk saw it. "Looks like there's a forcefield operating in the city."

"No life signs," M'Benga reported.

"Someone's got to be keeping that shield going," Christine said. "Going for high resolution on the surrounding area. Putting it onscreen."

The dying continent that slowly moved below them was replaced by a false-color enhanced image of one small section of the main city. The widest thoroughfares were familiar to Kirk. They were the same ones laid out when the colony had been founded, the same streets he had walked when he had been a boy.

Near the intersection of two of the largest streets, a large amorphous shape pulsated—indicating the area protected from sensors by forcefields.

"Jim," Christine asked, "any idea what that installation is?"

Kirk frowned. "If that's the old center of town, it's about where the Starfleet administration center was. But that was more than a century ago."

310

On the screen, a map overlay appeared, labeled: CITY PLAN, NEW HAVEN, TARSUS IV.

The Starfleet delta was positioned directly over the sensor-opaque area.

"Looks like it still is the Starfleet center," Christine said. "Bones, any chance there's a team from Medical down there we don't know about?"

"Not without a support ship on orbit," M'Benga said.

Christine made her decision. "Then that's it. We've found your base, Jim. What happens next?"

Kirk didn't have an answer right away. He hadn't expected the base to be so easy to find. Either the Symmetrists were overconfident, or—

Kirk's hands flew over the helm and reconfigured the controls for warp flight. "Brace yourselves! Get ready for—"

The viewscreen blasted the bridge with blinding white light as the ship screamed and spun to the starboard, throwing the crew from their chairs.

Kirk scrambled back to the helm as Barc squealed and every alarm on the bridge clanged, wailed, and beeped at once. Shadows danced crazily from all the flashing warning and overload lights. An irregular vibration pulsed through the deck.

"Damage reports!" Christine shouted over the cacophony.

The screen cleared slightly, enough to show the planet below them, and then a golden sparkle of light appeared and—

The *Tobias* seemed to fall as artificial gravity failed in the impact of another explosion. Kirk hooked his feet under the console and pulled M'Benga back into position. If they got hit again before gravity was reestablished, inertia would smash them against the ceiling, deck, or bulkhead.

"Barcs!" Christine shouted. "Inertial control! Full gravity now! What are they hitting us with?!"

"Transporter mines," Spock said. "They are being beamed directly into our path from the surface."

This was exactly what Kirk had suddenly realized. For the Symmetrists' base to be so obvious meant they had to have exceptional defenses.

"Barcs! Forget the environmentals! Get us out of—"

"New mine materializing, fifty meters astern," Spock said.

Kirk braced himself, but he knew it would do no good. When that mine went off, the *Tobias* would lurch forward at hundreds of kilometers per second, while the inertia of her crew kept each person at relative rest until the back wall of the bridge hit them and reduced them to little more than organic paste.

Kirk stared at the screen, at Tarsus IV below him, knowing it was not supposed to end this way.

It didn't.

The transporter mine didn't detonate.

"Spock?" Kirk called as he twisted to look behind him. "What's happening out there?"

But Spock, anchored to the science station beside Christine, merely pointed forward at the main screen.

Kirk twisted back.

Just in time to see the enormous but familiar white disk of a starship's command saucer eclipse the screen.

He didn't even have to wait to see the lettering on the hull to know what ship it was, and who commanded her.

So much for thinking Picard would stay behind to search Vulcan instead of following the *Tobias*.

The screen flashed once, and a direct visual communications feed began.

Jean-Luc Picard appeared, inexplicably still in his small flight deck, but most definitely the captain in control.

"Greetings, *Tobias*," Picard said with a smile. "I was wondering if we might offer you the services of a slightly larger vessel?"

Kirk hit the comm switch on his console. "Just so there're no misunderstandings, we have a mission to perform here. And you're not taking us back until we're done."

"I don't think you're in a particularly strong position for stating your terms, Jim, but we have no intention of taking you back. In fact, since we both have missions here, perhaps we could work together, instead of trying to ram each other out of space?"

Kirk slowly settled back into his chair as Barc brought the gravity online again. He could only guess that the *Enterprise*'s shields or firepower or both were keeping them protected from the transporter mines.

"What, exactly, is your mission?" Kirk asked.

"You're here for the Symmetrists," Picard said. "We're here for the virogen cure. And as far as our sensors are concerned, we'll find both directly below us."

"You've got yourself a partner," Kirk said.

Picard smiled. "You're welcome."

THIRTY-SIX

☆

Beneath the dark clouds that covered the main city, the Great
Seal of the Federation was fifteen meters across, carved from
the distinctive bluestone of Tarsus IV, and inlaid with a
mosaic pattern of minerals from each of the fifty-two worlds
who were members at the time it was dedicated.

As a teenager, Kirk had stared up in awe at the monument
outside the Starfleet administration building. But now the
seal was cracked, the top third fallen off, most of the mosaic
stones missing. Like the Federation it represented, the monument was crumbling in the aftermath of the virogen.

Kirk materialized before that monument, still in his new
Starfleet uniform, though now with a jacket and a hand
phaser. Spock, Christine, Barc, and M'Benga resolved beside
him. Barc and Christine carried phaser rifles. M'Benga a
hand phaser and a medical field kit.

Kirk studied the cracked seal for a moment, but quickly
dismissed it as a mere symbol. Throughout history, people
had been obsessed with creating similar icons, imbuing them
with power, rallying around them, going to war for them. But
not Kirk. There had been other symbols in the past, there
would be new ones in the future. The Great Seal of the

314

Federation was not the reason he and the others were here today. The ideals from which those symbols arose were far more important.

Kirk leaned out from behind the decaying monument and checked the state of the Starfleet installation beyond.

A domed forcefield rippled around it, enclosing it safely and completely, impenetrable to everything except limited wavelengths of visible light.

Kirk tapped his comm badge. He was beginning to appreciate how convenient this type of communicator was. "Kirk here. The buildings inside the forcefield appear to be intact."

Riker's voice responded. "Can you see any guards?"

"None visible," Kirk said. He glanced around at the rest of what he could see of the main city. Burned-out buildings, crashed flyers, signs of looting. Scans from orbit had failed to pick up a single life-form in the ruins larger than a rat. He thought of Chal and Teilani. "I don't think there's anything left to guard."

"They've got to know we're coming," Christine said as she slipped in beside him. "They targeted the *Tobias* precisely, so they must have seen the *Enterprise.*"

"Commander MacDonald's right," Kirk said as he touched his comm badge. "If the Symmetrists have guards at this installation, then they'll all be inside, waiting for us."

"Then let's not keep them waiting," Riker replied. "Stand by. *Enterprise* out."

A moment later, two new columns of transporter energy appeared by Kirk's team. They resolved into Picard and Beverly Crusher.

"Nice of you to drop in," Kirk said. "But I thought starship captains were supposed to mind the store these days."

Picard looked around, his grip on his phaser rifle almost casual, as if he did this every day. "Beverly and I have already been exposed to the virogen, which makes us perfect volunteers for this mission."

"I hate to disappoint you," M'Benga said, "but I can eliminate the virogen from animal carriers."

Beverly looked at M'Benga in delight. "Dried *trannin* leaves?"

M'Benga returned the smile. "You read my report?"

The two doctors excitedly introduced themselves to each other, shook hands. "Medical's already sent out the replicator programs for your compound," Beverly said. "It's a brilliant piece of work. And how fortunate that Klingon folk healer was on your world."

"Klingon . . . folk healer?" M'Benga repeated. She glanced at Kirk. He shook his head, not wanting the attention. "Right. A real mystery man. Never did catch his name."

"A shame," Beverly said. Then she looked around, saw Spock. "Ambassador, may I have a word with you, please?"

Spock looked surprised. "Dr. Crusher, this is hardly the time."

But Beverly insisted. She motioned for Spock to step away from the others with her.

"Is something wrong?" Kirk asked Picard.

"A medical matter," Picard said.

"Bendii Syndrome?" Even as he finally said those words, Kirk hoped his suspicions were incorrect.

Picard was impressed. "How did you know?"

"I've known Spock for . . . forever. The way he's been behaving these past few days, it hasn't been like him at all. But I read the reports of Sarek's death—the official results. The symptoms seemed the same."

Kirk and Picard watched Spock and Beverly in whispered conversation. "Bendii can't be confirmed without specialized procedures," Picard said. "But blood tests suggest he has been deliberately exposed to the same pathogen that killed his father."

Kirk felt a wave of inexpressible sorrow pass over him. "Is there any chance of a cure?"

"It might not even be Bendii, Jim. Just a poison that mimics its effects."

"Any idea how he was exposed?"

"Not yet."

Beverly gave Spock an injection from a hypospray.

"That will help him maintain control," Picard said. "For a little while at least."

Spock returned to the group, his face revealing nothing of his conversation with the doctor.

Kirk allowed his friend his privacy. "What now?" he asked Picard.

"Now, my first officer and my engineer will show off a new technique they're quite proud of."

"A new technique for what?" Kirk asked. "Shouldn't we be starting a bombardment to wear down that forcefield?"

"Welcome to the twenty-fourth century," Picard said. Then he tapped his comm badge. "Picard to *Enterprise*. You may begin."

Instantly the air filled with a powerful transporter harmonic. Picard gestured to the others to look past the protection of the monument at the forcefield.

Kirk was startled to see what appeared to be an umbrella of . . . cargo containers? They were materializing along the precise boundary of the domed forcefield.

Interference patterns formed, sending ripples of energy disturbances across the field, so bright that the low dark clouds were illuminated from below. Kirk squinted to bring the scene into clearer focus.

"Watch your eyes," Picard warned him.

Then at least two dozen Starfleet personnel in black phaser armor materialized *within* the forcefield on the dead lawn of the administration building.

"Punch through!" Barc snarled. The Tellarite beamed in delighted approval. "Interference disruption and transporter punch through! Absolutely brilliant! Not that there aren't twenty different settings I could make to stop it from ever happening again," he added.

"It works best on atmospheric shields," Picard said. Then he ducked and a moment later Kirk saw all the cargo containers disappear, followed by a series of explosions that covered the forcefield's surface.

Some of the troops in phaser armor stumbled under the force of the overhead blasts, but they were all quickly up on their feet and running for the building.

The surprise and the novelty of their attack had been so unexpected that fully half of them had burst into the closest building before the first shots of defensive phaser fire were directed at them. There *were* Symmetrist guards hiding inside.

Picard tapped his comm badge as the last of the armored crew dived into cover. "Picard to *Enterprise*. The second team is in. No casualties."

Kirk could hear Riker's grin in his reply. "All transporters standing by, sir."

Then, from far away, Kirk could hear muffled explosions, the whine of phaser fire. No more than a hundred meters away, the troops from the *Enterprise* were fighting the Symmetrist defenders—fighting and dying, and for what?

Kirk could almost hear Kodos's reply: *Survival depends on drastic measures. . . .*

Then a larger explosion rumbled through the ground. Kirk saw the forcefield shimmer, then wink out.

Riker's voice came from everyone's comm badges.

"The shield is down. Third team is beaming in now. We will transport targets out at will."

318

Picard nodded at Kirk as he hefted his phaser rifle. "Right now, minding a store doesn't seem like a bad idea."

Kirk smiled. He suspected that he and Picard were more alike than either of them knew, or would admit.

Then the transporter claimed them again and the real battle began.

THIRTY-SEVEN

———————— ☆ ————————

Christine's ears popped as she materialized in a dark underground room, somewhere in the lower levels of the old administration building. The blueprints from the main computer libraries of the *Enterprise* had shown that this building had originally been equipped with deep shelters for the city's population. Tarsus IV was close to the Neutral Zone, and the colony's founders had decided to be prudent.

In the attack's planning sessions, conducted while the crippled *Tobias* had been unceremoniously towed from orbit by two of the *Enterprise*'s shuttles, Spock had reasoned that the underground shelter complex would be the perfect setting for the antivirogen installation Picard expected to find. Thus, Picard's team had been chosen for the deepest penetration into enemy territory.

Christine swung her phaser rifle up to cover the area as Kirk and Picard, Spock and Barc, and the two doctors took form beside her. Crusher and M'Benga were crucial to this part of the operation. Both Kirk and Spock agreed that the Symmetrists would have outfitted their installation with self-destruct charges. The two doctors would be responsible for locating and isolating samples of the antivirogen before those

320

charges could be detonated. Picard and the others would be responsible for getting everyone out alive.

An explosion rumbled from somewhere many levels overhead.

"Was that a phaser hit?" M'Benga asked nervously.

Picard shook his head. "An explosive. And my people aren't carrying any."

Christine understood what that meant. Kirk and Spock had been right about the self-destruct charges, and they were already being activated.

"The Symmetrists are fanatics," Picard reminded everyone. A second explosion thundered from far away. "If they're destroying this installation, they'll do it methodically, whether they feel they can escape or not. We only have a few minutes at most."

Dr. Crusher moved her medical tricorder back and forth, then pointed toward a narrow doorway in a distant corner. "Diffuse life signs," she said. "Plant-based. Maybe in a growth medium."

Picard motioned ahead with his rifle, exchanged a tight smile with Kirk. Together, they ran to the doorway. Spock ran with them.

Despite the gravity of the situation, Christine had to fight down a sudden rush of elation. She was on a mission with Kirk and Spock, *and* Picard. The Symmetrists, however fanatical, didn't have a chance.

Another explosion shook the floor. This one was closer. Christine told Crusher and M'Benga to run ahead, she'd follow with Barc.

"Feels like we're making history, doesn't it?" she asked the engineer as she ran beside him.

"*Rrr,* I'd rather be juggling antimatter in a variable gravity field."

As they reached the doorway behind the others, an even closer explosion cracked the air around them. "Careful what you wish for, Barcs." Then she and the Tellarite ducked through the door and ran on.

Ahead of them, a pipe-lined corridor stretched about fifty meters. Crusher and M'Benga used their tricorders at every closed door on either side, but all readings indicated the strongest life signs came from straight ahead.

That was where the corridor opened into a large, well-lit storage chamber, at least three stories high, with white-tiled walls, holding five enormous, spherical white tanks ringed by catwalks, plastered with warning placards, and attached to diagnostic pressure displays.

Kirk and Picard ran to opposite sides of the storage chamber, checking each likely hiding place among the alcoves, computer stations, and stacks of packing crates. Since the main lighting sources were centered in the ceiling, there were impenetrable shadows everywhere—under the tanks, under catwalks, even on the catwalk ringing the top level of the chamber.

Crusher and M'Benga cautiously approached the tanks with their tricorders. Each tank was positioned on thick metal legs that raised it high enough for workers to walk under it. From a protected position between two large packing crates, Christine peered into those shadows.

"This tank is full of virogen culture," Crusher announced from the first tank. She read the results of her scan from her tricorder. "This must be where they were growing it in the first place."

"Virogen," M'Benga confirmed at the second tank.

Barc slung his phaser rifle over his shoulder and pulled out his own engineering tricorder. He started scanning for explosives.

Christine peered up at the highest reaches of the chamber. There were shadows enough in each corner of the catwalk to hide two or three watchers, or soldiers with weapons.

"More virogen cultures," Crusher said from beside the third tank.

"Dr. Crusher," Christine called out to her. "Could you sweep those balconies for life signs?" She indicated the shadowed areas with the barrel of her phaser rifle.

"Certainly," Crusher said. She adjusted the setting on her tricorder, pointed it up, and began to move it.

Then she screamed as an orange disruptor bolt blasted her back into one of the tank's support legs and sent her tricorder flying.

Instantly Kirk's and Picard's voices echoed in the chamber. "Everyone down!"

Christine saw where Picard fired to try and pick off whoever shot Crusher. Christine began firing to the right and left of Picard's target zones.

"Over there!" Barc suddenly shouted.

Christine saw where the Tellarite was pointing—at the catwalk circling the fifth tank—and fired at a moving shadow just as Picard fired again.

But another disruptor bolt shot down and hit Barc, throwing him squealing across the floor.

Christine wheeled as Kirk leapt to cover beside her. She was surprised to see he hadn't drawn his phaser.

"There are two of them," he said in a low voice. "On tank five, and on the catwalk up in that corner. M'Benga's safe under the fourth tank. Picard's standing by in the far corner. I'm going after Dr. Crusher and pull her under the tank for safety. When I draw fire, you go for the one on the catwalk, Picard goes for the one on the fifth tank."

"When you draw fire?" Christine said. "You're not a target!"

"Someone has to be." He gave her his phaser. "And I can't do this anymore." He got ready to run into the open area.

"Jim, wait!" Christine said.

He turned, just for a moment, to face her.

It was now or never. She reached out for him, kissed him. He was startled. Pulled back. "This isn't . . ." he began.

And then it was too late.

Christine shoved the phaser rifle into his hands, pushed him down between the packing crates, and charged out across the chamber floor, heading for Dr. Crusher.

She heard the crackle of a disruptor bolt hit the floor behind her, but she kept pumping her legs and arms, never slowing.

Phaser whines screamed behind her, from two different sources. She smiled, knowing that Kirk was doing some of the shooting.

A scream rang out, but it came from the wrong place to be either Kirk or Picard. It had to be one of the two other shooters. The Symmetrists.

She dived behind a stand of pipes at the base of the third tank and slid in beside Crusher. The doctor was conscious, barely, and Christine jammed one arm around her and dragged her to shelter beneath the tank.

She blew her hair up off her forehead and peered back the way she had run.

Kirk was kneeling where she had left him between the crates, phaser rifle in his hand, perfectly positioned to pick off more attackers.

She felt proud of herself for having outmaneuvered him. She wondered if Kirk would forgive her the kiss.

And then she felt the cold emitter of a disruptor dig into the back of her neck.

"Resourceful," a familiar voice said. "For a human."

Christine turned around as a powerful hand gripped her hair and sharply tugged her off balance to keep her from trying anything sudden.

But she already knew who had captured her.

The voice belonged to Srell.

THIRTY-EIGHT

─────────── ☆ ───────────

Kirk breathed heavily, from exertion, from anger, he didn't know which.

He could still hear the scream of the man he had shot on the catwalk. The man who had then fallen three stories to certain death on the chamber floor.

But he also still tasted the unexpected softness of Christine's lips on his.

Life and love in the face of death. The juxtaposition had been enough to let her take him by surprise.

She had changed the rules. On him.

He didn't know whether to be angry or proud.

He decided to think about it later. He touched his comm badge. "Kirk to *Enterprise.*"

No response. He could hear the hiss of a jamming device in operation. The Symmetrists had been thorough in the defense of their installation.

Then he heard another explosion roar from the corridor that had led to this chamber. If a communicator signal couldn't get through, he knew the *Enterprise* could never lock on a transporter beam. From the sounds of the explosions, all

325

the exits were being shut down, so there would be no physical way out, either.

He tapped the comm badge again. "Kirk to Picard."

"Go ahead," Picard answered. The communicators still worked over short distances.

"I picked off the one on the catwalk." There was no pride in Kirk's voice. He had merely done his job.

"The one on the tank didn't show himself," Picard said.

Kirk was relieved that Picard didn't ask why Christine, and not he, had made the run to Beverly. "Do you think he might have left the chamber?" Kirk asked.

"There's one way to find out."

Kirk knew what Picard had in mind. Another run across the chamber to draw a sniper's fire. But then the loudest blast yet detonated on the level three stories directly overhead. Tiles and chunks of extruded silicon rained down from the ceiling. Overhead pipes burst and water sprayed in one corner, gushing forth and splashing like a waterfall.

Kirk checked on Barc. The Tellarite was unmoving in the center of the chamber floor, but he hadn't been hit by any debris.

A new voice came from Kirk's comm badge. "Spock here. If the explosions we have been experiencing are following the pattern I have discerned, then the next sequence will begin on the level directly above us. And the sequence after that, on this level."

"Do you have a suggestion, Mr. Spock?" Picard asked.

"To proceed with dispatch, Captain Picard."

Kirk laughed silently. If Spock wasn't careful he might become a comedian in his old age.

Then Kirk's laughter froze as he saw Christine stumble out from beneath the third tank, a dark figure holding a disruptor to her head. When the figure spoke, Kirk's heart froze as well.

"Kirk! The rest of you! Reveal yourselves or the commander loses her head!"

Kirk didn't stop to think. He was on his feet at once, striding forward, ready to use the weapon in his hand, ready to use his hands alone if he had to, to rip out Srell's throat.

"That's close enough, Kirk. Drop the phaser."

Christine gasped as the young Vulcan jammed the disruptor against the base of her skull.

Kirk threw the phaser rifle away as if it were a spear. It clattered noisily among the debris that had fallen from the ceiling.

"Where is the logic in betrayal?" Kirk demanded.

"Spock!" Srell shouted to the chamber's ceiling. "I need your counsel!"

No reply.

"You're too exposed where you are," Kirk said, taunting Srell. "There are at least three other weapons pointing at you right now. Give up and you'll live."

Srell was unimpressed by the threat. "You're not from this time. Otherwise, you would recognize what's behind me."

Kirk saw that Srell stood close to a display panel. "So?"

"We are not dealing with the modified phaser that led you to believe I had been killed in spacedock. If a misplaced phaser bolt hits that panel, the tank explodes." Srell shouted again. *"Spock!* All you others, come forth now or I shall kill the commander *and* Kirk."

"Save your breath," Kirk said. "They're not coming out." He took two more steps toward Srell. They were only three meters apart. "This is a war. Soldiers die."

"Without knowing the symmetry of all things, you cannot understand the meaning of death," Srell said. He tightened his hand on the disruptor. "But I shall be your teacher."

Time stopped for Kirk. This time he had no doubt.

Srell was going to fire.

Christine was going to die.

He started forward, knowing he could never reach her in time.

327

And then, like some dark avenging angel, Spock dropped from the sky, from the catwalk on the tank above them, and landed on Srell as Srell's weapon discharged.

As if in a low-gravity ballet, Christine spun away from Srell's grip and the two Vulcans tumbled to the floor.

A halo of disruptor energy shimmered endlessly through Christine's hair, setting it ablaze.

Then time snapped back into place. Kirk threw himself at her and caught her in his arms as they both fell to the floor.

He gasped as he felt a sharp crack in his ribs, but his outstretched arms broke her fall.

He pulled himself up, gathering her close in his arms.

He couldn't speak as he felt how limp she was.

He touched her face, so young, still warm. Turned her head to see the ruin of scorched hair and charred skin that blackened her scalp.

But just a small part of her scalp.

Kirk spoke her name.

Touched her neck.

Felt a pulse.

Christine opened her eyes.

Smiled at him despite the pain he knew she felt.

". . . not bad for a hundred and forty . . ." she rasped.

He squeezed her hand, unable to speak. Then M'Benga was beside Kirk, pushing him away. A glittering medical instrument already whirring in her hand.

"She'll be okay," the doctor said. "Just give me room."

Kirk stumbled to his feet, holding his arm around his chest where his rib had cracked. Then he saw Spock and Srell locked in combat on the floor.

Spock lay on his back. Srell held him down, squeezing Spock's neck with all the ferocity of youth.

Kirk saw Picard running forward, aiming his rifle, ready to take his shot.

But this wasn't Picard's fight.

Spock was in danger. And that meant Srell belonged to Kirk.

Kirk charged forward and kicked at the youth's head as hard as he could.

The violent impact threw Srell from Spock. The young Vulcan's body hit the floor, rolled, then lay still.

Picard skidded to a stop. "It's under control," Kirk said, each breath a victory over the stabbing pain that lanced his side. "Beverly needs you."

Picard ran on to the *Enterprise*'s doctor. She was sitting on the floor under the tank, cradling her head, still shaken by the disruptor blast she had taken.

Kirk held out his hand to help Spock to his feet.

Spock rose and looked at him. Eyes blank.

"Spock, it's all right."

But Spock shoved Kirk aside and went to Srell, lifting him one-handed by his neck. Then Kirk watched in disbelief as Spock struck the youth, keeping him upright by clutching the front of his tunic, not letting him fall.

"Spock, no!" Kirk shouted. But then he coughed weakly as his cracked rib robbed him of breath.

Spock's closed fist struck Srell again. One of Srell's eyes was closed, dripping with green blood.

Kirk caught Spock's fist to stop another blow.

"Think what you're doing, Spock."

Spock glared wildly at Kirk, breathing through his mouth in spasmodic gasps. "This is what I *feel*," he raged.

"It's Bendii! Picard told me! You've been poisoned. Infected. This isn't you!"

Spock spoke through clenched teeth. "Dr. Crusher has treated me. Perhaps Bendii affected me in the past. But not now." He stared at Srell with murderous intent. "Now I am in perfect control."

He wrenched his fist from Kirk's grip.

Then a gigantic explosion burst through the far wall of the

chamber at the second-story level, causing a hailstorm of pulverized tile and shards of stone. Fire crackled along two exposed power conduits, sending sprays of sparks to hiss in the spreading water released from the already broken pipes. The main lighting flared, then dimmed. Low vapor began to form against the floor.

Spock lost his balance in the concussion of a second blast, releasing Srell.

The youth fell heavily to the floor, tried to push himself up. Could barely move.

"Get up!" Spock spit at him. He swayed on his feet, one arm half-raised as if ready to strike again. Both Vulcans were near total collapse. Srell, physical. Spock, emotional.

Srell stared up at Spock with contempt. "Kill me here. Finish your assignment."

Spock dropped to his knees, looked at Srell. The clipped style of Vulcan speech returned to him. "Explain."

Srell sneered at him, all pretense at control lost in the primal emotions of their conflict. "You have known all along." He coughed up green blood, spit out a clot of it on the chamber floor. "You were manipulated, Spock. Just as you said on Babel."

"Why?"

Srell raised a shaking hand to his swollen face. "It was so logical. The lesson had to be taught. The ecology is weak. The systems too complex." Srell stopped to taste the blood on his cracked lip. "Our projections showed the Federation would collapse on its own in less than thirty years, beyond the power of anyone to stop. The virogen was a necessity."

Spock's voice was deep, congested. "But the Federation is collapsing now, precisely because of the virogen."

"Because today, it *can* recover on its own. But thirty years from now . . ." Srell's gaze was locked on Spock. "The fall of a galactic civilization, Spock. Can you imagine the waste?

The horror?" Srell turned his head toward Kirk. "That is the death you must understand! Billions! Trillions! On your hands!"

Kirk stood over Srell. "How can the Federation recover?" His voice was commanding, compelling.

"We're . . . we're making an antivirogen here."

Kirk widened his eyes in shock. "You released the virogen *without* having a cure?"

Srell opened and closed his mouth like a drowning fish. "We *had* a cure. But . . . the virogen mutated. Our cure doesn't work. That's why we needed the alta mist. A new mode of delivery." Srell looked up at them both, madness growing in his eyes. "It is the symmetry of all things. . . ."

Kirk felt near to collapse himself. The Symmetrists had sought to teach the Federation a lesson about the complexity of the environment, without first understanding that lesson themselves.

"Why manipulate *me?*" Spock asked, seeking understanding of his own.

Srell doubled up with a violent cough. Green blood bubbled at the corner of his lip. Kirk looked over to see M'Benga still treating Christine. Picard was still assisting Beverly. Medical attention for Srell would have to wait.

"You were to test us, Spock. Your fine mind put to our use, to find the weak parts of our plan. And I was to follow beside you on your investigation. The dutiful student. Correcting any errors that you found. Obscuring any clues that others might discover. As long as we could be sure you would not report what you found to anyone but me, the plan was perfect. Even to the perfection of you seeing me die so I would never be suspected of betrayal."

"Not logical," Spock said wearily. "Eventually, I would have to tell someone else."

Srell shook his head. Blood dripped from his mouth to the

floor. "Mendrossen's confession. The holoprojector the Klingon brought you. The first time you touched the switch to play it."

"Bendii," Kirk said. *"That's* how you infected him."

Srell stared up at Kirk with almost an expression of admiration. "Not exactly Bendii, Kirk, but a poison so close that no doctor would suspect the difference."

"Your plan was flawed from the beginning," Spock said.

"My plan was perfect. It worked on Tarok. It worked on Sarek. It—"

Too late, Srell stopped, as if just realizing what he had said.

Spock lurched forward, raised a fumbling hand for Srell's tunic. *"Explain."*

Srell tried to crawl away but couldn't escape Spock's grip. "Sarek knew the Federation was doomed," he gasped. "More than a century ago. His work gave our cause the scientific basis we needed to proceed here."

"Here?" Kirk asked. "On Tarsus Four?"

"The lesson must be taught," Srell whispered. "If anything is to survive, an example must be made. But Sarek denied the logic of the fate that awaits us. He knew the time had come for the Federation to experience its future while steps could still be taken to avoid collapse. But he wanted to stop us."

"What did you do?" Spock demanded.

"I was a soldier in a cause!" Srell muttered. "There were things to be done. Terrible things!"

Spock raised trembling hands to reach for Srell. *"What did you do to my father?!"*

"I killed him!" Srell said. *"For the good of the many—Sarek had to die!"*

Spock covered his mouth with his hand, stifling the terrible sob that tore through him.

But something other than anguish for his friend tore through Kirk. Long-buried memories broke free. Finally unleashed.

There were things to be done. Terrible things . . .
For the good of the many . . .
Sarek . . .
Here, on Tarsus IV . . .

Kirk lifted Srell to his feet. He grabbed Srell's hand, spread his fingers, thrust them against the *katra* points of his own face.

"Show me," Kirk said. "Show me, damn you!"

And in fear, in terror, and, at last, in relief, Srell revealed his final secret, and opened his mind to James T. Kirk.

THIRTY-NINE

―――――――――― ☆ ――――――――――

At first in Srell's mind, there was pain.

But Kirk knew pain. The nanites had brought him that.

Then there was Srell's fear of death.

But Kirk had died. There were no mysteries there.

Confusion came next, terrifying for a Vulcan like Srell for whom logic and order were the cornerstones of life, built on the sand of the universe's indifference.

But confusion was a necessary part of being human, and Kirk knew it well. He willingly accepted all of Srell's youthful failings, his pain and fear, because he had felt them all before.

What Kirk sought in Srell's immature mind was unexpected wisdom.

Brought there by the touch of other minds.

Older minds.

With the disciplines he had learned from Hugh and his clan of reclaimed Borg, with the secrets culled from a thousand assimilated worlds, Kirk controlled the meld. It was not his power that drove it, for that ability belonged only to Vulcans. But it was Kirk's will that harnessed Srell's talent and forced it to his own purpose.

Kirk moved through Srell's thoughts like a whirlwind.

He saw Stonn and T'Pring, knew they were secret conspirators with Srell. He saw a dozen other minds he did not stop to identify. For he only sought one.

And he found it.

Sarek.

My *mind to your mind,* Kirk *told Srell, peeling back the layers of the youth's experience to reveal that which Kirk sought.*

And then Kirk touched Sarek's mind again. But not for the second time.

For the third.

Because the second time had been in San Francisco. And the first had been here. On Tarsus IV. When Kirk had escaped from Kodos only because Sarek had saved him.

Kirk saw it all, felt it all, knew it all—every memory that Sarek had taken from him that night was now returned. And Sarek's memories came with them.

Kirk saw how Sarek had calculated the effects of disruption in the galactic food supply.

Kirk saw how others had taken Sarek's scenarios for destruction and had chosen to demonstrate them.

Understanding the horror of what he had wrought by accident, Sarek had risked his life and his career to brave the Neutral Zone and lead the relief forces here. He had saved thirteen-year-old Jimmy Kirk on the night he had arrived. And to insure the boy's safety, he had entered his mind to bring forgetfulness.

How like my son. . . .

The echo of that thought was here as well, poignant, bittersweet, brimming with emotion that Sarek could never express.

That night on Tarsus IV, Sarek had touched Kirk's mind as a father to a son, and had opened the boy's mind to the call of the stars. And Kirk in turn had touched Sarek's mind, sharing with him his youth, his wonder, his dreams for the future, all the possibilities that Sarek would never touch and know in his own son.

Filled with understanding, slowly Kirk withdrew from the mind of Srell, taking all that was there of Sarek and that night.

He heard Kodos's threats again in the swirling snow. He knew now why he had always felt that he would die alone—because that is what Kodos had told him. He knew now why he had always been pursued by the dark shadow through his dreams—because that was how Kodos had chased him.

Now, closer to the end of his life, Kirk had reached back to its beginning, and at last seen and understood how each part fit into the next in turn, and how the beginning had defined what would be the end.

That was why it had always been Sarek in his dreams.

That was why he knew his duty now.

The duty every Vulcan son had shared since before the Reformation.

Avenge me, *the voice of Sarek cried.*

And so Kirk prepared to be what he had always known he must become.

His father's son.

Avenger.

FORTY

☆

Kirk tore Srell's hand from his face, the knowledge of what he must do burning in his mind, and in his blood.

Another explosion tore apart the far wall. Debris thudded against the first tank, making its metal groan. Sparks flew, flames erupted, vapors swirled above pooling water.

But nothing could distract Kirk, or change him from his course.

Srell scrambled back from his pursuer, slipping on the wet floor. He stared up at Kirk, his eyes reflecting the chilling knowledge that he had no secrets from him.

Behind Kirk, Spock still knelt, trapped by the onslaught of emotions he had denied too long, not knowing how to escape them.

Picard moved quickly over to Kirk and Spock, Beverly at his side. "We have to leave. The next explosions will take out this entire level."

Kirk kept his eyes on Srell. "We need a sample from tank five," he said. He had seen the purpose of this installation in Srell's mind. "It has the alta mist they've engineered to carry the antivirogen."

Picard's face lit up. "Then they do have a cure?"

337

"Get the sample," Kirk said. Explanations could wait. There was little time left. Picard and Beverly ran for tank five.

M'Benga and Barc half-dragged Christine toward Kirk, Spock, and Srell, through the billowing white vapor that covered the floor. The commander of the *Tobias* was dazed, but alive and on her feet. Barc listed, as if Christine were supporting the Tellarite as much as he was supporting her.

Kirk took M'Benga's phaser before she could think to stop him.

Its controls were simple.

He set it to kill.

Picard and Beverly returned on the run. Picard held a small pressure cylinder from Beverly's medical kit. "We have it," he said.

From somewhere on this same level, a new blast made the air snap past them like a sonic boom. When the echo died, Kirk was aware of Picard's intense gaze, directed at the phaser he held.

"Kirk, whatever this man's crimes, we will need him for questioning."

"No," Kirk said.

"You're a Starfleet officer!"

"Not anymore."

"You have a duty to the Federation!"

But Kirk ignored him. "I've done my duty. More than enough."

In a lightning move, Picard grabbed Beverly's phaser from her side and swung it up to Kirk's head—

—just as Kirk swung his phaser to Picard.

They froze there, eyes locked, weapons held only centimeters from each other's neck, so close even a stun blast would kill, each only a finger twitch from oblivion.

No one else in that chamber dared move. Not even as the explosions continued, coming closer, growing louder.

"I will not allow you to kill that man," Picard said through clenched teeth.

Kirk's answer was equally to the point. "Then logic dictates that I kill you first."

Sweat glistened from each man's brow. The phasers they held kept their aim with unshaking precision.

"Listen to the words you're using," Picard pleaded. "You've shared another's mind. Someone else's thoughts are influencing you."

"Put down the phaser, Jean-Luc."

"You first."

Seconds passed, with neither man so much as breathing.

Then slowly, and deliberately, Kirk moved his phaser from Picard to Srell. "Then kill me," he said. "If you can."

Kirk waited then, his weapon locked on Srell. Until he heard, as he knew he would, the slow escape of breath from Picard. The captain of the *Enterprise* was an honorable man. He couldn't kill Kirk. "Jim, please . . ." Picard said. But that was all the protest he could make.

Kirk leveled his phaser at Srell. Somehow he knew the words he must say in an ancient Vulcan tongue he had never studied, or even heard of. *"Terr'tra stol nu, kRen jhal."*

. . . and so I avenge my father's death . . .

But Srell threw back his head, defiant. "You forget, Kirk— even as you looked into my mind, I looked into yours."

Kirk's phaser wavered as his hand trembled.

"Keep running, boy," the young Vulcan said mockingly, echoing Sarek's words to thirteen-year-old Jimmy Kirk. "Run as you've always run. From your past. From your failures. From yourself."

Another explosion, nearer, closer, louder, slammed into the chamber. But Kirk didn't flinch. It was as if he drew strength from its fury.

Because, however harsh they were, however damning, he heard the truth in Srell's words.

He *had* spent his life running. From his past. But not from failures. He had run from what he knew lurked deep within him, that hidden part that drove him to always find another path, a different solution, a way to change the rules.

Because at the heart of every confrontation he had faced, he had known there was always one simple answer: to release the beast that lay in the heart of every human and let it lash out and destroy all that was wrong.

Destruction and chaos whirled around Kirk and for the first time in his life, Kirk embraced it.

Let this base be blown to dust. Let the Federation fall. Let all the stars of all the galaxies be thrown into oblivion.

Nothing else mattered except this time and this place. This intersection of all the events of his life when he at last stopped running.

Kirk leveled his weapon at Srell and the Vulcan became for him the focus of all that was evil in his life, in his universe.

"Look into my mind," Kirk challenged him. "Tell me what you see *now*."

Completely unbidden, a wave of primal anticipation erupted in Kirk as he sensed the first weakness exposed in the youth's contemptuous Vulcan armor of superiority.

Whatever secrets Srell had seen in Kirk's mind, he was at last beginning to understand them, even as Kirk did. And Kirk could see that Srell at last recognized what he had freed.

The Vulcan raised his hands uncertainly. ". . . no . . ." he whispered.

But his final word was lost to the noise of the base's destruction. Lost to the raw fury of Kirk's unrestrained emotions.

Kirk thrust out the phaser before him as if it were a thunderbolt to be hurled from the heavens.

He shouted a cry that came from a place so deep within that it seemed to stop time.

And in that infinite instant Kirk at last threw off the final vestiges of his outer shell and became what he had struggled all his life to hold in check.

Pure passion.

Srell stumbled back, his eyes filled with the terror of total understanding of what was to happen next.

And it did.

Kirk fired.

And at the same instant the chamber reverberated with a sequence of escalating explosions that caused the closest tank to blossom like a dying flower, releasing a torrent of gelatinous growth medium in a solid wave that engulfed Srell even as the phaser's beam lanced toward him.

He vanished in the mist the phaser blasted from the thick swirling liquid, gone forever.

Kirk breathed deeply as time resumed for him. Whether he had killed Srell, or the liquid had consumed him, he might never know. But his intention had been clear. And that unexpected knowledge was enough.

Kirk let the phaser slip from his hand, to fall into the ankle-deep sludge of the growth medium that flowed across the floor, hidden by the billows of white vapor.

From somewhere far off, he heard Picard call for the *Enterprise.* This time, there was no answering hiss of a jamming device. Riker responded.

Then Picard's stern voice eclipsed the dying convulsions of the chamber and the Symmetrists' dreams.

"Six to beam up," he said.

Swept up by the ship they had all served, Kirk and his

fellows escaped destruction, just as the chamber blew apart around them.

But Kirk was not concerned.

He felt . . . clean, free of pain and doubt.

Sarek's death had been avenged.

As had Kirk's life of denial.

Even in the midst of destruction, Kirk was, at last, at peace.

FORTY-ONE

───────────── ☆ ─────────────

Kirk closed his eyes, and saw the flames of Tarsus IV.

Cleansing. Purifying. Costly.

The battle to take control of the Symmetrists' base had been brutal. Fourteen of the *Enterprise's* crew had been killed, along with fifty-two Symmetrists, half of them Vulcan. Another eight crew members were in sickbay, in intensive care. Only twelve Symmetrists had been captured, all so badly wounded that they had not been able to kill themselves. They were being treated in triage areas set up in the shuttle-bay, under constant guard.

Even now, a full day after the battle, the collapsed administration buildings in the main city still burned. Kirk had seen the conflagration only from orbit on the *Enterprise's* main screen, but he could picture how those flames rose into the night, illuminating the crumbling monument that had been the Federation's great seal. In that image, he saw the future.

Federation's end.

"I've finished my preliminary report to Starfleet," Picard said.

Kirk opened his eyes. He had been sitting at a workstation Beverly Crusher had set up for him in an alcove off sickbay.

Before him, he had laid out all the herbs and leaves Hugh's people had given him when he had left their world. La Forge's repair crew had recovered the botanicals from his quarters on the *Tobias,* and he catalogued them, recording what he knew of each, to be sure his knowledge wasn't lost. Though he knew that all anyone was interested in were the *trannin* leaves that had saved Teilani and the children of Chal.

Picard stood in the alcove entrance, still waiting for Kirk's reply. Behind him, at least twenty medical personnel worked at consoles and lab tables. A few were from the *Enterprise.* But most were specialists who had come in the emergency flotilla launched from Starbase 515. More medical vessels were arriving every hour as word of what had happened here spread through the stars.

"It will be a useful addendum to the reports we've received from Vulcan. Stonn and T'Pring have been arrested. They have confessed to the Symmetrists' complicity in Sarek's murder, as well as Tarok's. And they have named other members of the movement. Apparently, now that their plan has failed, they are eager to explain the . . . logic of their beliefs."

Picard held Kirk's gaze for a moment, as if deciding how he should continue. "My report states that Srell died when the tank burst," Picard said.

"That's not what killed him. I did."

"You can't know that for certain. The tank burst. Srell's body was swept away intact."

"It doesn't matter," Kirk said. "I fired the phaser. I wanted him to die."

Picard glanced over his shoulder, as if to check that no one in the work area behind him could hear what he said. He stepped into Kirk's alcove.

"I've read your biographies, Jim. I've worked with you. On Veridian Three. The Borg homeworld. Now Tarsus Four. And everything I've learned about you tells me that if what you say happened *is* true, then it was an aberration. A shockwave from an explosion made you reflexively press the firing stud. Or you weren't aware that the weapon was set to kill."

Picard was grasping at straws. Kirk knew it. He could see that Picard knew it as well.

"People change, Jean-Luc."

"Rarely so profoundly."

Kirk rested an elbow on the work surface, rubbed his face with his hand. How could a life like his be explained in a handful of words? "You're right. I take it back."

Picard looked intrigued by that admission.

"People don't change." He remembered what Kodos had told him, alone on the *Enterprise*. His *Enterprise*. "But after enough time has passed. After they've seen enough of the atrocities that make up our civilization, . . . they become tired, Jean-Luc. Impatient. And as I've grown older, I've found that . . . I no longer want to wait for the things that are important in life."

"Why would that young man's death have been important to you? For *honor?*"

"For vengeance," Kirk said, though he could see that Picard didn't understand the emotional wellsprings from which that answer had come. At least, not yet.

"Some people," Picard said, "would argue that a civilized society has no place for vengeance."

"And while those people argue, civilizations fall. I don't have the patience for arguing anymore. Time is the ultimate nonrenewable resource, and we are rapidly running out of it."

Kirk could see that Picard wanted to question him further, but Spock stepped up behind him, disturbing the moment.

Like Kirk, Spock had returned to his civilian garb, setting aside his ambassadorial robes. Instead, he wore an unadorned black tunic. One sleeve had been rolled up to allow for the small inducer pump on his forearm, through which his blood was continually filtered.

Beverly Crusher had finally identified the contact poison the Symmetrists had used to mimic Bendii Syndrome. It would take a month of treatment to cleanse Spock's system of it, but the total length of his exposure had been limited, and Beverly expected a full recovery. Though Kirk knew the scars of Spock's emotional outbursts, caused by the poison that had robbed him of his self-control, would take far more than a month to heal.

"Excuse me, Captain," Spock said to Picard. Then he looked at Kirk. "Dr. M'Benga is ready for you, Jim."

Kirk stood up, and smoothed the Vulcan trader's clothes he once again wore. He felt their simple design was preferable to the new uniform he had worn on the *Tobias*. And all the other old uniforms he had worn in the past, as well.

"Do you think this will be it?" Picard asked as Kirk stepped past him.

But Kirk had no answer. Only time would tell.

FORTY-TWO

───────────── ☆ ─────────────

Kirk, Spock, and Picard went to a lab off the main sickbay. All the parts of the puzzle were laid out on the large worktable at its center: a pressurized container of alta mist, whose importance had been discovered only by Picard's dogged pursuit of the mysterious destruction of the *Bennett;* a tray of replicated *trannin* leaves brought to Starfleet's attention only by Kirk's unexpected return; and a beaker of pure virogen culture obtained from Tarsus IV, the planet Kirk had identified as the Symmetrists' base, a base only Picard's *Enterprise* could have subdued.

It wasn't symmetry that had brought all these elements to this one place and time, Kirk knew. It was *tapestry,* the subtle interweaving of individual threads to create a picture greater than the whole.

Spock brought the tray of *trannin* leaves to Kirk. The Vulcan was the puzzle's final piece. For if not for Spock's pursuit of his father's murderer, then Kirk and Picard might never have been brought together.

"All right, everyone," Dr. M'Benga said to Beverly Crusher and the five other Starfleet doctors and technicians in the lab. "Watch carefully."

347

Feeling just a bit self-conscious at having to perform such a modest task, Kirk picked up the dried leaves and began to fold them in his fingers, feeling them crack, then crumble, exactly as Miko had taught him on the world whose sun had been a galactic core.

He let the fine leaf fragments fall like coarse powder onto a clean patch of filter mesh. After he had created a mound about three centimeters across, he stopped.

"See," M'Benga said. "That's the consistency we need. We have to crack it along the leaf veins to expose the resin compound without contaminating it with stomatic residue."

Kirk stepped back from the lab table to let the experts go to work with the sample he'd prepared. In principle, he knew what M'Benga and Beverly and all of Starfleet Medical were now working toward. The *trannin* compound could stop the virogen's reproduction, but it was useful only in animals. Alta mist was fine enough to circulate through a planet's entire biosphere, drawing nourishment only from the air, thus not interfering with existing food chains.

The medical team believed that if they could somehow insert the *trannin* compound into the alta-mist cells, so the cells would generate the compound and spread it as they reproduced, then Starfleet would have an antivirogen that could move through plant populations as quickly as the virogen itself, cleansing whole worlds just as the inducer pump cleansed Spock's blood of poison.

But thus far, no matter how precisely Kirk had prepared the leaves, no matter how rigorously the technicians had attempted to artificially re-create the compound's molecular structure at a smaller scale, the two critical components Kirk and Picard had discovered—the *trannin* leaves and the alta mist—had not yet joined together.

And with each day of failure, more systems fell prey to the destabilizing virogen contagion and the Federation moved another step closer to total collapse.

Kirk watched as a technician agitated a sample tube in which the *trannin* and the alta mist had been mixed. Beverly ran her tricorder over the tube. Shook her head. Still no progress.

"What exactly is the problem?" Kirk finally asked. How difficult could it be to mix two biological substances that should have a natural affinity? Especially for twenty-fourth-century science?

"We have to establish a precise degree of permeability for the membrane of the alta-mist cells," M'Benga said. "If we leave the cell walls too rigid, the *trannin* compound can't penetrate them. If we leave the walls too permeable, then the *trannin* gets in, but the cell's chloroplasts and nucleii can migrate out."

"The frustrating aspect of it," Beverly added, "is that the possible solutions to the problem are almost infinite. We just can't work fast enough to try all the different variations in a reasonable time."

M'Benga suddenly looked over at her colleague. "Dr. Crusher, maybe there's a way we can automate the process. Do you have an EMH?"

Beverly scowled. "Yes," she said, and to Kirk it sounded as if she were confessing to a particularly embarrassing crime. "I suppose that as long as I'm not letting it work on my patients, I can't really complain." She sighed. "Computer, run the EMH."

There was a flash of light and a holographic doctor took form beside Kirk. It looked exactly like the one he had seen on the *Tobias.* "Please state the nature of your medical emergency," the hologram said, as if even a technological illusion had more important matters to attend to.

Beverly and M'Benga briefed the nameless doctor on the tasks they wanted him to perform: the rapid trial-and-error mixing of different alta mist and *trannin* combinations.

"You consider that a medical emergency?" the doctor

asked. The irritation in his voice made it clear that his program certainly didn't recognize it as such. Not for the first time, Kirk wondered whether personality chose profession, or if it were the other way around.

"The fate of the Federation may rest in the successful completion of these experiments," M'Benga explained.

"Well," the doctor said reluctantly, "if you put it that way." Then he began rearranging the equipment on the lab table in order, he said, to make his work more efficient.

Kirk glanced over at Spock. Much of the twenty-fourth century wasn't so very different from what he was used to. But some of it was simply peculiar. "So where does that thing get its personality?" Kirk asked. "What there is of it, I mean."

"I believe it is a simulation based on its original programmer, augmented by a database of all the different medical experts whose specialized knowledge and experience were combined to produce—"

The hologram suddenly looked across the lab table at Kirk and Spock. "Do you two mind?" he said. "I'm taking critical measurements and your voices are causing minute vibrations."

Kirk gave Spock a bemused look. "Did a computer just tell us to shut up?"

"I'm a doctor, not a computer," the hologram muttered.

Kirk thought about that response for a moment, then walked around the table to Beverly, ignoring the hologram's sharp look of annoyance.

Kirk whispered a question into Beverly's ear. She nodded in agreement, though not understanding, then took Kirk to a medical display screen where she called up a list of all the medical personnel who had been modeled as expert systems and combined to create the EMH.

At the display screen, Kirk scrolled through the list until he found the one name he knew had to be there.

He typed in a command to isolate a single visual and

personality subsystem from the EMH program, then turned to watch in satisfaction as the image of the holographic doctor rippled. In moments, the prickly bald doctor in the black and blue uniform transformed into a prickly white-haired doctor in an old-fashioned wine-colored uniform . . .

Medical expert Leonard H. McCoy. Age seventy.

"Well, what the blazes are all you people just standing around for?" the simulated McCoy groused. "We've got a galaxy to save. As usual."

Kirk walked back to Spock with a grin as McCoy barked orders to doctors and technicians alike. M'Benga was assigned to clean sample tubes. Beverly measured *trannin* samples. McCoy completely rearranged the lab-table equipment into an ungainly, though apparently even more efficient configuration. "I'm a doctor, not an interior designer," he complained.

Kirk saw the look of affectionate amusement in Spock's eyes, and the sadness. Though the Bendii poison was being leached from his body, its emotional effects were obviously still present.

"Now that's what I call a simulation," Kirk said.

Spock agreed. "I think I would like to help it."

"For old time's sake?" Kirk said.

Spock tilted his head to one side, as if not comprehending the question. "To save the galaxy from collapse," he said earnestly.

Kirk watched with anticipation as the simulated McCoy looked up to see Spock. For a moment, the program paused, as if it had just received input which it could not categorize.

"Do I know you?" the program asked.

In an act of pure illogic, Spock said, "Yes."

"Well, then, haul your pointy ears over to the sterilization unit and set up a sterile field around the alta mist. You amateurs have so many contaminants mixing into these samples, it's no wonder you can't get the same answer twice."

Eventually, the simulated McCoy got around to ordering Kirk to keep the table wiped down. And within the hour, instead of facing an infinite number of possible mixing combinations, McCoy had narrowed the possibilities to a limited range. Instead of months of work, M'Benga said they were now within days of a solution. If the Federation could last that long.

By the time another hour had passed, a medical debate had broken out. Spock, Beverly, and the simulated McCoy were arguing about which strategy to follow for the next round of tests. M'Benga had removed herself from the discussion—it was outside her area of expertise. But she reminded everyone that because of the equipment configuration that would be needed, choosing the wrong strategy could delay the project by an additional day.

"Why are you people so dead set against harming the alta mist organism? That's what's holding you back," McCoy said. "I say, harm the beast, but then give it the tools it needs to repair itself *after* the *trannin* has been absorbed."

Spock rose to the challenge. "The alta mist is a one-celled plant, Doctor. It wouldn't know what to do with 'tools.'"

"Now don't get smart with me, you green-blooded hobgoblin. Stop trying to force everything in such neat compartments."

"It is called logic."

"Well, I call it a waste of time. Life has a logic of its own, and I suggest we use it."

Kirk was ready to wade in and break up the argument that was paralyzing the medical team. But it was a medical matter, and Beverly Crusher assumed the role of mediator before he could act.

"Dr. McCoy," she began. "Could you please explain your approach? What do you want to do here?"

The hologram rolled his eyes in exasperation. "I thought you'd never ask. I simply want to exploit the existing signal pathways for general defense and tissue repair in the alta mist cells," he explained, as if it were the most obvious thing in the universe. "We'll use elicitors: oligogalacturonide fragments of pectin polysaccharides; the *18mer* peptide, systemin; *and* fatty acid derivatives including jasmonic acid. The cells will repair themselves like that!" The hologram snapped its simulated fingers.

"That's it, do it the hard way," McCoy said.

Kirk blinked. The holographic simulation had just spoken, but its mouth hadn't moved.

"If you want to keep the wound repair process under control in plants, then forget all that fancy gene expression crap and stick to salicylic acid. Plain old aspirin."

Kirk suddenly realized that though the holographic McCoy was in front of him, the familiar gruff voice was coming from behind. Kirk decided it must be an equipment failure. But then he noticed everyone else in the lab looking behind him, even the holographic McCoy.

Kirk turned—

—to see Admiral Leonard H. McCoy, age 146, gaping right back at Kirk with as stunned an expression of surprise as Kirk knew was on his own face.

Starfleet's greatest doctor was frail, and moved with the aid of exoskeleton braces on his legs and the support of Data's arm. But there was no mistaking the brightness in his eyes, and the quickness of his smile.

"Hell. I thought you were dead, Jim."

"I thought you'd run off with some dancing girls from Wrigley's."

McCoy winked. "These days, they can run faster than I can."

With deference and great care, Data escorted McCoy into the lab, where the medical personnel stared at a legend in the flesh.

Then Kirk saw Data react to the presence of the holograph-

ic McCoy across the room. The android smiled delightedly at
Kirk. "Given the present conditions," Data said, "I think we
might say that I have on my arm the *real* McCoy."

McCoy peered up at Data as he pulled his arm away. "Since
when did you get a sense of humor?"

"Two years, two months, six days, eight hours, three—"

"Good Lord," McCoy muttered. "And I thought Spock was
bad."

McCoy made his way to the lab table on his own, his
exoskeleton braces humming as his legs moved with slow,
deliberate steps.

He steadied himself against the table, then looked around
at everyone who was looking at him.

"Well, what do you think this is? A picnic? I'm a doctor,
not a sideshow. Someone mix up an aspirin solution, get me a
chair—"

The holographic McCoy stepped forward. "In my opinion,
the proper strategy is to *elicit* cell-repair functions, not
degrade them."

"And somebody shut that damn thing off," McCoy
snapped.

Two technicians ran toward the medical control panel and
an instant later the EMH faded from view.

McCoy flashed a triumphant smile at Kirk. "By God, it's
good to be old." Then he turned to the rest of the workers.
"Well, don't just stand there—let's get this show on the
road."

They did.

Two hours later, McCoy had the cure.

FORTY-THREE

---------------- ☆ ----------------

In a violent and uncaring universe of chaos and uncertainty, there were still some absolutes that were never meant to change, and never would.

It was with that thought that Kirk stood with Spock and McCoy on the bridge of the *Starship Enterprise.* For just one perfect moment, he heard Teilani's words, that time had no dominion.

But from bittersweet experience, Kirk knew that moments had a way of passing, and that this new *Enterprise* belonged to a different crew: Picard in the center chair, Riker and Troi to either side of their captain. Data at ops, La Forge at engineering, and Beverly Crusher at the main science station.

Kirk gazed approvingly at the new team. All at their posts, so intent on their mission.

As he had finally come to know from all his voyages, it had always been the crew who had mattered most, and in this new team he saw the best of his own.

But then he looked to the main screen, and wondered if even they would be worthy of the challenges that lay ahead.

Challenges not just for them, for Starfleet, and the Federation. But for all the people of the galaxy: Earthling, Vulcan, and Klingon alike, humanity in all its colors, shapes, and chemistries.

"Coming up on terminator and planetary dawn," Data said.

Kirk looked to his friends. Spock stood with his hands behind his back, his expression at peace, hiding the inner turmoil that Kirk knew still ravaged him. McCoy rested his hands on the belt of his exoskeleton support, thoughtfully chewing his bottom lip.

A wash of golden light filled the bridge as the sudden flash of the Tarsus sun lit the thin shell of its fourth planet's atmosphere. An arc of that dying world slowly grew, glowing in the early dawn.

"Beginning sensor sweep," Beverly announced.

No one spoke. Kirk didn't have to be a Betazoid to sense the tension on the bridge.

Three days ago, after the *Enterprise* had replicated enough of McCoy's antivirogen to fill the auxiliary propellant tanks of five terraforming runabouts, the first full-scale assault on the Symmetrists' plan had begun.

For twenty hours, the runabouts had circled Tarsus IV, streaking through its stratosphere, releasing their cargo as a fine mist.

McCoy had said the effect would be noticeable within fifty hours after exposure.

If the antivirogen worked.

On the screen, a wedge of sunlight grew across the planet's surface as the *Enterprise* flew through her orbit. But the world that light illuminated was still black and brown and dying.

Then Kirk peered more closely at the screen. He pointed at the lower left corner. "Spock . . . do you see that?"

"Dr. Crusher," Spock said, "scan the southeast quadrant of the landmass directly below us at full resolution, if you would."

"Full resolution," Beverly confirmed.

The image on the viewscreen expanded until Kirk could see the shadows that individual clouds cast on the ground.

Green clouds.

"There!" Kirk said.

"By the mountain range!" McCoy directed.

Beverly's voice rang through the bridge. "Sensors detect *chlorophyll!* It's pure, uncontaminated alta mist! The antivirogen is working!"

As one, the bridge crew stood up from their stations and turned to McCoy. Their applause thundered.

"I'm getting returns from all over the southern continent," Beverly said, ecstatic.

McCoy grinned proudly at Spock. "Hear that? They're applauding *me* for a change."

"Doctor," Spock replied, "I am pleased that you think so."

Kirk cupped a hand to his ear. "Is someone applauding?"

McCoy's grin faded as he looked back to the screen. "I liked you both better when you were dead."

As the crew returned to their duties with elation, Picard joined the *Enterprise*'s honored guests at the side of the bridge. He smiled broadly as he spoke.

"Dr. McCoy, this is indeed a monumental achievement. I've instructed Lieutenant Rolk to begin broadcasting the antivirogen's complete replicator code on all subspace frequencies, Starfleet and civilian. Even with the current communications difficulties, within two weeks every affected system in the Federation will be able to begin combating the virogen."

But Kirk shared none of Picard's optimism, and for good reason. He drew Picard aside. "You mean, every system that's maintained an operational subspace communications system," Kirk said. "You saw what Tarsus Four was like. The city was torn apart before the evacuation was completed. How many other worlds are there like this one?"

Picard dropped his smile. "We shall find them all, Jim. Starfleet no longer needs to maintain quarantine blockades. Our ships are free to patrol our borders, to make contact with any world or colony that may have succumbed to. . . ."

"Anarchy," Kirk said flatly. "It's what happens when the system doesn't work."

"But the system *is* working," Picard insisted. "Food supplies are already arriving at their destinations. Because of what you and Spock and McCoy have done here, we are now able to release seed stores to agricultural centers without fear of contamination. And with the threat of further contagion eliminated, the unaffected sectors of the Federation *can* and *will* reach out to those in need. Jim, you should be proud of what you've accomplished. What we've all accomplished. The Federation *is* secure."

"For how long?" Kirk asked. "The Symmetrists did this because they wanted to teach us a lesson. Did we learn it?"

Contempt shaded Picard's reply. "The Symmetrists were terrorists, not teachers. Tens of thousands have died because of what they've done."

"And billions more may have been saved."

Picard's body stiffened. "Are you *condoning* what these maniacs have done?!"

"Of course not," Kirk said. "But that doesn't change the fact that *they are right!"*

"That's absurd."

Kirk gestured at the viewscreen. "Look at that world, Jean-Luc!" Despite the promise represented by the small patches of green alta mist that again floated in the air of Tarsus IV, the world below bore the scars of ecological collapse, and would for decades still to come. "That could have been Earth, or Vulcan! Unless we learn our lesson, someday it will be! And what's the Federation doing to *change* that future—*nothing!"*

No one else on the bridge spoke. The only sound was the background hum of the instruments.

Picard flushed with anger. "The Federation Council is holding emergency sessions around the clock. At this very moment, it is reviewing its colonization and expansion programs in order to identify and insure the integrity of the entire galactic ecosystem. New committees will be formed. New studies begun."

Kirk held out both hands to Picard. "Don't you see? That's what they did in my age. They haven't learned, Jean-Luc. They can't see what's coming."

"And you can?"

Kirk heard the reproach in Picard's question, and understood why it was there. Kirk wasn't a scientist. He had no special skills as an environmentalist or biologist. But he did have the capacity to learn from those who did have the skills and the knowledge that the future needed.

"I can see what's coming," Kirk said, "because I've seen through better eyes than mine. Experienced the thoughts of better minds. Sarek saw the future. There're a hundred other scientists throughout the Federation who know what he knew about how much more expansion and exploration and colonization the galaxy can absorb."

Picard stared at Kirk, and Kirk knew what he was thinking. It was one thing for two starship commanders to have a difference of opinion.

But Sarek was another matter.

"Thirty years," Kirk said. "That's it. You look at the statistics. The growing pattern of complexity. There are other virogens waiting out there, other environmental disruptions that we can't even imagine because we have no real conception of our interstellar environment and our place in it. Thirty years, and it won't be fanatics trying to teach us a lesson. It'll be the real thing. A complete and total interplanetary collapse."

Picard shook his head. "Thirty years is a long time, Jim. Surely, someone will solve this problem before then."

"But who?" Kirk asked softly. "I've done all I can. Now . . . it's up to you."

Picard held Kirk's gaze and did not look away. Kirk knew the challenge had been issued and accepted.

Picard held out his hand. Starship captain to starship captain.

"Somehow I feel that we will meet again," Picard said. A truce declared, despite their differences.

Kirk shook Picard's hand in turn. "When we do, let's hope we're still on the same side."

Later, Data escorted Kirk, Spock, and McCoy through the corridors of the *Enterprise,* on their way to transporter room two. In matching orbit of Tarsus IV, the newly repaired *Tobias* waited to receive her passengers. Commander Christine MacDonald had been given her orders by a grateful Starfleet Command: She would take Kirk, Spock, and McCoy wherever they wished to go, then return to collect the rest of her crew on Vulcan.

Also, in light of the result of her unauthorized mission to Tarsus IV, questions concerning matters of disobeying orders and outright mutiny had been set aside. A personal note added to her orders from Admiral Strak of Vulcan, suggested that Commander MacDonald might wish to discuss the historical precedents for this ruling with one James T. Kirk.

The doors to the transporter room slid open as Kirk and the others approached. Data stepped to one side and stood at ease. "I will wait while you say your good-byes."

Kirk, Spock, and McCoy looked at the android.

"To whom will we say these good-byes?" Spock asked.

Data looked from Kirk to Spock. "This is the transporter room. I assumed that after you two left, I would escort Admiral McCoy to a shuttlecraft."

"The hell you will," McCoy said. "I'm beaming out with my friends."

Data blinked in confusion. "My apologies, Admiral. But I recall that you do not like the transporter as a mode of transportation."

"Hell, son. At my age, if my molecules get scrambled it can only be an improvement."

McCoy laughed. Spock frowned. Kirk shrugged at the android. "I can't take them anywhere," he said.

The three friends started into the transporter room.

But then McCoy stopped and turned back to Data.

"Son, you remember what I told you when you headed out on that last ship of yours?" he asked.

"I do, sir," Data replied. "You specifically told me to remember what you said."

"Well?"

"You said, 'You treat her like a lady. She'll always bring you home.'"

McCoy gave Data a cautioning look. "You keep remembering that, son. And take *care* of this one for a change, all right?"

Kirk smiled at the android's bemused expression.

"C'mon, Bones," he said. "It's time to go home."

FORTY-FOUR

───────────── ☆ ─────────────

Mount Seleya beckoned, and this time Kirk heard her call.

He stood with Spock and McCoy on the windswept mountaintop, the crimson Vulcan sunset bathing them in the alien color of human blood, human passion.

In the distance, they could see the sprawling temple in which Spock had been returned to life so long ago, his *katra* rejoined to his reborn body.

But the temple was not their destination this night.

Instead, they stood before the *fal-lan-tral*—the Passage of All Mysteries.

A worn path paved with ancient blocks of dusty red stone led up to the opening of a cave in the mountain's side. Within, in a labyrinth of hand-carved tunnels and passageways which none but Vulcan eyes had ever seen, waited the *tral katra*—the keepers of the spirits of the past.

The secret of the *tral katra* had never been revealed to outworlders. Some rumors said they were enormous crystals which held the wisdom of the Vulcan departed. Others claimed the *tral katra* were Vulcan priestesses who sat in yearlong meditations, each holding the *katras* of a thousand dead.

But all that was known for certain by non-Vulcan investigators was that beyond that dark entrance into the cave lay the repository of Vulcan souls, the place to which each *katra* was returned.

That fathomless cave was Spock's destination. And, as Spock had said, it must also be Kirk's.

"Can you feel it?" Spock asked.

Kirk pulled his cloak closer as the mountain breeze cooled with the approaching night.

Spock was right. He could feel it. Somewhere in the darkness beyond, Sarek's *katra* was in repose—all that Sarek had been, all that he had known, saved from extinction by the power of the Vulcan mind.

"We must go together," Spock said.

But Kirk shook his head.

Spock put his hand on Kirk's shoulder. "You are his son as much as I am."

Kirk stared at Spock. Deep within himself, he acknowledged the special bond that had formed between himself and Sarek. He knew it explained so many things about his past, his present, and his future.

But Kirk also knew what Spock truly meant, and desired at this moment.

Absolution.

"You didn't abandon him, Spock."

Spock looked out at the fiery Vulcan sun as it touched the horizon, only minutes from setting. "Then help me tell him that."

"You go to him, Spock. Touch his mind. He'll understand."

Spock hesitated. "I find, with age, my emotions are no longer my own, Jim. I need yours to guide me."

Kirk knew Spock's confession had been difficult for him, but the truth was that time had eroded Kirk's own ability to experience his emotions, just as it had eroded Spock's ability to control his. "Spock . . . you're being illogical."

363

"But it was you who avenged my father's death."

"There was more to it than one man's life," Kirk said. He thought of the pilots he had consigned to death above the jungles of Chal. He thought of his decision—his *desire*—to fire his phaser at Srell. Was either action different from what Kodos had done? Or what the Symmetrists had attempted? Is this what age had brought him to? "It was my duty." And so complete was Kirk's catharsis that to himself, his voice was as devoid of emotion as a Vulcan's.

"Good Lord," McCoy suddenly said. "Is this what it's come down to?"

He had been their silent witness, wrapped in a long admiralty coat against the rising wind.

"Have you two grown so close that you've managed to switch sides? With Spock too full of confusing emotions, and Jim cut off from what makes him human?"

"Your point, Doctor?" Spock asked coldly.

"What is it that stops you two from seeing yourselves as you really are? Spock, Jim may be cut off from what makes him human—but he's *still* human. It's the way he was born. But *you*—you had a choice, and you chose to be Vulcan. And I'm going to hate myself for telling you this, but you're damned good at it. No matter how old you are."

The three friends stood together, huddled against the fall of night, before the cave that led to mysteries unexplored.

Above them, the stars of Vulcan slowly brightened, shimmering through the growing crimson twilight.

"Have we changed?" Spock asked.

Kirk held out his hand to Spock. He had been asked that question before. He knew the answer.

"Not us," he said. As the two friends clasped hands, Kirk was struck by a stunning bolt of clarity. He recalled his first glimpse of Spock, not when they had met, but the image that had been in Sarek's mind that night on Tarsus IV, when Spock had been a youth, no different from himself.

AVENGER

How like my son, Sarek had thought.

Kirk finally understood the ultimate mystery that had united them.

He *and* Spock were Sarek's sons.

And in that moment, Spock understood as well.

"You are my brother, Jim. I, of Sarek's flesh. You, of Sarek's mind."

"Go on," McCoy told them. "You have to." His coat fluttered around him like resting wings. On the horizon, the last spike of day flared against the fall of night. He smiled. "Don't worry. I'll still be here when you come back."

Above them, day had ended. Night was absolute.

Spock looked to Kirk, as if uncertain what to think about what would happen next.

Kirk looked to Spock, uncertain how he should feel.

But he *was* certain that the answer was just ahead. There was always an explanation to be found.

And with his friends, his family, at his side, those things without which no life has meaning, he was not afraid to take the next step on his journey.

Into his future.

Into the *fal-lan-tral.*

FORTY-FIVE

☆

The *Tobias* blazed through space, the stars a rainbow in her wake.

On her bridge, Christine MacDonald held the center chair. She ran her fingers along the inside of her uniform's collar. Counted the four metal disks that were now affixed to it.

Captain MacDonald.

Her final passenger smiled at her. She smiled back, realizing she had been caught.

"I know," she said. "It's not important. Just more trappings."

But Kirk shook his head.

"It was important to me when I was your age. It should be important to you." He looked ahead to the viewscreen, watching the stars pass, thinking of the cycle of the generations.

Christine reached out and took Kirk's hand, held it close. She spoke diffidently, but her true emotions were apparent.

"I don't suppose you're looking for another ship? There's still a lot of galaxy left out there."

Kirk felt the eyes of every member of her crew upon him. Barc and M'Benga, the blond communications officer whose

366

name he'd never learned, the blue-scaled helmsman whose species he'd never seen. This crew would take her far.

But not where he was going.

He gently slipped his hand from hers, and turned away from the stars to look at her in her chair—*the* chair—to remember one last time how it felt. "Explore it for me. And if you ever pass this way again . . ."

On the viewscreen, the stars stopped moving as the *Tobias* fell from warp, coming up on her destination—a world where blue oceans and white clouds beckoned once again, a planet healed.

"I'll know where to find you," Christine said.

Below him, Chal waited. His world. His dream. Teilani.

Kirk had come home to stay.

EPILOGUE

☆

That night he lay in Teilani's arms, listening to the gentle rhythm of her breathing.

She'd been surprised when he'd appeared in the doorway of their simple cabin. "You came back," she said, as if this time she'd believed he never would.

"The commander of that ship," Teilani said. "She was very young."

Kirk kissed the gray of Teilani's hair. "She was," he agreed. "She was very pretty."

Kirk traced the scar that ran across Teilani's cheek, beyond even the powers of this age's doctors to heal. He kissed her cheek. "Very pretty," he assured her.

"And you came back," she said.

"I came back."

Kirk had been to Mount Seleya.

With Spock at his side he had seen what no other human on Vulcan had seen. Touched the mind that had first touched his. And seen the beginning and the ending of his life reconciled.

Spock, at last at peace with his father, would remain on Vulcan for a time. But the fate of the Romulans still tugged at him, and would draw him out again.

McCoy had come up with some ideas for improving the EMH and was back where he had always been on Earth, working hard, complaining to all who would listen, and even more to any who didn't.

But in time their paths would cross again, Kirk knew.

This universe still had some absolutes.

That night he had carried Teilani to their bed and they made love. For the first time, for the hundredth. It didn't matter.

Time had no dominion.

Later, they lay in contentment, sheltered by the night and their love.

"This time, James, I was afraid. That you wouldn't come back."

Kirk held her close, but knew that she was right. Someday he would not return, because death was the way of all things. But now, for the first time since Tarsus IV and Sarek, he no longer had the knowledge of how his end would come. Freed of that burden, he had at last become like all other men, with the future stretching out before him, as endless and unknowable as the stars.

At last, in Teilani's embrace, James T. Kirk fell asleep.

And for the first time since Tarsus IV . . . and Sarek . . . he did not dream of falling.

For tonight, at last, his journey had ended.

For tonight, at last, the future could wait.

At least, until tomorrow . . .

James T. Kirk

Will Return in

Star Trek®: Spectre

Coming Spring 1998

From
Pocket Books